Off the Deep End

By
Lanie Hartford

Blue Canary Publishing LLC
Portland, Oregon

Copyright © 2025 by Lanie Hartford
Blue Canary Publishing LLC

Paperback ISBN: 979-8-9864717-3-0
E-Book ISBN: 979-8-9864717-4-7

Cover design by
Katarina Naskovski/nskvsky

Printed in the United States of America

For my family—
who have supported me my whole life
and never driven me to jump off of a ship.

✦

Author's Notes

A note on timing:

This book takes place in 2010—cell phones were not all smart, social media was not ubiquitous, and some people still used landlines. Wild times!

A note for geographically-inclined readers:

The island is an amalgam, meant to evoke a sense of adventure and wonder (with just a hint of magical realism) in its general perfection and improbable variety. It is not rooted in a specific location or culture.

A modern note about past events:

This novel is full of little nods and winks to my experiences in my twenties. Often, the details in the book are more than nods—they're exact thoughts, opinions, and experiences from my life when I was writing in the 2010s. (Not the yacht-jumping. To be completely honest, I've never been on a yacht. But a lot of other things!)

I understand that in a post-Me-Too world, certain male behavior in this book is not acceptable, nor was it ever. The neck-biting incident in particular was taken almost verbatim from a personal experience when I was freshly out of college. I in no way condone that character's actions. This book is intended as a fun and breezy read, and it certainly does not intend to undermine the importance of physical consent or make light of those boundaries being blurred.

I hope you enjoy Off the Deep End! I certainly enjoyed writing it and living the moments that I did.

—Lanie Hartford

Playlist

Be Okay - Ingrid Michaelson

La Isla Bonita - Madonna

Burning Down the House - Talking Heads

La Comparasita (the Italian Tango) - La Charanga Cubana

Coconut - Harry Nilsson

Je Veux - Zaz

Hit Me with Your Best Shot - Pat Benatar

Total Eclipse of the Heart - Bonnie Tyler

Golden Years - David Bowie

Hungry Like the Wolf - Duran Duran

Sweet Dreams - Eurythmics

Alone - Heart

Video Killed the Radio Star - The Buggles

The Promise - When in Rome

Pame Mia Nihta Sto Feggari - Manolis Michalakis

Sway - Rosemary Clooney

Alors on Danse - Stromae

Are You Gonna Be My Girl - Jet

I'd Go the Whole Wide World - The Monkees

Sea of Love - Israel Kamakawiwo'ole

Chapter One

Cassandra Dillon had never liked the ocean. She didn't like how cold it was. She didn't like how deep it was. She didn't like how full it was of things that could eat her if only they got close enough. And she had never liked any of these things less than the moment she leapt over the railing of a fifty-foot yacht and the ocean came rushing up to smack her in the face with all its cold, deep danger.

She broke the surface of the water, sputtering and flopping her arms in a manner that vaguely resembled swimming, and tried not to panic.

"You're fine," she told herself, treading water and watching the ship speed away with everything she knew about herself and her life as the cold seeped deep into her bones. But it was a lie. She wasn't fine. She was having a nervous breakdown.

"Well, that's just great," she said aloud. All she needed to round out this horrible family vacation was a nervous breakdown. She could just hear her mother's voice now.

If you needed some time to yourself, darling, you could have booked a massage when we docked. You didn't need to jump overboard. And in that outfit. Honestly, Cassandra, what were you thinking?

But she hadn't been thinking. She had just acted. She'd been standing alone on the deck of the ship well past midnight, thinking about the expansive void that was her future. A future she had no idea what to do with. A future that would never again include Gram. A future that, for the next three months, would exist entirely of ocean and expectations and staving off sunburns and well-meaning judgements from her ever-present parents. She felt trapped. Frantic. Failing. Flailing. Thinking there had to be *something* that would shake her out of this funk and get her life on track. And it definitely wasn't this cruise.

She'd looked up and seen a shooting star. A sign. Then her eyes fell to the shadow of an island. Distant but possible, and maybe…maybe it was destiny. She hadn't thought it through, hadn't stopped to consider the consequences or the practicality or the logistics—if she had, she certainly never would have done it. With terrifying, impulsive clarity, she jumped over the railing. Then the water hit her.

Half a second later, so did reality.

And now she was bobbing in the middle of the ocean like a lunatic. Good lord, what had she done? A large wave rolled over her as the yacht left her in its wake, and Cassandra resumed panicking.

Her mind raced and her heart pounded as she madly tread water. This was not the way she had wanted to spend her summer. Too much water. Not enough space. Too much pressure. Nowhere to escape. She needed land. She needed distance. She needed time to think and make some real-life decisions without her family "helping" her to death.

And speaking of death, if she didn't start swimming, she was going to die.

"Swim now, think later," she panted, and began pulling herself through the water, heading toward the island that loomed large against the dark night sky. It couldn't be more than a quarter-mile away. People swam that far all the time, right? She would be fine.

Cassandra tried to focus all her energy on closing the distance between herself and land, but despite her best efforts, she couldn't stop her thoughts from wandering in dark directions. She was going to die! She could drown, or die of hypothermia, or get eaten by a shark…the thought of sharks in the water momentarily paralyzed her mind. If she came face to face with a shark, she wouldn't have to wait for it to attack her—her heart would just explode and that would be the end.

Cassandra screamed when a squid floated across her path, then felt both stupid and relieved when she realized it was actually a piece of kelp.

She shook her head to clear it and choked on a mouthful of seawater in the process. As she kicked her feet to launch herself forward, one of her sandals slipped from her foot and Cass imagined it sinking slowly into the abyss, lost forever to the fathoms below. She could be next.

"Swim now, think later," she repeated.

Swim now, think later. Swim now, think later.

This became her mantra as she floundered along, swallowing salt water with every other breath and cursing the ocean with every fiber of her being.

She hated the ocean! Her parents knew that. Why had they thought that spending the summer on a yacht would be a good idea?

We're only trying to help, darling!

Helped her right into a fit of insanity, that's what they had done. After two weeks of helpful hints and loving "suggestions" about her future, she had snapped. And now she was going to die by shark attack.

Swim now, think later.

Her movements, which at first had been awkward and stilted, became smoother and stronger as she found her rhythm, and Cassandra began to feel strangely sanguine. Liberated, even.

So, she'd had better plans.

Okay, she admitted, detouring around another piece of kelp, *every plan I've ever had was better than this one. Every plan* anyone *has ever had was better than this one.*

This wasn't a plan so much as a crazy, reckless impulse.

Deep breaths, she told herself. *This is good.*

There was a distinct possibility she was going crazy, and that was bad, but overall, this was good. She'd wanted time alone. She'd gotten it! She'd wanted distance from her family. Gaining more every second! This was exactly the opportunity she'd been hoping for.

Well, maybe not *exactly*. She could have done without the quasi-near-death experience and possible insanity, but hey! She had taken action. She was taking charge of her life again. And *that* was exactly what she needed.

She also needed land. She was not cut out for life at sea. If she didn't reach the island soon, she wouldn't be cut out for life at all. Her muscles ached and her breathing was beyond labored, but the island was getting closer with every arduous stroke, so Cassandra pressed on. She refused to die now. She wouldn't give the ocean the satisfaction.

If I die, it will be on solid land, the way nature intended!

Her arms and legs felt like they were slowly turning to stone, her lungs were on the point of bursting, and at some point, she had lost her other sandal to the depths, but she could make out the outline of the shore.

"Take that, ocean! I'm going to live!"

Something brushed against her leg and she thrashed and screamed again, propelling herself though the water with renewed force.

That's what you get for taunting the ocean, she chided herself. *Keep your thoughts to yourself until you feel sand under your feet!*

The beach was getting closer and Cassandra could make out the silhouette of a behemoth structure, probably a resort of some kind. That was a stroke of luck. Someone was bound to be on duty at the front desk. She could just go in and tell them…what, exactly? That she had jumped off a yacht? Hardly.

Swim now, think later.

She could figure all that out later. First, she had to make it there.

"Land! I'm coming!"

Soon she was close enough that she could touch down with her feet, reveling in the feeling of sand squelching between her toes.

Lumbering through the water like a fly through molasses and wheezing like an asthmatic lapdog, Cassandra finally reached the shoreline and collapsed on the beach, panting with her cheek pressed to the ground as the foamy waves washed over her.

"Land!" she gasped. "Land!"

Cass lay there, repeating 'land' every few seconds just to express her joy at being back on it. She thought about kissing the ground, but already had sand in more places than she cared to name—she didn't need it in her teeth as well. Gradually, her breath and heart rate slowed to normal and Cassandra began to process the situation.

She had made it!

She had jumped off a yacht like a loon, but she had made it!

She felt exhausted and jubilant and alive and *free*.

And overwhelmed.

Now what?

Swim now, think later.

Wait, that wasn't right. She was done swimming. Now was the time to think.

"Alright," she said with conviction, and attempted to push herself to standing, but her arms gave out and she crumpled back to the shallows, face splashing in the salty water.

Good grief, I'm paralyzed! she thought as every muscle in her extremities screamed in protest. Now that the adrenaline of swimming for her life was fading, her body appeared to have checked out for the evening.

She lay like that for several moments, weighing the pros and cons of attempting movement again. On the upside, if she stayed there forever, she could ignore the fact that her body had turned into a limp noodle and her sanity clearly took the term 'vacation' far more seriously than she realized. On the downside, if she didn't regain contact with civilization, she might die. Exposure to the elements, carried away by the undertow, suckered to death by a mutant man-eating starfish…anything could happen.

Cassandra paused her mental cataloguing of potential catastrophes, struck by the idea, and a slow smile crept across her face.

Anything could happen.

For the first time in a long time, she liked the sound of that.

Wiggling her fingers and toes, which seemed to be working just fine, Cassandra slowly, gingerly, propped herself onto her forearms.

Success! Next step: stand up.

She carefully pulled herself back to her feet and took a step in the direction of the resort. She stumbled but caught herself, then grinned in triumph.

"Ha! You can't keep me down, ocean. I'm on my way back to hot showers, soft mattresses, and flaky pastries."

Cass made her way along the shoreline and slipped in an uneven patch of sand, falling headlong into the shallows and effectively re-covering herself in sand and water.

"Well, that's just great," she said, brushing soaked hair out of her eyes and leaving a dark smudge of sand on her forehead. She scowled at the horizon.

"You had to have the last laugh, didn't you, ocean?"

Cassandra slogged her way up the beach. With every step, sand flew up and stuck to her legs with what she felt to be a deliberately cheeky efficacy. As she tramped along, muttering darkly about the ocean and crazy people who jumped into it, Cassandra's mind flashed back to dinner that evening—one of the last conversations she'd had with her family before spontaneously abandoning ship in the middle of the night.

"Barbara Wellington's daughter just got an internship at Microsoft," her mother had informed her.

"How nice for Barbara Wellington." Cass deliberately ignored the hint she knew Miranda was trying to drop.

"And Suzanna Sherman's daughter is planning her wedding for next spring!"

"Brittney Sherman is only engaged because she blackmailed her fiancé into proposing," Cass's sister Beth had cut in. Cass grinned at her over their mother's sharp glance.

"I'm just saying, darling! Everyone else seems to be moving forward in some direction or another. We just want you to find yours!"

Well, she had a direction now. North. Or maybe East. Whatever direction the resort was in. She was moving forward—toward the resort—and she was moving forward with purpose, damn it! Her mother would be thrilled.

The closer she got to the structure, the nicer she realized it was, and the grubbier she became: sodden, grimy, and grumbling.

Highly manicured lawns, immaculate topiaries, and high-rising stone walls loomed judgmentally in the dark. She glared self-consciously at a particularly beautiful gladiola and was fairly positive that it glared back, swaying sanctimoniously in the cool night air.

You're getting paranoid, she told herself. *The shrubbery is not mocking you. Just go in there and ask to use the phone. Figure it out from there.*

Entering the lobby of the swanky resort, Cassandra did her best to appear as if she belonged, but she was uncomfortably aware that she was wet, windblown, and barefoot, tramping sand across an otherwise pristine entryway. She approached the front desk and smiled in what she hoped was a charming manner at the tight-lipped receptionist who had been frowning at her with clear disapproval and growing suspicion since the moment she'd walked through the gilded double doors.

"Hi," Cass began, as good an opening as any, but apparently not good enough to thaw the icy exterior of the woman eyeing her distastefully from across three feet of highly polished mahogany.

Cassandra went on unfazed, radiating normalcy as hard as she could, just a nice girl in an unfortunate situation.

"Hi…Judith," she continued, reading the woman's nametag, "I'm Cassandra Dillon, and I'm afraid I'm in a bit of a situation." Cassandra smiled an unsinkable smile, focusing all her energy on getting this iceberg of a woman to smile back.

No such luck.

Judith sniffed primly and reluctantly answered, "At the Silver Sands resort, we strive to make all our guests' stay as pleasant and comfortable as possible. I'll be glad to be of service in any way I can." All of this was said in a tone that suggested she would *actually* be glad to call security and would certainly do so given the slightest opportunity.

"Oh, I'm not a guest here, but if I could just use the phone, that would be an enormous help!" Cassandra smiled gratefully, a silent and subtle encouragement for Judith to cooperate.

"The telephone is reserved for resort guests only," Judith responded with a smile of her own, looking like a delighted crocodile.

"Okay, not a problem! I'd like to book a room, please," Cassandra reached for her purse, not excited to discover the amount she would have to charge her credit card to stay there, but she stopped dead when she realized she didn't have her purse. Of *course* she didn't have it! She'd jumped ship in a fit of pure madness, and now here she was, without a single worldly good to her name—no money, no identification, no *sunblock*—talking to a woman who, if the jubilant gleam in her eye was any indication, was about fifteen seconds away from having Cassandra physically escorted from the premises.

Cassandra laughed faintly, and Judith smiled coldly in return. An impatient crocodile.

"This is going to sound very strange," Cassandra began, "but I fell off a yacht today."

Judith raised her eyebrows, disbelief evident on her face.

"A yacht," she repeated, monotone.

"Yes, a yacht," Cassandra said defensively, staring Judith down.

Judith stared grimly back, not at all amused.

"You don't believe me?" Cassandra challenged. "Two hours ago, I was happily on my father's boss' yacht with my family." (She mentally blanched, knowing that 'happily' might be stretching the truth.) "It's called the Sea Dancer. I'm sure you could verify that in some registry somewhere. We were sailing past the island this evening, and I was enjoying the night air by myself on the deck. I thought I saw a dolphin, so I leaned over the rail, but then we hit a big wave and I was tossed over."

There, she thought to herself. *That sounds plausible. There's no way in hell I'm telling her that I jumped on purpose.*

"It was the middle of the night," she went on. "No one was around to hear me call for help. I'm lucky to be alive—I could have drowned! I'm cold and I'm wet and I'm traumatized and the least you could do is let me use the phone," she finished with a reproachful look at Judith, who gazed back, completely unmoved.

"The telephone is reserved for resort guests only."

Cassandra exhaled in frustration.

"Judith, you seem like a reasonable woman."

The secretary blinked impassively, and Cassandra reassessed her tactic. Judith seemed like Attila the Hun with a gold nametag.

"You're dedicated," Cass went on, choosing not to share her comparison out loud.

"Hardworking. Passionate about the rules. I understand that! I'm a rule-follower myself."

"I believe there are very specific rules about climbing railings on boats."

"There was a dolphin, Judith," Cassandra said flatly. "I got carried away. And I've learned my lesson! Getting thrown headlong into the ocean in the middle of the night and having to swim for my life is punishment enough, don't you think? I've paid my dues and learned never to break the rules again, and if you could just let me use the phone—"

"Company policy is quite clear," Judith interrupted, voice heavy with righteousness. "The employee manual explicitly states, 'use of resort telephones is to be limited to—'"

"It's admirable that you're so dedicated to company policy, but don't you think you're taking it a little far in this case? I just fell off a boat, for heaven's sake! My family is probably frantic. I'm sure the administration would understand if you let me call my parents to tell them I'm alive."

"I'm afraid I just can't risk it. Rules are made to be followed." Judith looked pointedly at Cassandra from under tight-knit, criticizing eyebrows.

"Judith," Cassandra smiled again, but the receptionist pursed her lips and neatly cut Cassandra off.

"No, I'm sorry," she said, dropping all pretenses of a stern but polite receptionist and moving straight into open hostility. "The Silver Sands is not open to the general public. We do not exist to cater to the whims of some soggy vagabond washed up on shore, no matter what her sob story may be."

Cassandra blinked in disbelief. "You can't be serious."

"Oh, I'm serious, missy. You can just go blink those eyes at somebody else. If you need to use a phone, there are other buildings on this island. Go tramp sand all over their foyers and demand that *their* staff break well-founded policies for you. I'm not having any of it here." She crossed her arms with an air of finality and looked down at Cassandra from atop her moral high ground.

"Wow," Cassandra said.

This was really more than she could take. She understood that her story was hard to swallow. She understood that she might not fit the standard of the resort's usual clientele. She understood that she was asking this woman to go against company policy, her better judgment, and clearly her nature as a whole by asking to use the telephone, and if that wasn't an option, Cassandra could accept that.

But she could not accept the attitude. She could not accept being called "missy" by this condescending desk clerk in a snobby resort on some god-forsaken island she didn't even know the name of, at the end of one of the worst days of her life. The stress of the whole night's ordeal, preceded by months of pent-up frustration came rushing to the surface and Cassandra took a deep breath to unleash a verbal fury on Judith, the likes of which she had never known and was not likely to recover from any time soon.

"Listen up, lady," she began, narrowing her eyes—but as quickly as the rage had come, it dissipated. The wind went right out of her sails. If Judith wouldn't let her use the phone, there wasn't much she could do about it. It was clear that the only way Cass would get that phone was by prying it from Judith's cold, dead hands. The thought held some appeal, but Cassandra just didn't have the energy for it.

"You're honestly refusing to let me use the phone?" she confirmed.

"I'm afraid I'm going to have to ask you to leave." Judith's eyes sparkled victoriously.

Cassandra exhaled, knowing she was beat. "You're a hard woman, Judith. A hard woman."

She turned on her heel, head held high, and marched proudly out the door, pretending not to notice the quiet squeak of her damp bare feet on the polished marble floor.

As soon as she was outside and safely out of view from judgmental Judith, Cassandra slumped against a wall, defeated.

Now what?

She could go in search of another phone, but it was the middle of the night. Most places were probably closed, and she wasn't likely to be met with any more warmth or understanding than she had at the Silver Sands, even if she did happen to find another establishment still open. More than that, her body was at a breaking point. Her muscles felt like lead, her skin and hair were caked with salt, her eyes burned with the desire to close and not open again for a week, and her brain was getting heavy with sleep.

Her adrenaline had abandoned her completely, maxed out by the night's aquatic adventure and ensuing run-in with Judith the human sunbeam, and Cassandra was exhausted. She just wanted to get out of these clothes, curl up under a blanket and sleep until she was thirty. She could then wake up, mature and wise, knowing exactly what to do with her life because she'd spent the last six years carefully planning it out in peaceful REM cycles. But for now, since she had no clothes, no blanket, and nowhere to enter said comatose state, all she could do was decide which bush to curl up under.

That was her only option, right?

At least, that's what her muddled brain was telling her: sleep under a bush. Or next to one, anyway. Just sleep somewhere. There was nothing more that could be done tonight, in this state, and if there was, she didn't know that she cared. She just needed sleep. And the resort seemed as safe a place as she was likely to find on the island. There was no telling what she'd discover if she ventured farther out tonight—maybe the rest of the island was populated entirely by criminals and psychopaths. But, since she was probably the craziest person the Silver Sands had ever inadvertently allowed onto its grounds, chances were good that she would be safe here. Right?

Right, her exhausted brain replied. *Stop rationalizing and just sleep.*

"Well, shrub, it looks you're stuck with me whether we like it or not," she said, choosing to sleep near the sanctimonious gladiola out of a sense of vengeance, with her head under a hibiscus bush and her feet by the self-satisfied stalk of blooms. "I hope I kick you in my sleep."

The grass was cool and the ground was solid, and as she closed her eyes and sleep claimed her, the last thing to cross her mind was how absolutely delightful it was not to be in the ocean.

Chapter Two

Cassandra woke up with a twig digging into her cheek and somebody horrible poking her shoulder. Her arms prickled with goosebumps and her entire body was mad at her—every muscle silently shrieked as she shifted, still mostly asleep, while half a dozen sharp rocks assaulted her spine. This was clearly what death felt like.

But she was resigned to meeting her end as long as she could do it without resuming full consciousness. She adjusted her position so that the twig was no longer stabbing her face, but the poking at her shoulder refused to subside. Who was this horrible person? Why wouldn't they let her die in peace?

"Go away, please; you're horrible," she mumbled, trying to roll away, but the poking escalated to shaking, and Cassandra yelped, snapping fully back to reality.

"Why?" she gasped, opening her eyes and taking in her assailant for the first time.

Cassandra found herself face to face with an unexpectedly good-looking man in his mid-twenties looking quizzically at her from under a mess of blonde hair.

She said nothing, but squinted blearily at the stranger. He seemed to be waiting for an explanation, but Cassandra was in no mood to provide one, hoping if she stayed quiet long enough, he would get bored and let her go back to sleep.

Finally, he broke the silence.

"So. Interesting evening?" His eyebrows were knit together with something resembling concern, but mostly he looked like he was trying not to laugh.

Well, that was just fantastic. First she was sneered at by Judith, and then she was shaken from a blissfully deep albeit uncomfortable sleep to be laughed at by this interloper. She would not be recommending this resort to other travelers.

"Oh, you know." Cassandra propped herself up on the backs of her arms, wincing as they burned in protest. She glared at the stranger. "Just a typical Tuesday night. Now if there's nothing I can do for you, Mr..."

"Drake." He held out his hand, which she grudgingly shook, shifting her weight to one aching arm. "Finnegan Drake."

"Nice to meet you, Mr. Drake," she said, purely out of a sense of social obligation. It would be nice if he would let her sleep, that's what would be nice. "But like I said, if there's nothing else I can do for you..." she trailed off as she lowered herself carefully back to the ground.

"I don't think so." He put his hand behind her shoulder and pulled her back to sitting. She groaned but didn't shrug him off.

"You look like you're having a rough night, but trust me, you're much better off talking to me than security. What's your name?"

"Cassandra Dillon."

"So, Cassandra Dillon, what's your story?"

Cassandra sighed, resigned to at least several more minutes of consciousness while this sadist interrogated her.

"If you must know, I fell off a yacht today."

***

Finn guffawed, but then he took in her sand-encrusted clothes, matted hair, and deadpan expression.

"Wait, you're serious?" His voice rose in alarm.

"Mr. Drake, I'm sleeping under a bush. How playful do you think I'm feeling right now?"

Finn sat back on his heels and closely surveyed the sodden, possibly mad woman in front of him. Her face was smudged and there were shadows under her eyes and a twig in her hair. He noted the crazy strawberry blonde curls (currently thick with saltwater and sand, and peppered with earth where she had been sleeping on it), the small button nose and the curve of her lips, her still dampish clothes, the dark streak of dirt contrasting starkly with her pale forehead, and the defiant gleam in her big blue eyes.

He'd seen her earlier that night, sparring with Judith from across the lobby. Even from a distance, her energy had been palpable—insistent, almost frantic, definitely hovering somewhere close to the edge. She'd been polite, but there was something slightly volatile about her—like she was suppressing the urge to scream. Or laugh hysterically.

Combine that with her then-sopping clothes and the fact that her hair and body had been caked with sand, and it had been obvious she was in some kind of situation. She had clearly been getting nowhere with the stolid receptionist, but just as he had decided to intervene, he'd been waylaid by a colleague. By the time he'd gotten free, she was gone. He'd chalked it up to "not meant to be" and left it at that.

Then he'd come across her on the lawn, looking bedraggled but adorable—though still slightly crazed—murmuring in her sleep and cuddling with the local flora. She was either completely off her rocker or in serious need of assistance. It didn't really matter; he knew he'd help her one way or the other. There was no denying it—he was intrigued. This girl had a story. And, he couldn't help noticing, really nice legs. She'd also allegedly fallen off a yacht today. It was pretty much a chivalry no-brainer.

"How did you end up here?" he asked, wanting to keep her talking to confirm whether she was genuinely sane.

"It's like I told your delightful receptionist," Cassandra began with a yawn, and then proceeded to tell him a story about a family vacation and a dolphin sighting that seemed plausible enough.

"And when Judith steadfastly refused to let me use the phone, I decided there was no better option than to lie down right here and figure it all out in the morning," she finished.

Finn openly grinned, picturing the interaction between this disheveled spitfire and the hotel's stalwart front desk manager. From where he'd been standing, it had been quite a showdown.

The scent of coconut drifted toward him, which he was fairly certain wasn't coming from any of the plant life surrounding them. He ignored the smell and said, "Well, it's technically morning now. What's your plan?"

He watched her whole body deflate as she said on a sigh, "I have no idea. I have no money. No ID. No clue what to do next. I can't pay for a hotel room. I can't call my family to have them arrange a hotel for me. And I'm so tired I can't think straight. I just want to lie back down under this wretched bush and sleep forever." She cast a baleful glance at the blossoms hovering near her face and looked like she was thinking about smacking them.

Finn shook his head. "That's ridiculous. These plants are clearly not meant for sleeping…they're all scratchy and twiggy…at least find a nice grassy patch somewhere."

"After the night I've had, I can handle some twigs."

"How about a mattress instead? You can sleep in my bed. Alone," he added quickly, as her eyebrows shot up and her eyes narrowed. "I'll sleep on the couch."

He flashed the same smile he'd been using to talk himself out of scrapes since his second-grade teacher had caught him emptying the contents of his juice box into Jennifer Templeton's backpack. In his experience, people found it charming. Cassandra Dillon was no exception, and he watched her relax a little, though she was obviously carrying out both sides of a vigorous mental debate.

Her mouth screwed up to one side, her brow furrowed, and her eyes darted back and forth as she quickly calculated the wisdom of going home with a man she'd just met. He was fascinated by how much movement she managed to convey while standing completely still.

"You can use my phone to call your family," he offered. "And if it helps, I promise not to murder you." Finn smiled again, endeavoring to look as non-threatening as possible and willing her to say yes. For reasons he didn't bother to analyze now, he wanted to get to know this girl.

***

Cassandra raised her eyebrows, appraising the man in front of her. Finnegan Drake. Potential psychopath. Or, if she were a glass-half-full kind of girl, which she was about half the time, he could also be a potential godsend. At this point she almost didn't care. Glass half empty, glass half full…the only glass she had any interest in at the moment was the kind that came with a little umbrella in it.

He seemed nice enough.

Famous last words, she grimaced, *but let's review. I could stay here and when I wake up in the morning, I won't be any better off than I am right now. Or, I could go home with this guy, who, if he turns out not to be a killer (fingers crossed), could possibly be very useful. So, I either continue to sleep outside tonight, or sleep in the bed of a man I met five minutes ago. Not great options. Either way, I probably have a fifty-fifty chance of getting mugged and left for dead…if I go with him, at least I'll get a blanket out of the deal.*

Taking a deep breath, she looked Finnegan Drake straight in the eye and said, "If you murder me, I will haunt you mercilessly."

His smile widened to a grin.

"Fair enough," he agreed.

"Lead the way, Mr. Drake."

Stifling a yawn, Cass hauled herself to her feet, groaning but managing not to fall over as her muscles reminded her what questionable choices she'd been making lately.

She took a few steps before she remembered that she was wasn't wearing shoes.

"Is it a pokey walk?" she asked drowsily.

"What?" The man looked at her with confusion in his bright blue eyes.

"My feet," she said simply.

"Aha," he said, looking down. "Give me just a minute. Don't fall asleep!"

"No promises," she said to the spot where he'd been standing as he jogged off in the direction of the resort entrance.

She stared tiredly into space, blinking in progressively longer intervals until he came jogging back, holding a pair of disposable-looking flip-flops.

"Compliments of the front desk," he said, and she looked at him in disbelief. How had he sweet-talked Judith into giving him shoes?

"They keep them on hand for spa-goers and pool-users," he explained.

"Thank you," she murmured, slipping the sandals onto her feet and wobbling a bit in her exhaustion.

He held out a hand, prepared to steady her if necessary but giving her space.

"Thank you," she said again when she was situated. "I'm ready."

He started walking and she trailed behind the stranger in the dark, absentmindedly wondering if she had ever done anything this stupid before…previous events of the evening notwithstanding. Doing a quick scan of her life up to this point, she decided, nope, this was pretty much a low point.

When she was six, she had wandered away from her family during a camping trip, following a butterfly and a trail of mushrooms because she was sure they would lead her to fairies. (She was still pretty disappointed that they hadn't.) It had taken her parents hours to find her, but no real harm had been done.

Then when she was twelve, she had tried to shave her little sister's head because she'd wanted to donate hair to Locks of Love but hadn't wanted to part with her own.

As a teenager, she'd scraped her mother's car against a fence, scratching most of the paint off of one side. She'd tried to cover it up with nail polish, and then she'd had to go buy twenty more bottles of the same color to make the whole thing match.

Her freshman year of college, she had started a small kitchen fire in her dorm trying to bake cupcakes for the cleaning staff.

She had a history of acting without entirely thinking through the consequences, but this blew everything else out of the water, so to speak.

Cassandra was interrupted from her reverie when she realized her guide was talking to her.

"Hm?" she managed to say, not feeling up to complete sentences if avoidable.

"I said my place is just another couple of blocks away. Not too far."

"Mm, that's nice," she murmured sleepily.

"Do you smell coconut?" he asked suddenly.

"No…" Through her haze of drowsiness, she thought that was an odd question. Maybe he was unbalanced after all. "Oh, wait, yes. My sunblock."

My sunblock! she realized with a sudden burst of horror. *I'm stranded on a tropical island with no sunblock! What was I thinking? I'll be burnt to a crisp in two days…I'll look like a barbequed hot dog!*

"I don't want to look like a hot dog," she muttered out loud.

Finnegan Drake looked puzzled and she realized she must sound nuts, but she had other things to focus on. Like continuing to put one foot in front of the other rather than giving into the urge to collapse on the sidewalk and fall asleep right there. To hell with a blanket.

She was vaguely aware that the stranger had started to make small talk—probably to gauge whether she was actually crazy—asking questions about where she was from. She did her best to respond, but her answers were becoming increasingly incoherent. She just wanted to fall asleep and put this whole day behind her.

Happily, they soon rounded a corner and stopped in front of a small, comfortable looking bungalow.

"This is it," he announced.

"Hooray," Cass said groggily, leaning against the side of the building while he fumbled for his keys.

If he gave her a soft place to lie down, Cassandra decided he could kill her if he wanted to. Just as long as she was allowed to sleep.

***

As he opened the front door and stepped aside to let Cassandra in, Finn felt strangely self-conscious. He didn't usually bring strangers into his home, and now that this girl was standing in the middle of his living room with her wide, wandering eyes, things that seemed innocuous and functional when he was by himself suddenly appeared bland and spartan. He was aware of his mason jar cups in the kitchen, his surfboard on two crates that served as a coffee table and took up practically his entire front room, and the almost total lack of decor that made a living space inviting.

Granted, he was only staying here for the summer, but maybe he should get a plant or something…brighten the place up a little. Not that she was judging him. She had slept under a bush and gone home with him less than five minutes after meeting him…Cassandra Dillon seemed like a pretty easy-going individual.

He watched her out of the corner of his eye as he gathered spare blankets and a pillow, surreptitiously trying to kick dirty socks under the couch and whisk used dishes into the sink without her noticing. She smiled softly as she sank down onto his overstuffed brown couch.

"I'll sleep here," she said, eyes already closed. "No point in you giving up your bed."

He started to protest, but she was half asleep already, so he laid a blanket over her and placed an extra one on the surfboard easily within reach.

"Can I get you anything? Glass of water? Extra pillow?"

"No, I'm fine," she said dreamily. "Thanks for letting me stay here. If I'm still alive when I wake up in the morning, I'll appreciate it very much…" Her words trailed off and she was out like a light.

His lips quirked in a smile as he looked down at her, unkempt and unconscious on his sofa. Poor thing. She'd had a rough night. Exhausted to the point of incoherency. But she'd be alright. Asleep she seemed innocent, vulnerable…but he'd seen the flash in her eyes when he'd woken her up and the stormy expression from across the room as she'd argued with Judith. Cassandra Dillon could take care of herself.

Although, something about her story didn't make sense. If her family's boat had been on route, it should have been pretty far out to sea. Even strong swimmers would have had trouble with the distance, especially when taken by surprise. And in the middle of the night, no less. How had she not drowned? Adrenaline, maybe?

And if she'd fallen, why wasn't she more shaken up? She seemed flustered and frustrated, sure, but not particularly disturbed by her close encounter with death. It didn't entirely add up.

He shrugged, not overly concerned. She seemed sweet and spirited—slightly neurotic, maybe, but overall, it was hard not to like Cassandra Dillon.

In the morning he'd help her get in touch with her family and figure out how to send her back to them. By tomorrow the whole mess would be sorted and it would be like she'd never been there. The thought didn't hold much appeal. He was intrigued by her situation and drawn to those wide blue eyes and long pale legs. The thought of her disappearing from his life so quickly felt like a missed opportunity. But like he'd said, they would sort it out in the morning.

Chapter Three

Cassandra woke to the furtive bangings of someone trying to make coffee quietly and failing miserably. She propped herself up on one arm and looked around, momentarily confused as to where she was and why her body hated her. Her limbs ached to their cores, her tongue felt like an old sponge, and her skin was dry and tight. Then the events of the previous evening came back in a rush.

Oh, right. She had lost her mind the night before. And now she was defenseless in a strange man's house. What had she been thinking?

Her gaze wandered to the kitchen and she couldn't help but smile when she saw the man from the previous night tiptoeing around the small alcove, wincing and making silent shushing motions whenever something made a particularly loud clang. He looked up and seemed surprised to see her sitting upright.

Smiling apologetically, he held up a mug.

"Coffee?"

She shook her head and smiled cautiously back.

"No, thanks. I'll take a glass of water, though."

So far, so good. Serial killers didn't usually offer their victims coffee first, right? Maybe going home with him hadn't been rash and dangerous. Maybe she wasn't crazy after all!

She shifted on the couch, feeling contrite when she saw how much sand and debris littered the upholstery. If this man was officially not a murderer, she would offer to vacuum his cushions. Right now, he was offering to hydrate her, so he was okay in her book. All the salt on her skin and hair was making her feel mummified, and she was parched.

Shuffling into the postage-stamp-sized kitchen to stand beside him, she was a little taken aback by how much taller and broader he seemed in close quarters. He turned to hand her the glass, hitting her with the full effect of those dimples and electric blue eyes, and she felt her pulse kick up a notch. At the resort, she'd observed vaguely that he was good-looking but had been too manic to really notice. Now, standing six inches from him in a cramped little kitchen, she was acutely aware of it.

She blinked, rapidly trying to bring her mind back to the situation at hand. Water—right!

"Thank you, Mister…Drake, wasn't it?"

"Call me Finn. We've already spent the night together…I think we can skip the formalities."

Oh, my. She'd spent the night in the home of a veritable Adonis and passed out on the couch while he slept in the next room. Just her luck. To top it off, she probably looked like hell. Her hand unconsciously went to her hair, which felt coarse and gritty after her late-night swim. Maybe if she pulled her hair back…her eyes flicked to the hair band around her wrist and she felt a small jolt of respect for the thing—it was a stout bit of elastic to have stayed on throughout her ocean jaunt. That was more than she could say for her treacherous sandals…

"I was just about to take a shower"—Finn interrupted her thoughts and Cassandra's brain momentarily glitched, picturing this man wet and naked— "but there's a phone in my bedroom, just through here." He led her through a doorway off the main room.

"Feel free to call your family as soon as you'd like. I'm sure they'll want to know you're safe."

Cassandra felt a stab of guilt. Here she'd been having carnal thoughts about a stranger when her family was probably going out of their minds with worry.

"Thank you! They're probably in a panic by now."

"Sure. I'll give you some privacy. Just holler if you need anything."

He closed the door to the bathroom behind him and soon Cassandra heard water running. She turned to the landline with a feeling of doom. This was not going to be a fun conversation.

Sorry, Mom and Dad, but your hovering was driving me crazy, so I jumped off the boat to get some time to myself.

Probably not the best approach.

Sorry Mom and Dad, but the thought of spending my entire summer with you and Beth on a floating prison was making me crazy and there was no way that all that time together was going to help me sort out my life, so I jumped off the boat to get some time to myself.

Hm. Maybe there was just no other way to spin it.

Taking a deep breath, she lifted the receiver and dialed the number for her mother's cell phone.

"Hello, Miranda Dillon speaking," her mother answered breezily.

"Hi, Mom," Cassandra said tentatively.

"Cassandra?" Her mother sounded confused. "You silly thing, what are you doing calling from the cabin? Just take six steps outside and talk to us in person."

"What?" Cassandra was taken aback. "I would, Mom, but—"

"Honestly, darling, I know you're not one for sunlight or mornings or the outdoors, but your father and I had breakfast hours ago. And you'll have to get used to the sun eventually. Just slather yourself up with sunblock and come have breakfast before it's lunchtime."

"Mom, I can't—"

"Why, are you not feeling well?" Miranda's voice was momentarily sympathetic, but the moment was short-lived. "If you'd just take a Dramamine like I told you to, you wouldn't be getting seasick."

I don't believe this, Cassandra thought, but her mother rattled on.

"We'll be on this yacht all summer, darling. At some point, your body will have to adjust. You can't spend the whole cruise with your head in the toilet, or how will you ever make decisions about what to do when the summer is over? No, the best thing to do is to take some Dramamine and come out for breakfast when you're feeling better."

"Mom, I don't need Dramamine!"

"Of course, you need Dramamine, Cassandra!" her mother argued. "Why else do you think you're sick?"

"I'm not sick, Mother!"

"Then what on Earth are you still doing in your cabin?" Miranda demanded.

"That's what I've been trying to tell you!" Cassandra said, exasperated. "I'm not *in* my cabin. I haven't come out for breakfast yet because I'm not on the boat."

Cassandra was dimly aware that the sound of water in the other room had stopped, but she focused on her mother's reaction.

"Of course, you're on the boat; don't be silly. Where else would you be?"

"No, Mom. I'm not."

For a brief moment, Miranda was speechless, and Cassandra took advantage of the rare silence to say in a rush, "Look, it's a long story, but I fell off the yacht last night. Don't worry, I'm fine, but I'm still sorting things out, and I'll probably need your help later today. I can't talk now so I'll call you back soon! I just wanted to let you know that I'm safe. Give my love to Dad and Beth!"

"Cassandra?" she heard her mother say, but she hung up before she could be bombarded by questions to which she had no answers.

Knocking on the door of the bathroom, she heard a confused, "Yeah?" and burst inside, sailing right past a very surprised-looking Finn to begin pacing back and forth.

"I don't believe this!" she exclaimed, waving her hands wildly. "Nobody even noticed I was gone! Can you believe that? Their daughter disappears in the middle of the night and they don't even miss a beat on their way to breakfast!" Cassandra shook her head, outraged. "Breakfast! That's what my mother was going on about! I fall overboard and she's prattling away about breakfast and Dramamine!"

"Your mom eats Dramamine for breakfast?" Finn asked around his toothbrush, and Cassandra paused from her tirade to look at him, noticing for the first time that he was wearing nothing but a towel wrapped low around his hips, staring at her with raised eyebrows and a toothbrush in his mouth. Cassandra stared back, trying not to let her eyes wander or notice the droplet of water running down his chest, and trying particularly hard not to wonder what was underneath that towel.

"What?" she asked, her train of thought completely derailed.

He took his toothbrush out of his mouth and said, "Nothing. They didn't notice you were gone?"

Cassandra cleared her throat. "No, can you imagine? It's ridiculous!"

She paused thoughtfully for a moment and continued, "Although to be fair, it was late when I fell…they were all asleep when it happened and I don't exactly have a habit of getting up with the sun. It's not unusual for me to be in bed until about now anyway. I guess I shouldn't be surprised," she finished with a sigh, sinking down onto the edge of the bathtub, "and I should just be glad that they weren't worried for nothing."

She shook her head and glanced at Finn, then quickly looked away again.

"Sorry to interrupt. I was just a little shocked…I was all prepared to reassure a frantic mother that I'm not dead at the bottom of the ocean, and I end up having to explain that I'm not lazy or puking, just missing."

"Much less upsetting," Finn said, toweling off his hair with a hand towel.

Cassandra's eyes drifted to his arm, bicep casually flexed while he stared at her, waiting for a response.

"Anyway," she said, standing abruptly, "I'll let you finish. Up. Here."

She needed to get a grip.

Say something normal and stop ogling the stranger!

"Do you want me to make some breakfast?" she offered.

"You don't have to do that!" he insisted.

"Oh, please. It's the least I can do to say thank you for saving me from the streets last night. And for not murdering me in my sleep. And to apologize for barging in on you just now."

"And for ogling me," he added with a wicked grin.

She had the decency to blush.

"That, too. Though if you're going to parade around wet and in a towel, you should expect to be ogled."

"I wasn't parading! I was safely behind closed doors when you crashed in here and compromised my virtue." He tried to look pious and failed by a long shot. "Actually, I don't mind. It's a shame you didn't come in a few minutes earlier—you missed all the good stuff."

"Right," Cassandra squeaked. "I'll go make breakfast then. Do you like French toast?"

"Cassandra Dillon," Finn said seriously, "I may ask you to marry me by the end of the day."

She gave a strangled laugh and brushed past him, shutting the door behind her with decided firmness, creating a solid barrier between herself and all the towel-clad temptation standing not three feet away. Finnegan Drake and his willingness to help her were the only assets she had on this island. It seemed like an unequivocally bad idea to risk compromising that by getting involved in a tawdry fling with him, no matter how appealing the idea might be.

"Get it together, Dillon," she told herself sternly, and headed toward the kitchen.

***

Finn grinned as the door shut with a loud click and he heard an audible exhalation coming from the other side. There was a moment of silence before he heard Cassandra mutter something to herself, then footsteps retreating from the bedroom. Turning to face his reflection in the mirror, Finn saw himself looking patently amused. He probably shouldn't have teased her like that, especially when he was mostly naked, but she had come barreling into the bathroom, talking a million miles a minute, and then she abruptly stopped mid-rant to look at him like he was made of chocolate. Frankly, he was proud of himself for not boosting her up onto the sink and taking her right there.

He had a brief vision of Cassandra, eyes closed, back arched, pale legs wrapping around him as he let the towel fall to the ground. Then he shook his head to banish the image and resolved not to make any more suggestive comments. She needed his help and he wasn't about to go taking advantage of a vulnerable girl in a tough situation, no matter how nice her legs might be.

He took his time getting dressed, figuring it couldn't hurt to give his libido a while to recover, and by the time he wandered back into the kitchen, he found her, golden red curls pulled back into a ponytail, expertly flipping two slices of French toast and adding them to an already substantial pile next to the oven. She had laid out butter, syrup, and a plate of sliced fruit on the table.

"I hope you don't mind me making myself at home," she said with a sideways glance.

"Are you kidding? This is great! I feel a little guilty letting you work this hard, though. Shouldn't you be focusing on how to get back to your family?"

"Oh, apparently they're not that worried about getting me back, and truth be told, I'm not all that anxious to be getting back to them. I love my family, but they drive me crazy."

Something in her tone brought back the feeling that he was missing something important about her story, but he was distracted by the wafting scent of cinnamon as she carried the finished stack of French toast past him into his tiny dining nook. He pulled some passion fruit juice from the fridge, got two mason jar glasses from the cupboard, and joined her at the table.

"And why is that?" he asked, referring to her family as he loaded his fork with French toast and took his first bite. "Holy crap," he said before she had a chance to respond. "This is delicious! This is not normal French toast…what did you do to it?"

"Oh, I added a few things beyond the typical vanilla and cinnamon…orange zest, almond extract…nothing too exciting."

"No kidding. Where did you learn to cook?"

"I roomed with a culinary student the semester I studied abroad in France. I picked up a few things."

"Apparently. You're amazing."

"I almost never set things on fire," she said truthfully. "I have to say, though, I was surprised to find any of those ingredients in your kitchen. I didn't expect such a well-stocked spice cabinet."

She politely didn't say *because the rest of your place has the warmth of a walk-in freezer,* but Finn followed the logic. He appreciated her tact, though.

"You must cook," she concluded.

"Simple stuff, sure. I manage not to starve but I've never actually touched most of the things in there. I'm renting this place for the summer from an old family friend—Andre. He owns a restaurant on the island, so the pantry came well furnished, even if the rest of the place didn't."

"And you work at the resort?"

"Among other things."

"Do you need to be getting into work soon?" Cassandra sat up straighter, looking concerned as the thought occurred.

"No, it's fine. I'm a bartender. My shift doesn't start until this evening, and I'm actually working somewhere else tonight." Finn leaned back in his chair and crossed his arms behind his head. "I'm free all day."

Apparently relieved to know that there was nothing pressing she was keeping him from, Cassandra continued, "So you're only here for the summer?"

"Yeah. I just finished the last semester of my master's degree in anthropology and I like to spend my summers doing odd jobs in different places to observe the local culture."

"You see a lot of local culture at the resort bar, do you?"

"I also bartend at Andre's restaurant, so between the two places, I get the full spectrum of life on the island. The resort tips better but the restaurant is a lot more fun. And it's fascinating to see the juxtaposition of the two environments, how the two sides of life on the island clash and intersect, how interwoven they are. In so many ways they're polar opposites, but they necessarily feed off of each other. They've created this symbiotic relationship—" Finn broke off as he realized that he was rambling to a captive audience.

She was probably trying to figure out when she could catch the next ferry out of here and he was waxing eloquent about the paradoxes of tourist culture. Cassandra grinned at him over her juice and he cleared his throat.

"Anyway, it's interesting stuff."

"It sounds interesting," she said. "I was a French major in my undergrad. I love hearing about different cultures—food, language, history, traditions—it's all the best parts of life."

Finn looked at the woman sitting across the table, beaming at him and nodding with interest at the phrase *symbiotic relationship* around forkfuls of the best French toast he'd ever tasted. Cassandra Dillon was rapidly becoming his idea of the perfect woman. But that didn't change the fact that she was leaving this island as soon as circumstances allowed, and he had taken it upon himself to help her on her way. As much as he hated to admit it, it was about time to get down to brass tacks.

"I agree," he said, "and I would love to sit here all day talking food and history, but I'm sure you want to be getting back. It shouldn't be too difficult to get you to the next port before the ship docks. If you're in a hurry, I'll bet we could even contact your parents and arrange to drop you off mid-way. A buddy of mine has a boat that I'm sure he wouldn't mind lending to the cause. We'll have you back tanning on deck with your family in no time," he finished doubtfully with a glance at her pale skin, realizing that this was probably not a girl whose skin suffered from an overabundance of UV rays.

"Well-connected guy," she mused, sounding almost moody.

"Is something wrong?" he asked.

Suddenly Cassandra was looking everywhere around the room except at him.

"I'm not really sure how to tell you this," she said, "but I don't actually want to go back."

Finn perked up at the thought of her staying on land a while longer, but he said, "I'm confused. You fell off. In the middle of the night. I imagine that kind of put a damper on vacation with your family. Don't you want to get back?"

"Right," she said nervously, "about that...I didn't exactly fall, so much as I jumped off the ship."

"You what?"

She took a deep breath and met his eyes. "I jumped."

"You jumped."

"Yes."

"Off of a yacht."

"Yes."

"Into the ocean."

"Yes."

"Why?"

"I know it sounds crazy—"

"Yes."

"—But I just sort of...lost it."

"Lost it," Finn repeated. He knew there had been something fishy about her whole story.

This girl was nuts.

"It was a whim, a crazy impulse, a stupid, spur of the moment decision. I was alone on the deck, feeling overwhelmed..." She was speaking quickly now, hands flying and ponytail bouncing all over the place. "My whole life kind of caught up with me and I just...lost it. I saw an opportunity to get away and I made a break for it. Snap reaction. Simple as that."

"Cassandra, there's nothing *simple* about that."

"Listen, Finn," she leaned forward earnestly, and he got slightly lightheaded looking into her crazy blue eyes. "I know this sounds bad. And I truly appreciate everything you've done for me…you've been absolutely wonderful. You didn't have to do any of it and I will be grateful to you until the end of time. If you decided to turn me out on the streets right now, I wouldn't hold it against you one bit. But if you can believe that I had my reasons for doing what I did, unbalanced though they may seem, and understand that now that I've done it, I absolutely from the depths of my soul do not want to go back to that ship, maybe you can help me find a way to make it work. And if you can do that, then you will be a prince among men and I will personally look into having a statue erected in your honor."

She crinkled her forehead and looked so damn sincere that Finn knew he had no choice.

He tried without success to feel aggravated at the prospect of helping Cassandra Dillon out of this mess. She was a nut, but she was open and electric. The idea of spending more time with her was the most intriguing opportunity to cross his path in ages.

Affecting an exasperated sigh, he asked, "What can I do?"

***

Cassandra couldn't quite believe her ears.

"Really?" A wide smile lit up her face as she launched herself at the man across the table and kissed him soundly on the cheek. "Finnegan Drake, you are an angel!"

"Yeah, yeah," he said, looking a little dazed. "I want my statue made of gold. None of this silver or bronze nonsense."

"You can have it made of caviar and diamonds. Whatever you want. You are an absolute saint!"

"I haven't actually done anything yet. You may want to hold off on all this unbridled admiration until I've contributed something useful."

"Not necessary," Cassandra said confidently. "I'm sure you'll come through beautifully! I have absolute faith."

"I'm not sure I've earned that." He looked dubious.

"Don't worry about it! Nothing could be simpler...I'll just call my mother back and tell her I won't be joining them for the rest of the summer, then I'll ask her to send my things. In the meantime, I'll work on finding a place to stay and a means of supporting myself. You help out wherever you think you can." She smiled beatifically, pleased now that she had a plan.

Again, it wasn't quite a plan so much as a loose outline of a vague direction to take from here, but it was more than she'd woken up with that morning. And what was more, her secret was out and Finn hadn't thrown her to the streets or had her committed. All in all, she considered the day a victory thus far.

"So, here's what I think we should do," she continued. "I'll clear away all this breakfast stuff and then, if you don't mind me using your phone again, I'll call my parents and fill them in on what's happening. Then maybe you and I can brainstorm some ideas about where I might stay for the summer? You know the island, so I'm hoping you'll know some places I could look into."

"I'll clean up," he replied, already stacking plates and silverware. "You made breakfast…I can't let you do the dishes, too. That would be cruel. Go make your phone call."

"Thanks, Finn!" Cassandra bounded into the bedroom and shut the door behind her, feeling positively gleeful until she got to the phone. Then her bubble burst.

Edging her way toward the nightstand where the phone sat, she eyed it with distaste, feeling less sure of herself now that the moment had arrived to actually tell her parents that she was abandoning their summer trip. In theory it was liberating and exhilarating, claiming her independence this way. But in the jarring light of reality, it seemed ungrateful and more than a little harsh. There was no getting around it, though. It had to be done.

Sitting on the edge of the bed with a sigh, Cassandra slowly dialed her father's number. Her mother was probably in a tizzy by now, and Cassandra didn't think she could explain the situation without making it worse.

"Robert Dillon." Her father's voice came through the line sharper than normal—tinged, Cassandra noted with a pang of guilt, with anxiety.

"Hi, Dad."

"Cassandra? Thank God! Your mother told me what happened—where are you?"

"Um…" Cassandra floundered, realizing with horror that she had no idea where she was. She had never thought to ask.

"Could you hold on for just one second, Dad?"

"Cassandra—"

"Just one second!" She ran back into the kitchen and asked, "What island is this?"

Finn stopped in the middle of scrubbing a plate and looked at her in amazement. "You don't even know what island you're on?"

"Not now! My dad's on the line. Will you just tell me where I am?"

Finn gave her the name and shook his head in disbelief, chuckling as he did so. Cassandra shot him a look of pure venom and dashed back into the bedroom.

"Sorry about that, Dad! Had to check on something."

She gave him the information and he responded quickly, "That can't be too far away. We'll turn around right now! Just as soon as we pull up the coordinates."

"Actually, Dad…" Cassandra closed her eyes.

Just say it.

"I don't want you to come back for me."

"Have you arranged a way to rendezvous with us instead?"

"No, Dad, I mean I won't be meeting up with you again at all this summer."

Silence.

"Here's the thing," she blurted out. "This has been a rough couple of years for me. Post-grad funk, moving back home, and then everything with Gram…" Her throat tightened a little at that, but she ignored it and went on. "I've been floundering and we all know it. I know that this vacation was supposed to help clear my mind and get me focused, but I hate the ocean! And I don't like cruises. And I love you guys, but I need some time away to make my own decisions and live my own life. I think this is for the best. I've met someone who is going to help me find a job and an apartment for the summer. I'm safe and I'm happy and I feel like this is the right place for me to be."

There was a long pause while she waited for her father to process everything she had just thrown at him. It was a heavy, pregnant pause, full of unspoken alarm, and Cassandra could practically see her father's normally placid face wrinkled with paternal distress.

"Who is this person? Are you sure you can trust them?"

"His name is Finn and he's been nothing but helpful so far—"

"He?" The concern in her father's voice was now palpable. "Cassandra, if this is about some boy—"

"Of course not! This is about me figuring out my life. For heaven's sake, I have enough to worry about without complicating everything by bringing some guy into the picture!"

"Alright." Her father still sounded wary. "I just wanted to be sure. Well, Cass, if you think this is what you need to do, of course we'll support you. Beth will be disappointed, though."

Cassandra smiled affectionately. "Beth will hardly notice I'm gone. Every time you dock, she'll be heading straight to the nearest beach, looking for cute college boys. A few of the islands on the itinerary have topless beaches, don't they?"

"Don't even joke about it." Obviously, her father had had the same thought.

Cassandra laughed and asked tentatively, "I was hoping though, that you guys wouldn't mind sending me my things. I'll be looking for a job first thing this afternoon, but it will take a little time to get established. I have money in my checking account, obviously, but I don't have my debit card or any cash with me. If I could have you on standby to talk to potential landlords or employers who will need my information..."

"Of course."

"Thanks, Dad! And one last thing...would you mind explaining all this to Mom and Beth? I'll call them later, but I'm still feeling a little overwhelmed and I'm not sure I could justify this decision three times over today."

"I'll tell them."

"Thank you! I love you—I'll call again when I have more of an idea of how things will shape up."

"We'll talk soon, Cass. Be safe."

"I always am." Cassandra squinted at the semi-truthfulness of that statement, but hung up the phone feeling relieved and upbeat, if shaky.

That went well, she thought, feeling an immense surge of gratitude toward her unflappable father. *Now I just have to live up to this decision.*

With an exhale that was difficult to identify as a sigh of relief or groan of uncertainty, Cassandra went to find Finn and tell him the good news.

She found him putting away the last of the dishes and singing along while the radio played *Burning Down the House*.

Pausing for a moment to enjoy the view, she thought, *Nothing sexier than a hot guy doing housework.*

Finn put the final plate in its cupboard and shut the door with a flourish, spinning on his heel as he belted out about fighting fire with fire. He stopped short when he realized Cassandra was standing right behind him, and smiled at her sheepishly.

"Good song," she teased as he turned down the volume on the music.

"Hell yes!" he said, quickly recovering his dignity. "Gotta love the Talking Heads. So how did it go? Did they take it well?"

"Amazingly well, yes. My dad was much more likely to take it in stride than my mother or sister, so I called him instead. Mom will be convinced that I'm having a nervous breakdown and flutter around until she gets distracted, and my sister will assume that I'm shacking up with a hot islander and don't want to tell our parents."

Their eyes met and held a moment too long and Cassandra shivered, feeling the heat of that look in the pit of her stomach.

"Of course," she hurried on, "neither of those things are true. At least, I'm pretty sure I'm not having a nervous breakdown. I'm just taking some space and making some life decisions…my dad understands. He'll explain it to them."

"Speaking of decisions," Finn cleared his throat, "I've been thinking about where you might stay while you're here. I don't suppose you'll be happy sleeping on my couch the rest of the summer and I only have the one room—"

"Oh, I'll be finding a place as soon as I can!"

Cassandra briefly allowed herself to imagine sharing a room with Finn for the next three months, crawling into bed with him at night, pressing herself against his long, lean body, letting her hand wander down his beautifully sculpted torso—then promptly snapped herself back to reality and said, "I don't want to put you out any longer than necessary."

"It's no trouble at all," he said quickly. "You're welcome any time! But I kind of figured you'd feel that way, so I was thinking, I'd like to introduce you to my cousin Daphne. She's great, and she's actually looking for a roommate right now. If you guys hit it off, I think it would be perfect. It's a win-win."

"That sounds amazing! You are the best!"

"Hey, no problem. I'll call her right now if you want to shower and change out of those clothes. You can borrow a t-shirt and sweatpants, and I'll wash your things from last night while you're getting ready."

The prospect of getting out of her salt-encrusted outfit and washing all the sand out of her hair was absolute heaven.

"You are a god," she said fervently. "Keep up this kind of talk and I may just accept that marriage proposal."

***

Finn watched her walk away and told himself to get a grip. He wouldn't focus on the lingering glance they'd just shared or the flash of heat he'd sworn he'd seen in her eyes when she'd mentioned an island affair. And he definitely wouldn't think about the fact that at this very moment, she was taking her clothes off in his bedroom.

The sound of running water made his brain swerve rebelliously as an image of Cassandra in the shower flashed into his mind unbidden. For a moment, his thoughts wandered and he imagined himself in the shower with her, kissing water droplets off her shoulder, sliding his hand up her smooth torso to cup her breast, then moving between her thighs and making her moan—not that he would actually do it. She was just one room away, hot and wet and completely desirable, but he had promised to help her and that's what he was going to do.

Help, not seduce.

"Right," he said out loud, walking into the bedroom and picking up the receiver. "Help, not seduce. Remember that, Drake."

He repeated this to himself as the phone rang and he waited to hear his cousin's perky voice at the other end of the line.

"Hello," she chirped.

"Daphne? It's Finn."

"Hey, cuz, haven't heard from you in a few days! What's new?"

He laughed. "Funny you should ask…a lot, actually. But here's the punch line: I found you a roommate."

"Did you?" She sounded delighted. "I'm skeptical, obviously, but I'm prepared to be persuaded. Tell me all about them!"

"It's kind of hard to explain…she's new in town and sort of ended up on the island unexpectedly, but she wants to stay for the summer and she's looking for a place to crash."

"What does she do? What's she like?" Daphne asked without a moment's pause between the questions.

"Her name is Cassandra and she's smart and spunky and makes killer French toast—"

"I love French toast!" Daphne interjected.

"—and the two of you will have a blast together. I think we should all meet up for drinks and you can find out for yourself how much you'll like her."

Finn tactfully avoided telling his cousin that he had known Cassandra less than twenty-four hours.

"Sure, I'm game! Let's meet up at Andre's before your shift. Five o'clock?"

"Perfect. See you then! Thanks, Daph."

"Thank me later—I haven't agreed to anything yet. But I'm intrigued! See you at five!"

Chapter Four

Cassandra walked into the partially open-air restaurant and looked around appreciatively. She felt like she had just stepped into a Jack Vettriano painting. The front of the building was separated from the beachfront street by several decorative screens which allowed a gentle breeze to float amongst the tables. A large teak bar greeted patrons directly opposite the front entrance and Finn waved to the man serving drinks, but there was no one behind the hostess podium so he led Cass to a table in the middle of the room, nodding to several of the servers as they passed by.

On the edge of the table was a vase with a beautiful tropical flower that Cassandra had never seen before but smelled amazing, and the Italian tango was playing in the background. She danced a little in her seat as Finn passed her a menu.

"Shouldn't we wait for your cousin to order?"

"Nah, she'll probably have a free drink in front of her within five minutes of sitting down. Drew is on duty and he's been after her forever…I don't think

Daphne's had to pay for anything in this restaurant in weeks."

A cute, dark-haired waiter strolled over to their table, grinning at Finn and smacking him on the shoulder with a stack of menus as he approached.

"Hey Finn, shouldn't you be working? Who's your friend?"

"I'm not on duty for another hour, and your customer service needs work. This is Cassandra. Cassandra, meet Drew."

"Nice to meet you." He smiled. "You guys ready to order?"

Finn looked at Cass. "How do you feel about calamari, coconut prawns, and caprese flatbread to start?"

"Sounds great!" Cassandra scanned the menu.

"You got it," Drew nodded. "Anything to drink?"

"Just water for me—I've got to work soon. Cassandra?"

She stared at the menu with wide eyes and looked overwhelmed. "Everything looks amazing! This might take me a while. I think I'll wait for Daphne to make up my mind."

"Daphne's meeting you? Excellent! I'll be right back with two waters."

Suddenly, a perky little brunette in a purple halter top and flowy floral skirt blew into the restaurant like a hurricane on speed and plopped herself down at their table. She had impossibly curly hair that framed her face in tight, dark ringlets, and an open, sunny smile.

"Sorry I'm late," she shook her head, wild ringlets bouncing. "I ran into Mary Ella on my way out the door and we got to chatting about her birthday coming up. But here I am now! You must be Cassandra," she held out her hand for Cassandra to shake, fingernails tipped an iridescent turquoise.

"Daphne Drake," the woman dimpled at her. "So pleased to meet you. Finn hasn't told me much, but he says you're smart and spunky and I love smart and spunky! Tell me all about yourself!"

They were interrupted by their server returning with the waters, along with something red and frosty in a tall, shapely glass, lavishly decorated with various fruits, sword spears, and an umbrella. He placed the creation in front of Daphne with a wink and said, "Here you go, Daph. On the house."

She eyed him severely. "I will drink this free daiquiri, Andrew, but you know it won't do you any good. I've told you before, you couldn't handle me."

He grinned at her. "And I've told you before, we'll see about that. My plan is to ply you with free things until you change your mind."

"Suit yourself. But don't say I didn't warn you. As long as you're doling out alcohol, bring something for Cassandra. She's new in town."

He rolled his eyes. "The offer doesn't extend to everyone you know." But he smiled at Cassandra anyway and asked, "What can I get you?"

"Surprise me," she said. "Anything with an umbrella."

"You got it. One umbrella-ed something coming right up." He wiggled his eyebrows at Daphne and sauntered away toward the kitchen.

Daphne rolled her eyes. "What were we saying? Right! You were about to tell me all about yourself. Go!" She leaned forward eagerly and Cassandra laughed.

"Well…there's not much to tell. I'm twenty-four. Graduated with a bachelor's degree in French Studies. I moved back home after graduation to be with my family and help take care of my grandmother who was seriously ill at the time…in the last two years I've mostly spent time with them and working at a local café."

God, my life sounds boring, she thought.

"I live with my mom, dad, and younger sister, Beth, who just graduated high school. To celebrate, we were taking this summer to cruise around different islands on my dad's boss's yacht, but last night I fell off the ship and now here I am! That's me in a nutshell."

"Wait, what? You fell off a ship?" Daphne was incredulous.

Cassandra glanced at Finn, who gave her a subtle nod. They had both agreed that Cass should stick with the falling story, at least for now. No need to give Daphne any reason to doubt the stability of a potential new roommate.

"I can't believe it…" Daphne sounded astonished.

I guess I'm going to have to get used to that response, Cassandra thought, nodding her head and waiting for the onslaught of questions she was sure would follow.

"That's fantastic!" Daphne exclaimed, and Cassandra looked up, shocked.

"I mean, it's a little horrible, of course, but clearly you're fine, and my god, that's amazing! Fell off a ship, washed up on shore…it's like the beginning of a hokey mystery novel, but it actually happened to you! But if you fell, then why are you looking for a place to stay this summer? Don't you want to get back to your family?"

Cassandra hesitated. "Not exactly, no. I really don't like the ocean. And I'm not a big fan of boats. I see this little mishap as a golden opportunity—I wanted to spend the summer soul-searching, and never being able to get farther than a couple dozen feet from my family at any given time was kind of driving me insane. Now I'll be able to spend the next three months figuring out what I want without all that added pressure."

Daphne nodded vigorously. "You needed space. I get it. If I hadn't known right out of high school that I wanted to open a Pilates studio, I probably would have needed the exact same thing. So, you're soul-searching, huh?"

Cassandra nodded, a little dizzy from Daphne's rapid style of delivery and the earnest way she spoke. "Yes. Exactly! I'm not sure what I want to do with my life yet and I've spent the last two years focusing on everyone else—my sister's upcoming graduation, Gram's illness…I figured I would sort myself out once everything else had settled, but now it has and I'm still clueless. I know less now than I did when I graduated. When I was little, I wanted to be a fairy princess…eventually I accepted that the chances of that happening were slim to none, but I never really replaced it with a more realistic goal."

Daphne leaned back, delighted. "I think that's a wonderful goal! We'll see what we can do about making it happen this summer, and in the meantime, we'll be on the lookout for a decent plan B."

"So I'm staying with you?"

"Absolutely! I think Finn was right—we'll have a blast together."

Cassandra grinned and opened her mouth to release a stream of ardent gratitude, but she was once again interrupted by the arrival of Drew, this time carrying a tray piled with delicious-smelling appetizers and an abundantly garnished glass, which he placed in front of her with a flourish.

"One piña colada for the lady—*extra* colada— with an umbrella, as requested."

"That doesn't even make sense." Finn wrinkled his nose.

"It looks amazing," Cassandra countered.

"And keep them coming, Drew!" Daphne added, sipping her daiquiri. "Not only is Cassandra new in town, she's just survived a near-death experience and now she's moving in with me. We're celebrating on all accounts!"

"Anything for you, babe." He turned away just as Daphne lobbed a cherry at his head. It bounced off his temple and rolled merrily away, stopping at the feet of a man who, despite his small stature, projected an air of absolute authority. He looked at the small fruit with disapproval and glared accusingly in their direction.

Daphne looked contrite and Finn looked up at the ceiling and whistled, the picture of guilt. Cassandra simply blushed as the man stomped over to their table, muttering darkly in a language she couldn't quite place.

"What's all this commotion, eh?" he demanded. "Disturbing the peace, Finn? Shouldn't you be behind the bar?"

"My shift isn't for another half an hour, Andre," Finn answered reasonably.

"Drinking on the job?" The man eyed the table and drew himself up to his full height of five feet four inches, somehow managing to look incredibly imposing as he did so. "I should have Drew throw fruit at *you*. Or better yet, I'll just fire you!"

"Andre, you couldn't! You would miss me too much." Finn didn't look in the least bit worried. "It would be too awful for you! Besides, I'm drinking water. The cocktails are for the ladies."

Andre looked marginally appeased, unnecessarily smoothing the short, tightly curled hair that was already oiled flat against his head. He seemed to search for a reason to stay irritated and his eyes rested on Daphne, grinning at him from behind her daiquiri.

"Aha! I should have known you'd be causing trouble, Daphne Drake! Trouble flocks to you like pigeons coming home to roost."

"You don't mean that, Andre!" Daphne tried to feign injury but was betrayed by her wide smile. "You know I've never caused trouble a day in my life! I just usually happen to be around when interesting things happen." She bit another cherry off her sword spear. "I'm lucky that way. And you know you love me for it! I have to come around here every once in a while to spice things up for you or you'd get bored. We keep you young, Andre!"

The small man snorted, clearly making an effort to look disgruntled, but the corners of his mouth twitched, and he gave a short burst of laughter and shook his head. Lapsing once again into his native tongue, he uttered what Cassandra could only assume was a term of endearment since he smiled and pinched Finn's cheek as he said it.

"Now," he said, addressing the table in general, but turning his attention to Cassandra, "Who is this young lady I've frightened? I hope you two hooligans aren't corrupting her." He cast a stern look at her companions.

"Of course not, Andre!" Daphne exclaimed. "This is our dear friend Cassandra, who came only yesterday to our beautiful island. We've just decided that she'll be living with me for the rest of the summer. I think that calls for some celebratory cake," she hinted meaningfully.

Turning to Cassandra, Daphne added, "Andre makes the best desserts!"

"Add it to the list," Cassandra said, "because from what I've tasted so far, he also makes the best appetizers. These prawns are incredible!"

Andre looked delighted.

"I like this girl," he announced. "You two take good care of her. I have to go deal with a staffing crisis. My hostess quit on me today. No warning! Her boyfriend proposed last night." Andre shook his head, disgusted. "Apparently, he's a law student. And now she's dropping everything to plan the wedding." He heaved a sigh of great suffering. "Young people today!"

"That's perfect!" Daphne's face lit up. "Cassandra is looking for a job."

Andre cut his eyes to Cassandra and openly appraised her. "Can you smile at people? Make them feel welcome and show them to a table?"

Cassandra blinked back at him, taken completely off guard.

"People almost always like me," she answered, feeling dim.

"You see, she's adorable!" Daphne followed up. "Everyone will love her. And do you have a boyfriend, Cassandra?"

"No…"

Finn looked pleased.

"There, you see? She won't abandon you in the middle of the season to run off with some upstart law student. And you're saved the trouble of having to go through a job search. Everyone wins. Except maybe the law student. Now let's have some cake!" Daphne clapped her hands excitedly, considering the matter decided.

Andre smiled and held out his hand, which Cassandra shook in a daze.

"Welcome aboard, Cassandra. You start tomorrow. Four o'clock."

Cassandra's head reeled as she tried to process what had just happened while Daphne signaled Drew back over to the table. "We're celebrating again," she announced happily. "Tiramisu, please!"

"Cassandra's going to be working with us here at Andre's," Finn informed him. "Rachel just quit— apparently, that twit she's been dating proposed. Which means Cassandra is our new hostess. A definite step up if you ask me." He saluted her with his water glass.

"Hey, that's awesome! Congrats, Cass! I'll be right back with that cake and another round." Drew winked again and disappeared into the kitchen.

"Cass?" Finn glared at Drew's retreating form. "That's friendly."

Daphne shot him a surprised look.

"I don't mind being called Cass," Cassandra answered distractedly. "'Cassandra' is kind of a mouthful. It's 'Cassi' that I hate—it's a nice name, just not for me. I don't think I've ever *actually* kicked anyone for calling me Cassi before, but I think people can usually tell I'm thinking about it, because no one has ever called me that twice. Did I just get a job?"

"Yes," Finn saw her look of wide-eyed bewilderment and asked, "Are you going to be okay?"

"I worked as a busser in high school, a barista in college, and I've been a waitress for the past two years. I can be a hostess. It's just…Andre is a little…"

"Intense?" Daphne supplied. "Oh, if you're competent, you have nothing to worry about! Don't let him make you nervous. Andre is a cuddly little porcupine. He can be a bit prickly, but do your job well and he'll be eating out of your hand in no time! He's a big sweetie. Not to mention, a sucker for a pretty face. The two of you will get along just fine. Just be sure not to leave him to get married and the whole thing should be a breeze."

"Heavens, no!" Cassandra looked appalled at the thought. "I've sworn off men for the time being. They're too complicated."

"Really?" Daphne glanced at Finn. "That sounds prudent."

"Thank you! I think so too." Cassandra nodded. "I have plenty of time to meet a guy and let him cloud my judgment once I figure things out, but for now, while I'm making major life decisions, I need to be sure I'm making them for myself and no one else."

"Very wise," Daphne agreed.

"Well, I don't know…" Finn began.

"Finn, isn't it time you were getting to work?" Daphne interrupted.

"I've still got a few minutes," he said pointedly.

Daphne checked the time.

"No, it looks like you're down to the wire. You'd better go now or Andre will have your head. Don't you worry, I'll take care of Cassandra. You can swing by the apartment tomorrow morning to make sure she's settling in."

"Fine," he said, rising from his chair and shooting daggers at his cousin while she batted her eyes at him sweetly. "Cassandra, are you sure you'll be alright?"

"I'll be great!" she said, standing to give him a hug. It wasn't until his arms were around her that she realized this might be dangerous waters. Pressed close to him, she could smell the clean, fresh scent of his soap. His chest was solid against her, the planes of his back firm under her hands. She resisted the urge to run her hands up and down the muscles there, instead telling him, "This will give Daphne and me a chance to bond. Thank you again so much for everything you've done! I can't believe how quickly this is all coming together! It feels like fate."

"Happy to help," he said, pulling back to smile at her, close and warm and sincere. Her breath caught for just a moment before he released her and walked toward the bar, ducking a watchful Andre who loudly called after him, "You're late!"

"So," Cassandra said, turning to Daphne, "what now?"

"Well, later on, I'll take you to the apartment and show you around, and then we can see about getting you some clothes until your own stuff arrives. But for now," Daphne smiled as Drew approached their table, "we eat cake!"

***

Finn stood behind the bar and tried to focus on his job. Margarita for the woman in the blue sarong, gin and tonic for weird guy wearing a bowler hat and bowtie, restock the pineapple, remind Andre to order more cocktail napkins…but his gaze kept darting back to Cassandra, laughing with Daphne and sipping her piña colada, looking happy and hopeful and completely at ease. He couldn't believe that less than twenty-four hours ago, she had been stuck on a yacht, feeling confined and claustrophobic and overwhelmed. And less than one hour ago, she'd had nowhere to live, no prospect of a job, and had known absolutely no one on the island but himself. Well, him and Judith.

Now look at her. She'd had a minor nervous breakdown, thrown her life into complete chaos and uncertainty, and then hit the ground running without missing a beat. She was incredible. And she wasn't looking for a relationship. Well, that was just fine. They would be friends. He could live with that.

He watched her talking animatedly with Daphne, hands gesturing wildly, eyes wide with enthusiasm, pink lips parted in a relaxed smile, and Daphne threw her head back and laughed, enchanted. Finn was feeling pretty enchanted himself. He couldn't even hear what Cassandra was saying and still he couldn't take his eyes off her. She was effervescent. And she wasn't looking for a relationship. Well, what did that matter? He could be friends with her. Just friends. No problem.

Although… He knew that both of their summers would be a lot more interesting if she was feeling just a little less scrupulous about the opposite sex.

Or sex in general, he thought, and then felt guilty. She trusted him. He would keep his hands to himself while she did her soul-searching. He wouldn't be able to stop himself from thinking about the two of them together—he wasn't dead—but as long as he didn't do anything about it, they would be fine.

Because in the short amount of time he had known her, he had already begun to care about Cassandra Dillon. If she said she needed space to sort out her life, then he wasn't going to get in her way.

In theory, he respected her reasoning. He absolutely supported the decision to stay independent and avoid clouding her judgment with sex or romance. Good for her.

But in reality, he wanted to thread his fingers through all that strawberry hair and bite into that mouth. To hell with independence.

Cassandra looked up and caught his eye from across the restaurant. She smiled and waved and he felt her smile in the pit of his stomach. *Oh hell*, he thought. *This is going to be a long summer.*

Chapter Five

"Here we are!" Daphne opened the door and stepped aside to let Cassandra in. "Home, sweet home! What do you think?"

"It's fantastic!" Cassandra exclaimed. She stood in the doorway, taking in the room in all its technicolor glory. There were bright splashes of color everywhere—orange and yellow throw pillows on a plush red couch, a bright green vase on a blue end table, paintings of purple poppies on the wall, a chocolate brown armchair next to a crazy multi-faceted floor lamp—nothing matched and everything went together. It was warm and welcoming and Cassandra loved it immediately.

"Your bedroom is just through here," Daphne said, turning down a short hallway off the main room. "First door on the left, right across from the bathroom, and my room is at the end of the hall. It's pretty close quarters, but I think it's cozy."

"It's perfect. I love it!" Cassandra opened the door to the room she would be sleeping in for the next three months and smiled. The walls were painted a cheery yellow with more poppies decaled above the bed. A large, breezy window looked out on the water, coyly hidden behind gauzy white curtains. Most of the room was taken up by a large queen size bed, enveloped by an impossibly fluffy and inviting purple comforter. Cassandra couldn't wait to go to bed that night.

"It's not much—just the basics—bed, dresser, closet, but there shouldn't be anything else you'll need. I've got everything—fully stocked kitchen, bathroom stuff, towels, blankets...we'll just have to see about getting you some clothes. I've got an idea for that later—let me finish giving you the tour! You've pretty much seen it all, but still…" Daphne grabbed her hand and dragged her down the hall, showing her the rest of the small apartment and explaining where all the essentials were stored.

Twenty minutes later, Cassandra was sitting with her legs folded underneath herself on the big red sofa, one arm wrapped around a squashy throw pillow and the other holding a champagne glass full of mango bellini.

"You know, Daphne," she said with a smile, "I think I'm going to love it here. Cheers!"

They clinked glasses.

Daphne took a sip of her drink and said, "So! The last hurdle to overcome—at least for tonight—is how to go about getting you some clothes. You need something to wear to work tomorrow."

"I've been wearing these clothes for two days," Cassandra groaned. "I can't wait to get out of them!"

"Well, my clothes are a no-go. I'm a good six inches shorter than you." Daphne eyed Cassandra's long legs. "But I think I know just the person! I called her while you were in the bathroom and told her about your situation. She said we can pop over any time."

"Excellent! Who is she?"

"Mary Ella, our neighbor in 3A. She's over sixty, but she's your height."

"She's sixty?" Cassandra was appalled that Daphne thought she should be sharing clothes with a woman well over twice her age. After two days of wear, she knew this wasn't the most flattering outfit, but still…

"Mary Ella is one of the fittest women I know," Daphne continued, and Cassandra felt better. "She takes classes at my studio—yoga and Pilates *and* kickboxing. She does headstands, has the thighs of a woman half her age, and based on those kickboxing classes, I pity anyone who tries to mug her thinking they're knocking over a helpless old woman. She would destroy them. You'll love her! She's totally kick-ass. And she loved your story!"

Throughout Daphne's description, the picture in Cassandra's head evolved from a sweet little dumpling of a woman with white hair and glasses, to a svelte and sophisticated older woman wearing a pashmina, to a formidable elderly she-Rambo beating the stuffing out of some petty thief in a dark alley. Overall, Mary Ella sounded like a woman worth knowing.

"Then by all means," Cassandra grinned, "let's go meet her!"

"Yay!" Daphne bubbled, putting down her drink. "Follow me!"

They put their bellinis in the fridge to save for later and made their way to apartment 3A. Daphne rapped smartly on the door. It was opened by a tall, olive skinned woman whose dark hair was graying at the temples.

"Daphne!" she smiled. "You came."

The two women hugged and Daphne said, "Mary Ella, this is Cassandra, the girl I was telling you about."

"Nice to meet you, Cassandra." Mary Ella held out her hand, which Cass shook, simultaneously admiring the older woman's grip and her well-toned arms as she did. The definition of Mary Ella's biceps put her own to shame, and Cassandra felt silly for ever imagining this woman as a matronly old grandmother. She also felt that maybe it was time she visited the gym. She hadn't been since, well…ever, and if she was going to be sharing clothes with Mary Ella, even for a short while, she would have to step it up a notch.

"Nice to meet you, too!" she said. "Daphne's told me great things."

Mary Ella waved the compliment aside. "Don't listen to Daphne. She's a darling sweet girl but she'll fill your head with nonsense."

"Don't be ridiculous, Mary Ella! I lead your workouts—I know you have the legs of a twenty-four-year-old. Luckily for Cassandra, because that makes you the perfect person for her to borrow clothes from!"

"I'm sure we can piece together an outfit or two." Mary Ella eyed Cassandra expertly, sizing her up from head to toe. "How tall are you, Cassandra, about five foot eight?"

"On the nose," Cassandra answered.

"Come in!" Mary Ella ushered them out of the hallway and into her elegantly furnished apartment.

"Make yourselves comfortable and I'll gather up some options."

She disappeared into her bedroom and returned a few minutes later with an armful of clothes which she draped neatly over the edge of a Victorian wingback chair. "These should be a good start," she announced.

Cass thanked her heartily and scooped up the pile of fabric, making her way toward the bathroom per Mary Ella's directions.

"Come out and model anything that fits!" Daphne called.

Cassandra assured them she would, then shut the door behind her and stripped down to her bra and underwear, eying herself more critically than usual in the full-length mirror. She generally considered herself to be in good shape. Her mother maintained a nice figure without too much effort, and though Cassandra hadn't inherited Miranda's personality, priorities, or passion for garden parties, Cass hoped this would be one trait the two of them would share—chalk one up for genetics.

But good grief, Mary Ella made them all look like slackers! Cassandra was really going to have to start putting in some work if she wanted to be that fabulous when she was in her sixties. Or even in her twenties.

She held up a tastefully tailored white collared shirt and sighed. Mary Ella probably looked wonderful in this. And she was going to feel like a little girl playing dress up. Just like she had at four years old when she used to walk around the house in her mother's glittery black charity ball high heels. Collared just wasn't her style. Sleeves weren't really her style either. Cass preferred tank tops and jeans, with a loose cardigan thrown over when absolutely necessary.

Anything that came up to her neck made her feel claustrophobic and stifled. Sleeves were just a bummer. But she was deeply appreciative of Mary Ella for the loan, so she put aside her neurosis and systematically made her way through the stack of clothes.

Ten minutes later, she had several choices to show the others. When she emerged from the bathroom, Daphne said, "I just invited Mary Ella to come have a bellini with us when we're all finished here! Did you find some things?"

"I found plenty!" Cassandra said gratefully. She gestured to the outfit she was wearing.

"What do you think?"

"You look great!" Daphne said.

"It's a little tight in the bust," Mary Ella observed, "but you can just undo the top buttons. Better tips, that way, anyway," she winked. "If everything fits as well as that does, go ahead and take it all for now. No rush to get any of it back."

Once again, Cassandra thought how incredibly lucky she had been in the last twenty-four hours. The way everything was working out for her on this island was uncanny. Stars were aligning, pieces were falling into place, and every possible sign seemed to be pointing straight to the fact that she was right where she should be. Now she just had to live up to the opportunity.

"If that's all settled," Daphne chimed in, "let's go have that drink!"

***

When they got back to the apartment, Cassandra excused herself briefly to call her father again, this time to give him Daphne's address so that he could forward her things as soon as possible, and to leave a number where she could be reached until she had regained her own cell phone. He sounded immensely relieved to hear that she had found a roommate so quickly (particularly a roommate who wasn't male), and he told her that he had already made arrangements. She could expect her clothes, along with her wallet, cell phone, passport, and sunscreen ("My sunscreen!" Cassandra exclaimed) by the end of the week. In the meantime, they worked out a plan for her to make a cash withdrawal from a bank so she could pay for necessities until her things arrived.

When she got back to the main room, Daphne and Mary Ella were comfortably settled on the couch, waiting with a round of mango bellinis.

"We were just talking about how wild your story is," Daphne informed Cass as she folded herself into the big armchair and took the first sip of her drink.

"Falling off a ship and washing up on shore in the middle of the night! They could make a movie about you!"

They could call it French Major Loses her Marbles, Cass thought. Though maybe in the movie she really could fall, instead of jumping off the boat like a wackadoo.

"It's unbelievable!" Mary Ella remarked.

You're telling me, Cassandra thought, trying not to look shifty.

"I can't imagine what you must have felt," Mary Ella said.

"Well…" Cassandra began slowly. She didn't like lying to these women, both of whom had been so open and generous with her. She had confessed the full truth about jumping off the boat to Finn and he hadn't cared.

Sure, he'd looked at her like she was unhinged for a minute, but that minute had passed and now things were all the better for it! Maybe she should come clean to Daphne and Mary Ella—they had been nothing but kind, welcoming, and helpful so far…

On the other hand, they barely knew her. They had agreed to help a ship-wrecked soul-searcher who was a victim of her circumstances, not a crazy person who voluntarily flung herself into the ocean and deliberately threw her life into chaos.

Maybe a confession at this point, after less than twenty-four hours of acquaintance (and in Mary Ella's case more like twenty-four minutes) was a little *too* forthright. Daphne might decide that it was *not*, in fact, a good idea to rent a room to a person who, based on this one action, could very well be unbalanced. Cass could tell them about the jump later—when they were all established friends and could look back on the story and laugh.

That's settled, then, Cass decided before the champagne could loosen her lips and get her to admit things best kept quiet for now. *No full confessions yet. Just dodge the question!*

"It was scary," she admitted truthfully. "And it was a shock." *Also true.* "But once I got over the initial…craziness of it," Cass stumbled a little over the word, knowing it held more weight than Daphne or Mary Ella could realize, "I saw what a great opportunity it was. I needed a shake-up in my life. An awakening. Landing in that water woke me right up!"

"It's an impressive personality that can face turmoil and come out the other side with such a sanguine perspective," Mary Ella complimented.

"Oh, I don't know about that," Cassandra laughed awkwardly, taking a swig of her drink. "But when faced with the choice of going back to the boat—a summer full of loaded questions and high expectations and my parents staring at me, watching to see if inspiration had suddenly struck—or striking it out on my own here on the island, it was no contest. I'm just lucky I met Finn! Everything's fallen right into place thanks to him. Do you know Finn, Mary Ella? Daphne's cousin?"

"Of course! Charming boy. I'm sure he was only too happy to help you," Mary Ella exchanged a knowing glance with Daphne.

Daphne grinned and raised an eyebrow at Cassandra.

"Oh, stop!" Cassandra tossed a pillow at her. "It's not like that."

"Please!" Daphne scoffed. "He couldn't take his eyes off you at the restaurant!"

"He's helping me get settled! And he's been a perfect gentleman!" Cass defended. "Well, mostly."

"Mostly?" Daphne's eyebrows shot up and she straightened in her seat. "You never mentioned a 'mostly!' Did something happen?"

"Nothing happened!" Cassandra insisted. "It just…could have? Probably. There were a couple of moments. I accidentally walked in on him when he was getting out of the shower, he was kind of flirty…it wasn't a big deal."

"Flirty?" Mary Ella asked at the same time Daphne squealed, "The shower?"

"Yes," Cassandra answered them both. "But it was nothing!" she repeated, looking at the ceiling. "I've sworn off men anyway."

"Sworn off men?" Mary Ella sounded surprised.

"Temporarily." Cassandra downed the rest of her drink. Daphne topped it off and Cass sipped it gratefully.

"May I ask why?"

"It's not a good time for a relationship," Cassandra explained, squirming a bit in her chair. "I need to be soul-searching, and I don't want my life path to get thrown off course by a man."

"A wise decision," Mary Ella commended. "Especially from someone so young. It's important to know yourself well before stirring another person into the mix. I've always said that relationships are frosting on a cake, but self-knowledge is the cake itself. You need the latter as a solid foundation before you can add the former on top."

"Exactly! My cake is still baking," Cassandra saluted Mary Ella with her glass. "Dating would just be a distraction."

"Then it was not a specific person who led to this vow of singlehood?"

"No, no one specific." Cass shook her head. "My last relationship ended a couple of years ago. We dated in college but I never saw a real future together. When we graduated, I wanted to move home to be with my grandmother…he moved to the city to launch his career, and that was that.

"I've dated a few people here and there since then, but my life has been mostly family and work." Cassandra squinted into the past. A haze of restaurant shifts and family dinners, touring colleges with Beth and going with Gram to her doctor's appointments. Then more recently, funeral arrangements and sorting through Gram's things…her throat tightened and Cass brought herself back to the present. "Now that I'm getting a life beyond that, I need to be sure it's *my* life and not a life built around some guy."

"I think that's wonderful," Daphne said. "But does that mean you'll close yourself off to the possibility of something equally wonderful if it happens to fall into your lap? Isn't it possible to grow *with* someone rather than having to be fully grown when you meet them?"

"But then the direction of my growth will be influenced by that person." Cassandra frowned. "It's like a plant whose stem is bent because another plant is blocking its path! Or however plants work. I want to reach up toward the sun, free and clear, no restrictions. Metaphorically, of course…I don't go into the sun if I can help it."

"And what about sex?" Daphne asked.

Cassandra choked on her drink.

Goodness, straight to the point.

"No need to be coy, dear, we're all friends here," Mary Ella said. "And we're all adults. I think it's a very valid question. Relationships may complicate matters, but they do serve a useful purpose. Women have needs."

"You two don't mince words," Cassandra laughed.

Daphne pooh-poohed the idea.

"What's the use of subtlety amongst friends?" she asked. "So. What about sex?"

"I'll be fine," Cassandra assured them. "I'm not seventeen, for heaven's sake! I can control my urges. And I can take care of my own needs."

"Repressing your emotions is not healthy," Daphne tsked, shaking her head. "It makes people do crazy things."

Cassandra laughed again, recalling Tuesday night's mental breakdown. "Trust me, I know. But you're not talking about emotions. You're talking about hormones."

Daphne waved this aside. "Semantics," she said. "Repression is repression."

"A woman's sexuality is not something to be ignored," Mary Ella nodded. "It should be acknowledged and embraced."

"I'm not ignoring my sexuality," Cassandra assured them. "I'm just putting it on simmer for the time being. I've managed to exist happily, healthily and sanely for quite some time now without sex"—her inner self once again sneered at the relative truth of the term *sanity*— "so I am going to continue not having it until I've figured myself out."

There, she thought. *Completely sane. Rational and sane and sensible.*

"I think that's admirable," Mary Ella said, "but remember this, darling: it's one thing to know yourself. It's another thing entirely to stop your life from moving forward because you're too busy waiting for the 'right' time. No matter what it is…the right time for a career change, the right time for sex, the right time for falling in love…at my age you understand there is no 'right' time. All you have is the moment you're in. Just go out and start living."

Cassandra looked pensive but rebellious, and Mary Ella held up her hand. "Just something to keep in mind."

Glancing at the clock, the older woman said, "Oh, my, it's getting late! I should leave you girls to sleep. You both have work tomorrow. That's one of the many benefits of retirement: no one ever expects you to be anywhere at any given time."

She stood and headed for the door, turning to say, "It was lovely meeting you, Cassandra. Good luck on your first day tomorrow—you'll look wonderful! And remember what I said...just keep an open mind!"

With that, Mary Ella walked out the door, leaving Cass to consider her final words in the wake of her departure.

Daphne turned to Cassandra and said, "My instinct is to say, 'Let's have another drink,' but Mary Ella is right. We do have to work tomorrow, and even though you don't have to be in until four o'clock, I probably shouldn't send you to your first day working for Andre having gotten sloshed the night before. We've got all summer for girl talk and cocktails—let's call it a night!"

"Agreed," Cassandra nodded.

The two girls said goodnight and Cassandra made her way to her new bedroom. She closed the door behind her and sighed with pleasure as she surveyed the space, completely at ease for the first time in she didn't know how long. She was fairly certain that the glow she was feeling wasn't just an after-effect of the champagne, but was in fact the serenity that stems from having confidence in the direction your life is moving. Even though the rest of her future was a blank, she had a plan—an *actual* plan—for the next day, and for once, she felt like she had started down a path that was going to lead to something good. Finn and Daphne were the butterfly and mushrooms that were going to lead to her life as a fairy princess. Or whatever the grown-up equivalent of that was.

This felt good. This felt *right*.

It was funny, she thought as she slipped into a t-shirt Mary Ella had leant her for pajamas, that in order to get her life back on track, she'd first had to throw it completely off its rails.

"The universe works in mysterious ways, I suppose," Cassandra said, flipping back the covers and sinking down onto the mattress, snuggling into the pillow with another contented sigh. She just hoped that the universe was mysteriously directing her toward personal fulfillment, prosperity and ultimate happiness.

At least for tonight, she was pretty sure it was.

Chapter Six

Cassandra found herself sailing on choppy waters, floating in a lifeboat in the middle of nowhere. She looked around dolefully, completely at a loss as to how she'd ended up back in the ocean.

"Well, this is just fantastic," she said to herself, and was surprised when she heard a harrumph in response, emitted from a large and meticulously dressed walrus sitting at the other end of the dingy. He gazed at her mildly from behind a monocle and top hat, clearly having stepped right out from the pages of Alice in Wonderland, one of Cassandra's favorite childhood stories. Cassandra blinked at him in general disbelief.

"The time has come," the walrus said.

"The time has come for what?" she asked.

"For you to get your life together," the walrus said with what Cassandra felt to be undue condescension.

"And what would you know about it, Walrus?" she asked, affronted.

"Plenty," he replied. "I'm a life coach. Also, I have this watch." He pulled out a large pocket watch from the breast of his jacket and waved it under Cassandra's nose. The large hand was indeed pointing to the words *Cassandra gets her life together*.

"It was stuck for quite a while at half-past Cassandra graduates and Cassandra puts her life on hold for her family, but it's ticking along quite steadily now," he explained.

"This is a creepy watch, Walrus." Cassandra told him matter-of-factly.

"Nevertheless, it's accurate," he countered. "And it's telling me you're late for work."

Cassandra blinked again, and when she opened her eyes, she was standing in the center of a busy kitchen with a large white chef's hat falling over her eyes. In the background, Andre was yelling at her that he needed more mushroom sauce for the French toast. This was clearly a gross misjudgment on his part, but he was the boss, so Cassandra hurried to melt some butter in a skillet, but the chef's hat fell onto the stove and promptly went up in flames, creating a small fireball that narrowly avoided singeing off her eyebrows. She doused the flames with a bucket of water with a little umbrella in it, and when the smoke cleared, Cassandra was standing in a wooded glen, wearing an impossibly poufy princess dress.

She wandered through the trees, absentmindedly wondering where she was heading, when she came to a clearing with a waterfall. The trickling of the water beckoned her, and as she walked closer, she could see that someone was already there, standing underneath the falls.

Creeping to the edge of the water, Cassandra saw that it was Finn, looking every bit as good as he had when she'd walked in on him the day before, except this time, there was no towel. Unable to look away, she watched the trajectory of the water running down his lovely, lean body, dripping from messy blonde hair to his strong jaw, running down his neck, along his pecs, sliding down his stomach through a thin trail of hair, and as her eyes drifted lower, the walrus cleared his throat and said, "Enjoying the view?"

Cassandra jumped guiltily and asked, "What are you doing here, Walrus? Have you come to tell me it's time to stop creeping on unsuspecting men?"

"No. I've come to tell you that it's time to wake up."

Cass opened her eyes and looked dazedly around the room. The memories of the past forty-eight hours came rushing back, mingling with details from the dream, and she was momentarily disoriented.

"Ooh-kay," she said aloud. No more champagne before bed."

Stifling a yawn, she rolled to standing and wrapped herself in a blanket, padding out into the living room where her new roommate was folded in half at the hips, stretching in a tight hot pink exercise top and ruffled yoga pants. Daphne smiled at her upside-down, perky and alert, and Cassandra squinted blearily back, shrinking farther into the recesses of her blanket.

"Good morning!" Daphne said, cheery as ever. "Did you sleep okay?"

Cassandra snorted. "I had the most bizarre dreams last night. But the bed was amazing."

"Oh, I'm so glad." Daphne looked genuinely pleased. "Coffee? I don't normally drink it, but if you're a coffee person I can make some, no problem! Or I've already made an excellent smoothie, if you're interested."

"Smoothie?" Cassandra perked up at the mention of food.

"Absolutely! Coming right up," Daphne bounced into the kitchen and came back seconds later with a tall glass full of thick pea-green liquid.

"Spinach, carrot, pineapple, orange, mango, Greek yogurt, and ginger!" she announced. "Iron, calcium, vitamins A, C, and K, manganese, antioxidants, probiotics, and protein…breakfast of champions!"

"That's a lot of healthy things…" Cassandra said suspiciously. "How does it taste?"

"Amazing," Daphne said.

Cassandra took a tentative sip. She was right. It *was* amazing.

"You would be amazed how often healthy and delicious go hand in hand," Daphne informed her. "Black beans, avocado, sweet potatoes, obviously any fruit you can think of…and a lot of these foods are aphrodisiacs to boot! Nature is wonderful!"

Cassandra had her doubts about nature. She was all for food, but she was still harboring some feelings of hostility concerning her last up-close-and-personal encounter with the great outdoors. She hadn't ever been a fan of it before, and after what she'd been through Tuesday night, she was fairly positive that she would never feel anything approaching affection for the ocean. But she kept her thoughts to herself and quietly enjoyed her smoothie as Daphne expounded on the many treasures of the natural world.

Interrupting herself in the middle of a rhapsody about basil, Daphne said suddenly, "Oh! I meant to ask you earlier! I'm teaching a Pilates class at eleven o'clock—would you like to come?" she asked this with the same alacrity and zeal that Cassandra usually reserved for conversations about hot fudge sundaes.

Just last night she had resolved to be more proactive in her approach to fitness (which in her case meant approaching it at all), but now, in the light of day, with no Mary Ella around to make her feel like an underachiever, the couch was so cushy and the blanket was so cozy and leaving either one of them— particularly to squeeze herself into a pair of Mary Ella's exercise pants to do leg lifts and crunches— sounded categorically unpleasant.

But she would have to face Mary Ella again someday. And she had promised herself that she would start transforming into a woman of action. One Pilates class wouldn't kill her. Probably.

Stifling a sigh and pasting on what she hoped would pass for an eager smile, Cassandra said, "Of course! But you should know, I've never done Pilates before."

"Oh, you'll love it! It works your core muscles to improve strength and stability, while also stretching and lengthening your muscles to increase flexibility! Today is a mat day and we'll be focusing on abs!"

"Oh, good." Cassandra tried not to wince. A profound feeling of dread washed over her. Focusing on abs? What had she just agreed to? But Daphne looked so happy and her enthusiasm was so catching, Cassandra slowly began to feel less of an urge to flee. She shifted from a feeling of certain doom to one of mild alarm. She could deal with that. And anyway, it was a new experience. She had been wanting to have more of those…now was her chance.

***

Two hours later, Cassandra decided that new experiences were overrated. She was lying on her back, sweating profusely in a mirrored room full of toned and shapely women, all of whom were doing modified crunches more gracefully and effectively than she was. Her knees were bent toward her chest, hands behind her lifted head as she attempted to alternately stretch out one leg and pull the opposite elbow toward said leg, and she was actively trying not to scream in pain as Daphne effortlessly executed the same moves at the front of the class, calmly talking her students through the actions.

"Feel your abs," Daphne encouraged. "Let them control the movement as you alternate your arms and legs."

Cassandra gargled in pain. If she felt her abs any more acutely, she was going to have a hernia. They were doing the "bicycle crunch," which was the fourth type of crunch they had done in a row. Cass hadn't realized there were so many types of crunches. They had done regular crunches, crunches with one leg extended, crunches with both legs extended, and now this torture. It was hell on Earth.

"Last set!" Daphne chirped. "Just eight more!"

Cass wanted to cry.

"Great job!" Daphne said after they completed the final eight. "You guys made it through the crunch sequence. Now we're going to round off the class with The Hundred!"

The what, now?

Cassandra shuddered and felt every muscle in her body protest.

"Bring both legs straight into the air—feel free to bend at the knees if that's challenging—then squeeze your thighs together, activate your core to bring your head and neck off the mat, raise your arms in line with your sides, and pump! We're going to do this for one hundred pumps."

She's got to be kidding, Cass thought, but she dutifully followed her friend's instructions.

"Remember to squeeze your inner thighs and keep your glutes engaged!" Daphne's voice floated to Cassandra through the haze of agony. "Inhale two, three, four! And exhale two, three, four!"

Cassandra tried to exhale but it came out more like a strangled gasp. Inhaling was almost out of the question. Her whole mid-body was on fire. She was going to die here. After what she had survived just two nights before, this was not how she pictured her life ending. Wheezing in spandex. A most inelegant departure from this world. She had to live, if for no other reason than to survive for a less depressing death.

She told herself to suck it up. She could do this! They must be nearly done anyway. Then she heard Daphne say, "You guys are doing great! Almost halfway there!"

We haven't even done fifty?

Cassandra considered throwing something at her sprightly roommate if only she could spare the energy. Instead, she concentrated on breathing, squeezing her thighs together and "pulling navel to spine," which she was pretty sure was torture-code for sucking in her abs. She let out a small whimper but managed not to shriek her suffering to the four corners of the room when Daphne finally gave them the cue to relax.

Cassandra collapsed her legs onto the mat rather than "gently lowering them with control," and tried not to hyperventilate. Later, she would feel enormous respect for Daphne and the other women in the room, but right now, she was making an effort not to irrationally hate each and every one of them.

Mercifully, they had arrived at the cool-down portion of the class and Cassandra's heart rate began to resume its normal pace. If possible, she started sweating even more, but she gratefully let her muscles relax as she mindlessly followed Daphne's instructions for the gentle supine stretches that completed the session.

Gradually, the sweat began to dry, her breathing evened out, and she was left with an unexpected feeling of deep relaxation and an unmistakable sense of accomplishment. Hooray for her! She had just completed her first Pilates class and she hadn't even passed out! She deserved a treat!

Maybe Daphne would be up for coffee and pastries after the class. Cassandra could definitely use a cherry turnover right about now. Or a bear claw. Or an apple fritter. Yes. She wanted a baked good. The sooner the better. She had woken up early, drank a healthy smoothie for breakfast, performed laborious exercise before noon, and now it was time for something with trans-fats and sugar.

This is a good plan, Cassandra thought with keen excitement. She rolled up the studio's mat and stood, feeling proud of herself when she did not immediately collapse. Her legs felt like jelly and she was shaky on her feet, but she remained upright. She hoped Daphne knew a good bakery nearby, because after what she'd just endured, Cass wasn't sure how far she could walk.

Stepping with extreme care, she slowly made her way to the front of the room where Daphne was saying goodbye to the rest of her students. As the last woman filtered out, Daphne turned to her with a broad smile and asked, "What did you think? You were a trooper!!"

Cassandra smiled back. "It was touch and go there for a while. I wasn't sure I was going to make it! But you're an amazing instructor—very helpful and insightful cues. I'm pretty sure you saved me from injuring myself more than once!"

Daphne laughed and assured her that it got easier with practice.

"I'm sure it does," Cassandra agreed. "But in the meantime, it was killer and I think I need a reward. How do you feel about a snack? Is there anywhere to get a good Danish around here?"

"I know just the place," Daphne said. "Follow me!"

Cassandra followed Daphne down a street lined with colorful awnings and flower baskets hanging cheerfully from lampposts. She walked gingerly while Daphne bounced happily along beside her with her usual springy step.

"I love this street!" Daphne commented. "All the shops are so cute and everyone is so friendly!" As if to emphasize her point, she smiled and waved at a plump woman writing the daily lunch special on a chalk board outside a purple awning-ed café. "Good morning, Gladys!"

Gladys smiled back, pushing a dark curl out of her eye as she glanced up from her task.

"Morning, Daphne!"

Daphne continued on and said, "See? It's a great area! I was thrilled to get the studio nearby—it's my favorite part of the island! Although the beach is beautiful and there are some great vineyards further inland…"

Daphne went on to describe various districts of the island and Cassandra plodded along beside her, soaking it all in and growing more and more excited about her stay by the minute. She couldn't believe how lucky she'd gotten after her crazy escapade. She was overwhelmed with gratitude for the opportunity that had fallen into her lap. Or, more accurately, she had fallen into its lap. But one way or another, this seemed like the perfect place to begin her quest for self-discovery and fulfillment.

Starting with a pastry.

They turned into a small bakery, most of which was occupied by an enormous display case filled with the flakiest pastries Cassandra could ever have hoped to encounter.

"What looks good?" Daphne asked.

"Everything!" Cassandra said with wide eyes. "I have it narrowed down to about seventeen things."

"The bear claws here are fabulous! They make the best almond filling!"

"Sold."

They each ordered a bear claw and made their way to the sidewalk seating outside.

As soon as they were settled, Daphne remembered that she had promised to stop in at a gallery down the street.

"I want the owner to paint a mural at the studio and I told him I'd swing by this afternoon to chat about it. Do you mind if I run up and talk to him?"

"Don't worry about me," Cassandra assured her, gazing lovingly at the sweet roll sitting in front of her.

Daphne said something in reply and trotted off down the street, but Cass took no notice, as her full attention was now turned to the flakey almond-filled crescent on the table. Resisting the urge to talk to it and say something creepy like, "Alone at last," Cassandra picked up the bear claw and bit blissfully into it.

"Oh god," she moaned aloud as the taste washed over her. "Why do people ever bother to do anything but eat?"

She knew there were plenty of other perfectly valid ways for humans to pass their time on earth, but none came to mind at that precise moment. As far as she was concerned, ultimate happiness and food were one and the same.

"I think I'm in love," she breathed as she took another bite, then jumped about a foot in the air when she heard a voice beside her.

"Are you talking to that pastry?"

She looked up, startled, and saw Drew smiling a friendly but satirical smile down at her.

"Of course not!" Cassandra did a rapid mental review to make sure that she had not, in fact, spoken to the pastry. "I was addressing the world at large. Much saner."

"Sure it is," Drew pulled up a chair and dropped affably into it, propping his feet on the seat next to Cassandra. "What brings you here? Having an affair with a bear claw?"

"You can't fight true love, Drew," Cassandra said, savoring another bite. "What about you?"

"On my way to a lunch date," Drew reached for her pastry and Cassandra said, "I *will* kill you."

He held up his hands and leaned back in his chair, grinning.

"The girl's territorial about her baked goods...noted. So, how's it going, Cass? Adjusting to life on the island? You look like you've seen better days."

Cassandra looked down, surveying her rumpled exercise clothes. Her hair was in shambles and in the last hour she had sweat so much that her body was basically one massive salt lick.

"I'm embracing new experiences," she explained. "Apparently evolution is not always pretty. Daphne took me to one of her Pilates classes, and as a reward for surviving, I get this." She bit happily into her treat.

"And where is Daphne now?" Drew craned his neck to peer inside the bakery.

"Down, boy. You're on your way to a date, remember?"

"Doesn't mean I can't enjoy myself along the way."

"Based on your level of commitment, I'm hoping this is a first date?" Cass asked, by way of making conversation. She didn't really care what he did so long as he didn't make another grab for the pastry.

"Not many second dates in my life, Cass." Drew put his hands behind his head, lounging with great unconcern. "Keeps things on the island simple."

"Have you lived here long?" Cassandra asked, veering the conversation away from his love life.

"A few years."

"What brought you here?" Cass managed not to spew powdered sugar as she asked.

"Followed a girl." Drew shrugged.

"Of course," Cass snorted. "Well, there are worse ways to end up somewhere, and definitely worse places to end up."

"Yeah, once I got here, I never wanted to leave." Drew looked around fondly.

"I'm starting to feel the same way." Cass licked the last of the icing off her fingers and wondered why she hadn't ordered two pastries. "If only for the food."

"Simple needs," Drew smiled. "I like that."

"I'm back!" Daphne suddenly appeared in a whirl of dark ringlets and magenta Lycra. "He wasn't there—probably out on lunch, but I'll try back after my two o'clock class. Oh hey, Drew, what are you doing here?"

"'He?' Who's 'he?'"

"I've taken a lover, Andrew," Daphne said dramatically. "I hope you don't lose too much sleep over it."

"Ha! A likely story. With all this in front of you," Drew gestured up and down with exaggerated bravado, "why would you go chasing other men?"

"I was chasing a mural painter."

"You don't want some sensitive artistic type," Drew scoffed. "He'd bore you to tears."

"It's for the studio," Daphne rolled her eyes.

"Oh." Drew shrugged. "Well, gotta be off. Late for a date."

"Of course, you are," Daphne laughed. "Give her my sympathies."

Drew gave them a casual salute and took off down the street.

"That boy is ridiculous." Daphne shook her head.

"Yep," Cass agreed. "So, what are we doing now? Do you want to get some lunch? Personally, I could eat."

"Sure! Let's go home and get cleaned up, then we'll call Finn and see if he wants to meet somewhere for food before you have to be at work."

"Oh right. I have a job," Cassandra still looked a little dazed at how suddenly that had happened. "Okay, sounds good! Let's get going. I'm starving!"

***

An hour later, Finn was sitting on the patio of one of his favorite restaurants in the height of the lunch rush, tapping his foot nervously and telling himself it was ridiculous to be nervous. Cassandra Dillon was not a person to be afraid of.

Except that in the eighteen hours since he'd seen her, he hadn't been able to think of anything else and that alarmed him. A blonde flirted with him at the bar and he barely noticed. Her eyes didn't have that crazy glint that Cassandra's did. He went home and his place looked empty because Cassandra wasn't sitting on his couch smiling at him. He woke up this morning and missed the smell of Cassandra making French toast in the kitchen. If she was messing with his head this much after one day, what the hell would she do to him by the end of the summer? The prospect was frightening.

After a few more minutes of agitated tapping, he looked up and saw her walking toward him, radiant in the sunlight. She smiled as she approached and he tried not to stare at her mouth, then she plopped herself into the chair beside him and glared darkly up at the sky.

"I'm really not cut out for this kind of weather," she said, scooting deeper into the shade of the umbrella. "It's a wonder my skin hasn't fried into oblivion yet." She cast another accusing look up at the bright blue, cloudless expanse and then focused her attention back on him.

"Hi!" she said happily. "Daphne will be along in a minute. She met a friend on the way into the restaurant and stopped to chat."

"She always does," Finn replied, amused once again by how quickly her moods seemed to come and go.

"She sent me ahead because she didn't want to keep you waiting."

"Thoughtful of her," he said, glad to be alone with Cassandra, no matter the circumstances. "But I'm used to Daphne being late. She can't go anywhere without running into a friend or a neighbor or a student or her massage therapist or the guy who was her business class instructor. It's uncanny. She's a social woman, my cousin Daphne."

"I'm starting to pick up on that." Cassandra glanced through the menu and looked overwhelmed. Then she closed her eyes, jabbed her finger at a random spot on the page, opened her eyes, nodded her head, and closed the menu with a snap.

"So," she resumed, propping her elbow on the table, chin in hand, "how's your day going?"

Finn stared at her. "What was that?"

"'That?'" she repeated. "Oh, the pointing? That was strategy. Sometimes when everything on a menu looks good and I can't decide what I want, I close my eyes and let fate decide for me. I'm chronically indecisive, so it's a pretty good system."

"And what did fate decide you'll be having today?"

"The smoked salmon quinoa salad. It looks delicious. I'm very pleased."

Finn grinned and shook his head. He'd gotten it right the moment he met her—this girl was nuts. Adorable and nuts.

Deciding to move on, he said, "My day has been good. This is pretty much it so far. I got off late last night and since it was nearly daylight anyway, I hiked up to one of my favorite lookout points to watch the sunrise. Then I went home and crashed like a log. I woke up about forty-five minutes ago."

"You went hiking in the middle of the night?" Cassandra asked, horrified and fascinated. "After being up all day and working a full shift?"

"Sure. It was only a couple of miles. It's fun!"

Cassandra squinted, skeptical.

"I take it you don't hike for enjoyment very often," he guessed.

"Nooo…" Cassandra answered slowly. "I'm not opposed to hiking…it's just that I haven't done much of it. Nature and I don't always get along. I like it in theory, but up close it tends to be…"

"Intimidating?" he offered.

"Disgusting," she countered and Finn's face went slack with surprise.

"Not all nature!" she amended quickly. "Not most plants. And I like waterfalls and clouds and things like that! It's just…nature that…moves."

Finn laughed in disbelief.

"Again, I like it in theory!" she defended. "But a lot of the things I've seen in real life are disturbing."

"What am I missing?" Daphne suddenly appeared by the table, vivid in a yellow tube top and red capris.

"Cassandra doesn't like nature that moves."

"What?" Daphne looked confused.

"Okay, have you guys ever looked at wild animals up close?" Cassandra sounded defensive. "I mean really *looked* at them? They're not cute and cuddly or beautiful and majestic like you would expect them to be! No! They've got weird bumps or they're sickly and bedraggled or they're missing most of their feathers. I know they're found in the natural world, but they look unnatural! And they're creepy."

"Cassandra, what are you basing these opinions of wildlife on?"

"Zoos, mostly. And a wildlife safari I went on a couple of years ago. You should have seen this giraffe! Bumps all over its face! Very gross. And don't even get me started on the emu!" she shuddered.

"Emu?"

"They're modern-day dinosaurs!" she said emphatically, and Finn burst out laughing.

"Okay, I'll give you that one. But where exactly did you go on this safari?"

"Oregon."

"Cassandra, giraffes are not native to the Pacific Northwest! They don't belong in a temperate climate! You didn't really see a giraffe—you saw a sad shadow of a giraffe."

"It was a diseased shadow of a giraffe," Cassandra said flatly.

"This cannot be the way you view the world. Daphne, we have to do something about this."

"Definitely!"

"We're going to introduce you to nature," Finn said firmly. "You're going to love it."

"If you guys say so," Cassandra sounded dubious, "but don't get your hopes up. I have a history with the great outdoors, and it's checkered. Things tend to go awry when I step outside."

Take Tuesday, for example.

"Not to worry! We'll think of something great." Finn was confident. "We'll talk it over with Drew— he'll be working at Andre's tonight and he's always up to something fun."

"Yes!" Daphne said. "Drew may be an overgrown child, but he's always good for an adventure."

"But not too big of an adventure, right?" Cassandra amended. "Remember, I did take an unexpected plunge into the ocean not too long ago. I think I've filled my adventure quota for a while."

"Impossible," Finn shook his head. "You're fearless, Dillon. You just don't know it yet."

Cassandra blinked in surprise and then looked thoughtful.

"Okay," she said, hitting him with a smile that made his heart lurch sideways. "If the first adventure didn't kill me then I guess a second probably won't either."

"That's the spirit!" Finn clapped her on the shoulder. "It's settled then! We'll talk to Drew tonight."

***

Cassandra drummed her fingers on the table and tried not to look mind-whacked. Finn's words had hit her like a ton of bricks.

You're fearless, Dillon. You just don't know it yet.

He didn't mean anything by it; he was just being flippant. But he'd looked right at her with those killer blue eyes and in two offhand sentences he defined the indefinable feeling that had been nagging her for two years. She could have kissed him. She nearly did. Instead, she embraced the feeling of elated freedom that was slowly building up inside of her, filling her like helium inside a balloon. At that moment, she felt buoyant, weightless, like an enormous burden had been lifted.

She was fearless. She had just been ignoring it. For the past two years, she had been living everyone else's life—her grandmother's, her sister's, her parents'—stepping in to become whatever they needed her to be. She had been telling herself that it was because they needed her, and that was partially true, but she had also been hiding from the uncomfortable possibility that if she stepped out on her own, she would have no idea which direction to take. The fear of the unknown had stunted her, crippled her, allowed her to stagnate for two whole years. But she was not the kind of girl to be stagnant. She was the kind of girl who chased fairies and set fires and jumped off of boats. And it was time to start acting like it. Finn had known her less than two days before he'd recognized that.

Cassandra's epiphany was interrupted by the arrival of a harassed looking waiter who promptly took their orders and turned around, narrowly avoiding collision with a busboy and a tray full of water glasses as he made a beleaguered beeline back to the door.

Goodness, Cass resumed her thought process as the waiter disappeared into the sea of tables inside. *Clarity is happening a lot faster than I'd expected.*

Well, she certainly wasn't going to let all this new-found self-knowledge go to waste. She was going to go on an adventure. She was going to tap into the thrill of being alive. And she was going to love it. She hoped. One way or the other, she was going to try it. This was going to be great. But not until she survived her first shift working for Andre.

***

An hour after lunch, Cassandra was doing exactly that. She'd finished a lovely meal with Daphne and Finn (fate had chosen wisely when it delivered her the quinoa salad), changed quickly into Mary Ella's borrowed shirt, stared forlornly down at the top button stretched tight across her chest, thought *What the hell?* and popped it, then arrived at Andre's with ten minutes to spare. Andre spent those ten minutes giving her a crash-course training.

"It's quite simple," he said brusquely once he had given her a tour of the small restaurant, introduced her in passing to the various servers, handed her a clip board and guided her back to the podium at the front entrance. "Just smile and say hello to customers as they come in. Show them to a table or let them know how long the wait will be. If that twitty little dunderhead Rachel could do it, I'm sure you'll be more than capable. Off with you, now. You have customers!"

Cassandra turned to greet the large party that had just walked through the door and the next thing she knew, it was two hours into her shift and she hadn't even had time to blink. Andre kept a steady business through the happy hour and dinner shifts, and in no time at all, Cassandra found her stride. She welcomed patrons, soothed irritated customers, complimented little old ladies' jewelry, laughed at fathers' corny jokes, and winked at the children who rolled their eyes at the jokes. She developed an easy rapport with the wait staff, waved reassuringly at Andre every time he walked not-so-surreptitiously by to check on her, and generally delighted everyone she encountered. After five years in various restaurant positions, she felt completely comfortable in this homey little restaurant, moving with confidence and ease, and falling effortlessly into the familiar rhythm of customer service.

When Daphne and Finn showed up to see how she was doing, it was almost time for her break. She flashed them her wide *Welcome to Andre's—prepare to be thrilled* smile and showed them to a table with the assurance that she would join them in fifteen minutes. By the time she got back to them, they had flagged Drew over as well.

"How's it going, Cass?" Drew slugged her on the shoulder as she sat in the chair between him and Finn. "It looks like you're fitting right in on your first day."

"I see you're slacking on the job," she said with a light punch in return. "But it's been really great so far," she beamed at them all. "I'm so glad you guys brought me here!"

"Glad we could help! But listen, Cassandra," Finn said excitedly, "we were talking to Drew about your issues with nature—"

"I wouldn't call them issues," she interjected.

"—and he has a really awesome suggestion," Finn continued.

"Manta ray feeding." Drew cut in.

"I beg your pardon?" Cassandra said.

"Manta ray feeding," he repeated. "It's awesome! Manta rays eat plankton, which are attracted to light in the dark. There are tours that go out at night and shine spotlights into the water so all the plankton gather there and the manta rays come and feed. Some people like to snorkel or scuba dive with them, but we wouldn't make you do that. We'll just stay on the surf boards."

"Surf boards?" Cassandra couldn't help sounding appalled.

"Sure! Why would we pay money to go on some boat tour when we can just paddle out on the water ourselves. Finn's not working and you and I get off at the same time—it's perfect! We can go out tonight."

"Tonight?!" Cassandra repeated, now openly horrified.

"Be reasonable, Drew." Daphne countered. "Cassandra swam for her life like two days ago. And I already made her do Pilates today and she's been on her feet for hours…give her body a break. Let's go next weekend! Do you think you'll be recovered by then, Cassandra?"

Cass shot her a wide-eyed look. She was having trouble holding on to the fearless spirit of adventure she'd been so wrapped up in that afternoon.

"You know, I'm really not a huge fan of the ocean…couldn't we do something on dry land?"

"The manta rays are going to blow you away—really, they're amazing! This will be good for you!"

"I'm not entirely sure what a manta ray looks like, but I have a vague idea and it's terrifying. Are you sure we shouldn't start with something a little tamer next weekend?" Cassandra's voice was shrill. "You know…visit a nice pond? Feed some ducks?"

"Ducks can be vicious," Finn said darkly.

"Finn, you've got to get over that," Daphne rolled her eyes.

"The thing bit me, Daphne! Right on the arm! It was going for the throat next…I could tell by the predatory look in its beady little eyes."

"This coming from the guy who spent last summer leading white-water rafting expeditions in New Zealand."

"The *point* is this duck-free plan is a good one. Cassandra, you're going to love this."

Cass looked back and forth between the three of them, her face washed with concern.

"Have I mentioned that I hate the ocean?"

"Yes. This is going to give you a whole new understanding of it!"

"You know, guys…nature and I have maintained a very polite distance for a long time now. It works for us. I'm not sure we should mess with a good thing here."

"You can do this, Cassandra," Daphne assured her. "Finn and Drew have dragged me along on all kinds of adventures I thought sounded crazy, but I'm always glad I go in the end. Trust me. You'll have a great time!"

"As long as it doesn't end in a watery, sharp-toothed grave."

"Manta rays' teeth are tiny."

"Fine. But if I get eaten by a shark, I'm never speaking to you guys again."

"That goes without saying," Drew said, and Daphne kicked him under the table.

"What? That seems pretty obvious to me. But don't worry, Cass, the chances of you getting eaten by a shark are slim. Getting stung by a manta ray, on the other hand—" he was cut off by another kick.

"You're not helping," Daphne said. "Go clear a table or something."

"They can wait."

"Then go hit on that redhead. She's been making eyes at you for the last ten minutes."

"You notice when other women look at me?" Drew raised his eyebrows. "Jealous, Daphne?"

"She can have you with my blessing. Now go away or stop scaring Cassandra!"

"Alright, alright," he said, turning back to Cassandra. "Manta rays don't sting people. Those are stingrays. Manta rays don't have the poisonous barbs in their tails that stingrays do, so they couldn't sting even if they wanted to, which they don't, because they're peaceful. Seriously, Cass, you'll be fine. People do this all the time. It'll be great."

"If you say so." Cassandra felt somewhat reassured.

"What's all this?" Andre came stomping over. "Three of my workers shirking their duties?"

"Just Drew," Finn corrected. "Cassandra is on break and I'm off tonight."

"Thanks a lot," Drew muttered, casting a dirty look at Finn. Then he said in a louder voice, "It had to be done, Andre. We're planning Cassandra's first island adventure."

"Aha," Andre said, brightening. "What's on the docket?"

"We're going to paddle out to watch the manta rays feed next weekend."

"Andrew and Finnegan," Andre said severely, looking sternly over the rim of his glasses, "if you kill my new hostess, I will have your hides."

Cassandra let out a strangled laugh and nervously sipped her water.

"Oh, for heaven's sake!" Daphne cried. "Will you all stop scaring her? Cassandra, this is going to be fun!"

Cassandra nodded vigorously and kept on sipping.

"Andre, make this right." It was Daphne's turn to look severe.

"I'm sorry, my little chestnut," Andre smiled placatingly at Cassandra. "Manta rays are harmless."

Cassandra let out a deep breath and Andre continued, "It's drowning you want to worry about. You're a strong swimmer, yes?"

"That's it!" Daphne said as Cassandra went pale. "Cassandra, break's over! Go back to work and don't give them another thought. Trust me. *You will be fine.*"

Cassandra sighed and scooted her chair back to leave while Daphne rounded on Drew. "Now you!" she said accusingly as Cass got back to work, "Andre doesn't pay you to sit around terrorizing your co-workers. I'm sure you have plenty you should be doing! Start by bringing us some lettuce wraps." Her tone morphed from berating to beseeching. "Extra dipping sauce, please."

"Whatever you want, Daph." Drew stood and bent down to kiss her on the cheek, then chuckled as her eyes flashed and narrowed, and he scooted off toward the kitchen before she could retaliate.

"You three look out for Cassandra," Andre warned the remaining two. "She's a gem. I don't want her harmed."

"We'll keep her perfectly safe," Finn promised.

"See that you do." Andre's bushy eyebrows knit together, and he stared at them until they both solemnly vowed that the next weekend's activities would be completely risk-free. Shooting them one more reproachful glare, Andre stalked off in the direction of a large table, face transforming into a hearty smile as he spread his hands wide and asked the party, "How are you enjoying your meals, eh?"

"Geez, tough crowd," Finn said. "All this fuss over some night-time ocean sightseeing."

"Not all of us spend our summers thrill-seeking, Finn," Daphne countered. "I'm sure Cassandra has never passed three months working on an Alaskan fishing boat or guiding rafting tours."

"I don't spend my summers thrill-seeking. I spend them observing and experiencing various cultures."

"Last summer, all I heard about was white-water rafting and bungee jumping and spelunking."

"I was working while I was on those white-water rafts. And who goes to New Zealand without bungee jumping or spelunking?"

"I'm just saying, take it easy on her. Cassandra is spunky but she's going to be outside her comfort zone with this. We just need to make sure she doesn't get in over her head."

"I don't know why everyone assumes Drew and I are reckless." Finn was indignant.

"I don't know. But here come the lettuce wraps!" Daphne said happily. "Thank you, Drew."

"Let me know if there's anything else you need," Drew wiggled his eyebrows suggestively.

Daphne rolled her eyes and ignored him, digging into the appetizer.

"Drew! Stop harassing customers!" Andre called from a nearby table. Drew ducked his head, winked at Daphne, and strolled off to check on another party.

Meanwhile, Cassandra was giving herself an enthusiastic if unconvincing pep talk.

You can do this! she told herself, showing an unruly party of fourteen-year-old girls and one very frazzled chaperone to a table. *There is nothing to freak out about here. So, the ocean is one giant deathtrap covering seventy percent of the Earth's surface and you'll be floating unprotected on eight feet of narrow foam in the middle of the night. What's the big deal? It's not like you'll actually have to get in the water. What are the chances of something deadly bothering to swim up to the surface and chew on you?*

She immediately thought of half a dozen situations which would just as effectively kill her: currents, rogue waves, drowning after getting hit on the head with a surfboard, getting eaten by a shark, losing track of the others in the dark and slowly drifting out to sea and *then* getting eaten by a shark.

Pull yourself together, Dillon! Where's your sense of adventure?

Clearly it was holed up on dry land, very sensibly *not* swimming with giant sea creatures. Cassandra pictured her inner adventurer, curled up in a bathrobe and drinking fruit juice in the lounge of a spa, looking disdainfully at her for even considering such a ridiculous excursion. She glared at the mental image. It was obvious her sense of adventure had been on vacation for way too long. It was time to shake things up.

I'll show you, inner adventurer! she thought fiercely. *Next week, we're swimming with sea creatures.*

She got an image of the bathrobe-clad figure choking on her fruit juice and looking at her as if she were deranged. *Yeah well,* Cassandra told her inner self, *it will be good for us. This is happening.*

Chapter Seven

Cassandra eyed the surfboard Finn handed her with deep suspicion. She was standing on the same beach that just ten days earlier, she had stomped along, frantically retreating from the same ocean she was imprudently about to reenter. As the waves washed gently up on the shore, she was brought back to that moment of insanity on the deck of the yacht and she felt loopy all over again.

She was vaguely aware that Drew had begun to explain general safety precautions and she did her best to pay attention to what he was saying but kept getting distracted by the sound of the surf and the unsettling feeling it seemed to be having on her lately. Taking a deep breath to stave off any new crazy impulses that might be creeping up (like grabbing the board, smacking Drew across the face and yelling, "I don't belong in the ocean!" as she ran desperately in the direction of safety and solid ground), Cassandra focused on his instructions.

"Once you've found your balance," Drew was saying, "you're going to paddle out into the water. Finn and I have got waterproof flashlights around our necks, so you'll just follow us. We're going about a quarter of a mile out, and the tourist boat should already be there with its lights. We'll get there just in time for the action."

"Uh-huh," Cassandra said nervously.

"So, when you paddle," he continued, "alternate your arms rather than trying to use them simultaneously in a breast stroke. That will help you keep a consistent speed. If you start to lag behind or need a rest, just give a shout and we'll slow down. The last thing we want is for your arms to give out from exhaustion and we lose you in open water." Drew chuckled and elbowed her ribs and Cassandra gave a hollow laugh.

"Okay, any questions?"

"Yes. Are you sure I'm qualified to do this?"

"You'll be great! And if not, Finn's a certified lifeguard. He'll be watching out for you the whole time!"

"Not that you'll need it." Finn smiled reassuringly in the dark. "But if you do need me, I'll be right there."

Cassandra exhaled slowly, marginally comforted. If she trusted anyone to save her life in a watery crisis, it was Finn. She looked at him, broad and sure and smiling in the moonlight, and she felt her heart lurch sideways and her stomach drop out from underneath her, either from affection or lust or sheer panic at what was about to come. She wasn't sure which. Maybe all three.

"Okay," she said out loud. "I can do this."

"Yes, you can!" Finn encouraged.

"We'll wait until you're comfortable on the board before we head out," Daphne added. "Take your time feeling it out!"

"Just remember what I told you before," Drew said. "Put your hands at about chest level to bring yourself onto the board, and then keep your body straight with your chest lifted."

"Use your core!" Daphne chimed in. "Just like Pilates!"

Cassandra groaned but nodded to acknowledge all of their advice.

"Here goes nothing!" she said and waded into the water.

Even though the water was fairly warm, Cassandra inhaled deeply and suppressed a curse as the sudden cold of it seeped into her wetsuit and she felt her skin break out in goosebumps. The innocuous act of entering the ocean seemed foreboding as the events of the previous Tuesday flooded her mind.

Well, she thought, *at least this time I'm not having a nervous breakdown. This time I've completely thought through the situation.* She just couldn't believe that her thought process had led to the conclusion that she should actually *do* this. As far as Cassandra was concerned, her spontaneous flight to the sea had been far saner than the premeditated decision to enter it and seek out its giant inhabitants *deliberately*.

When the water reached her midriff, Cassandra awkwardly flopped herself onto the surfboard, aiming the length of her body toward the center of the board like Drew had taught her. She flailed for a moment and immediately began to slide backward into the water. Letting out a squeak, she gripped the sides of the board and tried to shimmy forward, overcompensating and dipping the nose of the surfboard into the water. With a gargled gasp, she spat out a mouthful of saltwater and mentally banished Drew and Finn to a deep circle of hell. As she struggled with the board, sloshing water all around and feeling like a child on a teeter-totter, she yelled, "I really don't think I'm cut out for this!"

"You're doing great, Cass!" Finn called back. "Just find your center! Not too far forward!"

Easier said than done, she thought as she half slid off the board while it rocked unsteadily from side to side. But eventually she wiggled herself into alignment with the midline of the board and felt it settle underneath her, bobbing gently with the water. She let out a relieved sigh and clonked her forehead on the slippery foam, raising her voice to ask, "Are we done yet?"

"We're just getting started!" Drew waded out beside her and easily pulled himself onto his board. Cassandra managed not to glare.

"You did an awesome job," Daphne said encouragingly, coming up on her other side.

"Yeah," Drew agreed. "You finally tamed the beast! It looked for a while like you were wrestling a sea monster."

Cassandra could sense Daphne shooting him a dirty look through the dark, but kept her forehead resting on the board as Finn paddled over, looking, she noted with disgust, completely at ease.

Get ahold of yourself, she chided.

They were all being great and she was being grumpy. For their sakes, and for the sake of her sedentary inner adventurer, she owed this a fair shot.

They spent a few minutes talking her through the mechanics of paddling, throwing out advice as she acclimated herself to the motion.

"That's it—one arm at a time," Daphne said.

"Use deep, rhythmic strokes." Finn's voice appeared close by her side and Cassandra blushed. Just her luck, she was wet and in the dark with a gorgeous guy thinking about deep, rhythmic strokes, and he was talking about surfboards. Well, this was the summer she had wanted: new adventures and no men to muck it up.

Embrace it, Dillon, she told herself, and focused on the task at hand.

Soon, she was moving about in the water with relative comfort and even some amount of directional accuracy.

"I think you're ready," Drew said. "That's probably enough practice—we don't want your arms tiring out before we've even gotten started."

"Are you ready for this?" Daphne asked.

Absolutely not! Cassandra thought, but she forced a smile and said aloud, "Absolutely!"

"That's the spirit!" Drew said. "Let's move out!"

"Yay!" Cassandra said with feigned enthusiasm, hoping that if she *sounded* excited, she might begin to *feel* excited, rather than feeling like she was about to hurl all over her surfboard.

They started paddling out to sea, veering slightly north.

This is insane! Cassandra's inner voice panicked. *We're heading defenseless into open water…we're all going to die!*

But she shoved these thoughts aside and concentrated instead on the steady pull of her arms in the water, just like when she'd swam toward the island. *Paddle now, think later,* became her new mantra. Things went badly when she let herself think. She focused on moving her arms in time with the others, matching her breath to the pace of her stroke.

When her arms began to burn and breathing was no longer enough to calm her nerves, she shifted her focus to the light hanging steadfastly around Finn's neck. If all else failed, she could forget everything else and stare at him for the rest of the trip.

He looked wonderful. Strong and steady, gliding through the water with no effort whatsoever. He grinned as he paddled, his eyes shining with the joy of being outdoors. Wet hair clung to his forehead and Cassandra was hit with the memory of Finn as he got out of the shower, toweling off his dripping hair and grinning wickedly at her as he stood there, gloriously and unabashedly naked under that towel.

Now his wetsuit clung to him like a second skin, hugging every muscle and plane of his body, and as she watched the graceful ease with which he moved, Cassandra's throat went dry. Stretched out on the board in the glow of the moonlight, she could see a perfect silhouette of the curve of his butt. It was exceptional. Round and firm—muscles a girl could absolutely sink her teeth into. Cassandra had a vision of Finn stretched out on top of her, imagined herself cupping that perfect butt, gasping with pleasure as he pushed hard into her, imagined their bodies moving together, and suddenly she felt a little lightheaded.

"Are you okay?" Daphne's voice broke through her reverie. "You look pretty dazed. Do you want to rest for a minute?"

Cassandra started guiltily. "No, I'm fine. Just daydreaming, I guess."

"We're nearly there, anyway," Drew said. "You can see the lights from the boat in the distance. We should be close enough to stop in a few minutes."

"Oh good," Cassandra said.

This piece of news was enough to jolt her from her fantasies completely. In just a few minutes she would be floating directly over a manta ray feeding ground. Which meant the beasts could very well be swimming beneath her at that exact moment. Her heart beat faster and Cass resumed deep breathing to stave off the panic that was rapidly welling inside of her.

Don't be ridiculous, she told herself. *For all you know, they've been swimming under you all along.* This thought only increased her surge of alarm and she started throwing shifty glances from side to side, searching for any dark shadows floating below. She was grateful that she had about a foot of surfboard blocking the view directly beneath her face, because if she looked down and unexpectedly saw a manta ray swimming along right under her, her heart would stop then and there.

"Hey guys," Cassandra called out tentatively, "I'm starting to freak out, here. You did say there are no sharks in these waters, right?"

"We never said that," Drew responded, and Cassandra nearly passed out.

"But don't worry, we probably won't run into any," he said casually. "Alright, gang, let's pull up here!"

Cassandra had been so consumed with visions of a shark-infested death that she hadn't noticed they had come within a couple hundred yards of the boat. It loomed in front of them, slightly off to their left, shining a massive spotlight into the water. A couple dozen people were crowded on the deck, leaning expectantly over the rails. Cassandra looked up at them with obvious envy, wishing there was something as substantial as a boat between herself and the water.

"What now?" she asked.

"Now we wait."

They all sat in their own kind of silence for several minutes. For Cassandra, it was tense. For Daphne, companionable. For Finn and Drew, anticipatory. Echoes of conversations drifted down from the tour boat, mingling with the constant sound of gently rolling waves, but the four surfers remained silent.

The hush was suddenly broken by an excited cry from someone on the boat. A wave of chatter rose up from the crowd as they all clamored to get a better view of the water. At the same time, a wave of nausea washed over Cassandra as she looked into the clear depths and saw two massive shadows moving swiftly toward the spotlight. The shapes grew larger and larger as they approached, moving through the water with unnerving speed and agility, and by the time they got close enough for her to make out their features, Cassandra nearly fell off her board from abject terror.

It was as if these dark, massive creatures had traveled directly from the bowels of hell—demons of the deep come to terrorize this unsuspecting group of pleasure cruisers. The smallest was easily twelve feet in diameter, the largest closer to eighteen. Strangely, no one else seemed upset, but Cassandra couldn't stop a small scream from escaping as the rays reached the spotlight and their otherworldly features were fully illuminated for the first time. Murky gray on top and ghostly white on bottom, their strange, flat bodies flew through the water like some kind of alien magic carpet.

Through her haze of fear, Cassandra noticed the markings on their undersides and was reminded of the carpet from Aladdin. A hysterical giggle erupted as she imagined grabbing onto one of the rays' antennae-like protrusions on either side of its head and hitching a ride, singing a watery rendition of A Whole New World.

Alright, time to get a grip, she told herself. *They're just fish. Giant, unnaturally flat fish with unnervingly large wingspans. No big deal. They won't hurt you. Like Drew said, they're harmless. Are you terrified of the fact that they're almost three times your size? No, you are not.*

Another equally large ray appeared from the depths, its gills rippling and giving it a frighteningly skeletal appearance as it passed not five meters below Cassandra's dangling feet and she concentrated on not hyperventilating.

Okay, she thought. *Okay, okay, okay. Remember, they're not dangerous.*

Losing consciousness, on the other hand, would be very dangerous. Although, if she fell into the water and half-drowned, Finn would have to rescue her and give her mouth to mouth and that would be a plus. Still, it probably wasn't worth the risk.

Breathing, that was the key. In and out. Inhale and exhale. By now, there were six shapes in total circling the light, looping and diving, bizarre oblong mouths open for an invisible feeding frenzy.

Swim away, plankton! Cassandra warned them silently. *You're about to be massacred!*

"Aren't they amazing?" Finn asked with awe in his voice.

"They're beautiful," Daphne breathed.

Another crazy giggle sounded and Cassandra echoed, "Beautiful."

That's right, she thought, *focus on the positive. They're not devil fish. They're beautiful. See how agile they are? Elegant. Not terrifying.*

Complete silence had fallen as thirty people stared enraptured by the scene before them. Cassandra looked at the mesmerized expressions on each of her friends' faces and then turned her attention back to the rays spinning slowly around the beam of light. When you didn't think of them as unholy demon spawn, there was something captivating about the way they moved. Gracefully, deliberately, turning loop after loop in an impressive display of acrobatics, triangular wing-like fins undulating noiselessly. It was almost like watching some kind of silent, unearthly ballet.

It was hypnotic, eerie, fascinating, and unlike anything Cassandra had ever experienced, watching these two-thousand-pound creatures weave an intricate underwater dance as they feasted on unseen organisms.

Cass's earlier horror faded and was replaced by wonder. She sat on her surfboard in the middle of the ocean, feet dangling in the water, unprotected and unafraid. Daphne had been right. There was a haunting beauty to these creatures and Cassandra stared at their movements, entranced. Suddenly it didn't matter that if they decided to, the rays could crush or drown her. Cass completely forgot about the possible dangers and just sat, bewitched. She could have watched this pageant of phantoms for hours.

The minutes passed and one by one, the rays swam away until only one remained. It turned its final loop and then began its retreat as well, gliding back the way it came, its long barb-like tail swinging like a pendulum as it disappeared into the darkness. The beam of light vanished from the water as the spotlight was shut off and the spell was broken. Chatter rose up once again from the deck of the boat, but the four friends enjoyed one last moment of quiet before coming out of their trance.

"Well," Finn said as all eyes turned toward Cassandra, "what did you think?"

Cass looked at them with wide, unblinking eyes. "That was *incredible*!" she said.

"Yay!" Daphne cried.

"See," Drew said, "I knew you'd come around."

"So you liked it?" Finn asked.

"I *loved* it!" Cassandra replied. "I mean, I was fairly sure I was going to die there for a while, but I didn't, and the manta rays were unbelievable! I've never seen anything like them."

"And none of them had mutilated fins or diseased looking bumps?" Finn teased.

"Their gills are incredibly creepy…it's unnatural for a living thing to have punctures in the side of its body and stay alive, but I chose not to focus on that. And I had a great time!" she beamed at them.

The tour ship's engines roared to life and the vessel began a 180-degree about-face, making its way back to port and creating a flurry of turbulent waves in its wake. Cassandra clutched her board to avoid getting thrown off and decided it was time to head to solid ground. Now that the magic of the manta rays' dance had ended, she was ready to be back on dry land.

The return trip was uneventful. The others chatted excitedly about the night's events, commenting on the size and number of rays and the hilarious look on Cassandra's face when she first saw them, but Cass barely heard them. She floated back in a daydream, head full of visions of wraithlike mantas turning slow circles around an ethereal beam of light. She was almost surprised when they reached the shore.

Sliding awkwardly off her board, she sloshed gracelessly through the shallows, splashing herself, Daphne, and Finn in the process, and then struggled with the slippery board, only dropping it twice before managing to get it into an upright position. The other three grinned at her ungainly exit from the water, but Drew clapped her on the shoulder when she joined them on the beach, shaky and exhilarated.

"You did good tonight, Cass," he complimented. "We're all impressed."

"Sure are," Daphne said, stifling a yawn. "You were a trooper! And on top of a full day at work and another Pilates class this morning, you did way better your first time on a board than I would have! But as much fun as this was, I've got to head home. I'm beat and I've got an eight o'clock kickboxing class in the morning. You want to come, Cass?"

"Daphne, I love you, but nothing in the world could induce me to wake up tomorrow at eight in the morning to kickbox. I'll catch it next time!"

"Okay!" Daphne blinked tiredly. "You ready to go home, then?"

"I guess so." Cassandra bounced on her heels. "It seems a shame, though. I've still got kind of an adrenaline rush from surviving another ocean adventure. Going to bed seems like a waste of an endorphin high."

"I'll stay up with you," Finn offered without missing a beat. "I was thinking of going for a late-night hike anyway."

"A hike?" Cassandra sounded dubious as she thought about it, but then smiled and shrugged. "Why not?"

She figured at this point in her day, what was one more trek through the great outdoors? And spending more time with Finn in the moonlight was too tempting to pass up.

"I'll take it easy on you." Finn nudged her with his elbow. "There's a nice, gentle hike with a great view not too far from here."

"Excellent," Cassandra said. "We're not exactly dressed for a hike, though," she added, looking down at her wetsuit.

"Not a problem! I've got some stuff in a locker in the staffroom at the resort. I'm sure we'll be able to find something for you, too."

"You guys are crazy." Daphne shook her head at them. "I've got to go to bed."

"Want some company?" Drew grinned at her.

"In bed, no. But you may walk me home. It's late and I don't want to be wandering the streets by myself."

"I'll protect you," Drew said, wrapping his arm around her shoulders.

"I'm a kickboxing instructor," Daphne said flatly, untangling herself from under his arm, "I'll protect myself. But in the event that we come across a crazy person with a machine gun, you may offer yourself as a human shield."

"Gee, thanks."

"Well," said Daphne brightly, "I want you to feel like you're contributing." She started walking down the beach in the general direction of her apartment. "It's a heroic death, sacrificing yourself for a damsel in distress."

"You're not exactly the damsel in distress type," Drew pointed out, trotting after her.

"Kickboxing will only get you so far against bullets, Drew."

They wandered off and Cass and Finn could hear them bantering all the way down the beach, their voices eventually trailing off as they disappeared from view.

"Those two really need to get together sooner or later," Finn said. "I don't know if I can handle the sexual tension much longer."

"I don't know," Cassandra said. "He's got a long way to go. Convincing Daphne that he's not just some yahoo trying to get into her pants is going to be an uphill climb."

"He is some yahoo trying to get into her pants," Finn said, "but there could be something there. And speaking of uphill climbs," he transitioned smoothly, "are you ready to go?"

Cassandra groaned. "That does not bode well. I thought you said it was a *gentle* hike."

"It is," Finn assured her. "That doesn't mean you won't have to walk uphill at least a little. And the view is worth it."

"Alright," Cassandra conceded. "Lead the way."

"We just have to make a quick stop by Silver Sands and then we'll get going."

Chapter Eight

Together, Cassandra and Finn ambled up the shoreline and Cass recounted the story of her previous midnight stroll along the very same beach—the way she'd lain there moaning when she washed up on shore, the way she'd tripped and fallen into the shallows when she'd managed to stand up again.

"After seeing the masterful way you handled that surfboard tonight, I just can't imagine that," Finn laughed.

"Yeah, well," Cass smiled," I'm never particularly graceful on land or in water…combine the two and I'm an absolute mess."

Finn's smile broadened. "What happened next?"

"I clomped through the sand toward the resort, severely questioning my sanity—as, I'm sure, was anyone else who saw me. I think I was muttering to myself the whole way and at one point I almost kicked a flower for mocking me."

"A flower?"

"Yes! Have you ever noticed how amazingly smug everything at the Silver Sands looks? Even the landscaping is pleased with itself."

"I hadn't noticed. But now that you mention it…" Finn said as they approached the fringes of the resort's ornate lawn and he surveyed the perfectly groomed terrain, "…I still would have a hard time believing the plants were judging you."

"Probably not *actually*, but I was in a weird place that night." Cassandra eyed the grounds defensively. "Although I'm still getting an aura of disdain from some of these topiaries."

She cast a leery glance at the surrounding hedges, then smoothed out her face and continued, "To be fair, I can't blame Judith for turning me away. I must have looked completely insane."

"You did," Finn chuckled. "At least by the time I could really see you. You were a mess. Muttering in your sleep, hair everywhere, that smudge of sand on your forehead…you looked deranged. I was walking through the grounds after my shift, expecting to go straight home and have a nice quiet end to my day, only to find this mad woman covered in sand and passed out under a bush, watering the lawn with her clothes. And then I thought you were going to bite my head off when I shook you awake."

"I was incredibly polite!"

"You *sounded* polite, but the look in your eyes said you were ready to go for the throat. You get those crazy eyes when you're riled up."

Cassandra glared at him.

"See, there they are now! You've got an impetuous streak, Dillon."

"Well, that's certainly true. I get that from my grandma. She would have jumped off a yacht and gone home with a strange man at two in the morning. And if he would have turned out to be a psychopath, she would have kicked his ass, rifled through his pockets for cab fare, and disappeared into the night."

"Sounds a lot like you," Finn said. They had reached a side entrance to the hotel and lingered by the doorway.

"She was quite a lady," Cassandra said wistfully. "And she would have loved this trip. If Gram had been standing next to me that night on the ship, she probably would have pushed me over the rails if I hadn't had the guts to go over myself."

"Did you tell her about your jump?"

"Oh. No. She died…" the words caught in Cassandra's throat. "About three months ago. Heart attack."

Finn could have kicked himself. "I'm sorry," he said, knowing this was a colossally useless thing to say even as he said it.

"It's okay," Cassandra cleared her throat. "It didn't come as a surprise. She had her first attack three years ago while I was away at college. That was the main reason I moved back home—to help take care of her. And she had a good life. Lived it to the fullest. Not only would she have watched the manta rays tonight, she would have been in the water with them. Gram was not a woman to pass up an experience."

"Sounds like an amazing woman," Finn said.

"She was." Cassandra's eyes were bright.

Not knowing how else to comfort her, Finn laced his fingers through Cassandra's and gave her hand a squeeze, dropping it before she could think he was trying to make a move.

"Thanks," she said, blinking rapidly. "It's nice to talk about her. I haven't much, since the funeral…" She sniffed, then paused for a moment and cleared her throat again. "But we have a hike to go on. And I'm expecting some pretty great scenery, so we'd better get moving!"

"Right," Finn said, relieved that she no longer looked like she was about to cry. "Just give me ten minutes and I'll find us some clothes."

***

Cassandra watched him jog down the brightly lit hallway. She shivered, wrapping her arms around herself in the dark and thinking sadly of her grandma.

She would have liked him, she thought.

He was exactly the kind of man Gram would have loved for her to bring home: charming and sincere, steadfast but adventurous, funny, thoughtful, sexy, intelligent…someone with an appreciation for food and 80s music, who looked damn good in a towel.

Okay, maybe now she was just naming off qualities *she* liked about him.

Oh, come off it, she told herself, dutifully reigning in her mind. *You barely know him.*

Still, she was grateful that he'd let her talk about her grandma. She hadn't opened up to many people since the funeral. Her family had been there for her, of course, and she for them, but none of them had been as close with her grandma as Cass had been. All Cassandra's life, the two of them had been kindred spirits. Since she'd passed away, Cass had felt lost, like a beacon she'd been following her whole life had suddenly been shut off.

It was sweet of Finn to let her talk about it, and not panic like so many men did when a woman got emotional anywhere near them. Finn had just listened and squeezed her hand. And his face had been so sweet, so concerned…

Get a grip, she told herself.

"Alright, I'm back!" Finn burst through the door unexpectedly and Cassandra let out a startled yelp.

He had changed from his wetsuit to a t-shirt, sweatpants and a pair of well-worn sneakers. He looked comfortably sexy and Cassandra couldn't help eying the way the t-shirt stretched across his chest. He went on, unaware that she was surreptitiously checking him out.

"Good news! I tracked down Ariana. She's a waitress in the bar and a hiking enthusiast, so she usually keeps at least one outdoorsy change of clothes at work. I think she's about your size…hopefully the shoes fit. You can go ahead and change behind the bushes…I promise I won't look." He wiggled his eyebrows.

"Or I could go find a bathroom inside," Cass stated the obvious. "I don't trust that eyebrow wiggle. Back in a flash!"

Cassandra trotted down the hallway, telling herself that it was stupid to be grinning just because Finn was flirting with her. He was a bartender, for goodness' sake—he flirted for a living. And anyway, she was on a dating hiatus. She was finding herself, damn it! And she was doing a pretty good job of it, considering the short amount of time she'd been on the island. There was no reason to get distracted just because she'd also found a sexy, interesting man whose lopsided grin made her stomach flutter.

Focus, Dillon! she told herself, veering at a sign for a restroom and heading down another long hallway. *Go on this hike, then go home and get some sleep, because you've got your life to figure out. Get your head in the game!* Then she chuckled because she was so completely un-athletic that using a sports metaphor was laughable, even in a mental pep-talk. Sports metaphors were for people who did *not* fall over playing hopscotch in the third grade.

But the point remains the same, she told herself staunchly. *Now is not the time to get swept off your feet by a killer smile and a degree in anthropology. It's a time for self-reflection and growth. Remember that.* She nodded in silent agreement with herself, committed in her resolve not to let Finn get in her head. Or anywhere else, for that matter.

***

When Cassandra located the bathroom, the door swung open just as she was about to reach for it.

"Pardon me," Cass said, pausing to make way for the person coming out. Then her eyes landed on the other woman's face.

"*You!*" Judith exclaimed. The receptionist's eyebrows snapped together in fury, taking in Cassandra's wetsuit, wet hair, and sandy sandals.

"Hi, Judith." Cassandra plastered on a smile. "Fancy seeing you here!"

Judith adjusted her spectacles and compressed her lips into a thin line. "Soggy again, I see. Young lady, the Silver Sands' facilities are *not* open to the general public."

"I'm here with Finn," Cassandra explained. "Finnegan Drake? He works here. We're just on our way to a hike."

Cassandra smiled and took a step forward, hoping to detour around Judith and cut the interaction short, but the intrepid employee held her ground, puffing herself up in front of the bathroom door like a dragon defending her hoard.

"I wonder," Judith mused, almost to herself, as if loath to address Cassandra directly, "if you've ever heard of a dress code."

"Oh, is there a dress code that I'm breaking?" Cassandra asked politely, stifling a sigh and resigning herself to at least another minute of Judith and her misplaced wrath.

Judith seethed, apparently caught against an inconvenient truth. She stared Cassandra down for a long moment.

"No," she finally said through her teeth. "Not as such. Not an officially stated set of rules. But there is such a thing as decorum, young lady. There is a time and place for *proper* attire and you seem to have a hard time grasping that concept." She scanned Cassandra up and down, practically hissing as she did. "You're *dripping* again."

Cassandra looked down at the small puddle forming at her feet.

"I am," she acknowledged. "I promise I'll clean it up once I've changed. We just went to see the manta rays feed," she said, hoping to prompt some semblance of a positive response. "Have you ever done that? It was amazing!"

Judith fixed her eyes on Cassandra. In them, Cass could see untold depths of disapproval—towering chasms and yawning caverns of boundless reproach. She took half a step back.

"Yes," Judith answered at last, voice flat. "It was magical."

Cass had never heard someone express a favorable sentiment so unwillingly. She pressed on, dauntless.

"I thought so, too!" she agreed, infusing as much chipper into her voice as she could. "So now we're moving on to a hike! More wonders of nature…keep the magic flowing..."

Judith folded her arms, unmovable. "The facilities are not open to the public."

With Titanic restraint, Cassandra managed not to groan in frustration or flick Judith between her ever-furrowed brows.

"I'm here at the invitation of a Silver Sands employee, Judith," Cass said, not worried that she might be getting Finn into trouble. He'd shown no concern whatsoever when she went into the hotel, and she couldn't imagine anyone else caring about the sanctity of a ground-floor bathroom as much as this pathologically dedicated front-desk worker.

"Finn is waiting for me outside," she said, inching her way toward Judith, who stood rooted to her spot like the bastion of a fortress. "I will be in and out in two minutes. Unless you'd rather I change here in the hallway or out on the lawn."

Judith gave a small gasp, then pressed her lips even more tightly together, so compressed that they paled at the edges.

"You most certainly will not!" she exclaimed with a voice of stone.

"I don't want to." Cassandra edged further forward, angling her hips around Judith's, who leaned her shoulders in, apparently wrestling with the perceived decorum of physically tackling someone on the hallowed premises of Silver Sands.

"Two minutes, Judith." Cassandra managed to lay her hand flat on the door, skirting around the bristling woman who looked half a second away from shouting, 'Sweep the legs!' and laying Cassandra flat on her back.

"Two minutes and then I promise I will wipe up that puddle and be out of your hair!"

Judith held her eyes for a long moment, clearly torn between the instinct to preserve the purity of Silver Sands by kicking a freeloading non-patron out into the night, and the practicality of avoiding a scene and getting rid of Cassandra as quickly as possible. In the end, practicality won the day. She turned on her heel with a huff and stalked away without a word.

Cassandra let out a heavy exhale.

So nice to see her again, she thought, and pushed open the bathroom door.

***

Finn was staring up at the night sky when he heard Cassandra's voice from behind.

"Ready to go!" she said, sounding perky as hell for someone who had just faced what was supposedly one of her biggest fears not even an hour ago. Although, being afraid of the ocean hadn't stopped Cassandra from jumping into it ten days ago. Hell of a girl.

"Did everything fit?" he asked, turning to face her, then stopped short as he saw for himself.

"Not exactly," she said, pulling on the hem of the t-shirt. "It's a little small, and the shoes are a no-go, but my sandals will have to be. Do you think that will work for the hike?"

Finn didn't respond. He had seen the exact same outfit on Ariana and been unfazed, but Cassandra had assets that Ariana did not. The scooped neck of the shirt dipped low and the pants hugged the curve of her butt and the shape of her thighs and Finn suddenly felt a little lightheaded. She had a great body. And it was off limits. He dragged his eyes back up to her face, which was regarding him with an arch expression.

The look quickly passed, as most of her expressions did, and was replaced by one of amusement. Watching this woman's face was like reading a book. She telegraphed exactly what she was thinking at any given moment and he loved it— Cassandra was purely guileless. Finn doubted she could hide something even if she wanted to. At the moment, he was just glad she hadn't called him out for leering. In an effort to bring himself back to the conversation, he said dimly, "Sandals?"

"Mmhmm," she said, grinning at him, and he had the decency to look sheepish.

She looked down and wiggled her toes. "It's not ideal, but better than going barefoot. Though if I get terrible blisters, you get to be the one who explains to Andre why his hostess is limping."

"If you get blisters, I'll just carry you the rest of the way." Finn hadn't meant for that to sound suggestive, but there was a long pause and Cassandra blinked at him. Maybe it wasn't actually suggestive, but the thought of touching her in any way was messing with his ability to discern innuendo from casual conversation. They had to get moving before he did something stupid like reach for her—trace his finger along the neckline of that shirt, pull it lower to echo the motion with his tongue, lick his way down the swell of her breast to—

"I'm sure your feet will be fine," he said abruptly. "Should we get going?"

"Right," she said with a small shake of her head. "After you!"

He started off in the direction of the trail and she followed a little way behind him.

"Tell me about this spot we're heading to," she said, jogging a few paces to catch up. "Is it far?"

"Maybe a mile away…we'll have to walk a while to get there, but not too far."

"How do you know about it?"

"I spent a lot of summers on the island growing up," he replied, slowing his stride. "My mom is a food critic and my dad writes for a travel magazine. This island is where they met—both of them were on assignment for work. It's always been close to their hearts, so we spent as much time here as possible. Daphne came with us when we were twelve and never wanted to leave, so she settled here as soon as she could after high school. Definitely not a bad place to spend your childhood," he said, looking around fondly while they walked along the shoreline. "Or adulthood, for that matter. The spot we're going to has a great view. We used to hike up there with a picnic basket and watch the sun sink into the ocean."

"That sounds wonderful."

"Can't complain."

"Where are your parents now?"

"Cannes, I think. Or maybe Nice. Somewhere in the south of France. They have quite a busy season lined up between the two of them, as usual, but they'll be coming to visit later this summer."

"Oh?"

"It's a standing date they have with Andre. My mom critiqued his restaurant when it was brand new. She loved his food and he loved her review and the rest is history. She and my dad went there on their first date. Andre served them free drinks all night, and the three became fast friends. Now, every year in July my parents travel here to celebrate the anniversary of the week they all met."

"That's a great story!" Cassandra sounded delighted. "And that's how you know Andre?"

"Yeah, he's always been a sort of honorary uncle to me and Daphne. He talks a big talk, but underneath his gruff exterior he's about as stern as chocolate cake."

Cassandra laughed. "So far, I love him. His restaurant is cozy, he's great with customers and employees, and eating his food is almost a religious experience. I'd take him on as an honorary uncle any day."

She went on with palpable envy in her voice. "I can't believe you got to grow up with that kind of amazing food! The way that man cooks is poetry."

Finn smiled. "Growing up with a food critic for a mother, I was introduced to a lot of gourmet food at a young age. And believe me, it's hard to appreciate endive salad, foie gras, or crab cakes with fennel aioli at the age of eight. Come to think of it, I'm not crazy about any of that stuff now. But eating at Andre's was always great…he makes a mean mac and cheese. And for a kid who regularly ate foods he couldn't pronounce, that was just about the best thing imaginable."

"I'll bet!" Cassandra sympathized. "But my parents were friends with businessmen, stock brokers and financial analysts. I'm sure there are plenty of lovely and interesting people in those professions, but none of them worked with my father. There were a lot of stuffy dinner parties, but not a lot of great food. It's hard to feel bad for you when I was stuck with weird food *and* boring people."

"Are you kidding? Don't feel bad for me at all! I got to travel, meet interesting people, stay at fun places, do exciting things…my childhood was pretty awesome. It's probably the reason I've never had any interest in a nine-to-five office job. My parents raised me to be fascinated by other cultures—they doomed me to a life of experiences and adventure from the very beginning."

"You poor thing," Cassandra teased.

"Yeah, it was pretty rough. How about you? Financial analysts, you say?"

"Yup. My dad's in the financial sector. There was never a chance of me following in his footsteps. I was good at math in school, but if I had to stare at numbers all day for a living I would snap after a week and try to run myself through a shredder. My sister Beth might have more of a head for it, although right now, she doesn't have much of a head for anything except boys. But she's eighteen—you can't really hold it against her. She'll mellow out sometime in college. We hope."

"What about your mom?"

"Ah, my dear mother. She's a suburban housewife. Very involved in her garden club and charity fundraisers. We get along just fine, but we don't have much in common. She doesn't understand how I made it all the way through college without getting engaged, and I don't understand how she spends so much of her time eating tea sandwiches to support humane societies and hurricane relief. I'm all for humane societies and hurricane relief, but I'm not sure why the tea sandwiches play such a big role."

Finn laughed. "Tell me more about yourself," he went on, switching tracks. "You were a French major in your undergrad, right?"

"*Oui. Mais malheureusement, je n'ai pas utilisé le français depuis deux ans.*"

Finn gave her a blank stare.

"Sorry," she laughed. "It's fun to pull it out sometimes. Yes. French Studies. How much farther is it to the path?"

"We're close. Just a couple minutes away."

Their surroundings had given way to lush trees, which grew thicker as they walked farther on.

"Is French Studies different from studying French?" Finn asked.

"French Studies focuses on speaking, reading, and writing the language, but it also encompasses the study of French culture through a much wider lens. History, geography, political systems, education, business, art, literature, music, food, film, philosophy...of course, we learn it all in French and a portion of our studies is devoted to grammar and vocab and everything else that you would expect from a language degree. There's just a lot more to it."

"That sounds a lot like cultural anthropology, but focused on one country. What did your parents think of it?"

"They were tolerant. My dad would have liked for me to go into something with more obvious practical application. My mother thought that if I was going to spend that much time preoccupied with French culture, I could have thrown myself into *haute couture*. But they never tried to talk me out of it and I'm grateful for that. It avoided a lot of pointless arguing. And they weren't paying for it—I had a scholarship."

"Impressive."

Cassandra shrugged. "Thank you. I always liked school and I was good at it. It's living in the real world that throws me." She looked pensive. "I'm not great with practicality."

"You just have a flair for the dramatic. And a different take on what's practical. That doesn't make you unreasonable. Here we are!" They had arrived at a dirt path that led at a slight incline into a densely wooded area.

"It looks pretty dark through there," Cassandra said uncertainly.

"Don't worry. On a night like tonight, a lot of moon and starlight shines in through the trees, and I've still got the big flashlight from earlier." He held it up. "There are no steep ledges and no dangerous animals living in these woods. Also, this trail is really well maintained. You might stub your toe or trip over a stick if you're really uncoordinated, but we've already decided that I will carry you if you manage to injure yourself."

"You underestimate my lack of coordination." Cassandra peered into the darkness. "But let's give it a shot."

She started up the path with slow, cautious steps. Finn rolled his eyes and caught up to her in two strides, grabbing her hand and pulling her along at a livelier pace.

"Since we are in fact humans and not snails or sentient molasses, and I would like to complete this hike before sunrise, you're going to have to walk a little faster than that," he told her.

"Sure, hurry us along if you want me to break my ankle," she said with mock reproach. "You'll have no one to blame but yourself when you hit mile four on the long trek home and your arms feel like they're going to fall off and I'm moaning about how the world is a cruel place full of harsh dangers.

"You know," she said, pulling him to a stop so she could bend down to smell a large white flower on a leafy green bush, "I haven't had a chance to see much of the island yet. Just your neighborhood and Daphne's and a little bit of the beach. This is beautiful. I could be cooped up in a tiny ship's cabin right now, staring at four dreary walls and listening to my sister talk in her sleep. But instead I'm here, stretching my legs, breathing in the night air, taking in the beautiful scenery..."

"Why, thank you."

"Not you!" Cassandra whacked his arm. "Although you're not bad either. I was talking about the island."

"I know you were. But I'm not bad either, huh?" Finn grinned.

"Don't fish for compliments." Cassandra blushed, continuing up the path.

"Of course not," Finn said, trotting after her. "I just wanted to make sure I heard you correctly. I thought maybe you'd said, 'you're not clad beaver.'"

"'You're not clad beaver?'" Cassandra repeated, voice heavy with skepticism.

"See, I thought it was odd, too. I wanted to be sure you weren't having a stroke. Make sure I didn't have to give you mouth to mouth."

"That is not how you assist someone who's having a stroke."

"Don't worry." He gave her another lopsided smile. "I'm a trained lifeguard."

"Changing the subject," she shook her head and they meandered up the path. "Tell me more about yourself. When did you get certified to be a lifeguard?"

"When I was seventeen. It was my first summer job. It made sense…I spent as much time as possible in the water during vacations when I was young. I figured if I had to work, I might as well get paid to spend time at the beach."

"We have very different relationships with the beach," Cassandra said, shaking a rock out of her sandal.

"We already learned tonight that you don't surf. And you've made it clear you're not a big fan of the ocean. What *do* you do at the beach?"

"Wear a lot of sun block." Cass shrugged. "Read under an umbrella. Try not to get sand in my eyes or anywhere else unpleasant. It's an uphill battle."

"That's pretty grim."

"The beach is a grim place."

"You're kidding, right? Tell me again what beaches you've been going to."

"I'm from the Pacific Northwest." Cassandra paused to examine a clump of purple flowers. "Our beaches are cold and grey and windy. Other people love them—I've just never had a great time."

He looked at her, openly appalled. "Cassandra, that is tragic. You're on a tropical beach now! Keep an open mind and I promise you'll start to see the ocean differently."

"I did tonight," she conceded, renewing their pace. "I let you take me into open water to look at marine life, two things which I historically despise, and I had an incredible time. See? I can evolve." She gingerly stepped over a tree branch.

"I never doubted it," Finn said, enjoying the rhythm of their steps as they fell into sync. "So, you finally found something to like about the ocean."

"I've always liked the sound of it," Cassandra countered. "And I like to eat certain things that come out of it." She considered this point and then amended, "As long as I don't have to look at them in their natural form. I tend to prefer them breaded and fried or slathered in butter. But that still counts for something."

Finn looked at her fondly, treading with unnecessary care along the path and pausing every so often to admire the foliage.

"You're kind of insane, you know that?"

She sniffed primly. "'I think I'm sweet.'"

"Well, that too," he said.

They continued on in silence for several minutes until Cassandra asked, "Is it my imagination or do I hear waves?"

"No, you hear them. We're almost to the lookout point. It's just over this ridge."

In another minute they were over the crest of the hill and suddenly they could see the ocean spread out before them. Finn heard Cassandra gasp and he turned to watch her take in the view. They stood on a small plateau at the edge of the trees. A dozen yards in front of them, the ground dropped off sharply in an abrupt cliff face. Beyond that, there was nothing but sand and ocean for miles. The moon hung low in the sky, bathing the sea in its glow, casting its reflection on the gently cresting waves. Cassandra's eyes glittered as she looked down at the water, lips parted in a smile.

"'You sure look lovely in the moonlight, Kathy,'" she breathed.

"What?" Finn asked, confused. "Who's Kathy?"

"Oh," Cassandra looked at him, jarred back to reality. "It's from Singing in the Rain. Gene Kelly creates a nightscape on a movie set for Debbie Reynolds using stage lighting and tells her she looks lovely in the moonlight. This is better."

"This is better than an iconic Hollywood love scene?"

"Well, you know…it's a better setting."

"I can live with that," Finn nodded.

"The 'I think I'm sweet' crack was also a movie line: Ruth Hussy in Philadelphia Story. I have to say, Finn"—Cassandra turned to him earnestly, a complete non sequitur—"these last few days have been amazing. I can't thank you enough for everything you've done for me."

"Don't mention it."

"No, seriously! Not everyone would have bothered to help a stranger off the street like you did the night we met, let alone open their home to one. And not everyone would have been so gentlemanly about it. In fact, I'm certain most men wouldn't have been. And they almost definitely wouldn't have gone on to help that stranger find a job and a place to live or taken her on adventures and brought her into their circle of friends."

Finn mentally acknowledged that she had a point, but once he'd met her, there had been no turning back.

"I'm so grateful to have met you," she continued intently. "I don't know what I would have done without you…and I hate saying that because it makes me sound helpless and dependent, but it's the truth. I know I would have found a way to figure things out on my own, but it wouldn't have been nearly as easy, or I'm sure even close to as much fun as it's been with you. So, from the bottom of my heart, thank you."

"You're welcome," Finn said, loving the way the moonlight bounced off her curls. "But I wasn't as selfless as you're making me out to be."

"You've been nothing but helpful from the moment we met!"

"Maybe," he said, trying not to be distracted by the soft curve of her neck, or by how soft any of her other curves looked. She was trying to express genuine gratitude and he knew that thinking about how biteable her neck looked made him a cad, even as she was complimenting him for being a nice guy.

"When I offered to let you stay at my place, I never had any intention of making a move on you. But—" he confessed, "it's not like I didn't notice how attractive you are. I think fifteen percent of the invitation was based on your legs alone. Of course, I still would have helped someone with stubby chicken legs, but I wouldn't have been as enthusiastic about it."

"Oh," Cassandra said, looking down at her legs, nonplussed. "Well, thank you. For the compliment just now and for not being a jerk the night we met."

She took a deep breath. "And I suppose, if we're being honest, I have to say I noticed you, too. When I felt someone shaking me awake, I expected to find a snobby twit with a sour face and a bad attitude. You know…someone like Judith. I didn't expect broad shoulders and blue eyes and great hair. You were a pleasant surprise."

She thought he had great hair. He was a pleasant surprise.

Finn grinned at her. "Those are the best kind of surprises."

She looked up at him with those wide, blue eyes and he felt lightheaded. "Right. Nobody likes unpleasant surprises."

Her skin was pale in the dark and he wanted to touch her so badly he was dizzy with it.

"Nope," he said. "Unpleasant surprises are the worst."

What were they even talking about? This was the most asinine conversation he'd ever had. He wanted her so much it was making him stupid—he had to do something about it. He knew it was a bad idea, but he had to do it anyway. She'd said something in response, but he couldn't hear her over the rush of blood in his ears.

"Finn?" she said. "Are you okay? You look a little spacey…"

He cut his eyes to her and she blinked back at him with those huge, crazy eyes, and with his heart pounding in his chest and a voice screaming in his head not to do it, he leaned down and kissed her.

He felt her inhale in surprise, but then her lips parted and her hands slid up his chest and she kissed him back with an enthusiasm that caught him completely off guard.

He buried one hand in her hair, gripping the back of her t-shirt with the other.

She moaned softly and came up on her toes, kissing him harder, lacing her fingers through his hair, and when she slipped her tongue into his mouth, the world dipped around him and he lost himself in her breath and her lips and her lush, soft skin.

Moments passed and eternity stretched out in front of him—a hot, dark eternity filled with nothing but Cassandra's mouth on his and her hands on his shoulders and her breasts pressed against his chest. When he slid one hand inside her t-shirt, she gasped and broke the kiss, breathing heavily and taking a step away with wide, bewildered eyes.

"I'm sorry," he said, crashing back to reality and trying to get his own breath back under control. "I shouldn't have done that."

"No, it's not your fault," she said, still looking stunned. "I shouldn't have kissed you back."

"I enjoyed it," he said, losing himself again and taking half a step toward her.

She put her hand up and took a half-step back, maintaining the distance between them.

"So did I, but that's not the point. The point is I've sworn off men. I'm not supposed to be kissing *anyone* like that. The point is we just met and we're friends. I don't want things to get complicated between us. The point is I don't want to mess up the good thing we've got going and the *point* is—"

"It's okay," he cut her off as her tone approached panicked and she was starting to ramble. "It won't happen again. I know you don't want to get involved, so if that's what you want, I won't like it, but I'll respect it."

"Thank you," she said on an exhale. Then she squinted and asked, "Can we just pretend this whole thing never happened?"

"Of course," he said, feeling like hell.

"Thank you!" she said again, looking relieved. Holding out her hand to shake, she said, "Friends?"

Finn clasped her hand in his and thought about throwing himself off the side of the cliff.

"Friends," he repeated.

"Okay!" she said, forcing a lot of perky into her voice. "Should we head back?"

"That would probably be a good idea."

Cassandra turned and started back down the trail, talking as she went, filling the silence with idle chatter. Finn followed behind her, feeling depressed. He did his best to keep up his role in the conversation, but his heart wasn't really in it.

He felt like an idiot. Over the past week and a half, she had mentioned again and again that she didn't want to get involved. But, like an ass, he hadn't been able to resist going after her.

Even still, he couldn't regret it. That kiss had been phenomenal. They had chemistry—even she couldn't deny that. But she'd made it clear that she wasn't interested. Although if the way she'd just kissed him was any indication…

Forget it, he told himself. *She wants to pretend it never happened.*

Cassandra was still talking about something and he tried to find his place in the conversation…was she talking about making jam? How the hell had they ended up there?

"…and so it's really a lot easier than I thought! You just have to make sure you boil the jars properly…"

Wow. She was clearly rambling, trying to steer the discussion towards a harmless topic. She must really be feeling the tension if this was where she had taken them. Nothing more innocuous than home canning…

Finn felt bad, but after what had just happened, he absolutely could not focus on a conversation about jam. He said, "Oh really?" at what he hoped was an appropriate time and then walked on in glum silence.

"Oh, no!" Cassandra interrupted herself a few minutes later and smacked a hand to her forehead, jolting him out of his depressed detachment. "I just realized I have no way of getting into the apartment. There was no room in the wetsuit for a key, and I don't want to wake Daphne up when she has an early class in the morning!"

"It's no big deal. You can crash at my place again tonight."

They looked at each other hesitantly and Finn added, "Or, if you want, I have a spare key to Daphne's place at home. You could use it to go home tonight, but it's the middle of the night and it's an extra twenty-minute walk and there's no sense getting home late and disturbing Daphne anyway. If you want to stay with me, I don't mind."

"It *is* late and it's been a long day—but are you sure it won't be weird after…?" Cassandra trailed off.

"It's not weird for me," Finn said with a lot more surety than he felt. "Like you said, it never happened."

"Right!" Cassandra agreed. "There's nothing weird about one friend sleeping on another friend's couch. So that would be great! Thanks, Finn."

"Don't mention it." They continued in silence until they reached his bungalow, then he unlocked the door and they both stepped inside, loitering uncomfortably in the living room until Finn said, "I'll get you a pillow!" at the same time Cassandra said, "I need to use the bathroom!"

When she came back, Finn had made up the couch for her, brought her one of his t-shirts to sleep in, and put Daphne's spare key on the surfboard coffee table where she could easily find it.

"Is there anything else you need?" he asked.

She met his eyes and held the stare a moment too long. He could only imagine what she was thinking.

She looked abruptly away and said, "No, this is great, thanks."

Finn just stood there, looking awkwardly at her, not knowing how to end the evening. A kiss goodnight was out of the question. Was a hug too familiar? A hand shake would just be weird. Should they high five? Fist bump? Could he just say goodnight and walk away? Finally, he had been standing there way too long and he had to do *something*.

"Well, goodnight," he said, and did one of those ridiculous point-and-shoot finger gestures before retreating quickly to the safety of his own room.

That could have gone worse, he told himself, collapsing onto his bed with a sigh. Of course, it could have gone a hell of a lot better. Cassandra could have been in there with him right now. In bed with him, rolling hot under him, smiling up at him with that mouth. He could have been kissing his way down her neck, feeling her breath come faster as he worked his way down her stomach…

He shook his head to clear the image. It wasn't going to happen. Instead, she was sleeping on a couch in the next room, ignoring the obvious heat between them, pretending they hadn't shared a mind-blowing kiss in the moonlight not one hour earlier.

"Hell of a girl," he said, and shook his head again. He got up to brush his teeth, and prepared himself for a very frustrating night.

Chapter Nine

Cassandra woke up disoriented, confused as to why she was staring at a surfboard. Then it hit her.

Oh right. I attacked Finn's face with my mouth last night. Now we're up to speed.

She sat up on the couch and looked around. Apparently, he was still in bed. She knew it was cowardly to leave before he was awake…but he had left her the key, and she was still trying to process that kiss. That amazing kiss. So really, she should probably sneak away quietly before she did something stupid like crawl into bed with him to find out if he was as good with the rest of his body as he was with his mouth.

Yes, she should definitely leave. The fresh morning air would do her good. Clear her head. Gain some perspective.

"Well, that's decided then," she said aloud. "We're doing the cowardly thing."

She changed as quietly as she could, grabbed the key from the table, and considered leaving a note but decided it wasn't worth the noise of digging around to find a pen and paper. Instead, she simply folded the blanket and Finn's t-shirt neatly on the pillow, took one last look around the room and left, shutting the door noiselessly behind her.

The way back to Daphne's wasn't complicated, so she didn't have to pay too much attention to where she was going. After a week and a half on the island, she was feeling pretty well acclimated to the pockets of the island she spent the most time in. This was for the best, because her head was spinning and she didn't have time to worry about paltry things like getting utterly lost in an unfamiliar town. She was occupied with other things, like the fact that she had swapped tongues with Finn last night against the backdrop of a disgustingly romantic ocean setting. What had happened to her resolve? Her commitment to a summer free from men?

"'I give myself very good advice,'" she sighed, quoting Alice in Wonderland, "'but I very seldom follow it.'"

She made a couple of stops on the way home to distract herself from her dismal lack of discipline, then arrived back at the apartment to discover it empty. Daphne must still have been in class. Cassandra took advantage of the time alone to pace, sigh, brood, and chastise herself—all of which she found enormously comforting. When Daphne walked in, bouncing in her aqua yoga pants, she found Cassandra trying her hand at looking woebegone, sitting on the couch with her knees tucked under her chin and her arms wrapped around her legs.

"You're up!" Daphne trilled, and then saw the look on Cassandra's face. "Wait, what happened?"

Cassandra wrinkled her nose and looked contrite. "I kissed Finn last night."

"You kissed Finn? Yay!" Daphne exclaimed, unable to hide her initial excitement, then realized this was supposed to be upsetting news. "I mean, that's bad!"

"It *is* bad!" Cassandra protested. "I'm supposed to be swearing off men, remember? Figuring out my life?"

"But things are going so well for you so quickly!" Daphne encouraged. "Maybe getting involved won't be as distracting as you think. Maybe you can open yourself up to the possibility of some fun…"

"I've barely begun to settle in," Cassandra countered. She got up from the couch and resumed pacing. "I still have no idea where to go from here. If I let myself get distracted by Finn…" she let herself picture what that would be like—Finn smiling down at her, Finn sliding into her, Finn, with his hands and his mouth, making her breathless, making her—

"No!" She snapped out of it. "My life beyond this summer is a total blank! I have no plans, no direction, no aspiration that might lead to some sort of plan or direction…I'm still at square one." She stopped abruptly and looked at Daphne. "Are you hungry? I need some comfort food. How do you feel about Eggs Benedict?"

"I'm not sure we have the ingredients for that…" Daphne looked at Cassandra like she was slightly unhinged. Probably because she had been waving her arms around and starting to rant like a crazy person.

"I went by the grocery store on the way home this morning. We now have the ingredients. Just don't think about how much butter is in it. You work out for a living—you need the extra calories!"

"Wait," Daphne said, regrouping. "You stopped by the store on your way home *this morning*? Did you *sleep* with Finn last night?"

"Only in the literal sense. I crashed on his couch because his place was closest. We didn't have sex. Just the one kiss…I stopped it just as we were rounding second base."

"That sounds like a hell of a kiss."

"It was," Cassandra headed toward the kitchen. "And now I need Eggs Benedict."

"You need to talk through this," Daphne corrected.

"That too," Cassandra agreed. "But first, Eggs Benedict."

"Do you have enough for three? I think I'll go invite Mary Ella to breakfast. We could use her insight."

"By all means, bring her over!" Cassandra said, turning on the stove and pulling two sticks of butter out of the refrigerator. "I can use all the insight I can get."

Fifteen minutes later, Cass was in the final stages of whisking her hollandaise sauce and had sustained only one minor burn from the three thick pieces of Canadian bacon sizzling on the stove, when Daphne walked in, followed by Mary Ella and a black fluffy dog the size of a small horse.

"Goodness!" Cassandra exclaimed as the dog came barreling into her to sit on her feet and pant. "Who's this?"

"Good morning," Mary Ella chimed. "This is Sir Galahad. He belongs to my gentleman friend, Felix, but he stays with me sometimes during the day."

"He's huge! And adorable!" Cassandra said, reaching down to scratch him between the ears. He looked up at her adoringly. "What kind of dog is he?" she asked, gently shifting him aside so that she could wash her hands.

"Many kinds," Mary Ella supplied. "Felix likes to say he's part lab, part chow, part woolly mammoth."

Cassandra laughed. "Sounds about right. Does Sir Galahad eat people food?" she asked doubtfully. "I'm not sure there will be enough for him."

"There's not enough bacon on the island," Mary Ella replied. "He loves people food, but Felix recently switched him to a strict dog-food-only diet. He's taking it pretty hard. But, since this is a special occasion, he can have one slice if you're willing to make him one. Did you hear that, Sir Galahad?" she asked, bending down to scratch him behind the ears. "One."

Sir Galahad lolled out his tongue and looked resigned.

"Sure," Cassandra said. "I was just about to poach the eggs and toast the muffins, and then we'll be ready to go! We should be eating in ten minutes!"

"Excellent! I brought fresh squeezed orange juice and champagne," Mary Ella said. "Based on what Daphne told me, it sounded like mimosas were in order. She implied you had quite an interesting evening last night."

"I'll say!" Cass said. "But I'll fill you in on the whole story when breakfast is ready to go. Just give me a few minutes!"

In no time at all, three beautiful plates of Eggs Benedict were on the table—toasty English muffins topped with crisp Canadian bacon and a perfectly poached egg, smothered in decadently creamy hollandaise sauce. Cass had accidentally dropped one of the English muffins after taking it out of the oven, but no one had noticed except Sir Galahad. She had gotten to the muffin before he did and made sure to set it aside so that it ended up on her plate instead of anyone else's. It was probably fine, but just in case, she wanted to make sure she wasn't serving breakfast that tasted like floor.

The three women sat down eagerly. Sir Galahad, who had already inhaled his *one* piece of Canadian bacon and been denied an English muffin, looked longingly on from the sidelines.

"Cassandra, this looks divine!" Mary Ella complimented. "I had no idea you were such a chef!"

Cassandra shrugged. "I find it relaxing. And as an added bonus, I get to eat afterward!"

They all dug in, taking a few moments to savor their first mouthfuls and express their delight with the meal before Daphne piped up and said, "So tell us everything! Mary Ella doesn't know anything. I just told her you have news that you need help digesting."

"Okay," Cassandra paused to collect her thoughts before beginning. "Mary Ella, you know that Finn was the first person I met when I washed up on the island."

"Yes," Mary Ella confirmed.

Cass nodded. "We've already become good friends. He introduced me to Daphne, set me up with this apartment, got me my job at Andre's…so not only are we friends, he's sort of like my benefactor on the island. I would have been lost without him. And I wouldn't want to do anything to jeopardize that relationship."

She paused to take another bite of her benedict and inhaled in pleasure as the luxurious tang of the hollandaise flooded her mouth. The mild dread that had been lurking in the pit of her stomach ever since she stopped the kiss last night eased slightly and she continued.

"Also as you know, I'm on a soul-searching mission and part of that includes not getting romantically involved with anyone. I want to spend this time focusing on myself. We know this already?"

There were nods all around the table.

"That being said, I kissed Finn last night."

Daphne squealed and danced a little in her chair.

Mary Ella raised her eyebrows in surprise. "Really?"

"Well, technically, he kissed me. But I kissed him back, so it really doesn't matter. The point is, we kissed."

"How did this come about?" Mary Ella asked.

Cassandra sighed. "It was late last night after the manta ray excursion—"

"Manta ray excursion?"

"Daphne and Finn took me out to watch the manta rays feed."

"You went into the ocean voluntarily?" Mary Ella asked, impressed.

"I know!" Cassandra said excitedly, "I'm evolving. So anyway, I was all pumped up after seeing the manta rays and didn't feel like coming home right away, so Finn and I decided to go for a late-night hike…"

"Uh-oh."

"Yeah…now that I'm retelling it, I should have seen it coming. Of course, I've thought about the *possibility* of something happening, but I was never going to act on it."

"Wait a minute," Daphne cut in. "This is something you've been thinking about?"

"Of course, it is," Cassandra said reasonably. "He's gorgeous! He's your cousin, so you wouldn't understand just *how* gorgeous, but he's not *my* cousin and I'm not dead…just temporarily staying away from men. We hiked up to this beautiful lookout point—it was all moonlight and starlight and ocean for miles— and I can't even remember what we were talking about, but then suddenly he was kissing me and it was glorious, and then I realized that I wasn't supposed to be kissing him so I stopped. And that's it. What do you two think?"

"Are you sure you're not supposed to be kissing him?" Daphne asked. "Because I've watched the two of you, and I think you could be good together."

"That's not the point," Cassandra said, cutting into her English muffin with unwarranted savagery. "I'm not supposed to let myself get distracted."

"But you agree that you could be good together?" Daphne clarified.

"I don't know," Cassandra sighed. "I mean, maybe. Yes. If I was looking for a relationship right now, Finn is exactly the kind of man I would be looking for. From what I've seen, he's the whole package—smart, funny, attractive, interesting, and I love being with him—but I'm *not* looking for a relationship. I'm not even going to be on this island for more than a couple of months. It would be stupid to get involved at this point."

"*Or*," Daphne offered, "is it perfect? Maybe the two of you are meant to be together, and fate put you here just so you could meet him." She sat up straighter, clearly thinking she was on to something. "I mean, what are the odds of you falling off a yacht?"

Jumping, Cassandra mentally corrected, but she didn't say this out loud. They still didn't need to know.

"And then the very first person you meet is an unbelievably charming and eligible man who falls for you immediately?"

"Technically, he was the second person I met," Cassandra said. "The first person was Judith, an unbelievably uptight and critical receptionist who hated me on sight, but go on."

"I don't know, Cass. This sounds like destiny to me."

"See, I like the sound of *parts* of that, but overall, I disagree," Cassandra said. "I do feel like the universe has something important lined up for me here. I think this island is exactly where I'm supposed to be right now. And you're right, this whole experience feels fated—the way everything has come together is like something out of a dream! But if the universe has led me here, it's to figure out my life. My *whole* life," she clarified as Daphne opened her mouth to protest, "not just the romantic part. And I refuse to believe that my destiny centers wholly on a man, even one as great as Finn. That's insane. There's more going on for me here."

"Aren't we getting ahead of ourselves after just one kiss and less than two weeks?" Mary Ella cut in, supplying a much-needed measure of perspective. "Cassandra, no one is saying you have to spend the rest of your life with Finn after knowing him for ten days.

That's ridiculous. So here is the question you have to ask yourself: what is important to you right now? Do you want to spend the summer searching for your life path on your own, or do you want to open yourself up to someone else and let them in on the process? Is there really something between you and Finn, or did you just get caught up in the moonlight and the starlight and the ocean?"

"No, it wasn't just the setting. It was Finn," Cassandra said. "That much I'm sure of. But he's not what I want. At least not right now," she amended as Daphne sighed. "I owe it to myself to spend some time alone, making my own decisions, and if it comes down to it, my own mistakes."

Cass drained her mimosa and stared into the distance, picturing a summer spent with Finn.

"Imagine if we did get together," she said. "And best-case scenario, maybe it's amazing. Maybe we fall madly in love. Then at the end of the summer, the choice isn't where do *I* go from here, it's where do *we* go? What's *his* next step now that he's out of grad school? What makes sense for *us?* Part of me would always regret it. I would always wonder what would have happened if I had just maintained my resolve and figured out my own life first. And I couldn't live with that. So, for now I'm sticking to my guns. No relationships and no sex until I've sorted myself out."

Mary Ella smiled at Cassandra's decisive tone. "Then it sounds like you no longer need our advice. The solution to any problem of the heart already lies within us. We know the answer from the beginning…we just have to be wise enough to listen for it."

"The wisest among us has spoken," Cassandra said, standing up and beginning to clear away the dishes. "For now, Finn and I are going to stay just friends."

***

When Finn woke up that morning, the first thing he remembered was the kiss and the look on Cassandra's face when she'd pulled away from him. He groaned and tossed his pillow across the room. He'd known it was a stupid move, known it might scare her off, but he'd had to do it anyway.

Dumb, he chided himself.

He wasn't surprised when he padded into the living room and discovered that Cassandra had already gone, though her absence left him feeling decidedly bereft. He had entertained the brief fantasy of waking up and wandering into the kitchen to the smell of French toast and the sound of Cassandra telling him that her dating sabbatical was a stupid idea, that their kiss had been amazing, and that they should pick it up where they left off. Then he would boost her up onto the counter and lose himself in the scent of cinnamon and coconut, the feeling of her legs wrapped around his waist, the slide of her body against his.

Oh well, he thought, resigning himself to the sad reality of cold cereal and no Cassandra. *That's what you get for being a jackass.*

Now all he could do was hope that she was serious when she said she could pretend like the kiss had never happened and they could keep getting to know each other and try to just be friends. As little as that appealed to him, having Cassandra in his life platonically was better than not having her at all.

"Damn it," he said morosely, closing the refrigerator door with his foot and leaning against the sink to eat his disappointing cereal.

She had bewitched him with her French toast and her crazy hair and crazy eyes and now life seemed boring without her—he looked down at his rapidly congealing cereal—boring and mushy. He had to convince her that celibacy was a terrible idea.

He sighed and let his head fall back against the cupboards, knowing even as he thought it that he wouldn't try. He was a decent guy and most of the time he acted like it. If being alone was what she wanted, then he would deal with it. No matter how terrible he thought the idea was.

***

Later that day, Cassandra was relieved to begin her shift at Andre's. The work kept her busy and left no time to dwell on her situation with Finn. Today there was Greek mandolin music in the background, the customers were friendly, and everyone on the wait staff was in a good mood. It all put her in such a positive frame of mind that when Finn came in for his shift an hour later, she was able to wave and smile as if nothing had happened.

Well that takes care of that, she thought as he grinned and waved back. *We really are back to normal.*

Customers continued to come in at a steady pace until after the dinner rush when they hit a lull. Cass took advantage of the time to straighten up the menus, check in with the servers, and determinedly *not* look over at Finn who was undoubtedly looking gorgeous over at the bar.

Okay, she told herself, *just one look.*

They weren't going to be kissing anymore, but that didn't mean she couldn't enjoy the view.

Nonchalantly, under the guise of restocking the mints, she angled herself so she could see him behind the bar. He was shaking a martini for an old man with wire rimmed glasses who said something to make Finn laugh. She simultaneously admired his forearms and his smile before a party walked through the door and she forced herself back to work.

"Hey, Cass," Drew waved the next time he passed by, "what time do you get off tonight?"

"Eleven," she answered, somewhat suspicious since he was clearly supposed to be chasing Daphne, not asking about her plans. "Why?"

"Me too," he said, "but Finn's stuck closing. Want to grab a drink after our shifts and heckle him?"

"Sounds good," Cassandra laughed. This would be perfect. Having a third-party present for her first interaction with Finn since the kiss would be ideal. Just to be absolutely positive there wasn't any lingering awkwardness. And with Drew there, she would be sure not to get swept away by Finn's great arms and his dimples and lean across the bar and say, "I was an idiot last night; take me now." Not that she would, of course…she was resolute in her plans for self-discovery. But it never hurt to have a buffer. Just in case.

***

"I got Cass to stick around for a drink after work."

Finn looked up from polishing a glass to see Drew looking pleased with himself.

"You're welcome," Drew said. "It's the perfect chance for you to make a move."

"I made a move last night." Finn resumed polishing. "She's not interested."

"You struck out, huh?" Drew nodded sympathetically.

"I did not strike out," Finn corrected. "She kissed me back. Hard. But then she stopped. She's not interested in any man right now."

"Whatever you need to tell yourself," Drew clapped him on the shoulder. "Should I tell her to forget about drinks?"

"No, it's fine. We're going to be friends."

Drew snorted. "Sure, you are. We get off at eleven. I expect a whiskey soda in front of me by eleven o' one. It's been a long shift and your cousin is driving me to drink."

"Like you need any extra encouragement."

Drew went on as if he hadn't spoken. "She yapped at me all the way home last night and then turned me down flat when I offered her a little extra company."

"Shocking. You didn't actually expect her to say yes, did you?"

"No," Drew shrugged. "But she'll come around." He slid off the barstool and started to walk away. "They always do."

"You're kidding yourself," Finn told him, but he was already gone.

When Drew showed up again at eleven, laughing with Cassandra about something he had said before they were within hearing range, Finn glared at his friend and slid a whisky soda on the bar in front of him.

"That'll be eight dollars."

"You're kidding right?"

Finn ignored him and turned to Cass. "And what can I get you?"

"I'm not sure," she answered, still smiling from whatever Drew had said, which on the one hand made Finn irrationally irritated, and on the other hand he enjoyed watching. She had a great smile. But noticing her mouth made him remember what she could do with it, so he focused on her eyes instead.

That didn't help. Her eyes were beautiful, too. He stared at her right eyebrow, which was nice as far as eyebrows went, but it wasn't particularly alluring.

"I loved the piña colada Drew brought me the other day," she told him, "but I'm supposed to be trying new things and I don't want to get stuck in a rut. Surprise me!"

"One mystery drink, coming up." He began muddling lime, mint and sugar for a mojito while Drew turned to Cassandra.

"So, you survived the manta rays. What are your next plans for the island?"

"Well, I don't know—that's why I have you guys. I'm not sure what else there is on the island. To be honest, I'm not even sure exactly where on the globe it's located."

"You're kidding," Finn paused in the middle of adding rum to the shaker to see if she was joking.

"The cruise covered a lot of ground. Or water, I suppose," Cass defended. She guessed a body of water that sounded plausible.

"Wrong," Drew told her. "But you're not too far off. Don't worry about it, Cass, you don't need to know where you are to have a good time."

"That's kind of shady advice." Cassandra squinted but didn't look overly concerned. "So tell me what there is to do here. Preferably on land. I'll venture into the ocean again at some point, I'm sure, but for my next adventure I'd like to do something that involves solid ground."

"That's a shame because this place is great for kayaking," Drew told her. "But that's fine, there are lots of landlocked options, too. What have we got, Finn?"

"Well," Finn started, handing the drink to Cassandra, who said, "Thank you!" and sipped it, looking delighted. "There are the ruins on the coast, the castle inland, the vineyards on the mountain, the butterfly gardens on the west side…"

"Where is this place?" Cassandra cut in. "Narnia? You have a castle and ruins *and* vineyards *and* mountains *and* manta rays?"

"Don't tell her about the safari on the north side," Drew said over his drink.

"What?" Cass gulped her drink, looking incredulous. "You have safari animals here? Where *are* we?"

"Kidding!" Drew said. "I hear you have a thing about giraffes."

"I do not have a *thing* about giraffes. I saw a creepy one once."

"What about the market?" Drew snapped his fingers. "There's a great open-air market downtown every Saturday. Lots of cool vendors. You should check it out."

"That sounds fun and easy!" Cassandra looked enthusiastic. "Do you guys want to go this Saturday? I'm working the dinner shift so I have the first half of the day free."

"Can't," Drew said. "I'm rock climbing with a buddy and then I've got a date. You and Finn should go."

"Do you want to?" Finn suddenly found himself accosted by those eyes again, looking up at him, excited and expectant. What else could he say but yes? He loved the market anyway—all the people and the colors and the noises and the smells—and if he and Cassandra were really going to be friends, they'd have to spend time alone together eventually. Saturday was as good a time as any.

"Sure," he said, and Cassandra's smile widened. "I'm bartending at the Silver Sands in the evening but I'm open through the afternoon."

"Perfect!" Cass finished her drink and slipped off of her seat. "Sounds like a plan—but for now I should be heading home—I'm exhausted! It's been an eventful week." She chuckled at what a gross understatement she'd just made and then said, "Thanks for the drink!"

When she was gone, Drew leaned back and said, "Again, you're welcome."

"For what?"

"For getting you more time alone with her," Drew explained like he was missing the obvious. "That's a perfect first date. You can try again."

"I told you, we're not doing that," Finn reiterated.

"Of course, anything you mentioned would have made a good date, but I thought it would be better to start off with something low key."

"Low key like swimming with manta rays?"

"We weren't swimming with them. And that wasn't a date. This will be just the two of you."

"We've done things with just the two of us."

"Yeah, and how did those work out for you?"

"It doesn't matter," Finn said. "I don't need to get Cassandra into a date-type situation because she and I are not going to be dating. When did you become an expert on relationships anyway?"

"Just because I don't want to be in a relationship doesn't mean I don't know how to get into one. I can be romantic if I want to."

"Why don't I believe you?"

"Because I'm not trying to sleep with you."

Finn snorted. "I think you just proved my point."

"Whatever. Saturday's a perfect opportunity for you to have another shot with Cassandra. And I handed it to you on a platter. I say you owe me a drink."

"Get your own drinks," Finn told him. "Saturday is just an opportunity for me to get to know Cassandra better. As a friend," he added sternly when Drew began to grin.

"Sure," Drew said, unconvinced. "Friends."

Friends, Finn thought grimly. *Wonderful.*

Chapter Ten

When Finn knocked on Cassandra's door Saturday morning, she answered wearing a breezy blue tank top, shorts, and a wide smile. He focused on the smile so his eyes wouldn't slide down her body to her legs.

"Hey," he said in response to her greeting. "You ready to go?"

"Yes!" she said, reentering the house. "Just give me one second!" She grabbed a long-strapped shoulder bag and pair of Jackie O sunglasses from the coffee table and turned back to him.

"Okay," she smiled. "Let's go!"

Her ivory skin gleamed with an oily sort of sheen, and he smelled coconuts as she drifted past him onto the street, which made him think tropical thoughts. He imagined Cassandra stretched out on a beach, sipping piña coladas from half a coconut while he slathered oil on her shoulders.

He needed to focus on something else before his treacherous mind started imagining topless beaches.

"You put on your sunblock?" he asked innocently as they started down the street.

"Yes!" she answered, oblivious to his train of thought. "SPF 80. Good luck to any UV rays trying to penetrate *that*!"

His mind swerved again at the word *penetrate*, and he told himself to get ahold of himself. To get himself back on a friendly, platonic track, he asked how work was going and she started chatting animatedly about how great the restaurant was.

Finn chuckled at her impressions of working with Andre and they swapped stories about their boss until they turned a corner and the first canopies of the market came into view.

"Oh my gosh, it smells amazing!" Cassandra inhaled and Finn pointedly did not watch the way her tank top rose and fell, but instead enjoyed the aroma of the various street foods drifting through the air—the fragrant spices of falafel, the grilled meat from the kebabs, the warm scent of cinnamon wafting from the churros.

"Are you hungry?" he asked.

"Not quite yet," she said, eyes darting from place to place, taking in all of the sights while they stood off to the side. "I had a smoothie with Daphne this morning…strawberry, blueberry, spinach, and almond butter. She called it her smoothie interpretation of a peanut butter and jelly sandwich. It was surprisingly filling—I think she threw some Greek yogurt and flax seeds in there as well. But I'm not sure I care! The question won't be when to eat, but *what*."

"I vote a little of everything," Finn suggested.

"I like your style, Finnegan," Cassandra nodded approvingly. "Plan: eat everything. So, how do you like to do this? Do you have favorite vendors you go to first, do you go through systematically and hit every booth, do you wander around and see what jumps out at you…?"

"Let's just dive in and see what looks fun." Finn smiled. "Stop anywhere that catches your eye."

"Excellent," Cass said enthusiastically.

"Oh, look at that" she said, leading him over to a stall filled with colorful scarves.

She picked out a light, gauzy scarf in varying degrees of purple and bought it as a thank you to Mary Ella for lending her clothes. An hour later, she had also bought a bright orange sarong and coral necklace for Beth, acquired a handmade wood-carved desk clock and matching pen for her father, eaten a hefty falafel pita and side of fries, and was in the process of purchasing a large basil plant to give to Daphne for their kitchen.

"Daphne will be thrilled," he said.

"I know," she grinned at him. "I've heard more about the nutritional wonders of basil in the last two weeks than the rest of my life combined. Did you know that it's considered an aphrodisiac?"

"Oh really?" Finn said mildly. The heady scent of the herb drifted toward him and he couldn't say he was surprised. He brushed aside the vision of a naked Cassandra covered in strategically placed basil sprigs. As far as fantasies went, it was kind of weird, but it left him feeling lightheaded nonetheless.

"What else has Daphne taught you?" he asked guiltily.

Cassandra left the plant with the vendor to pick up on their way home and then moved toward the next stall, rattling off a list of basil-related health benefits that was either a testament to her memory or proof of just how much his cousin could and would talk about nutrition given the opportunity.

"All that after only a couple of weeks," he observed, watching her browse through a stall of woven rugs. "Imagine what you'll know by the end of the summer."

"The mind reels," she laughed. "If all else fails, maybe I can make my living as a nutritionist based solely on the information I'll absorb from Daphne."

"It's good to have a backup plan," Finn agreed. "Speaking off all that, how's the search going?"

She shrugged, smiling at the woman selling the rugs before crossing the aisle to look at paintings on display by a young man with a tropical flower tattoo. Finn noticed the artist notice Cassandra, lurking in the background, waiting for her to look his way.

"I've been here less than a month," she said while Finn followed, keeping an eye on the lurking artist. "I'm not surprised that inspiration hasn't struck yet. It'll come."

"You don't sound too worried," he said as she flipped through a stack of postcard-sized prints.

"Today I'm not," she answered. "I'm just enjoying life as it comes at me. Mary Ella's advice. Give it a few more weeks...I might start to worry then. Oh, look!" she said, glancing up from the prints to an original hanging at the back of the stall, a nightscape of the viewpoint he had taken her to the night of the kiss. "It looks just like our hike!"

She went to get a closer look and the artist moved toward her, smiling appreciatively. "It's beautiful, no? One of the most breathtaking views on the island. You've seen it before?"

"Just the other day," Cass smiled up at him. "You've captured it perfectly! The moonlight, the water, everything! It's gorgeous!"

"Thank you," he smiled deeper and moved closer. "You're new to the island, then?" he asked, and Finn didn't like where this was going. "It's very romantic, no?"

Oh, brother. The guy was standing too close to her.

"Very romantic." Finn stepped up behind Cassandra and glared at the guy over her shoulder.

The artist eyed Finn and backed off, but Cassandra missed the whole exchange, still absorbed in the painting.

"It's almost like being there again," she said, fascinated. "You can practically hear the waves and smell the salt water and jasmine!"

She turned to smile up at Finn and he was dazzled, struck by the memory of the last time he had seen that view—Cassandra against a backdrop of ocean and night sky. That train of thought could only lead to trouble, so he turned to focus on the painting instead, and he had to admit it was beautiful. The lurker could paint, Finn had to give him that.

Even if Cassandra left the island in two months and he never saw her again, this painting could always be something to remind her of him and the one mind-blowing kiss they'd shared.

"Let me get it for you," he offered. "A welcome-to-the-island gift."

Cassandra laughed. "Like a roommate and a job weren't enough? That's very sweet, Finn, but you've done too much for me already. I can't let you buy me a present as well. I will take the painting though," she said, addressing the artist again. "I love it!"

"I couldn't part with it to a less deserving customer," he smiled down at her again and Finn smothered a scowl.

She paid for the piece and promised to return for it before the market closed.

"You're accumulating quite the haul," Finn commented as they headed further into the market.

"I've got something for almost everyone," she agreed. "I'm just missing you and my mother."

"You don't have to get anything for me," he said.

"Pfft!" Cass said and rolled her eyes.

"But your mother, huh? What do you have in mind for her?"

Cassandra exhaled. "I'm not sure. Everyone else is easy. But Miranda Dillon has never been an easy woman to shop for. She has very particular tastes."

"How about another painting?" Finn suggested. "Or a picture?" He pointed to a vendor selling photographs of the island. "Some type of art to let her share in your time here."

"*I* would think that's a lovely sentiment, but my mom tends to gravitate toward art chosen by a decorator rather than her daughters."

"Okay, how about a scarf, like you got Mary Ella?"

"She has pretty definitive opinions about style, too. I never know how to match her taste."

"So that also rules out jewelry, handbags, sandals, and hats." Finn gestured around to the various goods surrounding them on all sides.

"Pretty much," Cassandra said.

"How about a nice postcard?" Finn joked, thinking that Cassandra's mother sounded nothing like her. Cassandra's personality clearly stemmed from a different tributary of the gene pool.

"That might be my only choice," Cassandra laughed. "Maybe a kitten with a bikini photoshopped onto it. That would be right up Miranda's alley."

"That's settled then. Beach cat postcard it is."

"It would serve her right for being so picky," Cassandra mused, stopping at a hat stand and plopping one on his head. He posed, and she laughed and took the hat off, fluffing his flattened hair and saying, "I don't think wicker is your style."

She resumed wandering and went on to say, "You know, my grandma wouldn't have been nearly so complicated to shop for. I never could understand how my mother was her child. Not only did the apple fall far from the tree, it's like it came from a completely different orchard. Not that I don't love my mother!" Cass added. "She's just a very different person. Gram and I were two peas in a pod. She would have liked that painting. A memory come to life. Or better yet, she would have painted it herself."

"She was an artist?" Finn paused at a booth, removed Cassandra's sunglasses from her face and replaced them with an even larger, funkier pair.

"She was," Cassandra answered, putting a pair of purple cat eyes on him and standing back to survey the effect.

They mutually shook their heads at each other and put the glasses back.

"Do you paint, too?" he asked, leaving the sunglasses stand behind.

Cassandra guffawed. "No. That's one trait I definitely did not inherit. I have all the artistic talent of a bean."

"A bean?"

Cass shrugged. "Pick any non-sentient object. I am completely without creative ability. I have a cousin with a three-year-old daughter who can draw better stick figures than I can."

"So, I guess we can cross starving artist off the list of possibilities for your future."

"Correct!" Cassandra agreed. "Though if I had to make my living as an artist, I would definitely starve. But not Gram. She wasn't actually an artist by trade, but she did sell some of her work at galleries.

"I remember going to an exhibition of hers when I was seven. There was this painting of a waterfall in a forest scene that I just loved—sunbeams coming through the branches—I thought it was magical. I told her that it was exactly the kind of place where fairies would live. At the end of the night there was a sold sticker on it and I remember being sad that it might go to someone who wouldn't really appreciate it, but the next week a package came for me in the mail." She smiled at the memory and Finn guessed what was coming.

"When I opened it, there was the painting. She had added fairies, dancing around the trees. It was the most beautiful thing I'd ever seen." Cassandra's voice was wistful and her eyes became bright. "And even though she saw me almost every week, she had it mailed, because when you're seven, there's nothing as exciting as getting something in the mail addressed just to you."

"Do you still have the painting?"

"It's hanging in my room at home. I think of her every time I see it."

"You must miss her a lot."

Cassandra nodded, eyes too full to speak, but she blinked rapidly and tried to smile.

"You need food," he said to distract her—anything to get that look off her face.

"I do!" she agreed, wiping her eyes and laughing, willingly following the change of subject. "It's been almost twenty minutes since I've eaten anything. 'Feed me, Seymour.'"

"Who?" he asked, confused.

"Seymour…from Little Shop of Horrors. Don't worry about it! Just point me in the direction of churros!"

"Follow your nose," Finn spun her around by her shoulders and gave her a gentle push in the direction of the cinnamon scented cart, glad to have her back again. If she was quoting lines from movies that he didn't understand, things were back to normal.

They got their snack and stood in the shade of a brightly colored awning to enjoy it. The churros were perfectly crisp on the outside and light and soft on the inside, and Cassandra looked like she was in heaven. Watching her consume the pastry, Finn felt pretty much the same way.

"Oh my gosh," she moaned, licking the last of the sugar from her fingers, "I never want to go home. The food here is so much better!"

"So stay," Finn said, only half-joking.

"It might be worth it for those churros alone, but my pasty skin would never be able to handle it," she looked darkly up at the sunny, cheerful sky and moved further into the recesses of the shade. "Do I look like I'm starting to burn?"

"You might be getting a little pink," he answered, surveying the tops of her shoulders and the bridge of her nose.

"I knew it! Spending time outdoors always comes with a price. Do you mind holding my bag while I reapply sunblock?"

She pulled an enormous bottle out of her purse and relinquished the bag to his outstretched hand before squirting a huge dollop of lotion onto her palm and slathering it all over her arms and face. Another large blob and she got to work on her shoulders. The smell of coconuts drifted toward him again and he tried not to laugh as he watched Cassandra struggle to apply lotion to her own back. Her elbow was bent awkwardly behind her head and she turned in an ungainly semi-circle, looking vaguely like a dog chasing its tail.

"Need a hand?" he asked mildly.

"Would you mind?" she said, exasperated. "I wouldn't ask, except I once ended up with a hand-shaped sunburn on my shoulder blade and I'd like to avoid repeating the experience."

Finn laughed and took the tube of sunblock from her, squirting a quarter-size glob onto his hand. "I'm sure it wasn't that bad," he said as she turned her back to him and moved her hair away from her neck.

"There were stares," she told him while he smeared the lotion across her back, rubbing it into her shoulders, under the straps of her tank top and up her neck. "Incredulous stares. I even heard one woman say, 'That poor girl,' as I passed her in a restaurant."

He laughed again, deliberately ignoring how warm and soft her skin was under his hands, how she seemed to glow in the sunlight from the tropical-scented lotion. He took his hands off her as soon as he could and cleared his throat.

"There you go. No handprints burned into your back. You're safe for now, at least."

"Thank you!" She turned to face him again and smiled. "Where to now?"

"That cat postcard isn't going to buy itself. Should we soldier on?"

"After you." Cassandra gestured back to the throng.

Another hour later, they had explored every booth in the market, with Cassandra stopping frequently to visit with vendors, asking questions about their wares and learning more about the island in the process. As a result of her sociability, Finn had gotten contact information from several people he wanted to interview for a paper he was working on. It was still in its research and theorizing stages, but it promised to be interesting stuff.

He and Cassandra chatted easily about his research, her family, his travels, her degree...he was almost surprised when he checked the time and the afternoon had passed them by.

"Oh geez, it's getting late," Cassandra observed. "It's probably time to be heading back! I've still got to swing back home before work to change and drop everything off."

"How about some grilled pineapple for the road?" he asked.

"You drive a hard bargain, Finnegan Drake. But I give in."

They ate their pineapple and went to collect everything Cassandra had purchased earlier, including the exquisite hand-blown glass vase she had finally found for her mother.

"That was fun!" Cassandra said brightly as they trekked back in the direction of her apartment. "Thanks for coming with me!"

"Any time," Finn answered, glad to have spent the afternoon with her. Before today, he'd already felt that he knew a lot about her, considering how little time had passed since they'd met, but after spending the last few hours with her, he felt as if he'd known her forever. She was so open and forthcoming, he felt like he could ask or tell her anything. Aside, of course, from, "I think you're wonderful—how about ditching this whole 'just friends' plan and coming back to my place?" Other than that, they could talk about anything.

She asked him something about his studies and brought him back to reality. In no time at all, they arrived at her front door. He helped carry everything inside and unload it on the kitchen table. Suddenly, she straightened.

"I didn't get anything for you!" she said, distraught.

The look of utter dismay on her face made him laugh because it was so unnecessary.

"Don't worry about it!" he said. "I told you, you don't need to give me anything."

Actually, he could think of *several* things she could give him, but nothing she could put a bow on. Unless...he imagined Cassandra wearing nothing but a large bow and thought, *Leave before you say something stupid.*

"I'll find you something eventually!" Cassandra said, interrupting his thoughts. "Can I get you anything now? Water? Wine?"

"Nah, I should be heading back. I want to log those vendors' information and put together a few interview questions before I have to head over to the Silver Sands."

Spending time alone with Cassandra in a crowded public arena was one thing, but spending time alone with her in her apartment was more than he could handle at this stage in their relationship.

"Thanks, though."

"Of course." Cassandra got up and walked him to the door. "Let me know how those interviews turn out—I want to hear all about them."

"You'll be the first," Finn answered, pleased that she seemed so genuinely interested in his academic work. He left without hugging her, not trusting himself to touch her any more than necessary, and began the walk back to his own house. He took the scenic route, thinking of his research and Cassandra, and by the time he got home, he figured burying himself in his studies for the rest of the day was the wisest thing he could do. Much smarter than thinking about Cassandra and her coconut-scented skin.

Chapter Eleven

Daphne had gone into raptures over the basil plant, loving how the scent filled their little kitchen. She was still gushing over it the next morning while Cass tried to psych herself up for her very first yoga class. She didn't know much about it, but Daphne had informed her that yoga was more than a workout: it was a way of life. Cassandra conjured up what little she'd heard about yoga and imagined herself chanting and eating granola while twisting herself into a pretzel-like shape. She had her doubts about yoga.

"Did you know that historically, there were cultures where women put pulverized basil powder on their breasts to stop cheating husbands from straying again?" Daphne burbled on, and Cass was distracted from her musings.

"Really?"

"It's true!" Daphne confirmed. "But that's nothing! Did you know that the Aztecs didn't allow unmarried women to leave the house during avocado harvesting? It was thought to be too sexually potent to expose to maidens."

"You're kidding," Cass said, thinking of the avocado kale salad she'd eaten at Andre's the night before.

"I'm not!" Daphne promised, and continued her nutritional history lesson all though the walk to the studio. By the time she unlocked the doors to let them in, she'd segued into green tea's ability to decrease fat in the stomach cavity and along the intestines, and Cass was seriously reconsidering her stance on what she had heretofore considered a weak and worthless beverage.

"And that, combined with its anti-aging and health benefits, is why I no longer drink coffee," Daphne summed up, crouching front and center of the large, empty room and rolling out her bright pink mat with the soothing purple flowers.

Cassandra stood next to her friend and couldn't help but notice the smooth curve of Daphne's butt or the strong, graceful slope of her thighs, or the complete lack of self-consciousness with which she bent over, ass to mirror, in spandex pants that fit her like a second skin. Cass eyed her own body in the mirror, then looked around the cheery studio—its soft cork floors illuminated by warm, natural light streaming in from the windows and skylights, its large, mirrored wall reflecting the simply painted purple lotus blossom on the opposite wall—and imagined the room full of people. If she was expected to bend over in a well-lit room that was one quarter mirrors, she sure as hell wasn't going to do it up front next to Daphne.

Crossing the room to the far corner, Cass unfurled the spare mat she had borrowed from Daphne as close to the wall as she thought was appropriate.

"Not an exhibitionist, I see," Daphne teased as Cass sat cross legged in the middle of the slightly spongy green mat, mirroring Daphne's position.

"Be nice," Cassandra requested. "It's my first time."

"Oh, you'll be fine," Daphne's voice was reassuring as ever. "If you're ever confused about what's going on, watch me or look around at the other students. If you start to feel lightheaded or dizzy or need a rest, just sit or lie down on your mat, or go into child's pose. No one will judge you. We've all done it."

The first student arrived, chatted for a moment with Daphne, then unrolled her mat in the middle of the room and lay down on her back with her eyes closed as others began to filter in from the street. Even as the room filled, it stayed fairly quiet. A few people visited softly, some performed warm up poses for the approaching class, but most stretched silently out on their mats and looked like they were catching a quick pre-workout nap. Cass decided to follow the majority lead, laying down and closing her eyes, feeling safe and secluded in her corner.

The sound of two dozen people breathing deeply and rhythmically at their own intervals filled the studio, reminding Cassandra of gently cresting waves. Her thoughts drifted to a moonlit cliffside overlooking a secluded beach, the sound of the surf lapping against the shore, Finn standing beside her looking broad and beautiful against a backdrop of tropical paradise, smiling into her eyes as he leaned closer...

"Okay, everybody, let's begin!" Daphne chimed, and Cassandra was jolted back to her current surroundings, feeling a little disappointed. Kissing Finn in her imagination was probably better than trying to bend her body into unnatural shapes in reality. Except she wasn't going to be kissing Finn anymore so she'd better stop imagining it.

Dragging herself up to a seated position, Cassandra zeroed in on Daphne's introductions.

"Welcome back everyone, and hello to my newcomers! Is there anyone here who's trying yoga for the first time?"

Cass and one other woman on the opposite end of the room raised their hands, looking around warily.

"Excellent! Glad to see you here!" Daphne enveloped them both in an encouraging smile.

"Are there any areas in particular that people would like to focus on today?" she asked, addressing the class at large.

Voices piped up from around the room, requesting hips, thighs, lower back…one sadistic woman shouted out, "abs!" and Cassandra refrained from shooting her a dirty look. Her core had barely recovered from her first Pilates disaster.

"Alright!" Daphne beamed. "Let's start on our backs today."

Awesome, Cass thought, pleased with yoga so far. *This is the way to exercise.*

Then she had a grim flashback to how much time she'd spent on her back in Pilates and reconsidered. Happily, instead of instructing them to stick their legs in the air and squeeze their inner thighs together, Daphne invited them to close their eyes and take long, deep breaths in and out through their noses.

"Just relax," Daphne's voice was calm and even. "Allow your mind to clear, letting go of any thoughts as they come to you. Notice them, and then let them drift away."

She guided them through what she called the three-part breath, focusing air first into the base of the stomach, then also the rib cage, and finally expanding into the chest. Cassandra felt amazingly comfortable as the oxygen circulated through her body, astonished at the capacity of her lungs when she actually focused on her breath—something she had never done before unless she was short of it.

It was with great reluctance that she rolled onto her stomach when Daphne gave the cue, but she found that the first set of poses only deepened her sense of relaxation.

An hour later, Cassandra was flat on her back again, incandescently calm, feeling more serene than she could ever remember. A gentle sheen of sweat glistened on her forehead and chest, but she felt completely blissful.

She wasn't sure exactly what had passed in the last sixty minutes…there was a haze of forward bends, downward dogs, and chaturangas that made her think at the time that the backs of her legs might snap or her arms might collapse underneath her, and something about warrior poses that made her quadriceps burn, but somewhere toward the end Daphne brought them back down to the mat and led them through a series of stretches that left her with the oddly pleasant sensation of being a sponge with the water thoroughly wrung out of it.

Cassandra had stretched out and closed her eyes while every muscle in her body felt like it was melting into the floor. Daphne's voice faded into the background while Cass floated away on a freaking cloud. It was amazing.

Now Daphne instructed everyone to sit cross-legged on their mats. They ended the class with one resounding "Ommm" that reverberated deep in Cassandra's ears and chest, making her feel unexpectedly connected with everyone in the room, and solidifying her feeling of peace.

Slowly, she rolled to her feet and began to pack up her mat in a state of absolute tranquility.

Daphne smiled at her approach, wrapping up a conversation with another client to ask, "What did you think?"

"Yoga is so much better than Pilates!" Cass said fervently. "I could do that every day."

"Yay!" Daphne trilled. "We can make that happen!"

"So, you enjoyed it?" Mary Ella's voice sounded at her shoulder and Cass turned in surprise. She hadn't even noticed her neighbor in the class.

"I did!" She smiled beatifically at the older woman, who looked stately as ever in fitted black pants and a loose forest green top over a black undershirt, dark hair pulled back into a simple but elegant chignon.

"Do you think you'll come back for more?"

"Absolutely!"

"Wonderful. Perhaps we can all go out for gelato after class one day soon?"

"I never say no to gelato."

"Excellent! Well ladies, I'd love to stay and chat, but I have a lunch date with Felix this afternoon. I have to freshen up before meeting him on the north side of the island."

"You couldn't possibly look any better than you do now," Daphne declared, and Cassandra had to agree. Sophisticated even in sweats. There was something to strive for.

"You're a darling for saying so, but nevertheless, off I go."

"That woman is a paragon." Cassandra watched her breeze through the door and into the late morning sunshine. "I want to be her when I grow up."

"Don't we all," Daphne agreed. "What are your plans for the rest of the day? I've got another class in fifteen minutes. Any chance you want to stay for round two?"

"Tempting, but I'm not sure my body could handle *that* much flexibility in one day. I'll build up to it. And anyway, I have to work in a couple of hours. I think there will be just enough time to shower and call my family before I need to head out. But I'll see you for dinner tonight? I'm thinking stuffed chicken."

"Yes!" Daphne dimpled at her. "I will absolutely be home for stuffed chicken!"

***

"Come on, you chicken," Cassandra heard Drew say to Daphne a few days later as she joined them after her shift.

"What am I missing?" she asked, plopping down onto a chair at their table.

"Daphne is refusing to try bungee jumping," Drew scoffed.

"No, I'm refusing to try it with you," Daphne corrected. "I think you're trying to pump me full of adrenaline, hoping I'll get caught up in the rush and sleep with you."

"Stranger things have happened."

"Women do not jump off of cliffs and into bed with promiscuous men, Andrew. Your logic is flawed."

"It's worth a shot anyway. How about Friday?"

Daphne rolled her eyes and chucked a napkin at him, bouncing it off his forehead and onto his plate.

"You guys aren't going to make me try bungee jumping, are you?" Cassandra asked, concerned. "I'm still getting the hang of being adventurous on land and sea...I'm not sure I'm ready for airborne activities yet."

"Nah, we'll work up to that," Drew said. "But I'll pass the adrenaline theory along to Finn. Maybe he could use it—it worked for him after the manta rays."

Cassandra blushed and another napkin ricocheted off Drew's face.

"What did Drew do now?" Finn asked, joining them from the bar.

"He was being an ass," Daphne supplied helpfully.

"I was being colorful," Drew amended.

"A rainbow of wit, as usual."

"Anyway," Fin changed the subject, "who's up for continuing Cassandra's education of the island this weekend? I was thinking we could show her the butterfly garden on Friday."

"A whole garden of butterflies?" Cass was hesitant. "How close do they get?"

"Don't tell me you have anything against butterflies!" Finn laughed.

"Not from far away!" Cassandra tried unsuccessfully to defend herself. "But have you ever really looked at one up close? They're insects! No matter how pretty a butterfly's wings might be, insects are gross. Exoskeletons and antennae and all those creepy legs and buggy eyes..."

"The garden has more than just butterflies. It's like a tropical sanctuary. There are flamingos and koi fish and frogs and turtles and tons of different species of flowers..."

"You're not really selling this the way you think you are," Cassandra laughed. "*More* nature has never been a big draw for me. But I'm in." She looked around the table. "Anybody else?"

Drew shook his head. "As much as I would love to watch you freak out over a butterfly landing on your head, I'm going bungee jumping."

"Daphne?"

"Sorry. I have a meeting with my accountant."

"On a Friday night?" Drew raised his eyebrows.

"It's the only time both of our schedules were open."

"You know, I think that says something about the state of your social life. I could give you a hand with that."

"Drew, if I've said it once, I've said it a thousand times: your hands aren't going anywhere near my social life."

"You've never said that before."

"Not in so many words. But the sentiment was always there."

"*Any*way," Finn cut in again, "it looks like it's just you and me, Cass."

He grinned at her, bright blue eyes smiling into hers, and Cassandra's brain started flashing bright red warning signs at the feelings that smile stirred in the pit of her stomach.

"Danger, Will Robinson. Danger!"

She ignored the flashing and smiled back. "You and me and ten thousand butterflies. Sounds great!"

Chapter Twelve

"What do you think?" Finn asked when they walked through the entrance to the butterfly sanctuary late Friday afternoon. He spread his hands to encompass the expanse of garden that stretched out before them and Cassandra took it all in: lush foliage, brightly colored tropical flowers, the musical call of myriad birds echoing in the distance. Off to one side, a large pond was filled with koi and a turtle slowly wandered across a path to their left. It was the Garden of Eden, a kaleidoscope of sound and color, and Cassandra's inner voice told her that everything in it was going to appall her.

"It's beautiful!" she said out loud, because that was true, too. She was determined to silence her wet-blanket inner voice and enjoy this. It had to be the most vibrant place she'd ever seen, and her appreciation of it would not be dampened by the fact that birds and fish and insects were often disgusting. This was going to be a growing experience.

"You sure you're okay?" Finn asked, leading them towards a pond where several flamingos languidly waded. He stopped near the water's edge to examine the koi swimming lazy circles in the shallows. "I know this much nature puts you pretty far out of your element."

"Oh, no, I'm fine," she said, edging away from a flamingo, hoping Finn wouldn't notice her giving the bird a sidelong glance.

"What's wrong with the bird?" Finn asked, looking from her to the flamingo, not missing a beat.

"Nothing!" she said, fighting the urge to look shifty. "It's just…"

"Spill it, Dillon."

"*What* is going on with its eyes?" she blurted out. "They're like fish eyes in a bird face! It's unnerving."

"You aren't going to freak out about this like you did the emu, are you?" Finn's voice was mild.

Cassandra rolled her eyes and shot back, "This coming from the guy who's afraid of ducks. No, I'll be fine. I'll just look at something else. Oh my gosh, no I won't!" she said, throwing her hands up over her eyes as a large, vividly blue butterfly landed on an orchid in front of her, unfurled a tube from its face, and began to drink from the flower. "What the hell is that?"

"Cass, that's a butterfly."

"With retractable body parts?"

She took a deep breath and told herself to relax. Maybe this was normal. She wasn't sure that was a comforting thought.

"It's a proboscis. All butterflies have those," Finn explained. "It's how they get nectar. Have you never seen that before?"

See, Cass? It's normal…not terrible.

"I told you, I usually view them from a distance. I *knew* they would be disturbing up close! Look at those giant eyes!"

"You've shared the ocean with manta rays. You cannot be afraid of butterflies."

"I'm not *afraid* of butterflies. I'm frequently surprised by nature. There's a big difference. But not today," she said, squaring her shoulders and forcing a smile.

She was not afraid of nature. She was going to enjoy this, damn it! A butterfly fluttered past her, its wings a patchwork of reds and blacks, and she very carefully did not look at any other part of it.

See how pretty those wings are? You almost wouldn't notice the creepy built-in straw it can unfold from its body...

"Today is going to be great," she continued, starting down one of the paths that wound between the lavish trees and thick bushes. "Me and nature, together again, coexisting in perfect harmo—holy crap!" she jumped and then held very still as Finn turned to her, startled.

He took one look at her and burst out laughing. A bright green tree frog with huge orange eyes and sticky orange feet had leapt down from a branch, straight onto Cassandra's shoulder

"Well, you're just jumping right into this experience, aren't you?"

"Very funny. *I* didn't jump, the frog did!" She took another deep breath and avoided turning her head toward the creature, lest it decide to jump again, right at her face. She felt it adjust its toes on her shoulder and did some more breathing. *Just like yoga. With amphibians.*

"What do I do?" she asked, looking wide-eyed at Finn, who just chortled at her, the jerk.

"Wait until it decides to move?" he suggested.

They waited for several long moments while Cassandra stood like a statue and Finn looked amused. After a while, it became clear that the frog had decided to take up permanent residence on Cassandra's arm, and Finn said, "Well, I say you give it a name and get used to flies being caught near your ear."

"That's very helpful, Finn, thank you." The novelty of having a wild animal perched on top of her had worn off and Cass no longer felt like hyperventilating.

"How about Pete?"

"That's a terrible frog name! He's clearly a…" she looked out of the corner of her eye and turned her head a fraction of an inch to see him clearly, "Reggie."

"Reggie it is. Reggie the Tree Frog. Nice to meet you, Reg." Finn took a step closer to peer at the small creature and Reggie the Tree Frog stared placidly back, unimpressed.

"Do you think if we start walking, he'll hop away?" Cass asked.

"We can try."

They walked a few paces and Reggie gave no indication that he had any intention of ever leaving Cassandra's shoulder. He edged up a couple of inches toward her hair and stayed put, looking like he sat on the outskirts of some exotic forest underbrush, obviously quite content to live there forever.

"Finn, if this thing gets into my hair, we could have a problem."

They meandered down the path, passing a cornucopia of lilies, orchids and jasmine, dozens of butterflies flitting in the distance, while Reggie sat calmly on her shoulder.

"I see you've made a friend!" A jocular young employee appeared from behind a large flowering shrubbery, smiling widely from beneath his wire-rimmed glasses, pleased to be sharing in their special connection with nature.

"Indeed, I have!" Cassandra attempted to match the young man's enthusiasm. "It couldn't be helped, actually. He hopped a ride and could not be dissuaded. I think I may have a new pet."

"Tree frogs make excellent pets." The young man nodded vigorously, brown hair flopping over his forehead. "But it is exciting to see them here in a more natural habitat. Did you know that tree frogs change color according to their mood?"

"Really?" Finn was intrigued. "Reggie's bright green now—that must mean he's happy with his new home."

"Reggie?" The attendant looked confused.

"That's what we named him," Cassandra explained. "Since it seemed he might be with us for a while."

"Oh, of course!" The young man smiled. "I give the animals nick-names all the time. But obviously it's difficult to keep track of them individually. We have over seventy-five different species of butterflies alone here in the gardens. Over six thousand adults at any given time!"

"Oh, my!" Cassandra feigned eagerness, trying not to throw alarmed glances at the insects surrounding them. Imagine what would happen if that many butterflies decided to swarm at once. It would be like a reenactment of The Birds…with tubes instead of claws.

"Yes!" the worker continued earnestly. "Did you know that a butterfly's wings are made up of thousands of tiny scales? That's what gives them their color."

"Is that so?" Cassandra wanted to look fascinated, but she would have to settle for not looking horrified. Scales? So much for the beauty of butterfly wings.

"Of course, some people think that frogs have scales," he continued, gesturing to Reggie and chuckling at the folly of the masses while Cass wished he were just a little less knowledgeable about his job and so keenly excited to share his wisdom. "But that's what separates them from reptiles. Frogs are amphibians, so their skin is slimy instead of scaly. The slime comes from a layer of mucus that is excreted from the skin…"

"Well," Finn cut in as Cassandra turned pale and cast a horrified glance at the amphibian currently excreting mucus on her shoulder, "that is fascinating! But I've always been curious about the lifespan of turtles," he said, clapping a hand on the zealous garden attendant's shoulder and leading him back in the direction of the pond, while Cass hurriedly wandered further up the path and deliberately steered her mind away from scientific facts of the wildlife that besieged her.

More deep breathing. Clear the mind, that's the trick.

While she breathed and refocused her thoughts away from the technicalities of nature, she was able to view it through a lens of appreciation. As long as she didn't concentrate on the reality of tubes and scales, she could enjoy the abstract beauty of it all.

Gradually, she felt herself settling into the warmth of the air around her, the scents of the various blossoms as she rambled deeper into the gardens, the echoing songs of tropical birds in the trees. She inhaled deeply, breathing it all in, and soon she felt relaxed, contented even, reveling in the freshness and opulence. So much vibrancy, so much vitality—she felt more alive just being surrounded by it—like she was somehow soaking up the light and color and sound and becoming brighter and more vivid by simple association.

There was a deep, wholesome peace at the center of all this life. A rich, thudding heartbeat pulsing through every note of birdsong and vibrating in every lavish bloom. It reverberated in the beat of butterfly wings and resounded in the trickle of the softly flowing stream. Cassandra walked through it all, seeing with new eyes, every sense renewed, marveling at the beauty enveloping her, feeling its energy calling to something deep within her.

Maybe this was what people meant when they talked about communing with nature—this sense of energy, of connection, of boundlessness.

Contemplating this possible revelation, Cassandra leaned over to smell a blooming plumeria. As she did, Reggie leapt again, landing with sprightly ease on a wide leaf among the perfumed petals. He flexed his globular toes and blinked slowly at her. They stared at each other for a moment and Cassandra liked to think they had reached a mutual understanding—a reciprocal sense of respect. He gave her one last long look and hopped away.

She was watching the sway of the leaf in the wake of the frog's absence when Finn reappeared.

"You look happy," he observed. "Hey!" he said, pointing to her shoulder. "Is it because you finally offloaded Reggie?"

"Actually," she smiled genially, "I may be having a breakthrough!"

"That's good news. About what?"

"Life. Nature. My relationship to each respectively."

"Big stuff. We should celebrate."

"Any ideas?"

"There's a vineyard not too far from here. We could head over after we've finished up with the gardens. Great wine, wood fired pizza…you interested?"

"Pizza and wine?" Cass perked up. "I have to be at Andre's by eight, but I guess I could make time for pizza and wine. Come on, Drake," she grabbed his hand and propelled them down the path. "Let's go see some butterflies, because we have a vineyard to go to."

***

Finn watched as Cassandra bit into the sundried tomato and feta pizza (which she had chosen by closing her eyes and pointing at the menu), and enjoyed the blissful look that flooded her face. It was the same look she got whenever good food was involved. The same look she'd gotten after he kissed her in the moonlight. The same look he imagined she'd get right now if he leaned over and licked that bit of sauce off her full lower lip…

He cleared his throat and took a sip of his wine. "How's the pizza?"

"Amazing!" she said fervently. "This island has the best food!"

They were seated outside in the waning daylight, and Cassandra's hair was backlit by the sun sinking gradually lower in the sky. Flecks of gold and red glinted in her curls and her ivory skin was a pale contrast against the expanse of bright leafy vines that stretched out for acres behind her.

"How's yours?" she asked.

"Delicious, as always," Finn picked up a slice of his meat-lovers and bit into it so he wouldn't think about biting into the smooth curve of Cassandra's coconut-scented neck instead. This platonic thing was the pits.

"Thanks again for showing me another part of the island. It was a lot of fun! I think I grew today." She grinned at him and bit once again into her pizza.

"I'll say. You handled that tree frog like a pro. Next thing you know, you'll be wrestling alligators and swimming with sharks." An image flitted briefly through his mind of Cassandra wrestling an alligator in the mud, wet and round and slippery…ridiculous but erotic nonetheless.

"I'll leave swimming with sharks to you and Drew," Cassandra said resolutely. "I'm not sure I'll ever grow that much."

"Never say 'never.'"

"Never*theless*, it was a big day for me." Cass practically glowed as she reflected on it. "All that wildlife around me and I actually enjoyed it! Part of it *sat* on me and I still didn't mind! Eventually."

"Good old Reggie," Finn said fondly.

They went on to talk about her burgeoning taste for nature and Finn couldn't help but feel a growing sense of affection. Who else in the world would be so proud of spending an afternoon with flowers and butterflies? Most people would think nothing of it, but for Cassandra Dillon it was a major accomplishment. She was a sweetheart. Crazy as a loon, but a sweetheart just the same. Her ability to find joy in simple, innocuous things was infectious, and as he listened to her talk, Finn found himself viewing the gardens through new eyes.

"What's the screen for?" she asked toward the end of the meal, as the sky developed the first hints of twilight and the staff set up a large, canvas screen at the edge of the vineyard.

"They show old movies here every other Friday," he explained, and Cassandra's face lit up, delighted. "Random things—Casablanca, The Breakfast Club…last time I went, it was for a showing of The Princess Bride."

"'Inconceivable!'"

"Exactly."

"That's so fun!" Her tone was thrilled. "What are they showing tonight?"

"I saw a sign when we were coming in…I didn't recognize the title. I think it was Bringing Up Baby?"

"You've never seen Bringing Up Baby?" Cassandra sat up straighter. "Oh, you should. It's fantastic! A classic—Katherine Hepburn and Cary Grant. It's too bad I have to work or we could stay and watch!"

"It's a damn shame," Finn grinned, charmed once again by her enthusiasm.

"Katherine Hepburn is wonderful in it! Her character is absolutely crazy! Poor Cary Grant is this mild-mannered paleontologist who gets tangled up in all her antics but he can't help falling in love with her.

He just gets swept away by her personality. Never stands a chance."

Finn could relate to that. Based on what she'd just said, Cassandra could be describing a movie about herself. And he was on the fast track to becoming Cary Grant.

She seemed perfectly sane at first glance, but then she opened her mouth and you realized she was a nut. Or maybe it was that she seemed unbalanced at first, with that crazy glint in her eye, but then you got to know her and realized she was relatively stable. It was hard to say exactly which. On the one hand, she was level-headed, clear-sighted, seemed to have very sensible priorities. On the other hand, she jumped off yachts and let fate decide her meals for her.

It made everyone else Finn knew seem static and boring by comparison. He hadn't realized it before, but the people in his world had been gray and flat, and then Cassandra came along and everything became technicolor. She was the freaking Wizard of Oz of women.

"Sounds great," he said. "We'll have to watch it sometime."

"Absolutely!"

They finished their meal and Finn dropped Cassandra off at her apartment to get ready for work, feeling stupidly bereft once he'd left her.

He made his way back to his own place with the intention of getting some work done, settling onto the couch with a copy of Levi-Strauss's *Triste Tropiques,* but his mind kept wandering back to Cassandra. The look on her face when Reggie had landed on her shoulder. The way her eyes had shone when she talked about her growing experience. The rush of pleasure that had crossed her face when she'd sampled the wine at dinner.

He bet he could put that look back on her face if she'd give him the chance.

Finn opened his book and brought his mind back to anthropology where it belonged. This was going to be a productive evening, damn it! Focusing his eyes back on the page in front of him, he took a deep breath to concentrate.

And pictured Cassandra wrestling alligators.

Chapter Thirteen

"Well, Cassandra," Mary Ella asked after yoga the following week, "how are you moving ahead with your soul search?"

Cass spooned a bite of her coconut gelato brownie sundae and said, "I've been on the island a month now, and I've had a wonderful time, but I haven't come any closer to unlocking my destiny."

She ate her sundae to distract from her disappointing lack of progress and closed her eyes in happiness, enjoying the light sweetness of the coconut with the bone-melting richness of the chocolate. It probably countered all the caloric burn she may have achieved during yoga, but it was more than worth it. The leftover sense of well-being from the class combined with the almost sexual instant gratification of the sundae had her approaching nirvana.

Then she heard Mary Ella responding to her statement and remembered there was a conversation taking place.

"I'm sorry, could you repeat that?"

"I asked if you keep a journal. I've often found that writing down my thoughts helps me to sort through and make sense of them. Maybe keeping track of your experiences here will help you see that you're making progress."

"That's a great idea!" Daphne perked up from behind her mango smoothie. "I bet if you write things down, you'll be able to look back and see how much you're growing without even realizing it!"

Sir Galahad watched them all with palpable yearning from his spot on the sidewalk, but Mary Ella had already flatly refused him a frozen treat, placating him instead with a dog biscuit she kept in her purse. Sir Galahad was less than enthused.

"You could even do a dream journal!" Daphne expanded, looking pleased. "I kept one during a yoga retreat and it's really interesting! You can uncover all kinds of things your subconscious is trying to work though! Maybe it will help you realize some hidden desires."

My subconscious has certainly been bringing up a lot of not-so-hidden desires, Cass thought, remembering the hot dream she'd had about a freshly-showered Finn the previous night.

But she kept that to herself and said, "It's worth a shot! Nothing else I've been doing has led to any flashing neon signs saying, 'This is your destiny!' so maybe my subconscious will do it for me. Thanks, you guys—that's really helpful. I'll give it a try!"

***

Cassandra sat up in her cushy purple bed and stifled a yawn. She was probably late for work.

Stretching drowsily, she heaved herself out of bed and went to the dresser, gazing sleepily at her painting of the nightscape that hung above it. She thought hazily how beautiful it was, and then suddenly she was there, standing on the outlook once again.

"Well, this is nice, but I'm late for work," she thought. "Still, as long as I'm here, I might as well appreciate the view."

She walked toward the cliff's edge, enjoying the glow of the moon, which seemed even bigger and brighter than usual, and as she gazed down at its reflection on the water, she felt herself lose footing and go over the rim of the drop-off.

Before she had time to scream, she was floating on her padded green yoga mat, high over the ocean.

"This sort of thing doesn't usually happen in real life," she thought, feeling the fragile support of the mat underneath her. "Has my life really become Aladdin, or am I dreaming?"

"It's real," a voice said from behind.

She whipped her head around and felt the mat rock, then noticed a small green frog at the far end of the mat, all but camouflaged except for his weird orange eyes and toes.

"Reggie?" she cried. "I thought you might be the walrus. What are you doing here? Did you bring me here? Did you push me over the edge?"

"Of course not," he blinked at her, calm as ever, as if to say those were all silly questions. "The walrus is at a conference. And you brought yourself. You pushed yourself. Sometimes you need to take a leap of faith to put yourself back on the path to your life's journey, Cassandra."

"I already took a leap," Cass said, noticing that the mat had floated lower and brought them to hover right above the surface of the water. "I leapt off a yacht. I don't need to leap again."

"One act of faith is not enough," Reggie told her sagely. "You must continue to trust yourself."

She looked into the water and saw massive shadows coming up from the depths—manta rays back to haunt her.

"Oh, no. I am not getting in the water with those things," Cassandra said vehemently. "Looking at them was all fine and good, but I am not *swimming* with them."

"It's time for a leap of faith," Reggie said.

"Absolutely not!"

But the mat shuddered and she was flipped off, hitting the water with a pronounced feeling of dread. When she opened her eyes, Cass saw that the shadows were not manta rays, but butterflies, giant and surreal, slowly flapping their wings underwater and moving with a grace that mesmerized her.

One floated dreamily past her, its wings a flurry of purple, orange and red.

Scales, she thought, but she didn't care. It was beautiful. She reached out a hand to ask for a ride, but when her fingertips touched the delicate wing, the whole scene disappeared in a flash.

Cass sat up in bed, pretty sure that she was really awake now. Her alarm clock was buzzing and she looked at the painting hanging above her dresser. This time she stayed right where she was. Lack of teleportation was generally a sign of reality.

Rolling out of bed, she thought, *What the hell, subconscious?* but she jotted the dream down anyway before getting ready for work.

Later, having been talked into kayaking with Mary Ella and Daphne, Cass recounted the story.

"I don't think it gets much clearer than that," Daphne said, paddling gracefully upstream, circling Cassandra.

"What? A frog pushed me off a cliff, my yoga mat turned into a magic carpet, I swam with giant butterflies, and suddenly everything's clear?"

"You need to trust yourself! You're on the right path—you just need to keep at it!"

Cassandra squinted doubtfully, focusing half her attentions on Daphne's words and the other half on keeping her stupid kayak pointed straight, and Daphne went on, "If you want to get into basic dream analysis, I learned at the yoga retreat that water in dreams symbolizes your emotional state. At the beginning of the dream the ocean was far away, and by the end you were submerged in it. I think that could be your subconscious telling you that you've been analyzing your feelings and keeping them at a distance for too long, and now you have to stop avoiding them. It's time to dive in. Interesting that we're having this conversation in a river!"

Mary Ella nodded in agreement, paddling her kayak right alongside Cassandra's, helping steer her back on course and keeping pace with her easily. "I also think it's interesting that the manta rays, which you were initially so afraid of, turned out to be butterflies, which were beautiful. Perhaps if you face your fears, they won't turn out to be as frightening as you think."

Cassandra listened to their analysis and had to admit it made some sense. Reggie was still inexplicable, but you couldn't have everything.

"A leap of faith," she repeated, finally finding her rhythm and falling into sync with her two companions. She considered telling them about her recent very literal leap of faith—maybe it was time that they knew about the jump. But they were having such a nice day…and their conversation was about where her life was going, not where it had been. Having to explain about the jump would just distract from the more important discussion they were having now.

They floated comfortably down the river side by side.

"Reggie's leap of faith comment reminds me of Gram," she said, keeping the conversation on track and ignoring the nagging feeling that she was hiding something big from her closest friends. "One of the last things she said to me before she died was, 'Trust yourself. Don't overthink things. Go with your gut, because you're usually right the first time.' I guess my dream was trying to remind me of that advice."

"She sounds very wise," Mary Ella said.

"She was. You remind me a little bit of her," Cass observed, looking at the older woman, dauntless and serene, maneuvering effortlessly through the stream. "Not in looks, or even personality, really, but in spirit. Neither one of you are women to let life pass you by."

"Thank you!" Mary Ella sounded touched.

"One of the other things she said to me in the end was, 'Keep your sense of humor and keep trying. Remember: things change, and that's just life.' I've been trying to hold onto that as well. I know that all of this is just a phase, all this change. Her passing, Beth graduating and moving away, me finding myself. I know it's just the end of one chapter and the beginning of another, but I can't figure out what the next chapter is supposed to be about."

"Don't force it. It'll come," Mary Ella told her. "Just keep paying attention."

Daphne lightly splashed Cassandra with her paddle, smiling. "A few more dreams like that and your subconscious will practically be hitting you over the head with your life's purpose. You're bound to figure it out eventually."

"If I navigate life anything like I do this river, I might be in trouble," Cass laughed. "But for now, you guys are right. I just have to stick to the course."

***

Later that week, Cassandra regarded her phone without much enthusiasm. She had been plagued with guilt all day because it had been a couple of weeks since she'd last contacted her family, so she had vowed to herself while working the lunch shift at Andre's to be a good daughter and call them when she got home. Now, when faced with the actual task, her conviction was rapidly fading.

Daphne breezed through the door, home from a power yoga class, and Cassandra jumped at the chance to use her as an impetus to fulfill her familial duties.

"Daphne!" she said. "Make me call my family!"

"Call your family," Daphne said, plopping down on the couch next to her.

"No, I'm going to need more motivation than that. Here's the deal: Andre's special last week was a butternut squash risotto and I've been fantasizing about it ever since he replaced it on Sunday. I want to see if I can duplicate it tonight for dinner."

"Yay! Yum!" Daphne clapped, dark ringlets bouncing.

"But I don't get to make it until I pick up this phone and have a conversation with at least one member of my family."

"Right," Daphne said, furrowing her brows in determination. "Call your family. Feed me! I offered an extra kickboxing class today and if I don't have nourishment I'll pass out and probably die. Help me, Cassandra Dillon," she pleaded, holding out the phone. "You're my only hope."

Cassandra sighed. "I will make this call, Daphne. For your sake."

She grabbed her cell phone from Daphne's outstretched hand and retreated to her bedroom. Throwing herself onto the bed, she reveled as always in its cushiness, then propped herself up on her elbows and opened her contacts list, considering her choices carefully. Her mother would most likely spend the majority of the conversation talking about the events of their cruise, more or less forgetting there was another person on the other end of the line. The last time they'd spoken, Cassandra had gotten roped into a twenty-minute conversation about how, when her family had gone out to eat at the last port of call, the table linens had clashed terribly with Beth's choice of blouse and the server had been impressed that Miranda knew the correct term for a word that was spelled the same forward as backward. ("It's called a 'palindrome,' darling.") Cassandra shook her head. *No, thank you. Not today.*

Conversely, her father would spend the entire time grilling her about her time on the island: how was her job? How was the apartment? Did she feel safe? Was she carrying the mace he had sent her? Some of the clothes she had sent over were pretty revealing…was she being situationally aware? Was that guy Finn keeping his hands to himself? And so on.

Honestly, she loved her parents, but they could be exhausting. That left Beth. Beth would be okay. She was due to catch up with her sister anyway…she must have accumulated some good stories by now with the family docking and touring islands every few days. As she listened to the phone ring, Cass contemplated the amount of trouble that girl could get into on a dozen tropical beaches in the height of summer vacation. What had her parents been thinking?

Too late now, Cassandra thought as Beth's lilting voice came through the other line. "Hello?"

"Hey, Beth. How's it going?"

"Cass! I was wondering when I'd finally hear from you! Too busy gallivanting around tropical islands to call your little sister, huh?" Cassandra could practically see Beth shaking her blonde curly head in exaggerated dejection.

"Oh sure," Cassandra said. "Like you're just waiting sadly by your phone, hoping for a call from me. Mom gave me the family's itinerary, so I know you're at a resort this week. What are you doing right now?"

"Sunbathing," Beth said airily.

"It's a rough life, huh, kid?"

"Well, I put on a brave face."

"And how many boys also 'happen' to be lounging around nearby, waiting for you to notice them?"

"Probably only three worth mentioning."

"Only three?" Cassandra drawled. "Slow day?"

"I'm meeting one for tennis in an hour," Beth said blithely. "Mark. Nice eyes. Nice forearms. And then another guy, Zane, asked me to go dancing tonight after dinner. He's got a great butt. And yesterday I went swimming with Connor who's hilarious and has amazing abs. Oh, and then—"

"I get it," Cassandra cut in. "You've been busy. And all in what, four days?"

"Three," Beth said nonchalantly. "Dad looked like he was going to have a coronary yesterday when Connor showed up at the room to walk me to the pool. That boy can really fill out a pair of swim trunks."

Cassandra laughed. "Poor Dad. I don't think he knew what he was getting himself into this summer."

"He should have seen it coming," Cassandra pictured Beth shrugging her shoulders and grinning.

"You'd better watch it or all of our future family vacations will be spent touring monasteries."

"Well, we can't exactly call this a *family* vacation, can we?" Beth said with a hint of accusation. "You went off to have your own vacation and left me all alone with Mom and Dad."

"Yeah, Mom and Dad and Mark and Zane and Connor," Cassandra snorted. "Also, Beth, I *fell off* the yacht. I'm pretty sure you can't hold that against me."

Or you can't if you never find out that I jumped. And I'll never tell!

"I'm not so sure about that," Beth said wryly. "But anyway, tell me all about it! Have you met any hot guys?"

"Yes," Cassandra answered honestly. "I've also met some wonderful *female* friends that I'm having a great time with."

"Sure, sure," Beth waved this information aside as irrelevant. "But tell me about this hot guy. Is he the one Dad sounded all suspicious of when you first disappeared?"

"Yes," Cassandra said again. "But none of this is to be repeated to Dad, understood?"

"Of course not," Cassandra could hear the eye roll in Beth's tone. "Tell me everything!"

"His name is Finn."

"Describe him."

"Six feet, blonde hair, blue eyes, chiseled jaw, broad shoulders."

"Holy crap."

"Pretty much," Cassandra said. "And you may be less interested to know this, but he is also intelligent, articulate, funny, adventurous, and incredibly sweet."

"Please tell me you're sleeping with him."

"Beth!"

"What? He sounds perfect!"

"Nobody's perfect, Beth."

"He sounds pretty damn close."

"He might be," Cassandra admitted.

"So, what's the deal? Why aren't you sleeping with him?"

"Because I've only known him for a few weeks," Cassandra said sternly and she could once again feel Beth rolling her eyes over the phone. "Also, I'm taking a break from dating so I can focus on myself. You know that mom and dad intended the cruise as an opportunity for me to do some soul-searching. I'm doing it on this island instead. And I'm taking it seriously. No dating."

"Forget dating!" Beth said. "And forget soul-searching! Go jump him."

"That's very enlightened, Beth."

"Enlightenment is overrated. Nirvana is a good make out session, not mental clarity."

"Bethany!"

"Cassandra!" Beth's tone mirrored her own.

"You're eighteen. You have no depth."

"Maybe not, but I have fun. And this Finn guy sounds like fun. I bet he's a good kisser."

"He is."

"What?" Beth squealed. "You kissed him? What happened to 'no dating'?"

"I was temporarily distracted," Cassandra said primly, "but it only happened once. It was nearly a month ago and things have been perfectly innocent ever since."

"Was it amazing?"

"You have no idea."

Beth squealed again. "This is fantastic! I think an island fling is the best thing that could happen to you! Forget your misguided principles and let this guy screw your brains out."

"Bethany Dillon, I am going to tell our father to lock you in your cabin and throw the key into the ocean. Also, it's not just principles that are guiding me—it's self-respect. You should try it some time."

"I have self-respect," Beth said reasonably. "But *I* also have a good time."

Now it was Cassandra's turn to roll her eyes. "I'm changing the subject," she said.

She told Beth about living with Daphne and working for Andre and meeting Mary Ella. ("You should see her dog, Beth! He's the size of a triceratops!") Beth listened with rapt attention as Cass described seeing the manta rays and laughed hysterically as she recounted the saga of Reggie the Tree Frog.

"Okay," she admitted when Cassandra had finished. "It sounds like you *are* having fun. But promise me you'll at least consider giving Finn a shot!"

"Now's not a good time, Beth," Cass sighed.

Beth groaned in frustration. "You are hopeless, Cassandra! But I'll leave you alone."

"Thank you," Cass said. "Now promise me you won't go too crazy with these boys? Give our dad some peace of mind."

Beth chuckled. "Let's not get carried away."

"We make quite a pair, don't we?"

"Like fire and ice," Beth said. "I've got to go get ready to meet Mark, but keep me posted, okay? You'll let me know if anything else exciting happens?"

"Sure," Cassandra pledged. "But if by 'exciting' you mean sleeping with Finn, I wouldn't hold my breath if I were you."

It was Beth's turn to sigh. "Good luck, Cass. Remember to have some fun!"

"I always do," Cassandra said. "And you remember not to have too much fun."

"Like that's possible," Beth laughed. "Talk to you soon!"

"Bye, Beth. Tell mom and dad I called, but leave out any details about my love life! If they ask, just do what you do best and skirt the issue. Love you!"

Cassandra hung up the phone and exhaled. Her little sister was being a handful as usual, but that was for her parents to worry about. Cassandra had a butternut squash risotto to tackle.

***

"That was delicious," Daphne said two hours later as she finished putting the leftovers in the fridge. "I don't know how I survived before you came along! Don't ever leave me—I'll starve."

Cassandra uncorked the bottle of white wine she had used in the risotto and poured them each a glass.

"I'm sure you would be fine with your smoothies and roasted vegetables."

"I still love my smoothies and roasted vegetables." Daphne stuck her tongue out. "But with you around, it's like eating at Andre's from the comfort of my own home! With the added bonus of not having to pay for the food."

"Where do you think the food in our refrigerator comes from?" Cass asked, bringing the wine into the living room and folding herself onto the couch. "The grocery fairy? We pay for this food, too. And I'm not nearly as good as Andre."

"You're pretty darn close," Daphne retorted, following her from the kitchen. "But no one is as good as Andre."

"Too true," Cassandra agreed. "That man is a culinary master."

"Well, you definitely know your way around a skillet," Daphne said. "I may have to start offering more classes to keep up with all these extra calories I've been ingesting since you showed up. Speaking of which," she said, brightening, "do you want to try out kickboxing this week?"

"Sure!" Cassandra said, feeling magnanimous now that she was full of food and wine. "It might be nice to release some frustration over not making any more progress toward my goals."

"That's not true!" Daphne protested. "I think you've had all kinds of growth these past few weeks!"

"Abstractly, I feel like I'm making at least some progress, but concretely, I'm still no closer to figuring out what I want to do with my life," Cassandra pointed out.

"That's not something people usually figure out in a month," Daphne countered. "Some people go their whole lives without figuring out what they want from it."

"Ugh!" Cassandra's head fell against the back of the couch. "That's not comforting."

"I think you should be telling yourself that you've *only* been here a month and you've already accomplished so much!" Daphne said encouragingly.

Cassandra looked skeptical.

"Think about it," Daphne said helpfully. "You've found an awesome place to live, made some incredible friends," she smiled and pointed to herself, "found a job at a restaurant that you love, experienced things you would never have done before and *enjoyed them*," she emphasized, "and you've been totally dedicated to your resolution of focusing all of your energy inward, despite great temptation for distraction," she finished triumphantly.

Cassandra looked thoughtful and Daphne added slyly, "Oh by the way…how are things going with Finn?"

"Fine," Cassandra said absentmindedly, still mulling over the points Daphne had just made. "We're getting lunch tomorrow before work."

"At Andre's?" Daphne asked.

"No," Cassandra answered, focusing once again on the conversation. "We're going to a café he likes somewhere inland. More help exploring the island."

"The two of you have been spending a lot of time together," Daphne said pointedly. "A lot of *romantic* time." She poked Cassandra's arm.

"Oh, don't start," Cass poked her back. "We're just going to lunch. It's harmless."

"Yes, but there have been a lot of *other* things besides lunch. A lot of *date-like* things. With him. And you. Alone."

"Yes, him and me alone. We're friends," Cassandra said rationally. "Friends do things together alone."

"Usually not friends who have made out," Daphne contradicted. "Not things that can be done in public anyway," she laughed.

Cassandra threw a yellow tube pillow at her and bounced it off her head. "Finn and I made out once," she said. "It was a fluke."

Daphne scoffed, unconvinced.

"I'm not pretending I'm not attracted to him," Cassandra clarified, "but we've established boundaries and I'm not going to cross them. Neither is he. Getting lunch together is completely innocent."

"It smacks of a date."

"It isn't a date," Cassandra rolled her eyes. "We're not in the third grade when sitting together at lunch and holding hands constitutes a date. We're grown-ups. We're allowed to eat together without people getting all atwitter."

Daphne shrugged and Cass said longingly, "Ah, the third grade…there was a simpler time. Tony Kukowski gave me a pansy and told me I had pretty hair and we spent the rest of the year 'going out.' What a dreamboat," she sighed, starry-eyed with memories. "He had a robot lunchbox and a pet hedgehog and took everyone roller skating for his birthday. I was pretty sure I was going to marry him."

Daphne laughed and launched into a story about Alex Newman, the love of her grade-school life. The rest of the evening was spent laughing and reminiscing over past crushes and schoolgirl romances, all thoughts of Finn for the time-being forgotten.

***

That same night, Finn was drowning his sorrows over a pint with Drew.

"So, you're still striking out, huh?" Drew asked, scanning the bar and only half paying attention to the conversation.

"I am not striking out," Finn corrected. "I'm not even swinging. Cass isn't interested in a relationship right now."

"Are you?" Drew asked, smiling at a redhead at the end of the bar who smiled back, coy in an electric blue halter top.

Finn slugged his beer. "In general, no. With Cassandra, it could be worth it."

"Worth going to bed with the same woman every night?"

Finn thought of how Cassandra's hands had slid up his t-shirt when he'd kissed her, how her fingers had laced through his hair, how her breath had shuddered when he'd slipped his tongue into her mouth...he thought of doing all that naked, of pulling her on top of him, seeing her creamy skin in the glow of lamplight, running his hands up those long legs, feeling himself slide deep inside her…

"Yes," he said shortly.

Drew shrugged. "Your funeral."

"What about you?" Finn said, exasperated. "Aren't you supposed to be chasing Daphne?"

Drew shrugged again. "She'll come around."

Finn snorted. "You keep saying that, but if that's what you think, you don't know Daphne at all."

"Hey, Daphne's cool, but I'm not going to sit around twiddling my thumbs, waiting for her to decide she's interested."

"Did you ever consider the fact that she might be a lot more interested if you twiddled your thumbs for a while?"

"She knows that's not my style," Drew said, unconcerned.

"That's probably why she doesn't trust you," Finn said.

"Daphne's a smart girl—I like that about her. That and her ass."

"That's my cousin you're talking about," Finn reminded him, shooting him a glare.

"I probably wouldn't trust me either," Drew continued as though Finn hadn't spoken. "Doesn't mean I'm going to stop trying."

He nodded at the redhead who raised her eyebrow archly with a half-smile and turned away, revealing that her halter top was mostly backless in the process. The bartender handed a couple of drinks to the redhead, who shot one last look at Drew before heading back to her table. Drew craned his neck to watch her, eyes sliding down the backless tank top as she sauntered away.

"Focus, Drew," Finn waved his hand in front of his friend's face. "We're here to work on my problem, remember?"

"Right," Drew said, shifting his attention back to Finn. "You striking out with Cassandra."

"I am not striking out," Finn said patiently.

"So why are you here with me instead of back at your place with her?"

"Because she doesn't want to get involved." Finn downed the rest of his beer and signaled for another.

"Then it sounds like you're screwed," Drew summed up the situation. "Or in this case, not."

"Thanks very much," Finn said flatly. "Is that all you have to contribute?"

"It seems to me you've got two options." Drew held up his fingers. "Number one: seduce her. Number two: accept that she doesn't want you and move on."

"Those are my only options?" Finn said, nodding his thanks to the bartender who slid a second beer in front of him.

"Well, I guess you could sit around twiddling your thumbs," Drew said sarcastically.

"I can't seduce her," Finn said, ignoring him. "She'd regret it and I'd be left feeling like hell, worse off than I already am."

"Then 'accept it and move on' wins the day."

Finn looked thoughtful, struck by an idea.

"Wrong," he said.

"You're going to sit around and wait for her to change her mind?" Drew's voice dripped with scorn.

Finn waited a beat before responding, following this new train of thought. "No," he said finally. "I'm going with option number three. I'm going to help her out with this whole 'quest to find her life path' thing.

Once she knows what she wants to do with the rest of her life, she'll be open to dating, and then I'll make my move. In the meantime, I'll help her figure it out. We're having lunch tomorrow. I'll start then."

"And what if her quest leads her to discover that she wants to study penguins in Antarctica? She'll be on a boat south and you'll be shit out of luck, buddy. You'll never see her again."

"Cassandra is not a fan of nature. I doubt she'll decide to devote her life to studying it…but I see your point. I might be missing my window here." Finn once again looked pensive, then took another pull off his beer and said, "We'll cross that bridge when we come to it. I think this is a good plan."

"I think you're insane," Drew said dryly. "But if you're happy with it, I'm happy for you. Does this mean I'm free to go after that redhead?"

"Have at her," Finn gestured with his beer. "But don't expect me to put in a good word for you with Daphne."

"Daphne will come around," Drew said again as he slipped off his bar stool and headed toward the blue halter top.

"Now who's insane?" Finn called after him.

Drew would figure it out eventually. And then maybe he would have a shot with Daphne. Finn, on the other hand, was already figuring it out. And he was determined to have his shot with Cassandra as soon as possible.

"Tomorrow it begins," he said, and turned back to his drink.

Chapter Fourteen

When Finn arrived at the cafe the next day, he found Cassandra waiting for him at a table outside, looking serene in a broad white floppy hat and oversized sunglasses.

"You're looking very Audrey Hepburn this afternoon," he greeted her, flicking the brim of the hat and pulling up a chair. The scent of coconut floated to him on the warm breeze.

She smiled broadly at him and removed her sunglasses.

"Thank you! Part of my ongoing quest to avoid UV rays. I love this place, by the way! It feels like the quintessential European bistro."

"I think that was the general idea," Finn said, taking in the charm of the cobblestone and wrought iron and climbing wisteria. "And if you like the atmosphere, wait until you try the food. Incredible. They bring out fresh bread with a local olive oil and balsamic vinegar dipping sauce…you'll die."

"God, I love this island," Cassandra said, closing her eyes in anticipation.

Finn smiled at her enthusiasm and couldn't help but wonder if Cassandra's intensity for food extended to any other appetites. Based on the way she'd gone for his mouth when he'd kissed her, he was pretty sure it would.

"How's your day going so far?" he asked, going for banality so she wouldn't notice he was staring at her.

While she chatted her response, he listened and nodded along, waiting for his moment to casually segue into helping her with her life mission.

"And how's the whole "life path" search going?" he asked after a minute, driving right past subtlety and barreling straight into open inquisition.

Cassandra exhaled. "According to Daphne, it's going better than I realize," she said, which made absolutely no sense to him.

"So, it's going well...?" he clarified.

"Possibly," Cassandra looked thoughtful. "Depends on who you ask. Daphne says yes. I say it's not going horribly. My mother would probably say I'm still not engaged and I have no career, nor do I have any solid prospect of accomplishing either of those things, so it's going dismally. But I think I'm choosing to listen to Daphne in this case. She's the most sensible one in the bunch, so it seems like a good choice."

"Well, if getting engaged would help sort things out..." Finn offered, only half-joking.

Cassandra laughed and said, "If that's a marriage proposal, I appreciate it, but that's low on my list of priorities at the moment."

"Okay," Finn said in a more serious tone, "what's at the top of the list?"

"I don't know, getting a grip on my destiny? Personal, emotional, and intellectual fulfillment?"

"Well, that should be easy," Finn teased. "I think we can have that sorted out by the end of lunch."

"If you can accomplish that, I will marry you on the spot. My mother will be thrilled," Cassandra said.

As far as Finn could tell, the response wasn't entirely sarcastic.

"So," he began, "how do we figure this out?"

They were momentarily distracted by the arrival of the bread, which smelled amazing as always. The look on Cassandra's face was one of sheer bliss. The waiter took their orders and Finn returned to the problem at hand while Cassandra dove into the appetizer.

"There must be a simple way of going about this," Finn said, but Cassandra wasn't listening. She reverently tore off a chunk of the steaming loaf of bread, soaked it in the dark vinaigrette and bit into it, her face immediately flooding with happiness.

"Oh my god," she said on a half-moan, "this *is* incredible!" She licked a drop of sauce off her lip and all the blood drained from Finn's brain. "I'm sorry," she said, regrouping, "what were you saying?"

"Uhh," Finn replied suavely, his grip on the conversation lost.

"That's right, a simple way to go about this," Cassandra supplied.

"Right," Finn said gratefully.

"If I knew what that was, I'd have tried it by now," Cassandra took another bite and inhaled deeply, closing her eyes from the pleasure. She swallowed, opened them again and went on. "I'm just completely overwhelmed. It feels like the possibilities are endless and I have no idea where to begin. You should have some of this bread—it's fantastic!"

"Right," Finn said again, tearing off a piece of bread and feeling like a moron. What were they talking about? He couldn't focus with her sighing like that. He took a bite to distract himself, hoping that if he put something in his mouth that wasn't Cassandra, it would bring him back to reality and he could remember what the hell he was supposed to be saying. The warm, chewy softness of the bread and the tang of the vinaigrette cleared his head.

"Okay," Finn said, slowly finding his way back to the relevant topic, "let's start with this: what did you want to be when you grew up?"

Cassandra smiled. "A fairy princess. I'm sure I would have been happy with either fairy *or* princess, but both would have been ideal. That was the plan until I was probably eight. Then I moved on to international spy or private detective. I would also have settled for ninja."

Finn laughed. "How long did that last?"

"Well into middle school, as I recall. I think I spent a lot of time listening around corners and following people at a distance to gather evidence for cases. Once I even got sent to the principal's office for trying to break into another student's locker. I told him it was in the name of forensic science, but he didn't seem to care."

"Shamefully un-academic of him."

"I thought so, too! And then I went through a phase of karate chopping my little sister." She looked pensive. "I got grounded a lot that year. But then in high school I started taking French and that was great. I loved everything I learned about the language and the culture, and that carried me through college, obviously. I thought for a while I might want to be a translator, but decided it wouldn't be for me."

"Why not?" Finn asked.

"I don't want to spend all my time listening to other people's conversations," Cassandra said with feeling. "I want to have my own. If I had become a translator, my entire life would have been spent serving as a medium for everyone else's accomplishments. I'm sure you meet a lot of interesting people that way, but it wasn't what I wanted."

"Fair enough." Finn understood her point. "So, no translator. Is there anything else you could do that involves your degree?"

"There are plenty of things I could do," Cassandra shrugged. "But nothing I feel really passionate about. I know that sounds silly…why did I bother to get a degree if there are no practical applications for it? But there are a lot of practical applications for it, just none I'm interested in. I loved everything I studied as academic theory and I love French culture as a way of life, but I'm not sure I'm sold on centering a career around it."

"Okay…" Finn said, at a loss as to where to go from here.

"This is depressing," Cassandra interrupted, waving her bread around. "Let's talk about you for a while. What's *your* plan? How did you figure out your life?"

"I haven't really," Finn said simply. "I figure there's no rush. Someday I might like to settle into a teaching career at a university, but that would involve at least two more years of school to get a PhD. For now, I just want to keep doing what I'm doing—travel around, immerse myself in different cultures, study them, write about them, support myself by working in the local communities. I'm happy doing it, so why would I change?"

"To plan for your future?"

Finn waved her comment aside. "I don't want to spend my twenties worrying about something I may or may not want in the future. I don't want to look back in thirty years on all the things I could have done with my youth but didn't because I was too busy planning for 'someday.' By the time someday comes around, your life is passing you by, and what good did all that planning do you? You have memories of obligations and checklists and deposits into your savings account, but what about experiences? What about adventure? What about all the things you've done and seen and explored? I want to take advantage of my life as it's happening and worry about the future as it comes. But that's just my opinion," he added hastily, realizing that his whole speech went directly against Cassandra's current goals.

"No, I see your point. And I think I agree with it. Don't bargain current happiness for hypothetical future happiness," Cass summed up the concept nicely. "But that's exactly the problem: what will my current happiness consist of? What will I do for the rest of my life that will bring me fire and purpose and joy? Sure, financial stability is necessary too, but I want more than that. You've already found what I'm searching for. You know what your passion is. I still need to discover mine. I know what I'm passionate about academically and theoretically…now I need to find what inspires me pragmatically. That's the whole point of this summer."

"Oh," Finn said, finally understanding what Cassandra had been talking about for weeks. "Okay then, what makes you happy?"

"Food. Cloudy days. 80's music. Classic movies. Lamp posts. Benches. Purple flowers. Polar bears."

"Really? Lamp posts and benches make the top of your list?"

"They're picturesque!" Cassandra defended.

"You could always go into designing parks and scenic viewpoints for a living." Finn squinted, trying to assemble this information into something useful.

"Thank you," Cassandra said dryly. "Not helpful."

Finn laughed. "What else did you say, cloudy days? Okay, obviously nothing outside—" Finn was once again interrupted by the arrival of food.

Cassandra took a bite of her pesto gnocchi, closed her eyes again and sighed. "My god, I love this place!"

Finn dug into his lasagna so he wouldn't lunge for her across the table.

"Right, so something indoors—" he began again.

"Look, Finn, it's sweet of you to try and help, but we don't have to solve all of my problems today."

"I don't mind helping…I *want* to help." Finn panicked as he felt the conversation turning in a direction that would *not* end with Cassandra's life goals solved, making her happy and available, and thus putting an end to both their problems.

"And I'm very grateful for that, but let's talk about something else. How are the interviews coming along?"

Finn sighed and had no choice but to go along with the change in subject. As always, he appreciated her interest in his work, but not being able to touch her was getting really depressing. They had chemistry and she was ignoring it.

But he knew it went beyond physical chemistry. There was an emotional and intellectual connection as well. They could talk about anything…their studies, their childhoods, their interests, their aspirations, her grief over losing her grandma…hell, after knowing him less than twelve hours, she'd confided in him that she'd jumped off a yacht. That had to inspire some level of trust. But she was still determined to pretend it didn't exist.

Even though he respected her reasons for doing so, it was starting to take its toll. If something didn't change soon, he was going to lose his mind.

***

Cassandra was still ruminating over their conversation the next day, lying on her yoga mat waiting for class to start. She agreed with Finn that life was too short to be spent always planning for the future. Carpe diem and whatnot. She didn't have to have everything figured out right now, but still, some semblance of a plan for the future would be nice. Something to work toward while she was enjoying herself in the now.

She was contemplating this balance when she heard Daphne say, "What the hell are you doing here?"

obviously surprised out of her usual professional courtesy.

Cass looked up from her spot in the corner to see what had caused such an uncharacteristic response, and saw Drew sauntering through the door, looking smug as he approached Daphne.

"I'm here for yoga," Drew stated the obvious, then rolled out his mat, front and center of the room, directly in front of the spot where Daphne taught class.

"Drew, this is my place of business," she told him flatly. "You can't just show up here and try to flirt with me."

"Would I do that?" he asked, stripping off his T-shirt and tossing it to the front of his mat while Daphne narrowed her eyes. Several members of the predominantly female class eyed him appreciatively. Even Cassandra couldn't help enjoying the view. The boy was built nicely. Every eye in the class was turned to the front, curiously watching the exchange between the instructor and the hot newcomer.

"Cass seems to be enjoying your classes so much, I thought I'd come down and see what all the fuss is about," Drew explained, but Daphne looked skeptical. "Plus, there's a lot of bending in yoga, right?" His tone was the verbal equivalent of an eyebrow wiggle.

"Out!" Daphne said, pointing to the door. "If you're going to make a joke of this, get out now."

"Please don't make him leave!" a voice called from the back of the studio.

"See?" Drew spread his hands to the room in general. "The public wants me. Besides, I hear you going on about the benefits of yoga all the time—you wouldn't deny someone the chance to reap those benefits, would you?"

"Of course not," Daphne said through her teeth. "But if you push me, I will ask you nicely one more time to leave…and if you don't, then I will make you leave. These people are here for yoga, but I'm happy to give them an impromptu lesson in kickboxing with you as the target." She leveled him with a look that wiped the smirk of his face and he nodded obediently. "And you are not standing right behind me the whole time! Switch spots with Cassandra."

Cassandra, who was very attached to her safe, shielded spot in the far back corner, was none too thrilled with this plan, but Drew shrugged and said, "You're the boss."

He rolled up his mat and ambled cheerfully over to the corner. Cass had no choice but to pack up her stuff and move to the front.

She could see Drew in the mirror, looking far too pleased with himself while he got situated.

You're treading on thin ice, buddy, she thought. *Daphne will throw you out as soon as look at you if you piss her off. Or, if you really make her mad, she'll make good on that kickboxing threat.*

But she had her own issues to worry about, like not falling over for the next sixty minutes, so she lay down on her mat and focused on breathing, trying to clear her head before class like Daphne always instructed.

An hour later, Cassandra was so relaxed that she was practically comatose, business as usual for the end of a session, stretched out on her mat and thinking of nothing but breathing and scenic benches on a cloudy day. She had forgotten all about Drew, but Daphne clearly hadn't. As soon as people started filtering out of the room, the usually perky brunette marched straight to the back corner and started hissing at him in a low whisper. Drew responded in a tone of characteristic unconcern, obviously enjoying himself.

Cassandra opened one eye and considered intervening, but figured she'd give them some space. She could go over in a couple minutes and make sure Drew wasn't in danger of having a yoga mat shoved anywhere unpleasant. In the meantime, any form of movement seemed like a needless exertion.

Soon, she heard Daphne's prompt, pert footsteps go past her ear, so she sighed and rolled to one side, dragging herself to a seated position. The room had cleared out completely, apart from the three of them, and Daphne appeared to be somewhere between furious and flattered. Drew seemed to be having that effect on her more and more lately, but Cass couldn't tell exactly which feeling it was. She wondered if Daphne herself knew.

Moving with deliberate efficiency, Daphne gathered her things and headed to her desk near the front door, entering figures into the computer with great purpose and general lack of concern for Drew.

Cassandra finally pulled herself all the way to standing and started rolling up her mat while Drew wandered over.

"I was just telling Daphne how much I enjoyed class," he explained. "Totally stretched me out. Exactly what I needed."

He sounded sincere and Cass felt suspicious, waiting for the other shoe to drop as the two of them made their way toward the front desk.

"Of course, I was hoping for more physical adjustments," he continued. "A little more hands-on instruction."

There it is, Cass thought.

"An exercise class is not an opportunity to get felt up by the instructor, Drew," Daphne spared a glance for him and resumed typing.

"I'm a tactile learner," Drew was affronted. "I understand things better when there's physical stimulation involved." His tone was so candid and forthright that Cassandra was very nearly shocked. She hadn't thought Drew was capable of saying, "physical stimulation" without sounding dirty.

Daphne shook her head and smiled in spite of herself. "If I didn't know you, Drew, that might have worked."

His thin semblance of innocence melted and Drew smiled his usual impish grin.

"Yeah, well, it happens to be true, but we both know I'm using it for immoral purposes in this case. It was worth a shot."

***

Finn's further attempts to draw out Cassandra's latent life path were just as futile as the first had been. Each time, he learned more about her and became more infatuated in the process, but each time the conversation ended with her waving aside his assistance and changing the subject.

It was frustrating him to the point of madness, which is why he was taken by surprise a couple weeks later when his parents showed up on his doorstep.

"Hi, you guys!" he said, mentally smacking himself when he opened the door to find them smiling broadly at him from his stoop. Their visit had been on his calendar for months but he'd forgotten all about it with Cassandra driving him to distraction ever since she'd fallen, quite literally, into his life.

His parents looked tan and healthy, the same as they always did after months of work and travel, and he was glad to see them—even if he felt guilty for forgetting they were coming.

Fifteen minutes later, hugs had been given, drinks had been poured, and they were all seated around his tiny kitchen table, catching up on lost time.

"So, have you met anyone special on the island?" His mom refilled his wine glass after they'd discussed his parents' latest assignments and his latest studies.

"Sort of." Finn tried to sound nonchalant. Discussing women with his mother was never his favorite topic. "We're not actually together, though. She's Daphne's new roommate."

He left out the fact that she was Daphne's new roommate because he'd introduced them when he'd found Cassandra asleep under a bush in the middle of the night after she'd had a minor nervous breakdown and jumped off a yacht. His parents didn't need that many details.

"When do we get to meet her?" his mother asked, delighted.

"I'm not sure…she's pretty busy," he dodged.

"Well for now, you can tell us all about her!"

"Mom, Cassandra is just a friend. We're not dating," he emphasized. "Don't get any ideas. Tell me more about France!"

"But if she's Daphne's roommate, of course we'll meet her!" His mother ignored his last question, not at all distracted. "Why don't you invite them both to dinner tonight?"

"Tonight?"

"Sure!" his dad chimed in. "We're going to Andre's for dinner, and we want to see Daphne as soon as possible anyway. Why wait?"

"I guess I could ask," Finn conceded, feeling cornered. He would be happy to introduce Cass to his parents, but since he'd forgotten they would be showing up today, springing this on her felt like an ambush. Not that meeting his parents meant anything significant for her. Since they were just friends.

"Let's call Daphne now!" His mother beamed at him from across the table. "This will be fun!"

Chapter Fifteen

Cassandra sat with Daphne at one of Andre's best tables, feeling nervous. Spanish guitar music wafted in the background, but the soothing melody did nothing to ease Cassandra's stress. Finn and his parents were on their way. Not that meeting Finn's parents meant anything significant for her. Since they were just friends.

Still, from the way Daphne talked about them, it sounded like she thought of them as surrogate parents, and obviously they were Finn's *actual* parents, and anyone that important to two such important people in her own life were people she wanted to like her. The pressure was on.

Also, both of his parents sounded highly successful in their respective fields, which were very *interesting* fields —a food critic and travel writer...*so* interesting!—so the fact that she did not *have* a field or any sort of direction toward a field made her self-conscious.

Also also, it might be uncomfortable to share a meal with the parents of a man she'd been thoroughly kissed by only a few weeks prior, had been *groped* by only a few weeks prior, and about whom she'd regularly had impure thoughts ever since.

Her thoughts continued in this anxious and slightly incoherent vein until Daphne shrieked with unmistakable joy and Cass looked up to see Finn walking through the door with an attractive, middle-aged couple who had clearly given birth to him.

Daphne bounced out of her seat as soon as they approached and launched herself at her aunt, who laughed and hugged her tightly. She then hurled herself at her uncle, who hugged her hard enough to lift her off the ground, then spun her around and set her back on the ground. All the while, Cass just sat there, smiling like an idiot, feeling like her stomach was going to writhe out of her body.

Once Daphne's enthusiasm had subsided slightly, Finn took the chance to include Cassandra in the reunion. He came to stand next to her, gesturing to the smiling couple and saying, "Cassandra, these are my parents, Lindsey and Christopher Drake."

"Nice to meet you!" Cassandra smiled and wished she had been able to come up with something about a thousand times less boring than, *Nice to meet you.*

"Mom, Dad, this is Cassandra—the friend I was telling you about."

"Daphne's new roommate," Lindsey said warmly, her tone implying that wasn't *all* she'd heard about Cassandra. Cass mentally gulped and wondered just how much she knew.

"The one on the soul-searching mission," Finn's father nodded, causing a swatch of silvery blonde hair to flop onto his forehead. Christopher Drake was a window into Finn's future—the picture of what his son would look like in another thirty years. And if his father was any indication, time would treat Finnegan Drake well.

Way to go, Mrs. Drake, Cassandra gave Lindsey silent kudos. Finn's father had kept the broad shoulders and slim hips of his youth, though he was a bit softer around the edges than Cassandra was sure he had been three decades ago. His blue eyes still twinkled and his hair was the same messy mop his son sported, although with quite a few more grays. He had a quick smile and an open manner that made Cassandra warm to him immediately, much as she had to his son. She felt her tension ease a little.

"So, Cassandra, how's the soul search going?" he asked, sounding just like Finn as everyone settled into their seats.

"I haven't found my calling yet, but I'm having a good time looking for it," Cassandra smiled. She liked the way he dove straight into the conversation without any awkward getting-to-know-you's.

"That's the most important thing." He nodded approvingly. "Enjoy the ride!"

"What kinds of things are you doing to help you find your calling?" Lindsay asked.

"Well, I'm not doing one particularly enlightening thing so much as I'm doing several *potentially* enlightening things," Cassandra answered, wishing she had a more substantial response. "I've been trying new things: Daphne's exercise classes, journaling, hiking…trying to take advantage of all the experiences the island has to offer."

"That sounds like a good start." Lindsay smiled.

"She paddled out with us to watch the manta rays feed," Finn put in.

"Wow." Chris sounded impressed.

"Hey, everybody." Drew wandered over to the table. "Finn, are these your parents?"

"Yeah—Drew, this is my mom and dad, Lindsey and Chris. Mom, Dad, meet Drew."

"Good evening Mr. and Mrs. Drake, I'll be your server this evening," Drew said, sounding politer and more professional than Cassandra had ever heard him.

"We were just telling them about how we took Cassandra out to watch the manta rays."

"Oh man, it was hilarious!" Drew nudged Cass with his elbow, his brief, shining moment of formality extinguished in a puff. "You should have seen her battling that surfboard! But honestly, for a novice, she did really well."

"Finnegan!" Lindsey scolded. "You took a novice out into open water?"

Finn looked sheepish but Drew went on, "No, she did great! But you should have seen the look on her face when the first ray came up from the deep. Priceless," he chortled, taking a pad and pencil out from the pocket of his black server's apron. "Can I start you off with anything to drink tonight?"

"Lindsey! Chris! My friends!" Andre boomed from across the restaurant. He made a bee-line for their table, nearly mowing down two servers and a frightened busboy as he strode purposefully toward them. Giving them each an enthusiastic hug and kiss on the cheek and speaking rapidly in his native language, he interrupted himself to smack Drew upside the head and say, "Why didn't you tell me they had arrived, eh?"

"I just found out they were here!" Drew said, ducking his head lest Andre decide to smack him again for not being more alert. "They're getting to know Cassandra."

"Ah, Cassandra," Andre said affectionately, coming around the table to rest his elbow on her shoulder. "My new hostess! Is she not a peach?"

"Oh, Cassandra's working for you?" Lindsey was delighted.

"Did I not mention that?" Finn asked.

"Shame on you, Finnegan!" Andre said darkly, muttering a curse in his native tongue. "How could you leave out that important fact?"

"We've *just* been getting introduced," Finn defended as Andre glared. "Cassandra was telling them about her different methods of searching for her life's true calling."

Everyone turned expectantly to Cassandra. Six eager pairs of eyes and ears, all watching and waiting to hear how she was fulfilling her goal of discovering her destiny.

"Well…" Cassandra began, at a loss of what else to say, "aside from the new experiences and adventures, I've also been eating a lot of great food— it's hard not to on this island—and I've been cooking quite a bit. It helps me relax and clears my head."

"Oh, you cook?" Lindsey sounded intrigued.

"Why did I not know this?" Andre demanded.

Uh-oh, Cassandra thought. The last thing she needed was to be grilled about her culinary skills (*Ha ha*, her frazzled mind paused to appreciate the pun) by a food critic and a gastronomic genius.

"Not professionally!" she answered quickly. "Not anything close to professionally!"

"But she's wonderful!" Daphne the traitor cut in. "I swear, I've never eaten so well at home in my life!"

"When she and I first met, she made me French toast that changed my life…I'll never be able to enjoy cereal again!"

Et tu, Finn?

"That's pretty high praise," Chris said.

"Why have I never gotten in on this?" Drew sulked.

"Because you're not invited to our apartment for dinner." Daphne shot him a withering look.

"Poor Drew," Lindsey sympathized.

"Cassandra, my dove, I knew you were beautiful and charming, but I had no idea you were also a goddess of the kitchen!" Andre beamed at her.

"I'm not!" Cassandra squeaked. "I just cook so I can eat!"

She's being modest," Daphne contradicted. "Cassandra, you should cook for them while they're in town!" she suggested, sounding thrilled.

That's it, Daphne, Cassandra thought, glaring mental daggers at her overly supportive roommate, *you're eating dry toast for the rest of the summer! No more Eggs Benedict for you, Benedict Arnold!*

"That's a great idea!" Finn agreed and Cassandra mentally cut him off of French toast for life. "You should show them what you can do! How about tomorrow night? We both have the night off—it would be perfect! Andre, can you make it tomorrow night?"

Finnegan Drake, you are on my list, Cassandra brooded.

"For such an occasion, I would clear my schedule any night of the week," Andre pledged. "But for now, I must leave you. I have a shirking busboy to terrorize.

Nico!" he yelled as he walked away, scaring the pants off a dark-haired boy who had been lounging by the entryway eating mints rather than refreshing customer's water glasses.

"Glad it's not me," Drew said. "Now, about those drink orders…" he began making the rounds of the table.

"That's settled then," Finn declared. "Tomorrow night, let's say seven o'clock? Daphne, is it alright if we all come over to your place?"

"Absolutely! But I'm sorry, I won't be able to join you. I have a date tomorrow night!"

"A date?" Drew's head shot up from his writing pad.

"Feel free to use our apartment, though!" Daphne said, ignoring him. "We have more space."

"If you're not going to be there, Daphne, do you want us to postpone?" Lindsey asked.

Or cancel, Cassandra thought.

"No, don't worry about it! There will be plenty of chances for us to get together before you leave!"

"Cass, if Daphne's not going to be around, I can come over early and help with prep work," Finn offered.

"Sure!" Cassandra said. "An extra pair of hands is always helpful."

You cornered me into this, Finn, and if the meal is a fiasco, I'm taking you down with me!

"Who are you going on a date with?" Drew demanded, sticking to the essentials and scowling at Daphne.

"If you must know, Drew, I'm going out with a man I met at the grocery store. He seems very nice."

"The grocery store?" Drew said, disgusted. "Who asks a woman out at the grocery store?"

"As opposed to the oh-so-romantic bars you hang around in?" Daphne shot back.

"I bet he was just hanging around the produce section, waiting for a hot girl to show up so he could make a comment about her melons."

"Yes, because that would have worked on me." Daphne rolled her eyes. "Not everyone flirts like a twelve-year-old boy, Andrew. Some men evolve as they get older. Stewart and I—"

"Stewart?" Drew was appalled. "Please don't tell me you're going out with a guy named *Stewart*!"

"There's nothing wrong with the name Stewart!" Daphne sounded irritated.

Finn's parents exchanged glances and Cassandra gulped down her water, wishing there was alcohol in it.

"I bet by the end of the night you'll be calling him Stewey," Drew made a face. "And he'll be calling you something nauseating like Daphy-doo."

"Because he's a four-year-old naming a Loony Toons stuffed animal? I don't think so. Don't you have work to be doing, Drew?"

"Have fun on your date, Daphy-doo," Drew called over his shoulder and went to take their orders to the kitchen.

The rest of the table lapsed into uncomfortable silence until Finn's mom said, "So...that's Drew?"

"That's a troglodyte," Daphne said flatly. "But anyway," she said, shaking off the unusual irritability, "like I was saying, feel free to use our apartment tomorrow!"

"Are you sure you don't mind cooking, Cassandra?" Finn's mother asked.

"Of course not!" Cassandra said a bit too brightly.

What could go wrong cooking dinner for the food-critic-mother of a man I frenched a few weeks ago? And my boss. Who is a world-class chef. No pressure at all!

"There's no need to be intimidated," Lindsey said as if she could hear Cassandra's thoughts. "I'm not always in food-critic mode. Heck, if I can eat the food Finn's father makes for me, I can eat anything!"

Chris nodded good-naturedly. "I'm a terrible cook," he admitted. "I've found at least eight different ways to destroy boxed brownies."

"But he tries, and sometimes his experiments yield really interesting results," Lindsey's voice was affectionate. "Like the apple omelet you made that time. That…had character," she finished diplomatically.

"I think it was the bologna chunks that really killed it," Finn's dad said sadly.

"It was a unique breakfast," Lindsey remarked. "In the end, he insisted on taking me out instead. I think we got waffles."

"Well, that's a happy ending to any story," Cassandra said. "You can't go wrong with waffles!"

"Ha!" Chris challenged. "Try putting the syrup *into* the batter. Things will go wrong."

"Oh," Cassandra said sympathetically.

"Yeah," he agreed. "But that's the beautiful thing about marrying a food critic! I don't have to cook, she doesn't have to cook, and we get amazing food all the time. I planned that well."

"Oh, right, you planned it," Lindsey scoffed fondly. "You planned stepping on my foot as I was coming out of a coffee shop and making me spill hot tea all over you?"

"It was all part of a master scheme to get you to go out with me." He winked at Cassandra. "And it worked. Now here we are, twenty-six years of marital bliss later." He spread his hands as if to single-handedly take credit for the last two and a half decades. "Just like I planned."

"I don't think you can take credit for planning kismet, honey," Lindsey said. "The universe might strike you down."

"So, Aunt Lindsey," Daphne said, switching topics, "how was Nice?"

"Nice, as always!" Lindsey quipped, and then launched into details about where they stayed.

The conversation flowed from there, and Cassandra was grateful for the shift away from her feeble attempts to find personal fulfillment. She swapped stories with Finn's parents about the various regions in France they had all traveled to, and they were delighted to be able to practice their French with her. She listened to tales of their adventures and laughed, soaking up stories and enjoying getting to know Lindsay and Chris and the insight they provided into her two closest friends on the island.

At the end of the evening, they both hugged her goodbye and Lindsey said, "It was so nice to meet you, Cassandra! I'm so looking forward to dinner tomorrow!"

"Likewise," Chris said. "And if you're not sure what to make, I can recommend a bologna omelet that will knock your socks off." He winked, and Lindsey elbowed him in the ribs.

"I'll remember that," Cassandra laughed, "but I have one or two things in mind already."

"You're missing out." He shook his head sadly.

They said their goodbyes and Cassandra and Daphne began the walk home.

"That went well!" Daphne said. "I think they loved you!"

"Yeah, they're great," Cassandra declared. "Do you mind swinging by the grocery store on the way home? I'd like to pick up a few things for tomorrow."

"Sure!" Daphne said.

"So, tell me about your date..." Cassandra said in a sing-song voice. "What's he like?"

"Well," Daphne said, and launched into a detailed explanation of everything she knew about grocery-store-Stewart, the Casanova of aisle six.

Cassandra swooned at all the romantic moments of the meet-cute, absentmindedly planning her menu at the same time. By the time they got home, she felt almost prepared. She still felt the night had the potential for disaster, but at least she had a plan and a well-stocked kitchen. She couldn't ask for more than that.

Chapter Sixteen

At five o'clock the next day, Finn walked into the apartment to find Cassandra singing along to *Hit Me with Your Best Shot* and filling a saucepan with water.

Pat Benatar, eat your heart out.

Cassandra poked her head around the corner from the kitchen and brightened when she saw him. Turning down the music, she said, "Hey! I'm glad you're here—did you get my message about the cognac?"

"Yup," he held up a bottle he had dug from the depths of the well-stocked liquor cabinet Andre had left behind in the bungalow before he rented it to Finn.

"Fantastic!" she said as he came into the kitchen and set the bottle on the counter with a clank. "I didn't want to buy a whole bottle of brandy just for one meal, and the chicken really would be fine without it, but it adds complexity to the flavor when you flambé it."

"Sure," Finn said, not entirely following but figuring he would find out what that meant later. "So, what are we making?" He surveyed the vast array of ingredients, pots, pans, and prep bowls she had spread across the counter with alarm, wondering if he had gotten in over his head. He was, after all, his father's son, and while he had not discovered half a dozen ways to destroy brownies, he had burnt the hell out of them more times than he cared to remember.

"Coq au vin," she said, pulling half a pound of thick-cut bacon out of the fridge, revealing what looked like the murder scene of an unnaturally purple chicken in a large stock pot. Legs, thighs, wings, and what looked suspiciously like a back bone floated in a dark wine sauce along with chopped carrots, celery and onions.

"What the hell did you do to that bird?" he asked, staring at the mess in the pot.

"I marinated it!" Cassandra sounded defensive.

"You massacred it! Is that its spine?"

"Yes," Cassandra told him and he felt queasy.

"You don't have to eat it," she said, seeing the look on his face. "It's there for flavor right now, but we'll take it out at the end."

"You know, I think I might be a little out of my depth here," he confessed while she pulled out a large knife and began cutting the bacon into small chunks. "I have no idea how to make coq au vin."

"That's okay—I do," she assured him. "It's not as intimidating as it seems. And I'm starting you on onion duty, so I think you can handle that," she said, gesturing with the knife to a bowl full of very small, unpeeled root vegetables.

"Those are onions?" he asked, looking at the miniature veggies with caution.

"They're pearl onions. I thought you grew up around food..."

"I ate the food. I didn't make it…by the time it got to me, it was already on a plate. I never saw things in their natural forms."

"You'll be fine," she said. "Just cut off both ends and pierce a little x in the root side, but be careful that it doesn't slip when you do. Trust me, it only takes one bloody thumb to teach caution in the kitchen. Then fill that pot with water, bring it to a boil and add the onions for about thirty seconds. Strain them, dump them in cold water, and let them cool. Then you should be able to pinch them right out of the skins to peel them. Easy as pie."

"I've made pie," Finn said dubiously. "That's a misleading statement. But this sounds simple enough." He got to work on the tiny onions while Cassandra turned up the music and continued chopping the bacon into small strips.

"You're boiling bacon?" he asked, horrified, watching over her shoulder as she scraped the meat into another saucepan and filled it with water.

"Calm down, I'll fry it up in a minute. Whoa, watch the knife," she said as she whirled around to explain, not expecting him to be so close. "I'm just blanching it first so that the dish doesn't get too salty. You focus on your onions. Stay away from large blades."

"Alright, I trust you," he said, mollified, but leery of the knife. "Why do I cut an x in the bottom?"

"It keeps the onions from falling apart as they cook," she informed him, assembling a bouquet of different herbs and tying them together with cooking twine, fumbling with the knot and muttering darkly to herself when the twine frayed, then smiling in triumph when she got it to tighten anyway.

"What's that?" he asked.

"Are you going to be this curious the whole time?" she laughed. "It's a bouquet garni," she said, which told him nothing. "It's just fresh parsley, thyme, and a bay leaf, tied together. We'll use it in a while to flavor the sauce. I'm making one for the chicken and one for the braised onions, and I'm doing it now so we won't have to do it later once everything else is in the middle of cooking."

He nodded at the logic and efficiency of her reasoning and returned to his task, relaxing into the monotony of the action, singing along with Def Leppard, Joan Jett, and the Scorpions. By the time he had all the onions peeled in a bowl, Cassandra had blanched the bacon, patted it dry, fried it and removed it to a separate plate. She had also strained the wine from the marinade and set it aside in a separate bowl, patted the freakishly colored chicken dry, seasoned it with salt and pepper, and was in the process of browning it in the bacon grease. The amazing smells of bacon and chicken filled the kitchen, and the sound of sizzling accompanied the opening bars of Bonnie Tyler's *Total Eclipse of the Heart.*

Classic, Finn thought.

Cassandra said, "Yes!" and turned up the volume, whipping around to face him and using her tongs as a microphone to sing along with Bonnie Tyler about how lonely she gets when he's never comin' round.

He grinned and sang the male counterpart, watching her as she did, eyes bright with laughter, crazy loopy curls bouncing in a ponytail, lips quirked in a half-grin as she oversold the lyrics, electric and exuberant. Together they belted about falling apart every now and then, singing the chorus and laughing whenever one of them went for a high note and failed completely, singing with enthusiasm if not great skill. Cassandra kept one eye on the chicken, turning it when necessary, but for the most part she was engrossed in the song, hamming up the words, pointing her tongs at Finn and belting out that she needed him tonight. He laughed and sang along, the onions abandoned. During the musical interlude, he wowed her with his awesome air drum skills, and she doubled over laughing. As the song wound down, she clutched her tongs to her chest, face scrunched up with passion as she sang Bonnie Tyler's closing lyrics.

The song faded out and Finn attempted the last, impossibly high line telling bright eyes to turn around, grinning at Cassandra as she laughed and smiled happily back.

"That is a fantastic song," she said, turning the music back down to a reasonable volume. "I love that you know it!"

"Everybody loves that song," he said.

"My last boyfriend didn't," Cassandra said. "He thought 80's music was cheesy." She snorted and shook her head, turning back to the chicken to see that it was browning evenly.

This was the first time she had ever mentioned an ex and Finn felt a twinge, which was ridiculous.

Don't be stupid, he told himself. *Of course, she's had boyfriends. You are not jealous.*

Still, he had the unreasonable urge to go find this musically challenged ex-boyfriend and punch him in the face. He set the feeling aside and said, "I've finished peeling the onions. Now what do you have for me?"

"I'll have you start braising them in just a minute, but this chicken looks like it's about ready, so for now can you help me with the flambéing?"

"Sure," he said. "What do we do?"

"Well, if you can get the cognac for me, we're going to set the chicken on fire," she said matter-of-factly, in the same tone she would have used to say, "We're going to roast it in the oven."

"What?" Finn asked, alarmed.

"Oh, it's fine!" she said. "It's fun! Of all the fires I've started, flambéing has never been the cause."

"That's good," Finn said. Then the other shoe dropped. "Wait, what?"

Cassandra waved her hands to brush aside his concerns. "Just measure out a quarter cup while I find a lighter."

"Somebody's going to lose their eyebrows..." Finn sounded nervous.

"Then don't stick your face in the flames," Cassandra said reasonably. "But as far as fire goes, this is relatively cool," she assured him. "People run it over their hands and along tablecloths for party tricks. It's not that dangerous. Seriously, though, don't stick your face in the flame," she repeated.

She pulled a lighter from a drawer and asked, "Ready?"

"What do I do?" he said, slowly edging over to the pan.

"Just dump in the cognac, step back, and I'll do the rest," she said, gripping the handle of the pan.

Finn poured the liquid over the chicken, leaping back as it began to sizzle and pop, then Cassandra angled the pan, held the lighter just over the steaming brandy and *whoosh*! Finn jumped about a foot in the air as a giant ball of blue and orange flame jumped equally high out of the pan.

"Whee!" Cassandra said excitedly, shaking the pan to subside the flame. "Isn't that a blast?"

"That's one way to put it," Finn said, checking to see that she was un-singed, sniffing the air for the smell of burnt hair. All he could smell was the delicious scent of chicken frying in the skillet. "What the hell does that do for the chicken?"

"Well, for starters it's fun!" Cassandra said, gleefully shaking the pan back and forth. "Also, the extra heat from the flame produces a caramelizing effect and un-sticks all the brown bits at the bottom of the pan so that they can be incorporated into the sauce. You know how when you brown up bacon or any other meat, it leaves all that crunchy brown residue in the bottom of the pan?"

"Yeah," Finn said.

"That's called *fond*. Flambéing helps free up all that flavor from the fond and it gets mixed in with the rest of the dish. Overall, you get a richer, more complex taste. It's not a completely necessary step, but you get to play with fire and in the end, the meal is all the better for it," she finished with a satisfied smile. "Can you hand me that bowl of wine we strained out from the marinade? We're ready for it now."

She dumped the deep red liquid into the pan, then supplemented with chicken broth until the meat was covered. "While I'm doing this," she said, "you can braise the onions. Just melt a couple tablespoons each of butter and olive oil over medium heat and add the onions. Roll them around for a while to make sure they brown evenly, then dump that chicken stock I've set aside over them and add a bouquet garni. Cover and simmer, and they should be done by the time the chicken is."

She explained all of this as she added garlic, tomato paste and the other bouquet of herbs to the chicken and wine mixture, then set a lid on the pan to let it simmer.

"Now we wait," she said once he had the onions swimming in a gently bubbling pool of chicken stock.

She pulled another bottle of wine from the wine rack and reached for the corkscrew. "The hard part is over—we just need to let everything cook for forty-five minutes to an hour, then I'll have you sauté the mushrooms while I thicken up the sauce and we'll be good to go! Thank you," she said when he handed her two wine glasses. "And thank you for your help tonight! I would have been frantic if I had to do it all on my own!"

"You seem pretty capable without me," he said, taking the generously portioned glass she held out for him.

"It's all about timing," she said, wandering in the direction of the living room. "It would have been a pain to have to prepare the main dish and worry about the garnishes as well. I could have done it but it would have been way more stressful. You helped me stay relaxed. And it was fun!"

"It was," he said, joining her on the couch, being careful not to brush her leg with his. "I'm not much of a chef, so this was a new experience for me."

"You were a natural." She saluted him with her wine glass.

They spent the next forty-five minutes in companionable conversation, talking and laughing, sipping wine and swapping food stories while the familiar hits of Duran Duran, Billy Idol, and the Eurythmics floated from the kitchen.

Finn felt completely relaxed, giving in to the intoxicating combination of good music, good wine and good company. Cassandra chatted away about a cherry glazed duck she had tasted during her stay in France, ("I swear, I wanted to find the chef and propose on the spot!"), and Finn watched her talk, once again enjoying the way she seemed to speak with her entire body—graceful, long-fingered hands flying; curly, golden-red hair bouncing; wide, expressive eyes glinting with amusement. She was poetry in motion.

Wow, that's cheesy, he thought. *I must be getting tipsy.*

Cassandra glanced at the lime green sunburst clock hanging over Daphne's bookshelf

"Oh, we should get going," she said, downing the last of her wine. "We've got a few minutes left before we need to check on the chicken and the onions, but there are a couple of things to prep first. Could you wipe down and de-stem the mushrooms while I make the beurre manié?"

"The what?" he asked, dumping the mushrooms from the paper bag on the counter.

"It's just flour and butter mixed together. The French use it a lot as a thickening agent in sauces."

"Sure they do," Finn said. "What did you want me to do here?"

"Just use a damp paper towel to wipe down the mushrooms, then pull out the stems and we'll sauté the caps before we're ready to plate everything up."

Finn started on the fungi, singing along to *Golden Years* with David Bowie, while Cassandra lifted the lid off the large stockpot that held the simmering chicken, which smelled phenomenal.

"Thanks for doing the mushrooms," she said, giving everything a stir. "They freak me out."

"Mushrooms freak you out?"

"They have gills!" she said, wrinkling her nose. "It's creepy. And colonies of mushrooms are connected underground…did you know that? It's just one mutant organism with bulbous, creepy, gill-studded protrusions sticking up out of the ground! Tell me that doesn't sound disgusting."

"You have some very weird phobias, Dillon," he said, wiping dirt off a bulbous gill-studded protrusion.

"I'm not afraid of them," she corrected. "They just make me uncomfortable."

"Whatever you say," he said, humoring her.

"I'm going to give the chicken a few more minutes," she said, refilling their wine glasses and boosting herself up onto the counter beside him, kicking her feet against the cabinets and watching him work.

"And you say you're not a chef!" she said as he tossed the last mushroom cap into a bowl and discarded the stems in the trash. "Look at you, de-stemming mushrooms like a champ," she beamed at him over her wine glass.

A white streak of flour stood out on her cheek. He crossed his eyes and threw a mushroom cap at her, hitting her square in the chest. She stuck her tongue out at him and he lost his train of thought remembering what she could do with that tongue and then she popped the mushroom into her mouth.

"So you eat mushrooms even though you're afraid of them?" he asked, trying not to stare at her lips.

"Not afraid," she emphasized. "And yes, I eat them. I just try not to think too much about it."

"You're a nut job." He shook his head.

"You like me anyway."

"This is true," he conceded.

In the background, Heart had started to sing *Alone*, and Cassandra said, "Ooh, turn it up!" sliding off the counter and bounding over to the radio to crank up the volume. When she came back, Finn grabbed her hand and twirled her around. The electric guitar blared and the chorus began and Cassandra sang that she'd always gotten by on her own. He pulled her to him and she fell against his chest, smiling, singing that she'd never really cared until she met him.

His hands were on her hips and her arms slid around his neck and they began to move to the rhythm of the music, smiling into each other's eyes until the chorus faded and the music slowed and suddenly Finn was aware of everywhere their bodies touched—the gentle pressure of her hands on the back of his neck, the soft curve of her breast against his chest, the sway of her hips as they rocked in time with his. The smile faded from her face and the laughter in her eyes was replaced by heat. It felt so good to have her pressed against him that Finn forgot that he had agreed to stay away from her…he only thought about how soft she was under his hands, how eagerly she had responded when he had kissed her on that cliffside, how much he wanted to do it again.

The warmth of the kitchen had flushed her cheeks, still smudged with flour. Without thinking, Finn reached up to brush the powder off with his thumb, and he prolonged the touch, slowing his movements and trailing his hand across her cheek and down her neck, hearing her breath catch in her throat. Somewhere far in the distance, the plaintive voice of Ann Wilson sang about how long she's wanted to touch someone's lips and hold them tight.

Their eyes held for a long moment and the heat rose, and finally, Finn bent his head to her neck, trailing his lips across her throat as she tilted her head back and sighed, eyes closed, lips parted. Slowly, he worked his way to her mouth, feeling her breath deepen and her body arch into him. The scent of coconut lingered on her skin and Finn breathed her in, loving how yielding she was under his hands. Sliding his palm to the small of her back to bring her closer, Finn moved his lips to hers, kissing her slowly, deeply, stroking the inside of her mouth with his tongue, making her shiver, then kissing her harder, rougher, with an intensity that built with each shuddering breath. All his resolutions to stay away from her disappeared, replaced by the need to have as little space between them as possible. He craved her after all this time of having her near, talking, laughing, smiling at him with that lush mouth—and after weeks of denying himself, he finally let himself give in.

He bit her lip and she moaned, clinging to him, and he backed her up against the cabinets, boosting her onto the counter and digging his fingers into her ponytail, pulling her head back to bite her neck while she wrapped her legs around him and dug her fingernails into his shoulders. Her fingers tangled in his hair and she yanked his head back up to her mouth, tightening her legs around his hips to bring him closer and he pressed into her, cupping her rear end with his hands and angling his hips to pull her tight against him, making her suck in her breath and bite down hard on his shoulder. His hands reached for the button on her jeans and he slid the zipper down and the kitchen timer went off with a beep.

"Fuck," Finn said as she jumped and pulled away, breathing heavily, lips red, pupils dilated, looking hot and dazed, jolted out of the heat. *Alone* had given way to *Video Killed the Radio Star*, and Cassandra laughed and let her head fall back against the cupboards as she came back down to earth.

"Fuck," she agreed.

Chapter Seventeen

"I have to finish the chicken," Cassandra said. *Or not. Touch me again.* She firmly shoved the thought aside, determined to be a stronger person now that her brain wasn't being scrambled by Finn's hands on her body.

"Another few minutes won't kill it," Finn said, leaning in towards her and she thought, *Yes, please,* but she put up her hands.

"In another few minutes we would have been naked." Her brain swerved at the thought but she ignored it and got down from the counter, shivering as her body slid against his.

"That would have been bad," she said shakily, moving to the stove and taking the lid off the stockpot to survey the chicken. It looked and smelled magnificent.

"I don't know." Finn's eyes followed her, hot and dark, but he didn't reach for her again.

She was grateful for that. Cass didn't think she had enough resolve to deter him twice in one night.

"I think it could have been pretty incredible," he said.

"Your parents are going to be here any minute!" Cassandra reminded him, removing the chicken from the pot and setting it aside on a separate platter. "Not to mention our boss," she said, stirring in chunks of the butter mixture to complete the sauce.

"I'll call them—tell them we're running late."

"You will not!" Cassandra said, stirring faster to stop herself from saying, *Great idea, call them now. Use my phone!* "That timer was a sign from the universe, telling me to keep my head on straight."

"What does the universe have against great sex?" Finn asked, sounding irritated.

"Nothing!" Cassandra squeaked, manically stirring in the last of the butter and testing the sauce with the back of a spoon to see if it was thick enough to coat it. *Perfect.* "It's just not crazy about major life decisions being made in a haze of lust."

"Bullshit," Finn said, and Cassandra turned to glare at him. "Look, Cassandra, I respect the fact that you want to make decisions without being swayed by anyone else's agenda. And I'm trying to give you your space, but you can't keep whipping me around like this, kissing me back and then pushing me away and saying, 'We can't do this! It's a mistake!' If that's the way you feel then you should slap me silly and tell me to back off when I try to kiss you, not wrap your arms around my neck and stick your tongue down my throat!"

Cassandra narrowed her eyes, angry because he had a point. But there was no way in hell she was going to take all the credit for this.

"Listen, you," she said, pointing her spoon at him, "I am not the only one to blame here! I've made it very clear what my stance is on both physical and romantic involvement this summer, and you keep coming at me anyway. I'm sorry if I respond in the heat of the moment— I'm not dead, for heaven's sake—but when I come to my senses, I'm going to remember my priorities and they do not include you." She winced inwardly as her last sentence cracked the air like a whip and a muscle twitched in Finn's jaw.

Maybe that was a little harsh, she thought.

Cassandra had never seen Finn mad before and she didn't like it now. It seemed unnatural.

"That came out kind of severe," she said, ready to attempt some damage control, but the doorbell rang and she said, "Shit! They're here! Can you please just answer the door and try not to look like you want to bash me over the head with that skillet? I have to sauté these mushrooms and pretend like everything is fine so we can throw a lovely dinner party for your parents and it is going to be delightful," she said firmly.

"This is not over," he said, going to let his parents in.

"Surprise!" Drew said when Finn opened the door. He stood on the doorstep, grinning nonchalantly and holding a bottle of wine.

"What the hell?" Finn said.

"I'm here for the dinner party," Drew said, moseying into the living room. "Hey Cass," he waved. "I heard such great things about your culinary skills last night, I thought I'd pop by and see if you had room for one more. I brought wine!" he said, offering the bottle to Finn.

"Are you sure you're not here because you want to spy on Daphne and her date?" Cassandra asked, peering around the door from the kitchen, suspicious.

"What?" Drew looked offended. "That's ridiculous! Daphne is a grown woman and she can make her own terrible decisions about twits in grocery stores. I came to check out your skills and to get to know Finn's parents better! I barely got to meet them last night."

"Uh-huh." Cassandra was not convinced. "I wouldn't expect Daphne home any time soon. They met for happy hour at five, but she was pretty excited about this date. I wouldn't wait up for her if I were you," she said, giving Drew a sidelong glance.

"Whatever," Drew said, going for casual indifference and missing. "I'm just here for the food. Does it throw off your portions if I crash your party?"

"Not at all," Cassandra said gallantly. "We made plenty. Do you think your parents will mind, Finn?"

"No," Finn said shortly, and Cassandra shot him a look.

Drew looked back and forth between the two of them, picking up on the tension for the first time. "Are you guys okay?" he asked. "Did I interrupt something here?"

"Not at all," Cassandra said again, brushing the question aside. "Drew, if you want to open your wine, we can let it breathe before everyone else gets here. Finn, will you set the table? I'm almost done here. I just need to finish the mushrooms and boil up some noodles to serve as a bed for the chicken."

Finn said, "Of course," with polite detachment and Drew's eyes darted curiously from Finn to Cassandra before rummaging around for the corkscrew.

"So, who is this clown Daphne's seeing?" Drew asked offhandedly. "It's probably a pity date, right?"

"Certainly not," Cassandra said crushingly. If Drew was going to skirt around his feelings for Daphne and then take potshots at the men she dated, Cassandra wasn't going to make it easy for him. "And based on what Daphne's told me, he's definitely not a clown or a twit. He's a highly successful architect who's in town because he's helping to renovate one of the cathedrals on the island. I forget which one. Apparently he sculpts, rock climbs, plays piano, and was a tennis pro in college. He seems like quite a catch," she finished, twisting the knife a little. Drew was being a jerk, expecting Daphne to fall into bed with him just because he showed interest and then fooling himself into thinking that his attraction to her was purely physical. Cassandra felt no pity for him.

"Trust me, there's something deeply wrong with Stewart," Drew guaranteed. "Nobody's that perfect."

"Daphne also mentioned he was six foot four and built like a Greek statue," Cassandra embellished and watched Drew's brow furrow and jaw tighten.

There. That will teach you to take someone like Daphne for granted, Cassandra thought while he sulked.

Five minutes later, the table was set for six—in the center lay a large platter of chicken on a bed of noodles, swimming in a gorgeous deep purple wine sauce, and garnished with perfectly braised onions and sautéed mushrooms. Earlier in the day, Cassandra had prepared a tossed salad and picked up two loaves of crusty bread from the market so her guests could soak up every last drop of delicious sauce. The wine was decanted and everything was in order, just in time to hear a knock on the door.

"We're here!" Lindsey smiled when Finn opened the door. "Is that Drew?" she asked, looking past her son's shoulder into the living room.

"Yes," Finn said, stepping aside to let them in. "He crashed the party because he hasn't gotten to try Cassandra's food yet."

"More like he wanted to check out Daphne's date and see what his competition is," Chris chuckled as they filed inside and Drew looked affronted once again.

"I hope you don't mind that I invited myself along," he said, recovering.

"Of course not. The more, the merrier!" Lindsey said. "Cassandra, the house smells amazing! And look at that," she said, when she saw the table. "Everything is gorgeous!"

"And you helped with all this, Finn?" Chris said, casting a doubtful look at his son. "I'm not sure I believe it…after all, the apple doesn't fall far from the tree." He ruffled Finn's hair.

"He was an excellent help," Cassandra defended, not meeting Finn's eye. "He was in charge of mushrooms and onions. And he helped me flambé!"

"And the apartment's still standing!" Chris said, suitably impressed. "Well done, you two."

"So, everything is ready to go," Cassandra said, offering the two newcomers wine

"We're just waiting on Andre and then we can eat!"

Right on cue, there was another knock at the door, and Finn opened the door to let Andre inside.

"Cassandra, my peacock, this place smells divine," he said as he shuffled in. "Andrew!" he muttered a curse in his native tongue. "What are you doing here, you miscreant?"

"He crashed the party," Finn summed up.

"Spying on Daphne," Andre said knowingly, and Drew said, "Oh, come on!" and downed his wine.

"Ah, and what do we have here?" Andre asked, handing Finn his coat and eyeing the beautifully adorned table.

"Coq au vin," Cassandra answered, suddenly feeling self-conscious. The dinner looked wonderful and smelled even better, but when faced with a first-class chef and well-established food critic, she began to doubt the relative success of her entrée.

"Coq au vin?" Andre raised his eyebrows and said with respect. "That's quite an undertaking."

"It was, but she handled it like a pro," Finn said, which, Cassandra thought, was pretty gracious considering the fight they'd just had. "But we'd better sit down and eat it before everything gets cold."

There was sense to this suggestion, but as they all took their places around the table, Cassandra thought, *I should have planned some sort of appetizer and aperitif...liquor them up a little before they had a chance to taste the main course.* At the same time, she knew she had nothing to worry about. This was a classic dish and she and Finn had executed it well. Everyone would love it.

"I would like to propose a toast," Andre said, raising his glass. "To old friends," he gestured to Lindsey and Chris, who raised their glasses in acknowledgement, "and to new," he saluted Cassandra, who smiled back fondly. "And to Cassandra!" he continued. "My darling little rabbit, who has prepared this lovely meal for us today."

"With help from Finn of course," Cassandra interjected.

"To Cassandra and Finn!" Andre amended. "For making this evening possible."

"Cassandra and Finn," the other three guests echoed, and then dug into the chicken.

"Oh my god," Lindsey said, perking up as she sampled the coq au vin. "Cassandra, this is wonderful!"

"Really excellent," Chris agreed.

Cassandra sighed as she took her first bite and experienced the dish for herself, tender chicken falling off the bone, beautifully caramelized onions lending their sweetness to the savory tang of the wine sauce, subtle herbs pulling the dish together in perfect harmony.

My god, this is better than sex, she thought, then flashed back to Finn's hand on her zipper, shoulders solid under her hands, his mouth hot on hers as he pressed into her, making her gasp, feeling him hard between her legs. *Well, maybe not quite.*

"It did turn out well," she said modestly.

"Well?" Lindsey repeated. "This is a triumph! What's your recipe?"

"Since this is a special occasion, I did take the time to do a few things that I wouldn't normally do if I were making this for myself," Cassandra admitted. "If I were by myself and craving coq au vin in the middle of the week, I probably wouldn't have bothered to marinade it overnight, or braise the onions rather than quickly sautéing them in the bacon fat, or use pearl onions instead of dicing up an everyday white onion.

Also, I don't often keep brandy in my liquor cabinet, so I would generally skip the flambéing. But all those extra steps help enhance the flavor and make for a more traditional dish."

"It definitely paid off," Chris complimented, sopping up sauce with a chunk of bread. "Where did you learn to cook?"

"I lived with a culinary student during my semester in Dijon. I learned a lot from her and she taught me quite a few traditional Bourgogne recipes. Before I studied abroad, I was a menace in the kitchen."

"Cassandra, angel, how could you have hidden this talent from me?" Andre accused.

"It's not really a talent," Cassandra said. "Just something that keeps me from going hungry."

"Not a talent?" Lindsey sounded shocked. "Cassandra, it's a gift! And I wouldn't say that unless I thought it was true. Andre, why aren't you training this girl?"

"It's a travesty!" Andre agreed. "A crime against humanity! I had no idea you had such abilities," he said, shooting another accusatory glare at Cassandra. "We must begin cultivating them immediately!"

"That's a great idea!" Finn exclaimed.

"No, no!" Cassandra panicked. The amount of damage she could do in a restaurant-grade kitchen was astounding. So many sharp knives and hot surfaces and people to accidentally injure…the mind boggled. "I'm not a chef. I just cook at home…in a controlled environment…where the potential stab victims are limited to just myself!"

"Nonsense!" Andre tut-tutted.

"This would be perfect for you," Finn argued.

"You should go for it, Cass," Drew spoke up. "This is some kick-ass chicken."

"Really, Cassandra, I think you've got something," Lindsey said. "If you're at all interested in a culinary career, you should let Andre work with you."

A culinary career? Cassandra considered it. She had never really thought about it before—her roommate had been the culinary whiz, not her—she cooked to relax, to unwind, to eat. Would she want to take an enjoyable hobby and turn it into a daily obligation? Wouldn't that take all the fun out of it?

She loved cooking—it cleared her head, focused her mind, allowed her to forget life's little troubles and concentrate solely on the task at hand. She loved following a challenging recipe to the letter or tweaking a well-known dish to see if she could improve it, loved that she could immediately enjoy the fruits of her labor—sometimes quite literally fruits—rather than slaving away at a project for hours and having nothing tangible to show for it. But would she want to do it for a living?

She thought about it. Getting paid to cook…huh. There were worse things. Going to a kitchen every day rather than an office…handling food rather than people or budgets or paperwork. That could be good.

"What the hell," she said. "I would love to work with you, Andre! Just remember I have absolutely no professional experience!"

"Not to worry, ducky, we'll get it all sorted out," Andre assured her. "Why don't I come by at the end of the week and we'll cook something together, eh? See what we've got to work with?"

"Sure," Cassandra said, repressing her fear of working alongside Andre in a kitchen.

They set a date for the end of the week and the conversation moved in new directions, flowing from one topic to another, the sound of laughter and the clinking of silverware punctuating the evening. After the chocolate mousse that Cass had prepared earlier in the day had been finished and coffee had been served, the late evening sun was sinking low in the sky and the three older guests made their way toward the door.

"Thank you for a lovely evening, Cassandra." Lindsey hugged her as Chris gathered their coats. "We'll have to do it again!"

"Goodbye, cherub." Andre pinched her cheek. "Until Sunday."

Chapter Eighteen

Cassandra closed the door behind her with a sigh. "Well, that was interesting. Did I just agree to cook with Andre on Sunday?"

"Yes, you did," Drew stretched out on the couch, crossing his arms behind his head and propping his feet up on the coffee table. "Better you than me. Andre is terrifying in the kitchen. Good luck with that."

"I think it's great," Finn said, shooting a glare at Cass. "This could be exactly what you've been waiting for. Maybe you'll find your calling and be able to move on with the rest of your life," he said pointedly.

"Let's not get carried away here. It's just one dinner." She glared meaningfully back. "Not the rest of our lives."

"Maybe one dinner can be the start of something bigger." Finn scowled.

"And maybe dinner is just dinner and people shouldn't get all worked up over it."

"I thought dinner was awesome," Drew said, totally missing the tone of their conversation. "Solid choice, Cass. You can cook for me any time."

"Thanks, Drew, I'll keep that in mind."

"It's getting kind of late…" Drew eyed the clock. "Daphne's date must be going well. I'll bet Stewey's charming the socks right off her."

"If you're lucky, that's all he's charming off her. But it's barely nine thirty…it's still light outside! If you plan on hanging around until she gets home just so you can spy on her, you might be in for quite a wait."

"They've been gone over four hours!" Drew said. "Not that I care, but how much talking can you really do on a first date?"

"I don't know, but if the date's going well enough, you can do quite a lot of not-talking."

Drew frowned. "Daphne wouldn't sleep with a guy on the first date."

Whether Daphne would or not, it would serve Drew right to have his confidence shaken a little.

"There are plenty of other things you can do on a first date. And Stewart didn't sound like your run-of-the-mill kind of guy. There are some men you bend the rules for."

Drew looked irritated and Cassandra was pleased until Finn said, "Is that so?" and then she thought, *Oh, for heaven's sake!*

She shot him a look that said, *Not now.* She was in no mood to continue their fight with Drew providing commentary from the couch.

"That's an interesting point," Finn said, ignoring her warning look. "When is it acceptable for women to break their own dating rules?"

"When the situation calls for it," she said vaguely.

"Like when there's a particularly strong attraction and undeniable chemistry? When she meets someone who she connects with on every level?"

"Maybe," Cassandra said between her teeth.

"I don't think Daphne's going to be getting any of those things from Supermarket Stewart." Drew scowled at nothing in particular, still completely oblivious.

"I'm going to wash the dishes," Cassandra said, giving up on both of them.

"I'll help." Finn followed her into the kitchen.

"Not necessary," she said as sweetly as possible, giving him a look that said, *I will break a plate over your head.*

"I insist," he replied gallantly, glaring at her as if to say, *Tough. We have unfinished business.*

"Do you guys need a hand in there?" Drew called from the living room.

"No!" they said together.

"We've got it, thanks!" Finn added.

"Suit yourselves." They heard Drew rummaging around in a cupboard and soon he piped up, "Do you guys mind if I stick in a movie?"

"Make yourself at home," Cassandra called back, filling the sink with water and pulling on a bright yellow pair of rubber gloves.

A moment later, the opening credits of Star Wars blared from the next room and Cassandra began scrubbing plates in determined silence while Finn stood next to her with a towel, looking broody.

Once he was sure Drew was fully engrossed in the movie, he turned to her and said in a low voice, "So Daphne's allowed to make exceptions but you're not?"

"I was being flippant to annoy Drew and you know it. That boy is entirely too comfortable with the idea that Daphne will get bored with any other man she meets and eventually crawl into bed with him. Somebody needs to light a fire under his ass." Cassandra kept her eyes firmly on the saucy dishes in front of her, not inviting any further conversation.

"Maybe you were being flippant, but I think you believe what you said: some things are worth bending the rules for."

"I'm not bending anything for you, Finn. It's not fair of you to ask me to."

"It's not like I'm asking you to give anything up. You want this just as much as I do," he insisted.

"That doesn't mean I'm going to do anything about it!" She dropped the plate back into the water with an irritated splunk, goaded into facing him and placing a soapy gloved hand on her hip. "We have boundaries for a reason. I did not invite you here expecting this to happen—you were here to make chicken!"

"Whatever." He waved his hands as if this was a technicality.

"No, not *whatever*," Cass argued. She turned back to the sink and renewed scrubbing with vigor. "We agreed to be friends. You offered to help me with dinner. I accepted. We were having fun. You couldn't let that be enough. You're not pinning this on me," she dropped the plate in the dish strainer with a severe clack and moved onto the cookware.

"So this is my fault?"

"Yes." She furiously scrubbed at a pot, knowing that this was a massive simplification, but too annoyed with him to be fair.

"I misread the signals," he continued flatly.

"There were no signals!"

"Oh, come on, Cassandra!" he said, toweling off the last plate and adding it to the stack in the cupboard. "There's something between us! Trying to pretend there isn't is just idiotic."

"Idiotic?" she said dangerously, raising her eyebrows and turning to face him, frying pan in hand, dripping soap and bacon grease onto the floor. She thought about smacking him over the head with it.

The expression on Finn's face morphed from anger to hesitation. He took half a step back and Cassandra realized she was wielding the pan like a club. She lowered it but took a threatening step towards him and said again, "Idiotic?"

"Yes." Finn looked nervous but he tightened his jaw and went on. "We have a connection and you're trying to pretend it doesn't exist. You're skirting reality, just like you always do."

Cassandra widened her eyes and seriously almost whacked him with the pan. "I beg your pardon?"

He was definitely nervous now, but also resolute. "You've said it yourself, Cassandra. You're great with things in theory, but not so much in practice. I think you're hiding behind your theories about destiny and the universe and life-callings so you can avoid what's really going on here."

"And what's really going on here, Finn?" she asked, unsettlingly quiet.

"You have feelings for me," he faltered, lame in the face of her unwavering disapproval.

"You unbelievable *ass*!" she said, taking another step toward him, simmering anger now boiling over into fury. "Whether I have feelings for you or not, do you seriously think that's more important than everything else I'm working toward this summer? Do you think that by giving into you, all my questions about what I want out of life will just disappear? You think that I'm running away from reality just because I'm refusing to settle into a relationship with you?" She jabbed him in the chest with the frying pan, leaving a long, wet smudge on his T-shirt. "Well, I hate to shatter your delusions of grandeur, bucko, but I've got a few other things on my plate right now."

"But you don't deny you have feelings for me," he pursued stubbornly.

"As I've said before, Finn, that's *not the point*!"

"That's ridiculous!"

"I'm home!" Daphne called from the front room, breezing through the door in a turquoise halter dress and purple shawl. "What the hell are you doing here?" she said, confronted with the form of Drew lounging on the couch.

"Oh, for heaven's sake!" Cassandra rolled her eyes and dropped the pan back in the sink, striping off her gloves and yelling, "Hi, Daphne! How did it go?" just as Drew replied indignantly, "I'm watching a movie!"

"We need to finish this," Finn said under his breath, grabbing her wrist as she walked by, but she shook her head and glanced pointedly at the other room where Daphne was saying, "Don't you have a TV at your own apartment?"

"I came by for dinner. Finn and Cass can't get enough of me, so I decided to stick around a while longer."

"That is in no way a fabrication of this evening's events," Cassandra said, crossing the living room to give Daphne a hug. "How did it go?"

"Wonderfully!" Daphne smiled. I'll tell you all about it later." She looked past Cassandra to stare angrily at Drew. "Did you come here to spy on me?"

"I just came for the food and entertainment," Drew held up his hands. "Why would I be spying on you?"

"You knew I had a date tonight."

"Oh, was that tonight?" Drew leaned back and grinned. "That's right, how was old Stewey?"

"Could I see you outside, please, Andrew?"

"You just got back from a date with another man and already can't wait to get me alone, huh, Daph? Was he that boring?" Drew asked sympathetically.

"Now." Daphne's tone brooked no nonsense.

The pair filed onto the porch and Daphne closed the door behind them with a firm click

Immediately, the muffled sound of arguing strained into the living room, Daphne's tone conveying unmistakable annoyance while Drew's occasional interjection sounded detached and vaguely amused.

That's not going to go well, Cassandra thought, then Finn said, "Where were we?" and she thought, *Damn it, neither will this.*

"We were just wrapping up because there's nothing left to discuss." Cassandra turned to see Finn looking mulishly at her from the kitchen doorway.

"The hell there isn't!" He stormed across the room, not stopping until he was standing right in front of her. "You want me, Cassandra," he said in an even tone. "We need to discuss that."

Cassandra glared up at him and took a deep breath. His face was inches from hers and she couldn't decide whether she wanted to kick him or rip his clothes off. She decided that the quickest way to end this conversation and avoid that decision altogether was honesty.

"If I say yes to you, I'll regret it," she said, feeling terrible when he looked like she had slapped him.

"I'm sorry, Finn, but it's true. Yes, I want you. Yes, I feel a connection with you. Yes, we might be good together. But if I say yes to you now, before taking the time to get my own life straightened out, I'll always wonder *what if*. If we stay together, the doubt and inevitable resentment will eventually weigh us down and tear us apart, and if we break up—for that, or any other reason—I'll feel like I threw away my best chance of finding myself by choosing you instead. Either way, we both lose."

Finn looked stricken. "You're serious."

"*Yes*," she said, exasperated. This is what she'd been trying to make clear for over a month now. But the irritation she had felt earlier in the conversation was ebbing away, replaced by sadness. He looked crushed and he had been nothing but sweet since she'd met him, and she had never wanted to hurt him but she had anyway and now she felt like hell.

"Well, I can't say you didn't warn me," he said, smiling with no humor whatsoever.

"Please, Finn, we've only known each other a month. Can't we just be friends for a while?"

"I'm not sure we can."

"Why not?"

"I don't know if I can handle being around you any more if I can't be with you."

"Are you giving me an ultimatum?" Irritation crept back into her voice. "Date you or lose you?"

"No." He sounded tired. "I'm just telling you how I feel. I'm sorry, Cass. If you're still sure that you need space to figure out what you want, I think I need to take some space of my own. I don't think we should see each other for a while."

The words settled over them like a wet, heavy blanket and Cassandra nodded, miserable.

"I guess that's fair," she said glumly. "If that's what you want."

"It's not what I want," he said, his voice hollow. "But I think it's for the best."

A silence stretched across the room. Finn and Cassandra stared at each other, finally at a loss for words.

"Ugh, good riddance!" Daphne said, coming back through the door alone and collapsing against it with a heavy sigh as she shut it firmly behind her.

"What's going on with you two?" she asked, looking quickly from Cassandra, eyes wide and glistening, to Finn, face wooden and jaw set.

"I was just leaving," Finn made his way to the door, carefully not looking at Cassandra. "Night, Daph."

"Good night," she looked up at him, confused. "You're not staying?"

"Nah, I should be heading out. I'll leave you two to your girl talk." He kissed her on the cheek. "See you tomorrow."

He walked out the door without a backward glance and Daphne shut it behind him, turning to Cassandra to ask, "What was that about?"

Cassandra sank down onto the couch, feeling tired and empty. "He left."

"Well, obviously," Daphne said, and then the other shoe dropped. "Wait, what do you mean?"

"He doesn't want to see me anymore."

"What?" Daphne sat down beside her. "That can't be right!"

"It is."

"What happened?"

"We kissed again. And then we fought. And now he thinks we should stay away from each other for a while." Cassandra blinked rapidly, feeling silly for getting emotional. This was what she wanted.

"Oh, Cass, I'm sorry!" Daphne put a hand on her arm. "Maybe he just needs to cool down for a while."

"No," Cassandra shook her head sadly. "But he's right. If I'm going to figure this out, I can't let myself get distracted. But then he comes around and we have so much fun together and I can't help but start to fall for him, then I push him away at the same time because that's not what I'm looking for. It's not fair to either of us. We'll be happier by ourselves for a while."

She blinked again, determined not to cry and Daphne laughed sympathetically and shook her head. "Oh, honey. You don't look happy."

"Maybe not right now," Cassandra sniffed. "But I will be. Anyway," she shook her head as if to clear away all thoughts of Finn. "How was your date? Tell me all about it!"

"It was awful!" Daphne slumped, and her shawl slipped from her shoulder.

"What?" Cassandra was shocked. "You said he was wonderful."

"Of course, I had to say that in front of Drew!" Daphne rolled her eyes. "I wouldn't give him the satisfaction of gloating when he heard that Stewart was a dud."

"What was wrong with him? He sounded so great!"

"On paper, he *is* great. Intelligent, handsome, successful, mature...but he was so boring! I swear, I almost fell asleep during the salad course."

"Salad course? I thought you went out for happy hour."

"That was the plan, but when we met up, he wanted to take me to this gourmet restaurant he had heard about. It was nice but it was so stuffy! And the food they were serving wasn't nearly worth the prices they were charging for it. But I got the feeling Stewart would be more at home with mediocre food in a chic setting than legitimately good food at a hole-in-the-wall."

"Was he snobby?"

"Not exactly. Just a little too...subdued. Proper. I thought it would be refreshing but instead he just bored me to tears. We didn't laugh once the entire time! He talked about buttresses for twenty minutes, Cass. Buttresses!"

"Oh, my."

"I know! Normally I love hearing people talk about their interests. And most of what he was saying should have been interesting! But the man cannot tell a story to save his life."

"But you were gone for five hours!"

"I know. Dinner lasted about two excruciatingly long hours and then he invited me back to his hotel room 'to show me sketches of the cathedral.' For most men, that would have been a ploy to get me into bed, but I think he actually meant it. I politely declined and told him I had some business to take care of at the studio."

"At seven o'clock on a Friday night?"

"In all honesty, there were some things that needed doing. Not necessarily tonight, but all the same, I figured if I was going to bother to make the excuse, I might as well follow up on it. I had him drop me off at the studio, we said a pleasant, boring goodnight, and I spent a couple of hours doing paperwork, preparing for my fall marketing campaign."

"Why didn't you come back to the apartment for dinner?"

"I had already eaten and I wanted to take some time to think. Your soul-searching has inspired me to take a closer look at my life."

"How so?" Cassandra asked, surprised.

Daphne took a deep breath. "All in all, I'm really proud of what I've accomplished so far. Figuring out my career was easy…I had a direction from an early age. When I was young, I was always petite and people assumed that because I was dainty, I wasn't strong or capable. Then in high school I started getting into Pilates and kickboxing and it changed the way I felt about my body. I wasn't just frail or willowy. I felt strong, inside and out.

"I knew I wanted to share that with other people—help them find their strength. So, after graduation, I got my certifications, studied up on entrepreneurship, and set about opening my own studio. I've known I wanted to settle here since middle school. It's just so beautiful and the people are wonderful! And I've done all that I set out to do—I'm established on the island, my business is doing really well between the locals and the tourists, and I love the relationships I've developed with my clients. It's romantic relationships that don't seem to be working out the way I want them to."

"Was Stewart really so bad that he made you question your entire love life?"

"No, Stewart was fine. In fact, I'm going out with him again next week. It might be fun," she rationalized when Cassandra raised her eyebrows. "I'm hoping he was just nervous on the first date and he'll loosen up a little next time. It didn't seem fair to give up on him after just one date."

"Fair enough."

"But he did make me question what I'm really looking for in a man."

"And what are you looking for?"

"I thought I was looking for a grown-up. Somebody responsible and independent and respectful. I've dated so many boys over the years—and they've been fun, I've had a lot of laughs—but I'm a driven person with goals and ambitions. I'm sick of dating men whose only motivations in life are to surf, drink, and have sex. And then I met Stewart and I thought, 'Finally, an adult, how exciting!' Then it turned out to be very, very boring."

"There have got to be men out there who are interesting *and* competent."

"Men like Finn."

"Daphne, Finn is your cousin."

"Not for me!" Daphne laughed and threw a pillow at Cassandra. "For you!"

"Oh," Cassandra chuckled. But then she sighed. "Daphne, we've talked about this."

"I know, I know!" The little brunette held up her hands. "I won't get into it. But just remember, Cass, there are plenty of people out there who would give anything for exactly the opportunity you're turning down. The chance to meet a good-looking, well-rounded, emotionally and intellectually capable man who thinks you're wonderful? Plenty of women would sign away their first born for someone like that. Just be sure you're not throwing it away because the timing is a little bit off."

"And you be sure you're not thinking of settling for a man who couldn't even keep you interested through dinner, let alone the rest of your life, just because you're tired of dating children."

"I wouldn't dream of it," Daphne said airily. "Now, what did you make for dessert, and is there any left?"

"Chocolate pots de crème, and yes!"

"Lead the way!" Daphne said. "Who needs men when you have chocolate?"

Chapter Nineteen

Cassandra woke Sunday morning from dreams of headless purple chickens dancing around, taunting her with carving knives and then trying to kiss her.

"Creepy," she said as she jotted the dream in her journal and got up to prepare for her lesson with Andre. Clearly, her subconscious was nervous about training with him.

Get a grip, she told herself. *There's nothing to be nervous about. The worst that could happen is that he tells you that you have no talent, and you won't be any worse off than you are now. In fact, you'll be better off because you'll be able to cross another option of the life path list for sure. So calm down and just have fun.*

When Andre arrived in the late morning, Cassandra had successfully put all her nerves all on simmer and was able to greet him with a broad smile.

"Cassandra! Hello, dew drop, are you ready to begin?" he asked, coming in with two armfuls of groceries. "I thought we'd prepare a pork roulade with a seared scallop appetizer and see how you fare."

"Sure!" Cassandra nodded too eagerly, feeling like a bobble head, and her heart pounded harder. She tamped down on her bubbling nerves—she could do this. "Are you thinking a beurre blanc for the scallops?"

Andre beamed at her. "Indeed, I am, you darling kumquat. Let's start by butterflying the pork loin."

Thirty minutes later, the stuffing was coming together and they were chatting away while Cassandra worked under Andre's close supervision.

"Did you always know you wanted to be a chef?" she asked him, stirring the Italian sausage she had added to the onions, fennel, and red pepper sautéing on the stove.

"Of course not!" Andre guffawed. "When I was three, I was going to be a pirate. At five, I was going to be an astronaut. When I was eight, the plan was to be a magic genie, and at ten, I wanted to be a meteorologist."

"A genie?"

"I thought it would be great fun to have the power to grant wishes. And don't you wish I would have figured it out?"

"That would have been pretty cool," Cassandra admitted, deglazing the pan with white wine when the fond on the bottom of the pan started to darken, and stirring to incorporate its flavor into the stuffing. "But the way you handle food is almost magic in itself."

"You're a sweet girl," Andre said, peering through his glasses over her shoulder.

"Beautiful! How much longer will you leave this to cook?"

"I figured a few more minutes will give the onions time to caramelize a bit more," she said, adding breadcrumbs to the pan.

Andre nodded approvingly.

Cass left the skillet for a moment to chiffonade the basil. "So how did you finally decide to open a restaurant?" she asked, cutting the herb into long, slim strips.

"I've loved food always, but I never thought I would make it my whole life."

Cassandra nodded, slicing away and then pausing to give the stuffing a quick stir. She could relate to that.

"But for my twenty-first birthday, my family took me out to a fancy restaurant to celebrate. The food was all presentation and price tag and no flavor, and I thought, 'Bah! I could do better than this!' So I did. Try to slice that a little finer…that's right! The kitchen was always the hub of the house when I was young—I grew up watching and helping mamma and nonna create dishes that were both beautiful and delicious, and the overly-priced, overly-garnished sludge they served in that so-called restaurant was an insult to my palate! I made it my mission to show the world what real food tastes like."

"And you did!" Cassandra said, removing the skillet from the heat and stirring in the stripped basil.

"Indeed. Perfect!" Andre sampled a bit of the filling. "Now, once this cools, let's spread it and roll up the pork. Do you know how to truss a roast?"

Once the pork was rolled into a nice, tight log, Cassandra struggled with the kitchen twine and Andre showed her how to bring one end of the small rope under the other side like the first step of tying a

                    Lanie Hartford

shoelace, then do it again once or twice for extra grip, securely holding the pork in place before completing a simple knot.

She seasoned the bundled pork all over with olive oil, salt, and pepper, and then used the same pan she had cooked the stuffing in to sear the meat on all sides, creating a beautiful golden crust on the outer flesh. The pork loin then went into the oven, fat-side up, roasting low and slow to keep the meat tender and juicy, while Cassandra and Andre cleaned up their prep dishes and got to work on the dressing for the scallops. Cassandra had learned this classic French butter sauce from her roommate in college, so she was confident in her ability, even though beurre blanc could be finicky. She had never made scallops, though, and she confessed this to Andre. He talked her through the steps, which turned out to be amazingly simple.

Cassandra set the first ingredients of her sauce to reduce—shallots, vinegar, white wine, and a splash of cream—then followed Andre's instructions to pat the scallops dry and remove the small side muscle. A pan went on the stove to get smoking hot, preparing for the arrival of the scallops, while she whisked cold chunks of butter, a couple at a time, into the reduced wine mixture to complete her sauce, which she set aside to stay warm. A splash of oil and a few minutes later, and she had a set of beautifully browned, perfectly crisp-on-the-outside and lusciously tender-on-the-inside scallops.

She drizzled the seafood with the velvety butter sauce and presented the plate to Andre, who eyed the dish with critical professionalism. They each speared a forkful of scallop, clinked them together in a mollusk-y *cheers*, and took a bite.

Wow, Cassandra thought, as the gentle tang from the sauce inundated her senses and the delicate texture of the scallop hit her tongue. If she were served this in a restaurant, she would be tempted to find the chef and kiss them full on the mouth.

"Gorgeous!" Andre praised, going back for another bite and scooping up more of the sauce. "Perfectly emulsified…a beautiful sear. Well done, crumpet!"

They ate the rest of the scallops, accompanied by a glass of white wine from the bottle that had been opened for the sauce, chatting away about their triumphant dish and swapping memories of favorite meals until it was time to take the pork out of the oven.

Cassandra checked the internal temperature with a meat thermometer—it was hovering right on the edge of one hundred thirty-five and one hundred forty degrees Fahrenheit, so she removed it from the heat, basted it with drippings from the pan, and stood back to admire her work.

"Very good, Cassandra!" Andre complimented as she began to clear away dishes. The pork needed to rest for ten to twenty minutes to allow the residual heat to fully bring the meat up to temperature, so she might as well clean up while she waited.

"Finnegan and Daphne were correct," Andre declared. "I believe you do have the makings of a fine chef! How about we start you off next week, say Tuesday, on a slow shift? You can come in between the breakfast and lunch rushes and do some prep work. We'll see how you do in a real restaurant setting."

Cassandra blinked. *Are you sure you trust me with that?* she wanted to say.

She was absolutely positive this was not how most people got their first job in a professional kitchen. Most people were probably actually *trained* before someone handed them a knife and said, 'Here, whip something up and we're going to charge those people out there to eat it.' But it seemed foolish and ungrateful to question Andre's offer, so she swallowed her doubts and said, "That sounds wonderful."

"Marvelous!" Andre clapped his hands once together and bounced on his heels. "Now that that's settled, I regret I must leave you."

"Aren't you staying for lunch?"

"Sadly not, lamb chop, I must return to my restaurant. Make sure the good-for-nothings I left in charge aren't burning the place to the ground. I will take a piece of this for the road, though! Maybe two." He winked.

They boxed him up a portion of the elegantly swirled pork loin, which he couldn't resist sampling, even though it had not yet fully rested. He proclaimed it a tour de force, and took one more slice for good measure.

"Thank you again, Andre, for everything," Cassandra said earnestly, walking him to the door.

"Not at all, rosebud, it was my pleasure! I will see you later this evening for your hostess shift, yes?"

"Yes," she assured him.

"Until then, Cassandra, my little cabbage, I bid you adieu," he said with a flourish.

"Au revoir, chef," Cassandra laughed and closed the door behind him.

Well, she thought, leaning against the doorway and smiling in the direction of the kitchen where her beautiful roulade lay. *Here we go.*

***

The following Tuesday went off without a hitch. Cassandra completed her first shift in Andre's kitchen without destroying any of the food, setting anything on fire, or maiming any of her coworkers.

So she had almost tripped and stabbed the executive sous-chef in the back of the thigh with a boning knife...the point was she *hadn't* and no one had noticed, and wasn't that all that really mattered?

In fact, Andre had been so pleased with her work that he had decided to let her pick up shifts on a regular basis. She kept her hostess job but began putting in time in the kitchen as well. Within three weeks, she had been promoted from low-key, in-between-meal-rush prep-work to full-on lunchtime sous-chef. Andre marveled at her efficiency, ability to remember recipes without having to be told repeatedly, and natural instinct for balancing the flavor of a dish. Cassandra was just grateful she hadn't singed off anyone's eyebrows.

When she wasn't worried about disfiguring herself or those around her, she was really enjoying herself. She hadn't been sure how she would respond to the necessity for speed or having to juggle so many dishes at once or the pressure of preparing professional-grade food. Her biggest fear was that someone would send back one of the plates she had worked on and she would damage the restaurant's reputation and disappoint Andre, making him regret giving her this chance.

In spite of all that, she found that the challenges of life as a chef (or chef underling) were actually quite exciting, and it turned out that the rapid pace increased her efficiency rather than damaging it. After a few minutes on the job, she would get in the zone and the hours would fly by in a colorful haze of chopping, dicing, whisking and sautéing, and before she knew it, it was time to go home.

She loved the constant clatter of pots and pans, the sizzle and pop of veggies and meat sautéing in oil, and the ever-present booming of Andre's voice in the background. She had expected to be intimidated by him when he was in his domain, or perhaps worse, that he would continue calling her names like "dumpling" or "pearl" and single her out as a pet. Instead, he treated her like everyone else, with the same pseudo-gruffness he reserved for all his employees. He would look over her shoulder while she was making the house mayonnaise and shout, "What are you doing to those egg yolks, Cassandra, trying to rock them to sleep? Whisk! Whisk like a machine!" And she would grin and whisk harder. It was good fun.

The only drawback to the whole situation was Finn. Half the time when she came into work, she ran into him and it was awful. She could avoid him in the kitchen, but during her hostess shifts there was no escaping him. It wasn't that he was rude or sulky—she probably could have handled that—he was just polite. Distant. *Almost* friendly in a reserved kind of way. He treated her like she was just some girl he had met a couple of times but didn't know very well or care to know better. It was really starting to depress her. She would be in the middle of greeting a party and he would walk through the door, giving her a tight smile and nod before making his way straight back to the bar without a word, and Cassandra would deflate. It always took a few seconds before she could remember what she was supposed to be doing and smile brightly to greet customers.

The worst part was watching him interact with the restaurant's female patrons. She would see him smile and wink at a pretty girl as he handed her a drink and Cass would forget the name the latest party had given her. She would hear him laughing with a blonde while he muddled her mojito and Cassandra's stomach would churn. Once, they locked eyes after Cassandra had been watching him with a particularly flirtatious brunette in a pink flowered sarong. She tried to smile but he just turned away, stone-faced. Cassandra had thought that she was going to throw-up.

It was horrible having him so close by without getting to talk and laugh with him, especially when he was so charming and easygoing with everyone else. Cass felt invisible.

But she was cheered by her culinary success, by how instinctive and enjoyable it was to be working in a professional kitchen. Andre had even mentioned trying her out during the dinner rush sometime soon! And of course, she had Daphne to console her. Poor Daphne, whose second date with Stewart hadn't been any more engaging than the first, but who still insisted on seeing where things went. ("He's really not bad," she insisted. "Just...mellow. But he's warming up! He even made a joke at dinner this time.")

And then, of course, there were Daphne's exercise classes: yoga, which helped clear her mind; kickboxing, where she could vent her pent-up frustrations; and Pilates, which she was convinced she would never enjoy, but which she occasionally went to anyway because Daphne swore she would warm to it eventually. As far as Cassandra was concerned, the only positive thing about Pilates was the fact that she could talk Daphne into going out for a pastry after each class.

Then there were lunches and hikes with Mary Ella and Sir Galahad, and the entertainment of Drew dropping by the apartment every few days, always with some lame excuse like, "I noticed you guys were out of orange juice and, you know, it's important to keep up your vitamin C." Once, Cassandra was convinced he had stolen some poor woman's sweater, just so he could run it by the apartment because, "he thought Daphne might have left it at the restaurant." Then Daphne and Drew would argue for ten minutes before she finally kicked him out, exasperated, while Cassandra watched, bemused, from the couch.

Between all this excitement and working double duty at Andre's, Cass almost didn't have time to notice the hole that Finn's absence had left in her life on the island.

Almost.

She missed their conversations, the way he grinned at her when she went off on a rant about something like barnacles, the flare of heat she would feel in the pit of her stomach when their eyes would meet and hold for a moment too long. But most of all, she missed the comfortable camaraderie they had established from the very beginning of her dive overboard (it seemed so long ago), how easy it was to be with him, how natural their friendship felt. She just missed him.

But Cassandra finally felt like things were starting to happen for her, like her path was finally becoming clearer, and she wasn't going to do anything to jeopardize it. If Finn was still hurt by the whole situation, she would give him his space. It was for the best…for both of them.

***

The last three weeks had been hell for Finn. He had to see Cassandra almost every damn day at work and he couldn't approach her, couldn't speak to her, couldn't touch her. It was driving him insane. It was easier when she was in the kitchen rather than greeting people up front. At least that way he didn't have to watch her smiling and laughing for hours at a time—watch her wide, expressive eyes dance as she welcomed each new guest, charming every person who walked through the door.

The greatest relief, though, came from his shifts at the Silver Sands. He had always enjoyed Andre's more, preferred the welcoming atmosphere and easy-going clientele, but at the resort he could take solace in knowing that Cassandra wasn't anywhere on the premises. Even when she was in the kitchen at Andre's, out of sight, he was still acutely aware of her presence. The urge to find her, patch things up, talk with her, laugh with her, seduce her, was too strong if she was anywhere within a hundred feet. It was better to avoid the temptation altogether. As far as he knew, she wasn't any more interested in moving things between them to the next level than she had been before, and he was still too drawn to her to just be friends.

He toyed with the idea of moving on to someone else—there were plenty of options between the two bars who would happily serve as a distraction—but he wasn't interested. None of the women he met had Cassandra's spark, her vivacity, her weirdly endearing quirks. They didn't have the same openness or intelligence or easygoing temper. Next to Cassandra, every other woman just seemed flat.

For weeks now, he had been turning down perfectly nice, attractive, interesting women, just because they weren't Cassandra. After he had gently rejected a gorgeous girl with large, green almond-shaped eyes and butterfly tattoo on her shoulder, Drew had come over to him and hissed, "Are you crazy?"

Finn had just shrugged and said, "She's never heard Total Eclipse of the Heart," and left it at that. It was getting to be a problem.

One afternoon during a phone call with his parents, his mother asked, "How are things going with Cassandra? Are you still showing her around the island?"

"I think she's been pretty busy at Andre's," he answered off-handedly. "You know, training. I haven't seen much of her lately."

"So, Andre is training her after all! That's excellent."

His father's voice chimed in. "I liked her," he said. "Plucky."

"Yes," Finn agreed vaguely, not encouraging further conversation about Cassandra.

"Don't you see her at work?" Lindsey followed up. "I thought the two of you were getting close."

"We were. Are. We're both busy, that's all," Finn said, hedging the issue.

Lindsey sensed the evasion. "Did something happen?"

Finn considered trying to get her to drop the subject, but he knew it was futile so he gave in. His mother was like a bloodhound when she picked up the scent of information she wanted. He remembered his abysmal failure to hide a pet raccoon from her when he was seven. Finn had never been able to pull anything over on her before or since.

Sighing, he said, "Cassandra and I aren't on great terms right now."

"What did you do?"

"Why do you assume I did anything? How do you know it wasn't her?"

"Was it her?"

"Not exactly," Finn said fairly. "I guess it was both of us. We kissed. She didn't want to get involved. I suggested we take some space. That's it," he said, keeping it as simple as possible.

"That's it?" He could practically see his mother raising her eyebrows doubtfully at him. "Why do I get the feeling there's something you're not telling us?"

"That's pretty much it," Finn insisted. "It's the same dance we've been doing all summer long. She says she can't be in a relationship until she's finished soul-searching, then we kiss, then she tells me it was a mistake. I got tired of it, so I told her we should step back."

"Who kissed who?"

"I kissed her." Finn hesitated, thinking, *I'm sure there are mothers who will go their entire lives without asking their sons that question.* "But she always kissed me back!" he defended.

"So, she was crystal clear that she wasn't looking for a relationship, you kept kissing her anyway, and then got huffy when she stuck to her principles?"

"I wouldn't say 'huffy'..."

"Finnegan!" his mother scolded. "You should know better than that."

"That was a dumb move," his father agreed and Finn could picture him nodding.

"Cassandra seems like a smart girl. She's not the type who would jump into a relationship with someone, especially not at a time like this."

"You can't rush a girl like that, giving her an ultimatum just because things aren't moving fast enough for you!" Lindsey chastised.

"It wasn't like that!" Finn protested, feeling just as sheepish as he had when his mom had finally discovered that raccoon. Nothing like parents to make practically two decades of experience and maturity fall away in an instant. "I didn't give her an ultimatum. I just told her how I felt and said if she didn't feel the same way, maybe we shouldn't see each other for a while…" he faltered as he realized that sounded a lot like an ultimatum, but he stuck to his guns. There was a difference. "I saved us both a lot of headache," he said. "We can't just be friends. She knows it."

"So now you're nothing. That doesn't sound better."

Finn glared into the air in front of him, annoyed. Mostly because his mother was right.

"Relationships don't happen overnight, Finn. You have to give them time to grow organically. Especially with a girl like Cassandra."

"We've known each other for two months," Finn said mulishly.

Lindsey laughed. "That's nothing. Your father and I were an exception, but we were an entirely different circumstance. We were both ready for something serious. Cassandra has other things to deal with first. You told us that yourself!"

"I know," Finn said. "It was just getting too hard to be around her without being with her."

"That means she's someone worth waiting for," Chris said.

"You have to be patient," Lindsey emphasized. "Understanding, respectful of her needs. You can't expect her to be ready to fall into a relationship just because you are. I think you should go find her and work this out."

"I agree," said Chris.

Finn shook his head. "It's too soon," he argued. "Nothing's changed."

"You don't know that," his father challenged. "And even if that's true, you don't want to burn your bridges now and regret it later. You don't have to make some sort of grand apology. Just a small peace offering to start things on their way. There's that event coming up at the Silver Sands next weekend—that dance or dinner or whatever—why don't you invite her to that?"

"It's the quarterly gala," Finn clarified. "They have some sort of event like it every few months. I'm bartending that night."

"That's perfect!" Lindsey said. "She and Daphne would have a great time. Don't the proceeds go to ocean conservation? I'm sure they'd both love to be involved. And it would pave the way for all of you to start spending time together again."

"I don't know," Finn said, but his anger towards Cassandra had been losing steam for days. Once he had cooled down about that *I remember my priorities and they don't include you* crack, he had started to realize that maybe he had provoked her. And maybe he was ready to admit that he had asked too much of her too quickly. At this point he just missed her. Maybe inviting her and Daphne to the gala wasn't such a bad idea.

"Alright," he agreed. "I'll invite her. But if we come to blows over champagne and shrimp cocktail, I'm going to blame you."

Chapter Twenty

Cassandra regarded herself in the mirror and let out a deep breath. She looked nice.

Daphne's face appeared in the mirror behind her and lit up with a smile. "You look beautiful!"

"Back at you," Cassandra took in her friend's red satin halter dress and matching heels. Beautiful was an understatement. Daphne looked stunning.

"This feels like prom," Cass said, running her hands over her own strapless turquoise gown. Luckily, her mother had insisted they all come prepared for formal events over the summer, so she had something appropriate to wear to this ocean conservation gala Finn had invited them to. This was her favorite dress—ruching along the bust, empire waist, silky, flowing fabric that rippled when she moved. It made her feel like a mermaid princess.

"This will be better than prom!" Daphne said. "We're adults now—legal drinking and no curfew. And since I'm going with you, I feel confident my date won't get drunk on pilfered booze and throw up on my shoes."

"Does that mean you want me to leave my flask at home?" Cassandra joked. "I've already made room for it in my clutch."

Daphne laughed. "I'm sure the Silver Sands would love that."

"I bet Judith can detect contraband from three floors away. I can just imagine her flying through a side door and taking me out in a full-on body tackle. Maybe she would even injure herself in the line of duty and management would award her some sort of medal. The Purple Heart of hotel service."

"She would be so happy!"

"Maybe we should sneak in a flask...just for old Judith."

"I might need it." Daphne slouched against the door frame. "Finn told me he invited Drew."

Cassandra tried not to perk up at the mention of Finn's name.

"Aren't you bringing Stewart?" she asked.

"Yes. This is his last chance. But I was really hoping Drew would never meet him. I purposefully haven't brought him around to Andre's."

"If you're hoping Drew will never meet him, you can't be expecting him to last…have you already made up your mind to break it off?"

"Not completely." Daphne sounded conflicted. "He still might come around. You'll have to tell me what you think of him."

"I think if you need somebody else to talk you into liking him, you should dump him immediately."

"Even so, I want to see what you think of him." Daphne stood on tiptoe behind Cassandra and rested her chin on her shoulder. "And what Finn thinks. You both have good judgment."

"How's he been?" Cassandra asked casually.

"Oh, don't pretend like you're not dying to know!" Daphne grinned and poked her, and Cassandra gently elbowed her in the stomach.

"I just haven't talked to him in a while. Not since..."

"Since he kissed you senseless and you turned him down again?"

"I had my reasons!"

"I know, I know!" Daphne waved her hands. "Life path and all that. But Cass, don't you think you've made really good progress at this point? Maybe even enough to expand your focus to other things as well…?"

"I've definitely made progress, it's true." Cassandra toyed with a particularly stubborn curl, attempting unsuccessfully to flatten it into submission. "Working with Andre has opened my eyes to the possibility of doing something culinary, and I'm starting to formulate ideas in the back of my mind, but I still don't have a definite idea of where this is all going. I don't want to do anything to ruin it!"

"Alright, I'll leave you alone," Daphne said. "Are you nervous about seeing him tonight?"

"Nope," Cassandra lied, giving up on the curl. "I'm fearless, remember? I do Pilates and swim with manta rays. Sort of. I can handle one potentially awkward night with Finnegan Drake."

***

An hour later, Cass wasn't feeling quite so confident as she entered the elegantly decorated ballroom at the Silver Sands and met Finn's eyes from across the crowded room. She steeled herself for a curt brush off, but he smiled and waved.

That's a good sign, she thought, making her way toward an empty table with Daphne. A waiter passed by with a tray of champagne flutes and she snagged one and sipped it gratefully, resisting the urge to down the whole glass in one go. She was feeling self-conscious back at the ritzy resort, just as she had that first night when she'd washed up on shore and dripped all over the foyer, but she reminded herself how far she'd come since then—not to mention how much more appropriately dressed she was this time around. She took a deep breath and another sip of champagne, enjoying the bubbles, and felt measurably comforted. Tonight was going to be fun.

Daphne waved to someone on the other side of the room and a tall, handsome man with sandy brown hair hedged around the dance floor to meet them. His shoulders were broad under his suit jacket and his hazel-green eyes were kind over his aquiline nose, but Daphne's smile seemed pasted on as he kissed her cheek in greeting.

"Stewart, this is my friend Cassandra," Daphne said, pulling back a little. "Cassandra, Stewart."

"Nice to meet you." Stewart's smile was genuine as he gripped her hand firmly.

"Likewise," Cassandra smiled back thinking, *So far, I don't see anything wrong with him.*

Clearly Daphne did. Her body stiffened when he put his arm around her, but she forced a wider smile and said, "So, what do you think of the party?"

"It's beautiful," he said, gazing at the wooden pillars wrapped with twinkly lights and the tables lavishly set with bird of paradise centerpieces and crystal stemware. "Of course, none of it compares to the way you look in that dress."

That's sweet, Cassandra thought. A little corny, but certainly not deserving of the barely-contained eye roll Daphne made when she primly answered, "Thank you."

Something was up. Stewart seemed like a nice guy—there was no reason for the normally bubbly Daphne to be acting frigid. It was hard to tell since her natural demeanor was so sweet, but Cassandra knew her well enough by now to notice—Daphne was bordering on downright hostile. Cass decided to jump in.

"Stewart, Daphne tells me you were a tennis pro in college."

"That's right," Stewart answered, swinging a forearm. "Full scholarship."

He launched into a story about a grueling doubles match and Cassandra listened politely, watching Daphne out of the corner of her eye the whole time. The little brunette nodded along with her date's story, but her eyes wandered around the room, clearly not dialed in to his tale of aces and advantages.

Cassandra laughed in dismay at the unexpected twist when the referee was hauled away on a stretcher due to blunt force trauma to the head, but Daphne's faint chuckle echoed a beat behind her own, betraying indifference to Stewart's story.

"Oh, that poor guy!" Cassandra said. She watched, puzzled, as Daphne's eyes darted from one corner of the room to the other. "I bet he didn't know what hit him."

"Well, I'm fairly certain he knew it was a tennis ball."

Stewart and Cassandra laughed in commiseration with the referee's plight (he had made a full recovery, Stuart assured her), while Daphne chuckled half-heartedly and downed champagne.

"I think I'll go get a drink," Cassandra said when there was a lull in the conversation, telling herself that Daphne needed some time alone with her date, not that she wanted an excuse to go over and talk to Finn. "Can I get anyone anything?"

"I'm fine, thanks."

"Vodka tonic for me," Daphne answered quickly. "Make it a double."

Ooh-kay. Daphne's on a bender tonight.

"Sure thing," she said aloud. "Be right back!"

Wandering over to the bar, she unconsciously fluffed her hair and straightened her dress when Finn looked up.

"Hey!" He smiled. "Glad you could make it!"

"Thanks for the invite." Cassandra smiled back, happy to hear him sounding so comfortable.

"What can I get you?" he asked.

"A vodka tonic, champagne with a splash of St. Germaine, and your opinion on Daphne's date. Have you met him yet?"

"Stewart?" Finn asked. "Yeah, I served him brandy about twenty minutes ago. He seems like a nice guy."

"That's what I thought!" Cassandra agreed as he splashed tonic water into a healthy shot of vodka. "But Daphne seems like she's about ready to bash him over the head with a flower arrangement. Have you noticed?"

"Not really," he admitted. "But they've been keeping me busy over here. You look really nice, by the way," he added, and Cassandra felt her cheeks flush.

"Thank you," she said, smoothing her dress once again. "I've been spending so much time looking like a crazy person in the kitchen with steam-frazzled hair and sauce smudged on my cheeks, it's nice to have a reason to get dressed up. Thanks again for inviting us!"

"Of course," he said. "It's for a good cause...ocean conservation...I know how much you love the ocean," he grinned.

"Of course," she laughed. "I can't get enough of it."

They smiled goofily at each other for several moments before Finn cleared his throat and got to work uncorking a champagne bottle.

"So, you haven't noticed anything odd about Daphne since she started seeing Stewart?" Cassandra recovered.

"I haven't seen much of her these past couple of weeks," Finn looked at her, not saying out loud what they both knew he was thinking: *because I've been avoiding you.*

"Right." Cassandra didn't meet his eyes. "Well, I think something weird is going on. He seems perfectly lovely but Daphne's been making him out to be a total bore every time they've gotten together. I've been wondering why she's stuck it out, but now I'm thinking that he's actually really great, but for whatever reason she's looking for excuses not to get involved. If they come by, feel it out and let me know what you think."

Cass mentally stumbled when she realized that she and Finn weren't exactly checking in with each other lately. He would keep an eye on his cousin, of course, but he might not be too keen on the idea of acting as a sidekick in Cassandra's dating detective plan.

She watched his expression to see if it became guarded, but he just looked thoughtful and said, "Sure. We'll compare notes later on."

Then suddenly he seemed wary and looked closely at her, so she said, "Great! It's a date! To talk. About Daphne. I'd better get these drinks to her!" Cass smiled brightly, grabbed the glasses, and walked away before either of them could get any more awkward.

They were both tiptoeing around each other, trying to gauge what the other was thinking without starting another fight, and Cassandra was pretty sure it was making them ridiculous. It was time to take a deep breath and get a grip on normalcy.

She returned to the table to find that Drew had arrived and was chatting away with Stewart, while Daphne stood a few inches apart from them, looking more morose than Cassandra had ever seen her.

Handing Daphne the vodka tonic, which her friend accepted eagerly, Cassandra asked in a low voice, "Is everything okay?"

"Hey Cass!" Drew greeted her before Daphne had a chance to respond. "Long time, no see! It's been almost, what, six hours since we saw each other at Andres? You were starting to miss me, weren't you?"

"I drink to stave off the loneliness." Cassandra held up her cocktail.

"Stewart here was just telling us about his work on the windows of the old cathedral," Drew filled her in.

"The cornices are particularly ornate," Stewart explained. "Classic example of gothic intricacy. The restoration of the southern façade alone has taken weeks."

"Classic," Drew repeated. "Fascinating. Isn't this just fascinating, Daphne?"

Daphne glared at him over her drink and Cassandra shifted uncomfortably.

"Oh look, they're bringing out the food," Drew said as tuxedo-clad waiters began parading around with the salad course. "Let's grab our seats and Stewart can tell us more about the cornices. Don't leave anything out."

Stewart talked architecture all through the first three courses and Cassandra started to see Daphne's point. He was a very nice man. Just a little bland. He was interrupted during the curried duck and mango chutney when an impeccably coiffed woman resplendent in a blue sequined gown approached the podium at the far end of the room and elegantly cleared her throat.

"Ladies and gentlemen," she began, "welcome to the twelfth annual August Gala to Support the Efforts of Ocean Conservation, hosted by the Silver Sands resort." She paused for effect and a polite round of applause sounded throughout the room. The woman went on to make a very detailed and impassioned speech about the importance of preserving the earth's precious resources, emphasizing the value of each individual's contribution to the evening. She talked through the entire cheese course and well into the serving of crème brûlée and Chantilly cream.

Despite her best efforts to listen attentively, Cassandra's mind began to wander. She already planned to donate to the gala's efforts—she and Daphne had talked about appropriate amounts when they were invited to attend. This woman's speech, while enthusiastic, was not for Cassandra.

Hmm, she thought, *the dinner was nice, but I think I could do better.*

Good lord, a couple of weeks of culinary training under her belt and she was getting delusions of grandeur. The Silver Sands had put out a very nice spread—but if she was being perfectly honest, the duck had been a little dry, the chutney a little runny, and the soup a little overly peppered. She had expected more from a place with this sort of resources. They certainly hadn't skimped on amenities, but they would have done better to fire their chef and hire Andre. Not that they could have gotten him, probably.

The bedazzled woman wrapped up her soliloquy by smiling graciously and telling them all to enjoy the evening, then stepped down to the tune of vigorous applause. Cassandra wondered how many people were clapping out of genuine appreciation for the themes of her speech and how many were clapping out of relief that it was over.

She smiled and thanked the server who cleared away the final dishes and he winked at her as music began to filter through the room's top-of-the-line sound system.

"Would you care to dance?" Stewart held his hand out to Daphne as couples filed onto the dance floor. She nodded and let him help her out of her seat, and Drew looked sullen for the first time that night.

Tearing his eyes away from Daphne's retreating figure, he asked, "How about you, Cass? Want to dance?"

From the dance floor, at least she could keep a closer eye on Daphne.

"Sure." She took his outstretched hand and he twirled her onto the floor. Over the loudspeaker,

Rosemary Clooney sang about marimba music starting to play and Drew whirled her around in a surprisingly smooth rumba.

"You can dance!" Cass said, delighted.

"Did you think I would have asked you to if I couldn't?" Drew looked pleased with himself.

"Well, most men stick to a basic sway," Cassandra laughed as he spun her out and back in against his chest.

"I took five semesters of ballroom dance in college," he said, gliding her past Daphne and Stewart, while Daphne watched in open-mouthed shock.

"'C.K. Dexter Haven, you have unsuspected depth!'" Cassandra cried happily.

"Who?" Drew looked confused.

"No one. It's from The Philadelphia Story. Great movie. Great line. Never mind," Cassandra shook her head. "Why did you take dance lessons?"

"For fun," Drew shrugged.

Cassandra's eyebrows went up in surprise.

"Plus, there were a ton of hot girls in the class."

There we go. "That sounds about right."

"It's a useful skill to have," Drew added. "You never know when you'll need a good waltz."

"Attend a lot of balls, do you?" Cassandra asked as the song changed and he pulled her in closer for a slow dance.

"I date," he clarified. "Women tend to like it if you can actually dance when you take them dancing."

"I suppose that's true," she agreed.

"Admit it, Cass. You're impressed."

"I do admit it...you're good."

"You want me bad, huh?" he wiggled his eyebrows and she rolled her eyes.

"Have some shame, Drew. Daphne's right over there."

"Yeah," he said glumly. "With Stewart."

"Oh, be nice," Cassandra tsked. "You've had your chance and you decided to mess around with other women and flirt meaninglessly with her rather than show her you're really interested. You can't be surprised when she doesn't take you seriously."

"I don't chase women," he said.

"Then you're never going to catch Daphne," Cassandra said airily. "But that's your choice. There are plenty of fish in the sea. At least there will be if the efforts of tonight's gala are a success."

He ignored her lame joke and looked over her shoulder to where Daphne was swaying with her date.

"I think I need some air," he said. "You want to go outside for a while?"

"Sure." Cassandra followed his line of sight.

This should be interesting. She wondered if time alone with Drew would get him to open up about his feelings for Daphne.

It's worth a shot, she thought, and followed him out the door.

*****

Finn watched his best friend walk out the door with the person he was pretty sure was the woman of his dreams and felt his stomach twist. Which was ridiculous. Despite what Daphne thought, Drew was a good guy and Finn knew it. Still, the two of them had looked awfully cozy out there, twirling around the dance floor. Finn thought Drew had pulled her unnecessarily close during that slow dance and Cassandra's arms had looked way too comfortable wrapped around his neck.

Don't be an idiot, he told himself. *There's nothing to get worked up over.* Still, he shook a martini with unnecessary force and tried not to imagine Drew and Cassandra arm in arm, taking a romantic moonlit walk along the beach.

Pull it together.

If he was getting this worked up just seeing Cassandra dance with another man—a man he knew had no interest in her and vice versa—he needed to fix this. Maybe his mother had been right (words no man in his twenties hoped ever to utter, but most probably did): he needed to go to her and make things right. Soon.

Tonight, he decided. *After the gala. I'll apologize. I'll get her back.*

Chapter Twenty-one

Well, that was educational, Cassandra thought when she and Drew returned to the ballroom. He had managed to evade all of her questions about Daphne, but it had been fun. And surprisingly enlightening in other respects...he had told her about growing up and eventually coming to the island, and there was a lot more to his story than Cass would have guessed. Drew joked around a lot but the guy had had it rough. And he'd pulled himself out on the other side, relatively well-adjusted. He still had a lot of growing up to do, but maybe there was hope for him yet.

By now, the party was in full swing. Many of the older guests had left and the music had morphed from classic crooners to modern techno-style. Cassandra had left a tasteful soirée and returned to a nightclub.

She spotted Daphne over by the bar and went to see how her friend was coping. "What's this?" she asked over the thumping music. "When did the Silver Sands become a disco-tech?"

"About ten minutes ago," Daphne shouted. "What happened to you? You disappeared. Finn has been keeping me company but he's busy now."

"I went for a walk with Drew," Cass yelled into Daphne's ear. "Where's Stewart?"

"He ran into a colleague and they've been discussing gargoyles for half an hour now. I think they're out on the patio. She's pretty. You went for a walk with Drew?"

"Yeah. He's around here somewhere..."

"He's getting a drink," Daphne pointed down the bar where Drew was leaning in to shout something at Finn, who nodded and then turned to his other customers.

Mercifully, the song ended and shifted to something more subdued, still from this decade, but with less of a spine-shuddering beat and more discernible lyrics.

"So how was your walk?" Daphne asked, finally able to speak at a reasonable volume. "I didn't think Drew could spend that much time alone with a woman without hitting on her." Her gaze flickered quickly to Cassandra's face as if to discover whether he had, in fact, hit on her.

"It was fun!" Cassandra said. "I think sometimes he goes on auto-pilot and flirts with any female standing within a fifty-foot radius, but it's just a knee-jerk reaction. We actually had a really nice conversation. I had no idea he emancipated from his parents when he was sixteen."

"Neither did I." Daphne looked surprised.

"Oh."

Crap. He'd mentioned it so casually, Cassandra assumed it was public knowledge. Maybe Drew had opened up to her more than she realized.

"He told you that?" Daphne was bewildered.

"In passing," Cassandra decided not to mention the conversation about working three jobs to support himself through college, then quitting to follow a girl to the island the semester before graduation. According to Drew, he had been ready to propose, but she ran off with a scuba instructor. When she had winced, he'd brushed it aside and said, "It's a cliché because it happens. But it's water under the bridge now. In the end it all worked out because I love this island more than I ever loved her anyway."

Obviously, since he had been comfortable telling her about his past, Cassandra expected that Daphne knew about it as well. Apparently not. But if Drew had kept Daphne in the dark, he must have had his reasons, and it wasn't Cassandra's place to enlighten her.

"So, Stewart just abandoned you?" Cass asked, shifting attention away from her accidental breach of confidence.

"Oh, he introduced me to his friend, but there's only so much shop-talk a girl can stand before she makes a break for it. After a few minutes I started counting the number of architectural terms I didn't understand, and once they reached ten, I excused myself and went to look for you. When I couldn't find you, I came to find Finn and a drink."

"And you found both," Finn said, wandering to their end of the bar. "Need a refill, Daph?

"I shouldn't," she shook her head. "I'll take a water, though."

"You got it."

"I'm sorry I left you!" Cassandra apologized. "You and Stewart looked like you were having a good time when we left."

"We were having a time." Daphne nodded and took the glass of water Finn offered. "Who knew Drew could dance?"

Cassandra felt like Daphne's train of thought had jumped the tracks a bit, but she said, "I guess there are a lot of things about Drew we didn't know."

She followed Daphne's gaze over to Drew, who stood at the other end of the bar, chatting up a raven-haired woman in a low-cut yellow dress. Daphne rolled her eyes in disgust.

"So, about Stewart..." Cassandra steered the conversation back to Daphne's less-than-desirable date. She felt bad for the guy. He seemed like a decent man—he just wasn't at all right for Daphne. Cassandra knew this, and she was pretty sure Daphne knew it too. It was about time Stewart found out as well.

"You don't exactly seem to like him," Finn jumped in.

"Do you guys?" Daphne asked.

"That's a moot point," Cassandra pointed out. "The question is: do you?"

"I should. I mean, I do. Sort of. He's smart and handsome and responsible and considerate..."

"You don't sound excited about any of this," Cassandra told her.

"He's exactly what I thought I wanted."

"But in reality?"

"I don't want him," Daphne sounded defeated. "There's something missing—a spark, or passion, or—I don't know, something to keep me interested. He's just not the one."

"When are you going to tell him this?"

"I kept hoping I'd change my mind, but now that I've said it out loud, I think I should tell him tonight. After the gala."

"I'd do it as soon as possible," Finn prompted. "If you know it's not going anywhere then tell him so. He'll bounce back. Men usually just want women to be straightforward with them."

Daphne nodded, looking grim. "I'll do it now. He's coming back in anyway."

Stewart entered the room with a petite blonde in pink silk. As they approached, Cass heard him say, "So then he said, 'Frieze! Against the wall!'"

The blonde erupted with laughter, swatting his arm and saying, "Stewart, you are hilarious!"

"Hey, gang," Stewart greeted them as they neared the bar. "I'd like you to meet my colleague, Bridget."

"Hi!" Cass shook her hand.

"Nice to see you again," Daphne smiled. "Stewart, would you mind stepping outside for a moment?"

"Of course," he said. "Bridget, would you excuse us?"

"No problem," she said. "I should go find Carrie and Ryan anyway. We'll talk later?"

"Apse-olutely."

Bridget giggled. "There you go again!"

Cassandra stared uncomprehendingly while Bridget disappeared into the crowd and Stewart turned back to Daphne. "So, my lady, what can I do for you?"

Daphne downed the rest of her water, squared her shoulders and said resolutely, "We need to talk." She gestured to the door and Cass watched sympathetically as she led her soon-to-be former date toward the exit.

"Poor Stewart," she said, turning to Finn.

"He'll be fine," he reassured her. "He's a catch. Just not Daphne's catch. But how about you?" he asked, clapping his hands together once to lighten the mood. "What can I get you? Any requests?"

She looked at him, broad and beautiful in his white shirt and tie.

I can think of several.

"I would love another champagne," she said instead, feeling her evening could use a little effervescence.

"Coming right up."

Fifteen minutes later, she was halfway through her drink and had turned down two offers to dance (while Finn, she couldn't help noticing, listened attentively from behind the bar).

Daphne wandered back over to her, looking tired. "How did it go?"

"Not bad. He said there were no hard feelings and thanked me for being upfront about it. I told him he was welcome to stay and enjoy the rest of the party, but he said he'd better be getting back to the hotel."

"Well, that's good..." Cassandra put as much encouragement into her voice as she could.

"Yeah..." Daphne's normally lilting voice sounded droopy. "Now I just want to forget about it. Wait, isn't that him?" she pointed to a man who was clearly Stewart, crossing the room in what was clearly Bridget's direction. The blonde smiled at his approach, he said a few words and motioned to the door, and the two of them promptly left together.

"Well, I feel better," Daphne perked up as she surveyed the progression. "He's obviously not heartbroken over me. I can move on guilt-free. Want to dance?"

"Of course!"

Three songs later, Daphne was looking much like her normal self again and the two friends paused to hydrate.

"See, this night is turning out to be fun after all!" Cassandra said while they waited for Finn to bring them two waters.

"It is!" Daphne bubbled. "Yay us! Way to turn the night around!"

Finn showed up and handed them each a glass and they clinked their drinks together.

"Ladies." Drew sidled up behind them. "Finn. Are we all enjoying the evening?" He looked around. "Where's old Stewey? I haven't seen him for a while."

"Stewart went home," Daphne said flatly. "Unless the two of you exchanged phone numbers, you won't be seeing him again."

"What a shame." Drew suppressed a grin. "You guys decided to call it quits, then?"

"We agreed we weren't right for each other." Daphne offered no further explanation.

"That's too bad," he said, no longer bothering to hide his glee. "I was really starting to like poor Stewart."

"Then you can date him," Daphne said, finishing her water.

Although you may have to fight Bridget for him, Cassandra thought.

"Nah," Drew shook his head. "He's from out of town. Long distance relationships never work out. I think I'll keep trying my luck with the locals."

"You've had no shortage of options so far," Daphne commented, unconcerned.

"How about a dance?" Drew asked, and Cassandra was surprised by how quickly he went in for the kill. Daphne hadn't even been single for twenty minutes.

We need to work on your pacing, Drew.

"No, thank you." Daphne shut him down with no hesitation whatsoever.

"It'll be fun," he prompted. "Cassandra can vouch for me."

"It's true," she said, feeling kindly toward Drew since their walk on the beach. She could help him get Daphne on the dance floor. It was up to him to keep her out there. "He's got moves."

"It will help take your mind off of things," he persisted.

"Fine," Daphne sighed. "One dance. If you get handsy, I'm done."

"Wouldn't dream of it." Drew winked at Cassandra and pulled Daphne towards the center of the floor.

"How do you think that will go?" Finn nodded after them.

"I guess we'll find out," Cassandra leaned against the bar to watch how events transpired. In no time at all, Daphne was smiling, swept up in the movement and the rhythm of Drew's steps

He said something in her ear and she actually laughed.

Well, what do you know? Cassandra thought. She relaxed a little and turned to say something to Finn, but he was busy at the other end of the bar.

A good-looking guy in a black shirt and red tie approached her and asked if she wanted to dance, but she politely declined. When she looked back at Daphne and Drew, she was surprised to see the two of them looking cozy together. They were both smiling as he spun her out and then pulled her back close against him. His hands slid low on her waist and she didn't seem to mind. When the song ended and transitioned into another, neither one gave any sign of noticing. They kept moving together, oblivious to the fact that Daphne's "one song" had come and gone.

The new song had a fun beat and since Finn was still busy with work, Cassandra decided to bop on out to the dance floor alone. She shimmied over in the direction of Daphne and Drew, who both acknowledged her with a smile and a nod but were too caught up in each other to really notice her. That was fine by Cassandra. If Drew had any hope of winning Daphne over, it was good for them to spend some time alone together without bickering the whole time. Let it last while it could.

She moved to the music, enjoying the rhythm and thinking how nice it was to let off some steam after the last couple of emotionally high-strung weeks, when suddenly she felt someone dancing right up against her from behind.

Oh, dear. And she'd been having such a nice time by herself. She didn't want to fend off random strangers—if that had been what she'd wanted, she would have said yes to one of the three who had asked her earlier. The stranger pressed his hips closer and tried to swivel in time with her own. Damn it. How did people behave in these types of situations? Cassandra had never been one for clubs. How did one politely communicate to a stranger, *back off buddy or you're going to lose a body part,* without having to say as much?

She shot a look at Daphne, but her friend was facing the opposite direction. The dance accoster put his hands on Cassandra's hips and she pointedly kept as much space between them as possible while deciding how best to handle the situation. Steer them closer to Daphne and Drew and wait for a good opening to join them instead? She didn't want to interrupt…things were going so well for them.

She darted another glance in their direction and thought, *Whoa.* Daphne was turned so her back was to his front, and Drew had his hands on her hips, pulling her tight against him. He bent down to brush his lips against her neck and Daphne reached up to tangle her fingers in his hair.

Careful there, Daphne, Cassandra spared a thought for her friend, but she had her own problems to deal with. She felt her own problem move her hair to one side of her neck.

This was getting ridiculous. She was just about to turn around and tell him that she needed to use the bathroom, which seemed like an effective exit strategy that wouldn't invite his company, when she felt his mouth on her—biting into the curve of her neck.

She whirled around. The rules of politeness no longer applied.

"What the hell?!" Cassandra pushed him away and took a step back, putting a healthy amount of distance between the two of them. Her assailant was a couple inches taller than herself, with dark hair, dark eyes, and a shocked expression.

"I'm sorry," he sounded confused. "Weren't we heading in that direction?"

"No!" Cassandra said, appalled. "Not even remotely!"

Daphne and Drew had stopped dancing and were watching the scene.

"What about my body language told you that I wanted you to sink your teeth into my neck like a vampire, you creep? Who bites someone before even bothering to introduce themselves?"

"I'm Neil." He held out his hand.

Cassandra stared at him in amazement. "You've got to be kidding me. You're lucky I didn't turn around and punch you in the esophagus, *Neil*!"

"Is everything okay, Cass?" Daphne appeared at her shoulder with Drew close behind.

"It will be once I give this jerk a piece of my mind!"

"Look," Neil said before she could begin, "I noticed there's a jealousy thing going on between you and these two—you've been watching them for the last three songs—and I just wanted to say, you're a beautiful woman and any man here would be lucky to be dancing with you. If he doesn't see that, he's an idiot."

Cassandra blinked at him, her fury now muddled with confusion. "What? I don't care about *him*! No offense, Drew."

"None taken."

"But the woman he's dancing with is my best friend and I was watching them to make sure she was okay."

"Oh." Neil looked taken aback. "I read that wrong."

"Yeah, you were way off there, buddy," Drew said sympathetically.

"You *think*?" Cassandra said, still outraged, though marginally less so, since it turned out that in his own, misguided way, Neil had been trying to pay her a compliment. "Even if that wasn't the case, what makes you think you have the right to put your mouth all over someone you haven't even made eye contact with?"

By now, the surrounding couples on the floor had stopped to watch the confrontation and Cassandra felt a little guilty at the spectacle they were making. This was a gala, after all. She stepped closer and took the edge out of her voice and slowly people began dancing again.

"Look, Neil, maybe you're a nice guy. I hope, anyway. Next time, try starting up a conversation with a girl before you go for the throat. It sends a better message."

"You're right—I'm sorry." Neil looked genuinely contrite.

"Is there a problem?" Finn's voice came from behind and sounded threatening. Neil looked alarmed now that she was flanked by two strapping men, and Cass couldn't believe it, but she was almost starting to feel bad for him.

"It's fine, Finn," she said, putting a hand on his arm. "There was a misunderstanding."

"It looked like more than that to me." He scowled at Neil, who was now looking like he'd rather be anywhere else.

"It's taken care of. Neil is going to keep his hands and his mouth to himself, and he was just about to go enjoy the party from over there." She gestured to where a group of people were dancing together.

"Yes, I was!" He looked at her gratefully and danced away.

Drew grinned at him as he passed and said, "Cheers," but Finn continued to glare daggers at him from a distance. "Are you sure you don't want me to call security?" he asked.

"No, it's fine, really." Cassandra brushed it off. "He needs to work on his opening, but I'm okay. And it seems like he learned his lesson."

They all looked over to Neil, who was in the process of introducing himself to everyone in the new circle, shaking hands with each person in turn and making a healthy amount of eye contact as he did.

"If you say so," Finn grumbled, clearly not pleased. "I've got to get back to work, but if you need me, I'll be right over there." He crossed the room to return to the bar and the other three wandered back to a table.

"So," Drew said, transitioning smoothly as ever, "who's up for another dance?"

Daphne glared at him. "You're kidding, right? You saw what happened! Some stranger just *bit* Cassandra! I had to break up with my date in the middle of the party. I say we call it a night before something else terrible happens."

"I don't know," Cassandra put in. "I don't really want to wrap up the evening by explaining to Neil that you should speak to women before you bite them. It's a sour note to end on. But if you want to go home, Daphne, we absolutely can!" she added supportively.

"See, Cass is up for it!" Drew said. "Stick around, see where the night goes."

"It's not going in the direction you're hoping," Daphne warned him.

"No?" He didn't sound concerned.

"No." She was firm.

"Give me a chance." He smiled down at her and put heat into his voice. "I bet I could turn your night around."

For a brief moment, Daphne looked a little dazed, but then she shook her head and said matter-of-factly, "Give it a rest, Drew. It's never going to happen."

"Don't try to deny it, Daphne," Drew leaned in and grinned. "You want me."

"Yeah?" Daphne retorted, clearly fed up with the whole night and losing patience. "And why do you want me?"

Drew's grin diminished and he looked caught off guard. "What?"

"You heard me," she said. "Is it because I'm smart? Strong? Independent? Buoyant and cheerful and charming? Or is it because of my ass? Because I'm pretty sure you look at me and you don't see *me*, you see a hot piece of ass you'd like to take to bed with you. Well tough luck, pal, because it's never going to happen."

Drew smiled the same smile he'd been using to charm the pants off women since he was fifteen. "Never say 'never.'"

Daphne narrowed her eyes. "Let's get something straight, Andrew. You can wiggle your eyebrows and make suggestive comments and dance with me all you want, but I am never going to sleep with you. Ever. *Ever*," she repeated, and Drew looked taken aback.

"Don't get me wrong," Daphne went on, "you've got a lot going for you. You're good-looking and funny and a hell of a good time, but we both know who you are—you don't get *involved* with the women you're involved with. You're the kind of guy who has his fun and then grabs his pants on the way out the door, trying not to make too much noise as you close it behind you. I have no interest in becoming another notch in your bedpost. There are plenty of other women in the world to fill that position. You don't need me."

"You're overthinking this, Daphne. We could have fun together."

"You couldn't give me what I want."

"I could get you where you need to go." Drew leaned in closer.

Come on, Drew, Cassandra winced. *Read the room.*

"Unfortunately for you, anywhere you could take me is nowhere I want to go," Daphne said with crushing finality.

Drew looked at her for a beat and then shrugged. "Your loss."

Daphne snorted. "You have that backward." She walked away without looking back and Cassandra followed her, giving Drew a curt nod as she did.

Drew watched Daphne leave, his mouth set in a grim line, but he didn't go after her. He stared at the exit long after she'd disappeared through it, then shook his head, headed for the opposite door, and went home alone.

Chapter Twenty-two

Out on the patio, Cassandra caught up to Daphne, who had practically speed-walked all the way from the ballroom.

"Hold up, there," Cass called. "These heels were not made for jogging."

Daphne stopped abruptly in front of a garden path and began pacing back and forth.

"That boy drives me crazy!"

Cassandra's eyes followed her as she marched up and down the path. "I've noticed."

"He's impossible!" she raged, stopping in front of Cassandra with fire in her eyes. "The minute you start to think, 'maybe he's a decent guy after all…maybe he actually has some potential,' he turns around and makes a crack about getting you into bed."

"Well, not *me*," Cassandra said fairly. "He only seems to do that with you."

"Me and every other single woman under fifty that he meets. He knows Finn is interested in you. He has *some* boundaries," Daphne conceded. "Just not many."

"Have you ever thought that maybe—"

"What are you guys doing out here?" Finn stepped out from behind a bush and both women gave a startled scream.

"Don't sneak up on us like that!" Daphne punched her cousin on the arm. "After the night we've had, we're both probably one moronic male comment away from snapping like twigs. The next bonehead who tries to cross us is going to get savaged!"

Cassandra nodded. There was some truth to that.

"I just came to check up on you. I saw you storm out, so I got one of the waitstaff to cover for me so I could make sure you're both alright."

"We're fine," Cassandra said. "Daphne is just recovering from a fallout with Drew."

"Yeah, I saw him leave after you did. What happened?"

"Nothing. Just typical Drew." Daphne sounded disgusted.

"Words were exchanged," Cassandra glossed over the fight. "Now I think Daphne is ready to call it a night."

"Cass, if you want to stick around and salvage the evening, that's fine!" Daphne said. "Honestly, the walk home alone might be nice. It'll clear my head…if I wasn't wearing heels, I would go for a run."

"I don't want you walking through the streets alone at night! Especially dressed like that!"

"Please," Daphne laughed. "At this point, if I feel threatened it would be a welcome excuse to release some aggression. I would love to beat the hell out of some guy right now."

"Yeah. Between Stewart, Drew, and neck-biting Neil, this has not been a good night for men," Cassandra agreed.

"So if you want to stay, don't let me stop you! I could use the time alone."

"I really don't want to end the night like this…" Cassandra said, torn between the appeal of reviving a lousy evening and the guilt of abandoning her friend. But if Daphne really wanted to be alone…

"If you want to hang out together after, I'll make sure you get home safe," Finn told Cassandra. "The party will be wrapping up soon anyway."

The thought of spending time alone with Finn was too much to resist. After three weeks away from him, she had been missing him anyway, but after this catastrophic night spent in the company of bores, cads, and bunglers, his company was more appealing than ever.

"Stay, Cass," Daphne insisted. "I'm going to go home, take a bath, and forget this whole night ever happened. You stay here and have a good time!"

"Are you sure you don't want us to walk you home?" Finn asked. "I could tell Leo I have to duck out early…"

"No, don't worry about it!" Daphne assured them, flapping her hands. "Stay, work, enjoy! I just want to go home and go to bed."

****

As Finn walked with Cassandra back to the ballroom, he tried to keep his excitement at bay. He was still working, after all, but the gala would be ending within the hour and Cass wanted to hang out afterwards. That was a good sign. After avoiding each other for weeks, any time she agreed to spend with him was a good indication of progress. Maybe she had actually turned a corner and was ready to give this a shot…

Let's not get ahead of ourselves, he warned himself. She was willing to spend time at his house. It didn't necessarily mean anything more than that.

Still, there was something different about her tone and the way she looked at him. Maybe things were finally getting back to normal, but maybe it was more than that. The difference was subtle, and Finn wondered what she was thinking. Had she figured out enough about her life path in her time training with Andre to feel like she was ready to give their relationship a try? He shrugged the feeling aside, figuring there was no point worrying about it until he found out for sure.

For now, he was just happy to be with her again. The deprivation had been driving him to distraction. Earlier tonight, when he had looked up and seen her in that dress, all curves and curls and huge blue eyes, he'd felt all the air rush out of his lungs. When she'd sauntered over to say hello, the slippery fabric of her dress slid against her body every time she moved, and he had forgotten the ingredients to a gin and tonic.

Then when he had seen that creep dancing with her, every muscle in his body had tensed, ready to go punch the guy in the face. He nearly had when he saw the jackass put his mouth on her. Finn had had one hand on the bar, ready to vault over it and knock the son of a bitch's teeth out, before he saw Cassandra whirl around, incandescent with rage, looking like she was about three seconds away from impaling him with her stiletto.

He'd calmed down, remembering she could take care of herself, but he had gone over anyway, ready to have her attacker hauled away by security as soon as she gave the word. He had no idea what the bastard had said to talk himself out of having his ass handed to him by a very angry strawberry blonde in three-inch heels, but by the time Finn had gotten there, she looked calm and the jerk looked contrite, so he had let the subject drop.

He went back to the bar and thanked Leo for manning the fort. The crowd had thinned out considerably, but several enthusiastic dancers remained on the floor. Finn told Cass she didn't have to stick around to keep him company, but she said she'd had enough dancing for one night and hung around the bar. She turned down another cocktail, so he made her a Shirley Temple with extra cherries speared onto a little umbrella and she was thrilled.

The rest of the party flew by as Cassandra chatted away, animated as ever, filling him in on everything he'd missed since they saw each other last, and he commented on her stories, occasionally mixing drinks for thirsty dancers. He and Cass were finally back to their easy pre-fight banter. Finn didn't know exactly what had happened to prompt the change, but he didn't much care as long as she was back.

She was in the middle of an anecdote about nearly adding cayenne pepper instead of cinnamon to an apple crumble ("but I *didn't*, and that's the important thing!"), while he smiled fondly at her and absent-mindedly mixed a martini for some guy in a purple shirt and blue tie. The dope was leaning coolly against the bar, trying to get noticed, but Cassandra didn't even bat an eye. She blazed on through her story

("…so without even thinking, I smelled it, and boy was *that* a terrible idea!"), completely unaware that a man was standing not two feet away, trying to get her attention.

Charmed as always by her artlessness, Finn's smile widened and he handed the guy his martini. Finn turned his full attention back to Cass in time to hear her say, "So I spent the next twenty minutes with ice cubes shoved up my nose, but the dessert was saved!"

She beamed at him, biting a cherry off the end of the umbrella, and he laughed.

"What a hero! Did Andre give you a promotion?"

"Oh, Andre never found out." Cassandra's eyes widened in horror. "And he never will! He raised his eyebrows at the ice cubes, but it wasn't getting in the way of my work, so he didn't ask and I certainly wasn't going to offer an explanation!"

When the gala was coming to an end, Finn made the announcement for last call—he whipped up two final cocktails, poured a glass of wine, and they were free to leave. The catering staff was in charge of cleanup, so there was no need to stick around.

Before they left for Finn's place, Cassandra needed to use the facilities.

"Between the champagne and all that water, I'm *very* well hydrated," she laughed. "Where is the nearest bathroom?"

Finn led her to it, navigating their way through the maze of marbled hallways, and popping them out at the far end of the main lobby.

Uh-oh. Cassandra stopped mid-chuckle at a story about Finn's latest interview when Judith's head snapped up from her computer and her gaze zeroed in on them with eagle-eyed precision and raptor-like ferocity.

The click of Cassandra's heels and the echo of Finn's laugh reverberated through the large foyer and Cass looked warily at the nighttime receptionist.

There's no way she can be angry with me this time, Cassandra thought. *I'm here for the gala. I'm nicely dressed...*

Still, as they walked, she pointedly stood on Finn's far side, placing him between herself and the fastidious watch of the sharp-eyed woman behind the front desk.

"Evening, Judith!" Finn smiled easily at her when they passed by.

"Finn." Judith's voice was as warm as Cassandra had ever heard it. The desk clerk looked at Finn with something approaching affection and asked, "Working the gala tonight?"

"Just finished," he confirmed. "How about you? Keeping everything ship-shape up here?"

"No trouble so far." Judith glanced severely at Cassandra, who smoothed her dress self-consciously.

"You won't be getting any from us." Finn gave her a reassuring smile and Cass was almost sure she heard Judith softly sigh. "We're just passing through so Cassandra can visit the powder room. Doesn't she look beautiful?" he asked, inviting Judith to share in the compliment.

Judith looked grimly at Cassandra.

"Very appropriate," she said, deadpan.

Cassandra and Finn both blinked at her.

To be fair, Cass thought, *that's the nicest thing she's ever said to me.*

Finn put his hand at the small of Cassandra's back and gave her a gentle shove in the direction of the bathroom, helping Cass escape from Judith's looming glare while he distracted her.

"Do you have plans for the Perseids this year?" Finn asked as Cassandra surreptitiously strode away. She didn't know what that meant, but it seemed to perk Judith right up, and Cass heard them discussing what sounded like stargazing while she made her way to the restroom.

By the time she returned, Judith was practically glowing at Finn while he wrote something down on a notepad embossed with the Silver Sands emblem.

"Can't go wrong with the view here," he said, tearing off the page. "Knocks my socks off every time." He handed the note to Judith with a wink, and she actually *giggled.*

Cassandra looked at Finn like he was a magician who had just pulled off a levitation trick.

How did you do that? she wanted to ask, but he said, "If you'll excuse me, ladies, I'm going to use the facilities myself."

He trotted off and Cass was left alone with Judith, whose glow immediately snuffed itself out.

She turned a flat expression on Cassandra and said, "Well, young lady, it seems you finally found a decent change of clothes and a hairdryer."

And there's the Judith I know, Cassandra thought. *No giggles for me.*

"It *is* a special occasion," Cass said brightly. "I thought about wearing the wetsuit to the gala since it would fit the ocean conservation theme, but I changed my mind at the last minute."

Judith stared back, obdurate and unamused.

There is no pleasing this woman, Cassandra thought. *The hell with it.*

"You should have seen what Finn almost wore!" she teased. "In the end he decided a speedo wasn't practical for work."

Judith sucked in her breath, and Cass wasn't sure if she was shocked by the scandal of the suggestion or mind-whacked by the idea of Finn in a bathing suit.

Either way, the concierge recovered quickly and snapped, "He seems to be spending entirely too much time with you. He's a good boy and I'm sure you're a bad influence."

Bite me, you barracuda.

"Actually, I have you to thank for that!" Cassandra said, struck by the thought. "If you hadn't turned me away that first night on the island, I never would have met Finn out on the lawn. He never would have helped me, we never would have become friends, and my life on the island may never have come together at all! So really Judith, thank you."

She looked squarely into Judith's reproachful eyes, feeling half earnestly grateful and half pleased by a perverse sense of justice that this woman who despised her was responsible for all of the good things that had happened to her since she'd leapt off that yacht. The older woman stared her down, and Cassandra could see that she was equally at odds with herself. Judith bristled like an agitated porcupine at the thought that she had inadvertently been of service to this soggy upstart, but in the face of Cassandra's genuine thanks, her suitable attire, and her general lack of disarray, the hard edges of Judith's face seemed to soften. Just a few drops melted from the tip of an iceberg, a handful of stones crumbling from the face of

a mountain, a weak ray of sun shining on a frozen
tundra…this subtle mollescence was no indication that
Judith was ready to make friendship bracelets and
invite Cass out for manicures, but it was the farthest
she'd ever looked from wanting to throw Cassandra
out of the building.

"Well, I wouldn't say…I didn't…" The woman
faltered, unsure how to proceed down this alien path
toward civility.

"I'm back!" Finn appeared suddenly at
Cassandra's elbow. "What did I miss?"

"I was just thanking Judith for all the help she's
been to me since I washed up on the island." Cassandra
smiled innocently when Finn looked at her with
momentary disbelief.

He recovered nicely and nodded along. "Always
ready and able to help—that's our Judith!"

"I'm beginning to see that."

Judith flushed. Maybe from Finn's compliment.
Maybe from a vague acknowledgment that his praise
did not strictly apply to her behavior toward
Cassandra. But Cassandra was willing to move on
from their checkered past. Perhaps there was a grand
reason behind all of Judith's animosity. It had been
necessary to set Cassandra on the right path.

"Well, we'd better be off." Finn put a hand on
Cassandra's shoulder and Judith's eyes flickered at the
gesture. Cassandra sensed a deepening chill emanating
once again from behind the front desk.

"I think you're right!" she said. "Thank you again,
Judith." Cassandra thought about reaching out to shake
the other woman's hand, but she didn't want to strain
the boundaries of their burgeoning truce. She was a
little afraid that if she made any sudden moves toward

Judith, the desk clerk would panic and try to ram a stake through her heart. Or more likely in Judith's case, a gold-plated pen.

Judith may have eased up a little in the face of Cassandra's appreciation, but she also seemed ready to charter herself as president of the Finnegan Drake Fan Club. As far as Cass could tell, either Judith would be marginally pleasant the next time Cassandra saw her, or Cass would soon receive an anonymous package of dog droppings in the mail. At this point, it was a toss-up.

Opting out of the handshake, Cass settled for a little wave and a parting smile. Judith looked caught between a smile and a frown and landed somewhere in the vicinity of a grimace.

Well, Cassandra thought when Finn offered her his arm and she took it, walking with him toward the door and hearing a strangled sound escape Judith behind them, *That's progress!*

Chapter Twenty-three

When they got to his bungalow, Finn offered her a beer—which she prudently declined—so he got them two glasses of water (he put an umbrella in hers anyway), and they settled down on the couch. She smiled, stuck the umbrella in her hair like a tropical flower and asked, "What now?"

Want to have sex?

He mentally smacked himself. If he made a pass at her now, she'd probably storm out the door and he wouldn't see her again for the rest of the summer.

He couldn't blame himself, though. That dress was damn distracting…everything kept sliding around. It made him want to run his hands over the smooth fabric, reaching around to lower the zipper so he could run his hands over her smooth skin beneath it. He bet the dress would glide down her body and pool at her feet like water. The image left him lightheaded— Cassandra standing in the middle of his living room wearing nothing but a pair of strappy blue heels.

He cleared his throat and said, "I have board games."

Nothing more innocent than board games, right? Hopefully she hadn't noticed that his face had gone slack with lust before he responded.

"They were here when I moved in," he explained. "The last tenant must have left them. I think there's Candy Land, Monopoly, and Clue, which kind of sucks with two people."

"Candy Land!" she exclaimed. "Oh my gosh, I haven't played that in forever! Do you think it's still magical when you're an adult or is it boring?"

"Let's find out," Finn suggested, digging it out from the storage closet.

Four minutes later, when Cassandra landed at the Candy Castle, she said, "Well, that settles it. It's very, very boring."

"I don't know," Finn defended. "There was an exciting moment there when...we…no. You're right. It was boring."

"Someone just needs to zaz up the rules!" Cass studied the instruction manual. "Did you say you also have Monopoly and Clue?"

"Yes..." he said, and she jumped up and got them from the closet, along with a bag of army men she discovered.

"Look what else I found!" she said, dumping the pieces of the various games out on the table. "Just give me a minute!"

Fifteen minutes later, Cassandra finished explaining an elaborate set of rules and asked, "Do you get it?"

"Not even remotely," he answered, thinking, *Couldn't we just play strip Candy Land? The first one to get naked means the other one wins?*

"You'll catch on as we go!" Cassandra said excitedly. "Can I be the red piece?"

"If I can be green," he said, resigning himself to at least twenty minutes of being very confused.

A few rounds in, Finn couldn't believe it, but he was actually starting to understand this crazy game. Cassandra took her turn and said dramatically, "Ooh, another red square! That means another murder! Poor Mr. Mint. Okay! You write down the killer, the murder weapon and the scene of the crime, and if I correctly guess one of the elements, that's an extra two hundred dollars for me!"

It was incredible, but he followed everything she had just said. On his next turn, he drew a card and said "Yes! A double purple! That puts me right through the Gumdrop Pass, *and* I get free parking!"

"Ugh!" Cassandra groaned. "I knew I should have built a hotel there on my way through the Gumdrop Mountains!"

"Well, there go all your plans to block me at the Licorice Castle. Even if it turns out that Miss Scarlet *did* kill Mr. Mint with the lead pipe, you'll never get the money quickly enough to build all the real estate you'd need to block my gingerbread army!"

But in a surprising turn of events, Finn got stuck in the Molasses Swamp for three turns in a row, and Cassandra came from behind to win the game.

"So *that* is a fun version of Candy Land," she said as they put all the games back in their respective boxes.

"It was," Finn said. "Even though you practically had the game handed to you. Who would have guessed that Plumpy was the killer? He seems so jovial..."

"No, there's definitely something sinister going on there," Cass pointed out. "Although I guess you could say the same for any of them...that game is full of surprisingly creepy characters."

"Too true," Finn said, packing the last of the games back into storage and plopping down beside her on the couch, not actually touching her, but close enough that he easily could have if he wanted to. And he wanted to.

It wasn't just that she was beautiful and was wearing a really sexy dress. Although that was there, too. It was everything about her—her energy, her intelligence, her effervescence, her charm. She was sweet and gutsy and a little bit crazy and it was the most captivating combination Finn had ever met.

"Oh, I never told you," he said, "I got a copy of Bringing up Baby. I borrowed it from Mary Ella. She said you were right and I definitely need to see it. It's been a couple weeks now, so she might be wanting it back," he lied, knowing full well that Mary Ella didn't care how long he kept it, but any excuse to keep Cassandra in his house was a good one. "Do you want to watch it?"

"You have a TV?" Cassandra asked, looking around his TV-less living room.

"It's in the bedroom," he said, hoping that didn't sound like a come-on. Unless she was for it. Then he'd be thrilled.

But Cass didn't seem to think twice about it.

She grinned and said, "This will be great! You're going to love it!"

He thought about offering her another drink, but that would definitely make him seem like a creep. *Why don't you go into the bedroom while I fix you a drink?* No.

Instead, he refilled their water glasses and set up the movie. There was a semi-awkward moment when Cassandra hesitated before getting onto the bed, but she kicked off her shoes (*Blue strappy heels*, he thought) and climbed on top of the covers.

He stretched out next to her, as careful as ever to keep space between them, but he was close enough to feel her warmth and it was all he could do not to reach for her. Maybe this wasn't a good idea. He wasn't sure he could sit through almost two hours with her on his bed without touching her.

She propped a pillow up against the headboard and snuggled into it, and he looked at the pillow with envy. Then he pushed the play button and settled back onto his own pillow, determined to be a gentleman if it killed him.

Amazingly, it wasn't as difficult as he'd expected. Within minutes, Finn was caught up in the film, watching meek and mild Cary Grant try to stand up to his shrew of a fiancé (*Well, they're clearly not getting married*, he thought), then meeting the charismatic, hare-brained Katherine Hepburn. In two scenes, she managed to unwittingly swipe his golf-ball, steal his car, ruin his hat, and destroy his chances at obtaining one million dollars, but she was clearly the most interesting person he was ever going to meet.

"You were right," he told Cass. "This is a good movie."

"I knew you'd like it." She turned her head to smile at him. Her face was inches from his, and showing Herculean restraint, he managed not to lean in and kiss her.

"You were also right about her being crazy," he said instead.

"I know—she's wonderful!" Cassandra agreed, turning her head back to the screen. "Just wait…it gets better."

For the rest of the movie, Finn enjoyed the antics of Hepburn, Grant, and Baby the leopard while simultaneously enjoying Cassandra's nearness. They laughed together at each outlandish plot twist and kept up a steady commentary throughout the film.

At the end of the movie, Cary Grant finally admits he's in love with Katherine Hepburn as she both saves his career and destroys the project he's been working on for four years. Cassandra clapped and Finn joined in while the two stars kissed and the screen faded to black.

"So you liked it?" Cass asked.

"I loved it," he answered.

"Yay!" She swung her legs around the edge of the bed. "I'm so glad! But it's late," she said, slipping her feet back into her heels while Finn watched, distracted. "I should probably be getting back home." Cassandra finished fastening the straps and stood.

Finn looked at the clock. She was right. It was late.

"You can stay here again if you want," he suggested. "I'm happy to walk you home, but it's pretty late to be out, so if you'd rather crash here and go in the daylight, that's fine. I'll take the couch."

"No, that's silly!" she protested. "I can't let you give up your bed."

We can share it, he thought.

"I'll take the couch," she finished. "If you're sure you don't mind."

"Of course not! I'll get you some clothes to sleep in. You can do whatever you need to do in the bathroom...there's an extra toothbrush in the second drawer."

"Thanks!" She slipped into the adjacent bathroom and Finn absently noted the click of her heels on the tile while he focused on finding clothes to put *on* Cassandra rather than taking them off her like he wanted to.

He gathered a T-shirt and sweatpants, then waited a couple of minutes before knocking on the door that separated his bedroom from the bathroom.

He heard a muffled, "Come in," and opened the door to find Cassandra brushing her teeth in her ball gown, looking more glamorous than anyone had a right to while getting ready for bed, still wearing that ridiculous umbrella in her hair.

"I brought you some pajamas," he said, reaching past her to set the bundle on the counter, brushing her shoulder as he did.

His hand had barely grazed her but he felt the light touch in the pit of his stomach. Her skin was soft and he was close enough to smell the now-familiar scent of coconut. Their eyes met in the mirror and held for a long moment and the scrubbing of the toothbrush slowed and stopped altogether until Cassandra finally said, "Thank you!" around the brush and resumed scrubbing.

She bent to spit into the sink and her rear end brushed against him and his whole body stiffened. She must have felt it too, because she went still for just a moment before she hastily stood up and rinsed the brush, then had no choice but to turn around, eyes wide, face hesitant.

They were inches apart but she didn't move away, didn't say anything—which in and of itself was unusual—and Finn knew he was going to kiss her. He had held out all night, held out for three weeks, but now, when she was standing in his bathroom, staring up at him with those huge eyes, the scent of his toothpaste fresh on her breath, she was more than he could resist.

Slowly, carefully, giving her plenty of time to back away, he bent his head to hers. Her mouth was cool like peppermint, and when he parted her lips with his own, she breathed a sigh of pleasure and he deepened the kiss, feeling himself grow tighter, wanting to make her breath come faster, wanting to feel her everywhere. He slipped his tongue into her mouth and she tasted sweet and hot and familiar, drawing in a sharp breath and pushing closer to close the space between them, sliding her arms around his neck and pressing her body against him without hesitation.

Finn broke the kiss and put an inch or two of space between them. He took a ragged breath and said, "Maybe we should stop. This could get out of hand."

She stared back at him, lips red, pupils dilated, looking more depraved than he had ever seen her. "I don't care," she breathed. "Kiss me harder."

She grabbed his collar and pulled him roughly back to her, biting into his mouth like he was a pastry. All the blood rushed from his brain and he slid his hands down her back, pulling her tight against him and kissing her back with no reservation at all.

Chapter Twenty-four

Cassandra shivered as she felt Finn's hands glide down her back, grabbing her dress and twisting the fabric like he wanted to rip it off. She ran her tongue along his lower lip and he sucked in his breath, sliding one hand up her back to bury it in her hair, lacing his fingers through her curls and pulling her head back to bite her neck.

Somewhere far in the distance, Cass heard the sound of crumpling paper.

"My umbrella!" she realized, pulling away from him, distraught, turning to look at the flattened purple paper lying forlornly in the sink.

"I'll get you a new one," he said, yanking her chin back up to reclaim her mouth, and she thought, *Yeah, I'm okay with that.*

He had her pinned against the counter, bent back over the sink, licking into her mouth, making her breathless, and as he moved his lips across her cheek towards the hollow under her ear, she tried to get her breathing under control and thought, *If I'm going to stop this, I'd better do it soon.*

Then he bit her earlobe and she thought, *Or later. Later is fine, too.*

Honestly, at this point, she couldn't think of a good reason to stop him. She was well on the way to figuring out her life, and she had thought about this so many times—what it would be like if she finally said yes, finally had him—and now here he was, and he was even hotter than she'd imagined.

His hand slid over breast and she moaned, feeling herself tense as he stroked her nipple with his thumb, separated from her only by a thin layer of fabric.

She sighed under his touch, loving his hands on her body and loving what he could do with them. He pulled her to standing and lowered his head to kiss her shoulder, sliding his hand around to reach for her zipper, lowering it slowly, and suddenly Cassandra felt the cool rush on her skin as her dress rippled along her body to her feet and she was standing there, naked except for three-inch heels. This was not the kind of dress you could wear underwear with, but she hadn't planned on anyone else becoming aware of that. Finn didn't leave her any time to feel self-conscious, bending his head to her breast, licking, sucking, making her mindless until she cried out from pleasure.

Just as she was growing impatient for more, Finn moved his mouth to her other breast, teasing her with his tongue and then sucking hard as his hand slipped between her thighs and she gasped, moaning as his fingers stroked her, circled her, making her muscles tighten and every nerve she had sing.

She rolled her head back, feeling his mouth and hands hot on her, but she wanted more, wanted to feel

his skin against hers, wanted to feel him everywhere.
Then he slid one finger inside her and she lost her train
of thought completely, unable to think of anything
other than how good it felt to finally have him
touching her, of the pressure he was building inside
her. His mouth was still hot on her breast and she
moaned, raking her nails down the back of his shirt as
he slipped another finger inside her, stroking higher.
The feel of the fabric under her nails triggered
something in her brain and her mind picked up where
it had left off.

Why am I the only one naked? she wondered. He
looked rumpled and sloppy and sexy as hell in his
dress shirt but she wanted him out of it, so she laced
her fingers through his hair, pulling his head back up to
hers so she could start to work on the buttons of his
shirt.

Capturing his lower lip between her teeth, she
sucked and he drew in a sharp breath as she ran her
hands over his shoulders, sliding his shirt down his
back, then moving her hands around to loosen his belt.
Easing down the zipper of his slacks, her hand
continued to explore until she found the long, hard
length of him. Shoving his clothes the rest of the way
down with her free hand, she heard his sharp intake of
breath as she wrapped her fingers around him and
began to stroke up and down, until he groaned and
grabbed her wrist, pulling her hand away and
intertwining his fingers though hers with one hand
while the other moved back between her thighs and he
began to kiss his way down Hart torso, licking the
hollow between her breasts, darting his tongue into her
belly button and making her gasp, gently biting the
sensitive flesh of her inner thigh. By the time he found

her center, she was wound so tight she almost came undone right there.

His mouth moved against her while his fingers moved inside her, licking, sucking, stroking, petting, taking her higher, making her shudder.

"Oh my god, Finn," she breathed, digging her fingers into his hair. His only response was to slide his fingers higher, and Cassandra cried out and arched against him, twisting a handful of hair. He removed his hand and Cass had half a second to be disappointed that he was stopping so soon before he boosted her up onto the sink and licked into her and her brain short circuited, nearly blacking out from the pleasure. She arched her back and moved against him, dimly aware that maybe she should be contributing more, but his hands were rough on her hips and his tongue was hot inside her and she felt too damn satisfied to care. She shoved aside her concern and focused instead on the heat he was building, on her breath coming from deep within, sighing as he brought her closer and closer to the edge.

She opened her eyes and was surprised to see that she was still wearing her shoes. The sight of the strappy heels against the muscles of his back was so sexy that that alone practically sent her over, but he gripped her hips harder and licked higher into her and she broke, throwing her head back as the pleasure rolled over her in waves, finally collapsing back against the mirror, temporarily too sated to move.

She was dimly aware of the sound of a drawer opening and foil crumpling, and then suddenly there he was again, coming back up to kiss her. His mouth tasted strange and exotic, and she blushed thinking about where it had just been. She hadn't had time to be self-conscious while he was down there, but now that he was done, she felt a little shy. At least, she did until she felt him against her and then she wanted him all over again. Two seconds ago, she wouldn't have thought she could handle any more pleasure, but now, feeling him press hard between her thighs, she wanted as much of him as she could get. She bit his shoulder as he slid into her, hot, slick, hard inside her, and the light flared behind her eyes as he rocked into her, pushing deeper with each movement of his hips. He groaned and licked into her mouth and Cassandra spread her legs wider, tilting her hips to take in all of him, breathing his name as he slid harder, deeper into her, filling her to the brim. He ran his hands down her back to cup her rear end, pulling her harder against him and she cried out against his mouth.

"Harder," she gasped, and he bit her lip, pulling her even tighter against him, rocking even higher into her, and she wrapped her legs around him and moved with him, each stroke of his hips bringing her closer to dark, beautiful oblivion.

"Oh god, there," she moaned when he changed the angle of his hips and hit something so good that Cassandra's world tilted around her. She clung to his shoulders, breath coming in short, shallow gasps as he bore down on her, pulsing into her again and again and again, bringing her right to the edge of ecstasy, closer, closer, closer, until she finally broke, crying out as her body was rocked by the force of her orgasm, until Finn shuddered against her and her own body quieted and they both lay still, panting in each other's arms.

"Wow," she said when she could speak again. "To think, we could have been doing that all summer."

Finn laughed. "That's what I kept trying to tell you," he said. "But I seem to remember something about a life path…" He brushed a curl off of her shoulder and kissed the bare skin there.

"Right," Cassandra pulled him back to her mouth and kissed him again. "Which, at the time, was wise and prudent and you should be impressed that you know such a level-headed person."

She slipped down from the counter and shivered as her body slid against the length of his

"But I'm going to be a chef. That much I know. The rest of the details are fuzzy, but I said I wanted a path, not a GPS tracking system, so I'm pretty sure the universe and I have come to an understanding and I'm allowed to date now."

"The search is over?" Finn looked hopeful.

"The search is no longer the only thing I'm allowing myself to focus on." She ran her hands up his chest, palms gliding across his nipples, and he looked distracted.

"So you're allowed to focus on me now?" he asked, sounding dazed.

"Yes," she answered, wrapping her arms around his neck. "In fact, I'm pretty sure that for the rest of the night, you're going to require all of my attention."

Chapter Twenty-five

"You and Finn finally got together?" Daphne shrieked the next day. "Yay! Wait, I am happy about this, right?" she asked, momentarily cautious, then jumped up and down and clapped, saying, "Of course I am, look at your face!" before Cassandra had time to get a word in edgewise.

"Yes, Daphne, we're excited about this," she told her exuberant friend, unable to suppress the silly grin she'd been wearing all morning, ever since she woke up in bed next to Finn.

"Yay!" Daphne cried again, still jumping. "This calls for celebration! Bear claws and mimosas!"

"Breakfast of champions," Cass grinned. "We have bear claws?"

"You have a bear claw. I have a mango."

"Mangos and mimosas?"

"Well, mangos and pineapple orange juice. You're a bad influence."

"That's fine, I'll skip the champagne. We're supposed to be at yoga in two hours anyway. But I'm eating that bear claw!" Cass declared. "And then I'll make you an actual breakfast. Wait a second! How was the rest of your night? It wasn't going well, last I saw you."

"Who cares about that?" Daphne exclaimed. "Tell me everything! How did this happen?" Daphne dragged her toward the kitchen and opened the fridge to dig out the juice.

"It was a lot of things," Cass answered, taking two champagne flutes out of the cupboard. If they weren't having the champagne, they could at least use the fancy glasses.

"But mostly, last night threw into amazingly sharp relief what a great guy Finn is, especially compared to all the other creeps out there."

"You can say that again."

"So, I found myself wondering why I'm resisting him so strongly when really everything between us should be so simple."

"Finally!" Daphne said. "I'll drink to that!" she saluted Cassandra with her glass, then took a sip and reached for a brown paper bag next to the sink.

"I still stand by my decision not to be with him up until now—oh my gosh, I love you!" Cassandra interrupted herself as Daphne pulled out her pastry, then resumed, "But now that I'm figuring things out—I really do love working at Andre's and I know that's what I want to be doing—there's no reason to keep pushing him away. He's sweet and funny and sexy and he's so easy to be with. When we're together, it just feels right. From the moment I jumped off that boat, he's been amazing."

"Jumped?" Daphne sounded confused, and Cassandra stilled.

Daphne still doesn't know.

"Umm…" Cassandra laughed nervously and her stomach started turning somersaults. "I planned to tell you this more officially, definitely with at least one alcoholic beverage in each of us, but yes…jumped. I didn't fall off the boat that night. I jumped."

She looked nervously at Daphne, watching her reaction—was her best friend about to tell her that she was crazy and demand that she pack her stuff and leave so Daphne could find a sane, stable person to live with?

Daphne looked at her in open-mouthed shock for a moment, then burst out laughing.

"Wow, you really did need a summer away from your family, didn't you?" she grinned and shook her head.

"This doesn't freak you out?" Cassandra asked, feeling a rush of relief surge from her chest all the way through her solar plexus.

"Of course not!" Daphne laughed. "If anything, I love you even more. Fate didn't push you around, you took charge of your life! You jumped into the ocean—you! The ocean!—because you needed to take control of your future. You've been brave and adventurous and steadfast and—other than a brief lapse on a boat—completely responsible this summer. So you had to do something a little crazy to make your life your own. Who cares? You, Cassandra Dillon, are one of my favorite people."

Cassandra stooped down to hug her roommate. "Right back at you, Daph. I love you."

"I love you, too," Daphne said. "Now! Tell me more about last night!"

Cassandra filled Daphne in on the rest of her evening with Finn—making up new rules to Candy Land ("I totally kicked his ass, by the way. I am the Clandopoly Land master!"), watching the old movie ("I couldn't believe he had gotten a copy—it was so sweet!"), and then glossing over everything that happened from the bathroom on ("I'm not going into detail, Daphne—he's your cousin. Suffice it to say, it was amazing!").

When Daphne had asked all her questions and they had discussed every reasonable detail, Cass said, "So that's me. How are you doing after last night?"

"Oh, I'm fine," Daphne brushed the question aside. "I walked it all off on the way home. Those run-ins always get to me."

"Yeah, breaking up with someone is always hard," Cassandra sympathized. "But Stewart seemed to take it pretty well. Bridget certainly looked pleased."

"Stewart? Oh. Yes, that too."

"What were you talking about? Drew?" Cassandra caught on belatedly.

"He drives me up the wall!" Daphne furrowed her brow and crumpled up the empty pastry bag, throwing it toward the kitchen with more force than necessary. "But I'm fine now," she said primly, smoothing out her face.

"Yes, I can see that," Cass laughed. "You might have a harder time convincing that grocery bag, though. Come on." She stood and held out her hand to Daphne, pulling her up from the couch. "I'll make you scrambled eggs. You need protein."

"Really, I'm fine," Daphne said again, and Cassandra looked archly at her over her shoulder, towing her through the kitchen door.

"Sure, you are. You just mutilate whatever inanimate object is on hand when Drew's name is mentioned. No one else gets that kind of rise out of you. Stewart certainly didn't."

"That's because Stewart was a gentleman." Daphne lifted her chin.

"No, that's because Stewart got you as excited as that paper bag and couldn't have kept you interested for all the cornices in the world." Cassandra pulled the egg carton out of the refrigerator and turned to the cabinets to grab a mixing bowl. "Drew might be able to give you a run for your money, though."

Daphne scoffed.

"Seriously, Daphne! You guys have chemistry."

"But he has the mentality of a fifteen-year-old! He has absolutely no substance!"

"I don't know," Cassandra countered, cracking eggs into the bowl. "I had an interesting conversation with him last night. Did you know that he's just one semester shy of a bachelor's degree in business?"

"Drew went to college?" Daphne looked surprised.

"Put himself through," Cassandra confirmed, going back to the fridge for cheese.

"Worked three jobs to do it. Something happened just before his final semester to derail his plans and he ended up here, but he's a smart guy and he could do well for himself if he wanted to. I bet he could even help you out with the studio. You should try having a real conversation with him someday. I think it would surprise you."

"I doubt it." Daphne got out a pan for Cassandra and set it on the stovetop. "He is without facets."

"You looked pretty surprised when you saw him dancing last night—dill?" Cassandra interjected, opening up the spice cabinet.

"Yes, please," Daphne nodded. Cassandra grabbed salt, black pepper, and turmeric as well. Daphne had once spent a whole lunch rhapsodizing about turmeric and Cass knew she would appreciate the addition.

"If he has those sorts of unexpected skills, why couldn't he have unexpected depth?" Cassandra asked, shaking herbs into the mixing bowl. "He even revealed some of it to me yesterday."

Daphne snorted. "Or, he was spinning a story to get in your pants."

"Oh, stop it," Cassandra scolded, clunking the mixing bowl next to the stove and turning on the heat. "We both know that Drew has zero interest in me. And he's a good guy. You can't deny it. He just doesn't know how to properly tell you he's crazy about you."

"You mean sleeping with anything in a bikini doesn't spell out true love to you?" Daphne drawled, topping off their orange juices.

"Okay, I admit he could be choosier," Cassandra conceded, pouring eggs into the pan. "But from his perspective, he doesn't have a shot in hell with you— you've been turning him down for months. He's twenty-six years old and male, living on a tropical island. You can't blame him entirely."

"Finn would never act like that."

"Finn is an entirely different person, with an entirely different past."

"What past?"

"Talk to Drew," Cass emphasized, folding the eggs when they began to solidify. "Clearly, there's something there or you wouldn't get so hot and bothered when he flirts with other women."

Daphne cast a withering look her way and she held up her hands, spatula included. "I call 'em like I see 'em. Really, Daph, talk to him. I think if you guys were able to connect on something real, he might finally be able to grow up and you could have a shot at something great."

"I'll think about it," Daphne said darkly.

"Good!" Cass said, satisfied. "Now what do you say we invite Mary Ella over for scrambled eggs and hash this out all over again?"

"Brunch and girl talk on a Sunday morning." Daphne heaved a long-suffering sigh. "Life is hard."

***

"So you and Cass finally did it, huh?"

The same morning, Finn sat, elated, on his surfboard with Drew floating a couple feet away, looking depressed. They came to this spot regularly—a sparsely populated alcove that usually had decent waves—but today the air hung heavy and still around them and the water moved in gentle ripples. They were stubbornly sitting on their boards anyway, just in case the weather took a turn for the exciting.

Finn didn't need a change in weather to lift his spirits—he was still giddy about the events of the previous night. He was happy just to enjoy the feeling of the cool water on his legs and the sound of the surf lapping against the shore, but Drew clearly needed a pick-me-up. He sat hunched on his board, face sullen under his dark hair, mood out of place amidst the bright sunshine and beautiful scenery. Finn didn't want to make matters worse by flaunting his own good fortune in Drew's face, but he was too happy to suppress it.

"Yup," he answered shortly, trying not to be obnoxious in his post-coital cheerfulness.

"Congratulations," Drew said in a tone that people normally reserved for talking about death or illness. "I'm really happy for you, buddy."

"You can be happy for me when you're in a better mood," Finn said fairly. "What's going on with you today?"

"Nothing."

Finn scoffed. "Sure. That's why you look like they outlawed bungee jumping. What's up?"

"I'm just thinking about the fight with Daphne last night."

"Yeah, she seemed pretty pissed. What did you do to her?"

"I didn't do anything!" Drew was defensive. "Nothing more than usual, anyway. We were dancing, having a good time, and then she flipped out on me. That woman is a loose cannon."

"Let me guess: you made a pass at her before she went rogue."

"Well, sure. I always make a pass at her—no harm in trying."

"And you've never stopped to consider that's not the best approach with Daphne?"

"It works with every other woman I meet."

"That's because all the women you go after are shallow party-girls," Finn said. "Daphne is the only woman of substance you've ever wanted."

"Yeah." Drew looked contemplative. "Why couldn't she have been just a little bit shallow?"

Finn splashed water at him. "Very funny, jackass. But she turns you down all the time—why are you moping now?"

"It wasn't a casual brush-off—she was saying no for good. She said I can't give her what she wants."

Finn squinted. Based on what he knew about his friend's track record and his cousin's relationship goals, there was probably a lot of truth to that statement. But Drew looked like hell so he wasn't about to come out and say that.

"Well," he began diplomatically, "you and Daphne don't want the same things. She wants someone who will commit. Someone who will build a life with her, love her. You've said so yourself: that's not your style."

"Not for a long time," Drew said, staring absently at the shoreline and Finn glanced at him, surprised. What the hell did that mean, not for a long time? When had Drew ever wanted to settle down with a woman?

A brunette in a barely-there black bikini was making eyes at them from the beach, but Drew didn't even glance at her. He gazed off into the distance, brow furrowed in thought. Finn looked from Drew to the brunette and back again, shocked that Drew genuinely didn't seem to notice her. Daphne must have really gotten to him if he didn't notice scantily clad women sending signals his way.

"I've never seen you get like this over a woman," Finn told him frankly. "Your attention span isn't usually this long. You've got it bad."

Drew jerked his head around. "No, I don't! She's a pain in the ass. She's always on my case about something. If I fell for her, I'd never have a moment's peace."

"She's usually on your case about sleeping with other women," Finn pointed out. "If you stopped, she'd have a lot less to complain about."

"It's just something she said last night that's bothering me," Drew went on as if Finn hadn't spoken.

"Just one thing?" Finn raised an eyebrow and Drew ignored him again.

"She said I don't really *see* her. She said I just see a random girl I want to have sex with."

"Isn't that how you see most of the women you hit on?"

"Yes, but I don't want her to think that's how I see *her*," Drew said. "It's not like I don't care about her—we're friends."

"Uh-huh," Finn said, not convinced. "Drew, friends don't spend months trying to get into another friend's pants."

"You spent two months trying to get into Cassandra's."

"Yes, but I'm in love with her, so you're not really helping your case," Finn said, surprising himself by saying it out loud. But now wasn't the time to dwell on it—they were focusing on Drew's love life, not his.

"Also," he went on, "friends don't spy on their friend's dates or look gleeful when they find out their friend has dumped said date."

"I've never looked gleeful in my life."

"And they don't get all broody when their friend tells them that they're never going to be together," Finn continued. "Face it, buddy—you're done for. But you should be proud of yourself," he said when Drew closed his eyes and passed a hand over his face. "If you were going to fall for someone, Daphne's a damn good choice. You've spent time with dozens of women who couldn't hold a candle to her."

"Don't you think I know that?" Drew said from behind his hand. "I know she's amazing."

"Have you tried telling her that?"

"She wouldn't take me seriously."

"You've never given her any reason to take you seriously," Finn said, probably with less sympathy than he should have had for his best friend. "So…just so we're all on the same page…you do realize you have feelings for her, right?"

"Of course, I do, asshole. What do I do about it? She won't go out with me."

"Ask Cass," Finn suggested. "I bet she'd have some ideas for you."

"Good call!" Drew snapped his fingers. "Women have all sorts of devious ways of tricking people into doing things."

"That's a healthy attitude to bring to the table," Finn said. "But sure, we'll get her help."

Chapter Twenty-six

"You want me to trick Daphne into going on a date with you?" Cassandra asked, voice heavy with skepticism. "You're joking, right?"

"Not *trick*," Drew explained. "Just help me get her to do something she wouldn't normally do."

"Like go on a date with you?" Cass clarified. "And how is this not a trick?"

"I know it sounds ridiculous," Finn said. "But Daphne was really mad the last time she saw him, and he's actually serious about wanting to work things out with her. Can you give him some pointers?"

"Prove it," Cassandra said. "Why should I help you?"

"Because I'm a stand-up guy?" Drew said hopefully.

Cassandra laughed. "Hardly! Okay Drew, I don't like to do this to you because I don't want to pry into your private life, but since you're asking me to do just that to my best friend, I need to understand some things about you. I need to ask you about your almost-fiancé."

Finn looked up, startled.

"I'm sorry to mention it," Cass said, "but if you want my help with Daphne, I think this is pertinent information."

"I told you pretty much the whole thing the other night." Drew shrugged.

"What?" Finn was outraged. "You were almost engaged?! And you told Cassandra, but you never told me?"

"It came up." Drew shrugged again. "Like I told Cass, I went to school with this girl, Sarah. We met junior year. I fell pretty hard. She was a bio major and came to the island during winter break of our senior year to study some rare breed of fish and I followed her, planning to propose before we went back for our last semester. Then I walked in on her screwing her sleazy scuba instructor and I broke things off. She went back to school; I stayed here. I didn't want to go back and see her around campus, so I decided to take a semester off and finish after she graduated, but by the time that came around, I had fallen in love with this place and I never looked back."

"You never told me any of this!" Finn said, indignant.

"It's over," Drew said dismissively. "It's not important now."

"Have you been with anyone since then?" Cass asked.

"I've been with lots of women since then." Drew wiggled his eyebrows and Cassandra smacked him over the head.

"Cut that out if you want my help! You know what I mean. Have you had any serious relationships since then?"

Drew shrugged. "Too much hassle."

"There, you see? You distance yourself from women because you don't want to get hurt again, so you go after the kind of women you know you don't have a future with. Daphne is the only exception."

"Thank you, Dr. Dillon."

"Am I wrong?"

Drew scowled at her. Cassandra raised her eyebrows and waited.

"Probably not," he admitted.

"See, this is good!" Cassandra clapped her hands and smiled. "Progress! Now how do I know you really feel differently about Daphne?"

"What do you want me to do, write you a poem?"

"Sure, write me an acrostic! D is for…"

"Do you really think I'm going to do that?"

"No. But convince me you're serious about her, and I will help you."

"What will it take?"

"Well, for starters, you can stop sulking around like a five-year-old. You're a man, for heaven's sake! Act like it."

"I don't sulk." Drew's tone reeked heavily of sulkiness.

"Tell me what you like about her."

Drew curled his lip, clearly not interested in discussing his feelings, but Cassandra crossed her arms and waited, so he sighed.

"She's beautiful," he started, staring straight ahead, not looking at either Cass or Finn.

"Obviously." Cassandra held out for more.

"And feisty." His lip quirked in a smile, still staring into the distance, and Cassandra grinned and quietly smacked Finn's arm several times. It was like pulling teeth, but Drew was going to express real feelings.

"And adventurous. And smart." Drew almost seemed to have forgotten they were there. "She's strong. She doesn't take bullshit from anyone, but she can take a joke. She's friendly to everyone. And independent. And driven. She expects more from me than what I give her. She's challenging. And exciting. And sexy."

"That's perfect!" Cassandra said, thinking that, now he had started, Drew would go on listing Daphne's many virtues until she cut him off. "Now tell her all of that!"

"I can't just come out and say that!"

"You need to start being more direct with her." Cassandra ignored him.

"I've been about as direct as I can be." Drew sounded frustrated.

"Hardly! You've never told her *any* of that."

"Daphne knows I'm interested in her and she shuts me down every time."

"Daphne knows you're interested in *sleeping* with her," Cass corrected. "Not the same thing. If you want Daphne, you're going to have to tell her how you feel, and then you're going to have to prove it."

"How?"

"By backing it up with action. No more sleeping around. And the two of you need to start spending actual time together. Not flirting or fighting or spending time with me or Finn as a buffer. You're both active people—go hiking or surfing or parasailing or something. Try taking her dancing again…that seemed to work. But—and I want you to listen to me very carefully here—you cannot try to sleep with her."

"I don't follow."

"Daphne's not stupid. She's going to assume that whatever you're doing, you're doing it to get her into bed. And given your history, that's a fair assumption. So, to prove that you really care about her, you need to take things slow. You can't jump into bed with her the minute things start to go well. It might take a while. But in the end, it'll be worth it."

"Not sleep with her," Drew repeated.

"Only if you want to keep her," Cass confirmed.

"Don't try to sleep with her." Drew nodded as he wrapped his mind around the concept. "Okay. I can do that. I think. But how do I get her to go out with me in the first place?"

"Why don't you try asking?" Cassandra suggested.

Drew laughed. "Yeah, right. Did you see her face when she left last night? It's going to take more than that."

"Listen, you dork, you don't need tricks to get Daphne to go out with you. You just need to be honest. As a matter of fact, I've already laid some groundwork and if you approach her and have an actual conversation—about your past and your interests and passions, and without making any cracks about sex—I think you have a shot."

"I told you!" Finn smacked him.

"If that doesn't work," Cassandra went on, "then afterwards, maybe we can work out some sort of grand gesture to help her realize you're actually serious."

"You already talked to her?"

"I was feeling generous after our chat at the gala. You have to let Daphne see that side of you."

"Thanks, Cass!" Drew sounded grateful. "You're amazing!" He kissed her cheek and she smiled.

"I do what I can."

"But if you already talked to her, why did we have to go through all of this?"

"Because I wanted to make sure that I was right about you. And I am. You're a good guy."

"The best." Drew winked at her. "And Daphne Drake deserves the best."

***

For the next several days, it seemed like Drew was all talk, because he didn't come around to the apartment at all—it was the longest stretch he'd stayed away in weeks.

Cass never got a chance to find him at work and ask for an update, because there was never a dull moment in the kitchen (though, Cassandra was pleased to report, still no fires, impalements, or lost appendages to date). Between her busy work schedule and budding romance with Finn, Cass didn't have time to wonder whether Drew would ever work up the courage to talk to Daphne, but based on a pseudo-nonchalant comment from Daphne earlier in the week ("Drew hasn't stopped by in a while"), Cass could tell she was noticing the absence.

Cassandra had almost given up on him until one night, while waiting for Finn to finish an interview for his paper, Cassandra and Daphne were watching Roman Holiday and swooning over Gregory Peck when there was a knock on the door.

Cass paused the movie while Daphne got up to see who it was, jolted out of her laughter when she saw that it was Drew.

"Hey, Daph."

Cassandra couldn't see him from her spot on the couch, but Drew didn't sound nearly as sure of himself as usual. Normally he grinned and leaned against the door frame and said something suggestive, cocky as hell, but tonight his tone was more subdued, almost nervous.

It seemed that Drew was about to make his move.

Cass thought about retreating to her room to give them some privacy, but she was too curious to see how it would all turn out. So instead, she resumed the movie and tried to look invisible, turning down the volume so it wouldn't disturb them or prevent her from eavesdropping.

That way, she told herself virtuously, she could step in and rescue Drew if things went south and Daphne decided to go for the throat.

"Did you bring me flowers?" Daphne sounded surprised and suspicious.

Cassandra surreptitiously scooted down the couch for a better view.

"Not exactly."

She saw Drew holding what appeared to be a bouquet, looking more sheepish than she had ever seen him. "I brought you a smoothie."

"What?"

"Well, ingredients for a smoothie." He held out the bundle, and sure enough, there was a banana, a mango, an orange, an avocado, and five strawberries, all skewered and wrapped inside four leaves of kale.

Daphne looked up at him, startled.

"You made me a smoothie bouquet."

"I figured it would be better than roses."

A cautious smile spread across Daphne's face.

"That's...unexpected."

"Look, Daphne. I don't know how to say this in a way that will make you believe me, but you're important to me. Really important. And I haven't had that in a long time, and I haven't wanted it in a long time, but I want it now and I want it with you. And I know you don't have any reason to trust me and it might be a long time before you do, but I'd like to take you on a date."

He'd made his speech in a rush, as if he needed to get it all out at once, but now he stood and waited without making a sound, nervous and vulnerable.

Cassandra openly stared from her spot on the couch, holding her breath while Daphne stared at Drew in silence.

"Would you like to go for a walk?" Daphne asked finally.

Drew let out a shaky breath and smiled, relaxing for the first time since he'd said hello.

"Just let me put this in the fridge." Daphne walked past Cass toward the kitchen, shooting her a buoyantly excited expression as she did.

Drew nodded and grinned at Cassandra from the doorway and she grinned maniacally back and gave him a double thumbs up.

Well done, Drew.

The couple exited and Cassandra leaned back into the couch, still smiling, and resumed the movie. They would be fine.

Just as Audrey Hepburn was breaking a guitar over a man's head, the front door rattled and Daphne floated back into the room.

"So," Cassandra switched off the TV to grin at her friend, "how did it go?"

Daphne couldn't hide her jubilation. "It was great! Oh, Cass, it went really, amazingly, surprisingly well! I learned more about him tonight than I have since we met!"

"That's great!"

"He was sweet! And genuine. And smart! I didn't know he had any of that in him!"

"I told you he had hidden depth! He's C.K Dexter Haven!"

"What?"

"Nothing. Tell me more!"

Daphne filled her in on the details of their conversation.

"He really opened up, Cass. He has layers I had no idea existed! And he didn't hit on me once! He left without making a pass. And that smoothie bouquet! I never in a million years would have seen that coming! Did you tell him to do that?"

"I had nothing to do with it."

Daphne fell back against the cushions, glowing.

"We're going for a hike on Saturday."

"Careful," Cassandra teased. "Those hikes can get you into trouble."

"I don't know." Daphne gave her a half smile. "I might be ready for a little bit of trouble."

Chapter Twenty-seven

The following days flew by in a happy blur of mornings with Daphne—sometimes accompanied by Mary Ella and Sir Galahad—afternoons and evenings at the restaurant, and nights with Finn. August was well underway, and Andre was beginning to ask veiled questions about her post-summer plans, but Cassandra mindfully ignored them for the time being. She had a fairly good idea of what she hoped to make happen at the end of the month, but it was such a big step that she was afraid to admit it out loud. For now, she was simply trying to enjoy each moment as it came.

One morning, she and Finn had been enjoying a particularly nice moment—she had made French toast again and the two of them had come up with some very creative uses for warm syrup—and they were just getting out of a much-needed shower when they heard a knock at the door.

"Daphne must have forgotten her keys," Cass said. She gave Finn a quick kiss and wrapped herself in a towel, saying, "You get dressed and I'll go let her in."

She padded across the living room, hair still dripping. When she turned the knob, she said, "Hey, Daph, it's not like you to forget your—Dad!"

She interrupted herself mid-sentence as the door swung open to reveal her father's placid face smiling on the stoop. He was flocked by her mother and sister, who were both grinning madly at her.

"Mom, Beth! What are you guys doing here?"

"Surprise!" her mother sang out. "We've come to see you!"

"I can see that," Cassandra said, mentally regrouping as fast as could be expected from post-coital satisfaction to surprise visit from family. Nothing like the sight of your parents to completely dampen a good afterglow. Belatedly, she smiled and gave them all hugs, clutching the towel closely and apologizing for her dampness.

"It's great to see you guys!" she said, pretty sure that that was the truth. "Sorry I'm all wet…I just got out of the shower. I can't believe you're really here!"

That was definitely the truth.

"We thought about calling but your mother wanted it to be a surprise," her dad explained.

"It is!" Cass felt water trickle from her hair down her back and wished she were wearing underwear. "It's a big surprise!"

"We decided to recharter our last excursion so we could come see you—we just couldn't resist coming to check up on you!" her mother exclaimed.

"That's their story, anyway," Beth cut in. "I think Dad just wanted you to distract me. But there are beaches here, right? Any cute guys?"

Before Cass could answer, Finn's voice came from the next room.

"Hey, Daph, have you heard from—oh," he said, stopping short as he turned the corner from the hallway.

"Hell-o," Beth said.

Mercifully, Finn was fully clothed, and Cassandra sent out a silent thank you to the powers that be that he hadn't come out wearing nothing but a towel. As much as she would have loved that under different circumstances, she could only imagine how her father, who was already frowning and eyeing Finn's wet hair suspiciously, would have reacted to that. Cassandra touched her own wet hair and tried her best to look un-ravished. Considering what Finn had been doing to her fifteen minutes ago, it wasn't easy.

"You're not Daphne," he finished lamely, stating the obvious.

"I take it you're not either." Her father glowered, now looking with patent disapproval at Finn's hair.

"Nope, this is Finn!" Cass said brightly, figuring if she didn't act guilty, they couldn't pin anything on her. "He's Daphne's cousin. Finn, this is my dad, Robert, my mom, Miranda, and my sister, Beth. They've dropped in for a surprise visit!"

She looked meaningfully at Finn, her tone telegraphing, *Isn't that wonderful?* as sternly as she could so that she would start to believe it herself.

"Mr. Dillon, Mrs. Dillon," Finn reached out to shake each of their hands in turn. "Great to meet you! You too, Beth!" he added, encompassing them all in an easy smile. "I've heard great things!"

"So have we," Beth piped up, eyeing Finn from head to toe and giving her sister a sly smile.

"You must be the boy who helped Cassandra that first day after her fall, poor thing!" her mother said.

Finn looked startled at the word "fall" and Cassandra's nervous system went into high alert—she had never told her parents that she'd jumped and Finn knew the truth. It all seemed so long ago that it hardly mattered, but still, she didn't want her cover blown now, after she'd managed to avoid hurting their feelings for so long. Let them think that her plunge overboard and summer on the island was an act of fate—rather than a deliberate decision on her part designed to get her out from under their loving, ever-present gaze. Her heart pounded nervously in her chest, but Finn just smiled wider and said, "That's me!"

Bless you, Finnegan Drake, Cassandra thought as her mother gripped his hand and said, "We just can't thank you enough, looking out for Cassandra this way! Goodness knows what would have happened to her if the two of you hadn't met!"

Cassandra slightly resented the implication that she wouldn't have been able to take care of herself on her own, but since she had previously voiced the exact same sentiment herself, she couldn't really hold it against her mother.

"We owe a lot to you," Robert said grudgingly, apparently able to set his fatherly disapproval aside for the man who, in their eyes, had saved their daughter's life.

Finn graciously brushed their thanks aside and said, "I just did what any good Samaritan would have done. I was happy to help!"

"Oh, pish!" Miranda fluttered her hands. "Let us take you out for breakfast! It's the least we can do! Have you eaten yet?"

Finn and Cassandra eyed each other guiltily.

"I actually made French toast not too long ago," Cass jumped in, "but if you guys are hungry, I can make some more now and we can go out for a late lunch in a while? Although, Finn, if you have to work..." she trailed off, knowing perfectly well that he didn't, but wanting to give him an out just the same.

Spending half the day with her entire family on such short notice was a lot to ask. He hadn't had time to mentally prepare. One minute he was licking maple syrup off her stomach and the next he was forced to make small talk with her parents from across the breakfast table. Not a fair turnaround. But, since he was a prince among men, Finn shook his head and said, "I'd love to go to lunch!"

"Excellent!" Miranda clapped. "That's settled, then!"

"I'll get started on the food," Cassandra offered. "If any of you want to freshen up or take a quick nap in the meantime, the bathroom is just down the hall and my bedroom is the first door on the left. Finn, could I get your help in the kitchen?"

"Of course!" He followed her out of the room and she called, "Make yourselves at home!" to her family over her shoulder.

She busied herself with gathering the ingredients, waiting until she heard conversation floating from the other room ("Well, isn't this place just darling! Beth, come look at this clock!") before giving Finn a quick kiss and whispering, "Thank you! You're officially going above and beyond the call of duty here! And thanks for not saying anything about the jump..."

"Of course," he said again, helping her crack eggs into a bowl. It probably would have gone faster without him—by now, Cass could simultaneously crack two eggs at a time, one in each hand, while Finn had to pause every so often to fish a bit of shell out of the egg goop, but it was cute that he was helping.

"I figured if you didn't tell them yourself, you wouldn't want me to do it. And I'm pretty sure that meals with the parents are fairly standard on the list of boyfriend duties."

Her heart lurched sideways at the term *boyfriend.* While it was obvious that they were together, neither of them had specifically used that word. But he used it now so casually, she decided not to make a big deal of it.

Get a grip, she told herself. But she felt giddy nonetheless.

"One way or the other, I owe you!" She came up on her toes to kiss him again. She'd meant for it just to be a peck on the lips, but he followed her down, reclaiming her mouth and saying in a low voice, "I can think of several things you could do to make it up to me..."

Reluctantly, she put some distance between them and said, "About that...can we keep this whole thing between us under wraps, just for now?" She squinted and bit her lip, hoping he didn't take offense.

"I hate to ask," she hurried on, "but it seems like the wise choice. They're going to ask me all kinds of questions about what I've done here and what I plan to do next, and when I tell them, I want them to know that I've made all of my choices with a level head on my shoulders. I just don't want them holding anything against you!"

"Okay," he said, taken aback but not angry. "But just so you know," he said, leaning in close, "several more things were just added to the list."

"We'll do them all," she promised, and kissed him again.

"Just not right now." She pulled away. "My parents and little sister are in the next room and I have to make breakfast."

"Right," he said, turning on the water to wash the frying pan she had used earlier. "They might notice."

Twenty minutes, a loaf of bread and a dozen eggs later, they were all sitting down to eat when Daphne swept into the room, her usual perky self, talking a mile a minute.

"Hey, Cass, I'm home! Oh my gosh, are you making French toast? It smells amazing! That's fantastic, I'm so hu—oh, hello!" She finally noticed the surplus of people in the room and stopped long enough to look at them all in surprise.

"Daphne, meet my family." Cassandra answered her unasked question. "They've come to surprise me."

"That's wonderful!" Daphne dimpled at them all. "It's so great to meet you! I'm Daphne, Cassandra's roommate! It's so exciting that you're here! I want to hear all sorts of stories about Cass as a little girl! I bet she was the cutest little thing anyone's ever seen!"

Cassandra smiled fondly at Daphne, who was completely unfazed by three uninvited guests sitting around her dining table. Cass may have been caught off guard at finding her parents on her doorstep, but Daphne had never had an awkward social interaction in her life. She was immediately lovable.

Beth smiled and pulled out the chair next to her. "Come and have some French toast and I'll tell you about the time Cass tried to use our house as an animal shelter for the stray cats on our street."

"That is so adorable!" Daphne was thrilled.

"Less adorable when you come home from Girl Scouts to find three feral cats hiding under your bed." Beth shook her head. "I still don't understand how she got them into the house, but you'd think she would have hidden them in her own room!"

"They were hissing! Your room was empty at the time." Cassandra shrugged. "It seemed like the better choice. And I lured them in with pot roast."

"I knew it!" her mother exclaimed. "Cassandra Elaine, you said you didn't know what happened to that pot roast!"

"The cats needed it more than we did, Mom," Cassandra said virtuously. "They were starving."

"Apparently they were still hungry enough after all that pot roast to try and eat *me*," Beth looked reproachfully at her sister.

"Oh, they did not!" Cassandra shook her head. "They were just being friendly."

"Friendly like a caged lion," Beth said darkly, and Cassandra said, "Eat your French toast."

"That is great!" Daphne bubbled. "I never had siblings—this goofball was the closest thing I had," she said, elbowing Finn.

They spent the rest of the meal and the next couple of hours getting to know each other—swapping zany childhood stories and talking about their summer adventures. Beth had plenty to say about her summer conquests, with her father coughing and shaking his head at the ceiling at the other end of the table.

Cass handed out everyone's presents from her market trip with Finn, and her mother was delighted with the vase. Cassandra smiled at Finn, sharing the victory, then her face changed, suddenly dismayed. She signaled for him to meet her in the kitchen, going in under the guise of filling beverages. He followed, presumably to give her a hand, but he shot her a confused look when he closed the door.

"I never got you a present!" She looked genuinely distressed. "I got something for everyone else but I never gave you anything!"

He laughed, relieved that she hadn't called him in with an actual problem.

"You've given me plenty," he said, sliding his hands low around her waist and pulling her toward him. "But if you're worried about it," he brushed her lips with his, "put a bow on tonight and we'll call it even."

"Deal!" Cass kissed him again, lingering against his mouth until her father called, "Everything okay in there?"

She sighed and rested her forehead on Finn's shoulder.

"Just making more juice!" she called.

She loaded herself and Finn up with a round of pineapple-orange-guava-filled glasses and shuffled back out to the living room.

Cassandra's parents filled her in on all the islands she had missed since she bailed on their trip, and Finn had questions about all of them—some he had been to and some he hadn't.

Cassandra told her family about all her antics on the island, seeing the sights, meeting the people, working with Andre...she left out the part about falling for Finn. That was a story for another time.

When the conversation died down, Daphne piped up. "How about a tour? Have you had a chance to see any of the island yet?"

"Not yet," Miranda answered. "You were our first stop—we couldn't wait to see how Cassandra was doing without us!"

Cass smiled and thought, *This is what I get for not calling more often.*

"Well, let us show you around!" she offered out loud. "We can start with our neighborhood—there are some great little shops and galleries around—and then we can make our way over to Andre's for lunch! He'll definitely want to meet you! And then I have to work, but while I do that, how about you hit the beach?"

"Sounds like a plan," her father agreed, and Beth asked, "Is there a nude beach on the island?"

"There'd better not be if you want to see anything beyond the four walls of this apartment while we're here," Robert warned.

Two hours of tour guiding and souvenir shopping later, Cass was settling into a table at Andre's with her mother on one side and her sister on the other. Her father was seated across from them with Finn looking surprisingly at ease next to him. Daphne sat across from Beth, animatedly telling a story about how Andre had once sang *Heartbreak Hotel,* doing a full Elvis Presley impression to cheer her up after a bad break-up. "You'll understand once you meet him," she told Beth. "It was amazing!"

Once they'd had a chance to peruse the menu, ("Everything looks delicious!" her mother exclaimed), Cassandra segued into the topic of accommodations. She and Daphne had discussed it while they were shopping—Daphne had offered to let everyone stay at the apartment while they were in town, which Cass appreciated greatly even if she hoped it wouldn't be necessary.

"Are you guys going to be staying with me and Daphne?" she asked, crossing her fingers that they'd gotten a room somewhere and feeling guilty for it. She loved her family, but she'd jumped off a yacht in order to avoid being in tight quarters with them this summer. Quarters didn't get much tighter than the ones she and Daphne shared. But because she did love them and she was a good daughter (aside from the whole yacht-jumping business), she said, "Dad, you and Mom could sleep in my bed and Beth could camp out on the couch. I'll take the floor."

"You could stay at my place," Finn offered, and suddenly the idea of her family invading her apartment seemed a lot more appealing.

"We booked a room at a resort nearby," her father answered, shooting Finn a you're-not-fooling-anybody look. "The Silver Sands. Do you know it?"

"Intimately," Cassandra shuddered. "That's where I landed my first night on the island. Finn works there part-time."

"The service has been so impressive!" her mother gushed. "The woman who checked us in was so helpful and welcoming—Judith, I think was her name."

Cassandra bit back a guffaw.

"She was a prune," Beth muttered.

"Well, I'm glad you're happy with it," Cass said. "But you guys didn't have to get a hotel—we could have made space!"

"That's sweet Cass," her father told her, "but I'm sure this will be much more comfortable for everyone."

At that moment, the waiter showed up to take their orders, and after he'd left, Beth had more questions for

Finn about the different places he'd lived and worked. Cassandra listened to his stories affectionately, loving how easily he adjusted to spending time with her family. He made Beth laugh, charmed her mother with his knowledge of different cultures, and even her father seemed begrudgingly impressed by the research he had conducted and the wide variety of work experience he'd gained. She was fairly confident that when they found out that she and Finn were a couple, they would be happy. Well, Beth and her mom would be thrilled. Her dad would be tolerant. But that was about as much as she could hope for from her father's approval of any man she was sleeping with, and between the three of them, it averaged out to happy.

In the middle of Finn's story about his stint working for the Red Cross in a village in Peru, Andre barged out of the kitchen and made a beeline for their table. "Cassandra, my apple blossom, Nico has just informed me that you arrived with your parents and neglected to introduce them to me!" He shook his head at her sadly as if grievously offended by this oversight.

"Of course not, Andre!" Cassandra said earnestly. "I just know what a busy man you are, and I was waiting for the right time to be sure we didn't interrupt one of your brilliant creations."

Andre looked appeased.

"But I'd like to introduce them to you now," she went on. "Andre, this is my mother and father, Miranda and Robert Dillon, and my little sister Beth. Mom, Dad, may I present the wonderfully talented Andre, master of the culinary arts, and my benevolent employer."

Andre bowed with a flourish at this auspicious introduction, then straightened and said, "Robert,

Miranda, it's a pleasure to meet you! And may I compliment you on what a fine job you've done raising such a remarkable, enchanting girl. Cassandra is my rising star! Truly a gem."

"Thank you, Andre! We're rather proud of her ourselves." Her father looked at her fondly. "And we're so glad to hear she's been valuable to you."

"Valuable!" Andre pshawed. "She has been my crown jewel! My priceless treasure! Such charm and skill! I will be heartbroken when she leaves me."

Cassandra coughed and shifted in her chair.

"The things she can do in the kitchen…" Andre kissed his fingers. "Beautiful!"

"Really?" Beth asked. "Geez, all she's ever made for me is spaghetti."

"Is this true?" Andre looked shocked.

"I haven't had much time to cook since college," Cassandra admitted. "Between taking care of my grandma and working at the cafe...I never was around early enough to make dinner."

"But this is a travesty!" Andre exclaimed. "To have such talent go unknown by your closest family! Cassandra, my little rutabaga, you must cook for them!"

"Oh, with all the amazing food on the island, they don't want to waste a meal here on something I've made!" Cassandra waved the idea aside.

"Don't be so modest, sugarplum," Andre boomed. "Of course they would!"

"Of course we would," her father echoed.

"We want to see how you've been spending your time here," her mother added. "See what you've learned!"

"I, mostly, would just like to eat," Beth said. "What are you going to make us?"

"I don't know yet..." Cassandra drew a blank.

"How about your paella?" Daphne suggested. "I about died when you made it for Mary Ella's birthday—it was incredible!"

"And that would give your family a chance to taste some of the delicious seafood we have here on the island," Andre agreed.

"Sure," Cassandra said slowly, mentally running through the long list of ingredients and feeling a little dizzy at the end—it was a lot of seafood. "How about we have a dinner party on Sunday for your guys' last night? We'll invite everyone—Mary Ella, Drew— maybe we'll finally even get to meet Mary Ella's Felix! And you'll come of course, won't you Andre?"

"For the chance to taste your paella, I would move heaven and earth!" Andre vowed.

"Okay, then! That's settled—Sunday night!" Cassandra smiled and looked across the restaurant to see Angelo coming toward them with the first round of plates.

"Don't get your hopes up too high, though," she warned her family. "Whatever I make on Sunday won't even begin to compare to what you're about to have now. Get ready for the best food you'll ever eat!"

Chapter Twenty-eight

Cassandra was busy at work, preparing for a large party that was about to arrive.

"Finn, how are those churros coming?" she shouted over her shoulder, but he didn't answer.

Instead, she heard a loud harrumph directly behind her.

She turned, and there was the walrus, dressed as meticulously as ever, but he had exchanged his top hat for a tall white chef's hat.

"You look ridiculous," she said, turning back to her prep work.

He ignored her.

"So. It seems that you finally figured it out," he said with his usual condescension. "Took you long enough."

"I don't have time for this, Walrus," Cass said, rapidly chopping mangos.

"Don't talk to me about Time!" The walrus sounded uppity. "I know Time."

"Oh right, your creepy watch," Cassandra sighed, pausing her work to face him, figuring he wouldn't leave her in peace until he had finished badgering her. "What does it say now?"

"I'm not here to just hand over the answers!" The walrus held the large pocket watch close to his vest.

"Then what on Earth are you here for? I have work to do!"

"Yes, you do. You've found your calling and now it's time to decide what to do next."

"Is that what the watch says? 'Cassandra decides what to do next'?"

The walrus clutched the watch closer and glared at her.

"That's it, isn't it? Well, the watch had just better be patient, because I haven't decided yet."

"Now who's ridiculous?"

"There's a lot to consider!" Cassandra was defensive. "I'm still weighing my options."

"Nonsense! The choice is clear. And I should know. I'm a life coach."

"Well then, life coach, tell me the clear choice so that I can get back to work."

"That's not how this goes! You already know the answer. Pay attention."

"I am!"

"Not to me. Your mangoes are on fire."

"What?"

Cassandra woke with a start. It was two o'clock in the morning and nothing was on fire.

"Damn cryptic walrus," she muttered as she scribbled the dream in her dream journal and then fell back into a dreamless sleep.

***

"That's a lot of seafood," Finn said when he walked into the kitchen on Sunday, dropping a bottle of wine onto the counter and giving Cass a kiss on the cheek.

She looked up from scrubbing a mussel to survey the scene around her. He had a point.

"It's a lot of people to feed," she countered. "Normally I wouldn't use lobster and crab *and* mussels *and* shrimp in one recipe, but this is a special occasion and my parents are footing the bill."

"How many animals died to make this dinner?"

"Two chickens, whatever goes into chorizo, and a lot of crustaceans. But don't worry, Finn, it's the circle of life. Before I boiled them, the lobsters waved their antennae at me in a way that said it had been the aspiration of their lives to end up in a dish as delicious as this is going to be. They're fulfilling a lifelong ambition here. It's very moving."

"How long have you been in the kitchen already?"

"Maybe an hour, give or take. I've made my broth, cut up the chickens, boiled and split the lobster, sliced up the chorizo, and now I'm washing all the shellfish. Daphne was helping me earlier, chopping onions and scallions and whatnot, but she had to duck out to teach a class. Plus, she didn't want to be around when the lobsters met their fate."

"How can I help?"

"There's not much dinner prep left, and I made hors d'oeuvres this afternoon. Do you want to take over rinsing so I can gather the rest of the ingredients?"

"Sure," he said, taking the mussel from her and looking at it like it was an alien. Cass couldn't blame him. That was how she felt about everything that came out of the ocean.

"So, I just hold it under the water?" he asked, and she thought it was adorable how a man whose leisure activities included jumping off cliffs, trekking through caves, and diving with sea creatures could look so unsure of himself holding a small shellfish. She loved him for always volunteering to help even though he was out of his element.

"Yes, just run it under the water and make sure that any sand or grit gets rinsed away," she said, rooting through the spice cupboard for smoked paprika, saffron and bay leaves. "We still have plenty of time before everyone gets here. Mom and dad are wine tasting, Beth is at the beach with Sir Galahad, and Mary Ella said something about going for a ride along the coast with Felix before coming over. Daphne and Drew are bungee jumping. They'll be along eventually."

"Well, if we have some time to kill…" Finn started to say, wiggling his eyebrows.

"Not that much time," Cass cut in. "My parents are leaving tomorrow and then we'll have all the time in the world."

"You mean all the time until summer ends," Finn corrected, finishing the last of the mussels. He sounded overly casual, and Cassandra knew he wanted to ask what her plans were once the summer ended, and what was going to happen to them when she went home. It was a subject she'd been skirting for weeks. At first, Cass had avoided it because she wasn't sure of her own answer, and now she was afraid of what his might be.

She pointedly ignored the hint and said brightly, "Well, for now, we only have an hour, which isn't nearly enough time to finish making dinner and do everything I've got planned for you later."

She slid her hands up his chest and came up on her toes to kiss him, slipping her tongue in his mouth and feeling his hands tighten on her hips, pulling her close.

"We have a *little* time, don't we?" he said against her mouth, and Cass felt the heat flare low in her stomach, so she steeled her resolve and pulled away before he could convince her that serving dinner a half an hour late wouldn't be the end of the world.

"Not enough," she said again. "If you're finished with the mussels, could you set the table, please?"

She gave him one more quick kiss and turned to the stove. Finn sighed, but opened the cupboard to begin gathering plates.

An hour later, the paella was resting, ready to be served, and Cass was just thinking that maybe they *would* have enough time, when there was a knock at the door.

"We're here!" her mother sang as she opened the door. "I'm so sad this is our last day on the island. This place is just beautiful! We've just finished a tour of the vineyards and the wine here is exquisite! And the views! Gorgeous! I can see now why you were so determined to stay, darling."

Her mother continued on in this fashion while her father silently filed in behind her and kissed Cassandra on the cheek. Finally, her mother paused for breath and took notice of the sights and smells around her.

"Oh, Cassandra, it smells wonderful! We can't wait to taste everything and see what you can do!"

Robert nodded his agreement.

"Thanks, Mom," Cassandra smiled. "We're just waiting on everyone else. Can I get you some more wine?"

Cassandra uncorked a bottle and listened to Finn making conversation with her parents from the other room, loving him for how well he got along with her family. Miranda talked incessantly and her father was gruff, but Finn's good naturedly went along with them both.

Presently, the door sounded again and Mary Ella walked in, followed closely by an attractive silver-haired man in a tropical polo and khaki shorts, which displayed an impressive scorpion tattoo on one of his muscular calves.

"Mary Ella!" Cass hugged the older woman and then stepped back to smile at her date.

"And you must be Felix! It's so nice to finally meet you!"

"The pleasure's mine," Felix winked and gripped Cassandra's hand warmly. "Mary Ella tells me you're quite the chef."

"Come in and have some wine before you decide for yourself!" Cass gestured them further into the room and went to fill two more glasses.

Soon Beth arrived with Sir Galahad galumphing along behind her. "These beaches are amazing!" she plopped onto the couch with a satisfied sigh. "And the guys aren't bad either," she added with a grin. "Do I get some wine?"

"No," her father answered decidedly before Cass had a chance.

"But you can have juice," she laughed. "We have peach mango guava, and you can have an umbrella."

"Excellent," Beth bounced off to the kitchen to retrieve her drink while Sir Galahad trotted lovingly behind, undoubtedly hoping he'd get a snack once they'd crossed into the room where food was kept.

Andre showed up a few minutes later and immediately began expounding on Cass's many virtues, talents, and perfections with her parents until Drew and Daphne arrived, looking flushed and happy.

"How was bungee jumping?" Finn asked.

"Fantastic!" Daphne gushed.

"I told you you'd love it." Drew grinned and put his arm around her shoulder

"Adrenaline," he winked at Finn. "Works every time."

Daphne rolled her eyes but she smiled and leaned into him.

Everyone drank wine and enjoyed appetizers until dinner was served, to great acclaim. Cassandra's family was suitably impressed by her skill and she was happy to be able to share it with them.

She was glad they'd gotten to experience the island for themselves and get a taste (quite literally) of how wonderful life was here. It would make what she had to tell them soon so much easier.

The evening went by in a happy haze of food and laughter. Cass looked around the room filled with all the people she loved most in the world and couldn't believe how lucky she'd gotten. Who would have thought on that warm Tuesday night three months ago, standing on the deck of a yacht she hated, dreading the summer before her, that Cass would have ended up here? Surrounded by beauty and friendship, filled with love and passion and purpose, looking forward to everything that life had to offer in the future. She had jumped off that yacht and straight into her destiny.

All she had to do now was tell everyone else.

After dessert (a flourless chocolate coconut cake), Cass asked Finn to give her a hand with dishes and left the guests playing charades in the living room.

"That was great!" she said, filling the sink up with water. "It's a shame your parents couldn't be here."

"Yeah, I think they're in Prague now. But I know they would have liked to see you again before you go home."

There was that overly-casual tone again. Cass cleared her throat and picked up a sudsy pan.

Soon. They would talk soon.

"Crocodile!" Beth shouted from the other room. "Mouse trap! Lava monster!"

A timer buzzed.

"Jaws," Drew said reproachfully. "'Lava monster?' Come on!"

"Sounds like a good time in there." Cass seized the opportunity for a distraction. "I'm so glad Beth is having fun."

"I think she would have slept on the beach if your dad would have let her. Her skin is now bronzed in a way I don't think yours is physically capable of. But despite your best efforts, Dillon, it looks like you've managed to get some sun." Finn stood behind her and kissed her coconut-scented shoulder.

Then he straightened and said in that guarded, casual way, "Though I'm sure at the end of the summer, you'll go home and return to your usual whiter shade of pale."

Damn. Apparently, he was not to be distracted.

Cass listened to the shouts and strains of laughter streaming from the next room and thought, *Now is not the best time.* She hadn't talked to anyone else yet, hadn't confirmed the details, and if he wasn't as happy about it as she hoped he'd be, everyone they knew was only one room away, ready to listen to them fight.

But she turned and looked up at his face, sweet and loving and anxious, though he wasn't saying it, and she wanted to tell him anyway.

"About that," she said, eying the wine on the counter and wishing she had a glass of it in her hand. There was no overstating the value of a little liquid courage at a time like this. "I've been thinking...I'm learning so much from Andre, it doesn't make sense for me to leave so soon. There's no way I could get training like this anywhere else! I know I only talked with Daphne about staying through the summer, and your plans here are temporary, too..." She trailed off, not sure how to say, 'but I think you should forget whatever your plans were and stay here with me.'

"Are you saying you want to stay?" Finn looked at her, eyebrows raised, and Cassandra nodded, terrified that he would say, 'Well, have a good time, I'm going to Argentina to work on a vineyard in three weeks,' or something else equally adventurous and transient.

Instead, a slow grin crept across his face. "Thank god!" he said. "I thought you were going to tell me you were leaving to go to culinary school in France or something."

She stopped, struck by the idea. Why hadn't she thought of that before?

"Don't go getting any ideas!" he said quickly, seeing the look on her face.

"No," she reassured him. "Andre is way more fun than a culinary school. But aren't you leaving at the end of the month? You were only supposed to be here through the summer."

"It turns out the impact of tourist culture here on the island is far more complex than I could have anticipated," he said with exaggerated seriousness. "Who knows how long it will take to research? Months, at least. Years, even. We'll just have to see."

"So you're not going anywhere either?" Cassandra asked, face lighting up as relief flooded her body.

"Not as long as you're here," Finn said, pulling her in for a kiss, and she felt more love for him now than she ever had before. Her head reeled from his news and her brain felt fuzzy from the kiss, and she pressed closer.

"Careful," Finn said, pulling away. "Your family is on the other side of that door."

"I don't care." She followed him, keeping him close, leaning into his solid, loving warmth. "They'll find out soon anyway—there's no hiding the fact that I've fallen for you."

He grinned and bent his mouth to hers. "You have?"

She nodded and kissed him again. "Completely off the deep end."

THE END

Acknowledgements

My profound thanks to…

Alissa, for being the best plotter and problem-solver, and the other half of my brain.

Malena, for always being there to talk through every detail of this book—and my life in general.

Emma, for getting this whole thing off the ground.

Kimberly, for one hundred thousand pearls of book-launching wisdom.

Alix, Jessica, Sammy, Sarah, and Tiffany for helping me to bring Drew out of the 2010s, requesting more scenes with Judith, and greenlighting my architectural pun.

Christy and Karen, for your unwavering attention to detail.

Professor Monica DeHart at the University of Puget Sound, for your contribution to Finn's library.

Michael, for making me French toast, introducing me to the Talking Heads, and more recently, for outlining how a professional kitchen actually works.

Pam Larsen, my wonderful third grade teacher, for the cake metaphor.

Dad, for talking boats with me.

Gamie, for giving me colorful and checkered life advice. "Live your life; make your mistakes; don't tell the world." Words to live by.

Mom, for everything.

About the Author

Lanie Hartford is a Pacific Northwest romance author who loves cloudy days and rainy nights. She happily practices yoga and reluctantly does Pilates. You can find her most days writing and sipping tea at her favorite spots downtown, and most evenings editing and sipping wine at her favorite local wineries. She firmly believes that food is love, and happiness is a well-placed semi-colon.